MW01154542

DIVINE POWER™

ROLEPLAYING GAME SUPPLEMENT

Rob Heinsoo • Richard Baker • Logan Bonner • Robert J. Schwalb

CREDITS

Design
Rob Heinsoo (lead), Richard Baker, Logan Bonner, Robert J. Schwalb

Additional Design
Greg Bilsland, Andy Collins, Matthew Sernett

Development
Stephen Schubert (lead), Andy Collins, Peter Schaefer

Additional Development
Mike Donais, Andrew Finch

Editing
Jeremy Crawford (lead), Jennifer Clarke Wilkes, Kim Mohan

Managing Editing
Kim Mohan

Director of D&D R&D and Book Publishing
Bill Slavicsek

D&D Creative Manager
Christopher Perkins

D&D Senior Art Director
Jon Schindehette

D&D Design Manager
James Wyatt

D&D Development and Editing Manager
Andy Collins

Art Director
Karin Powell, Jon Schindehette

Cover Illustration
Ralph Horsley

Graphic Designer
Emi Tanji

Interior Illustrations
Kyle Anderson, Ralph Beisner, Kerem Beyit, Concept Art House, Emrah Elmasli, Luvas Graciano, Rebecca Guay, Layne Johnson, Goran Josic, Mazin Kassis, Howard Lyon, Lee Moyer, William O'Connor, Lucio Parrillo, Michael Phillippi, Wayne Reynolds, Dan Scott, Georgi "Calader" Simeonov, Ron Spencer, Amelia Stoner, Matias Tapia, Kieran Yanner

Publishing Production Specialist
Angelika Lokotz

Prepress Manager
Jefferson Dunlap

Imaging Technician
Ashley Brock

Production Manager
Cynda Callaway

Game rules based on the original DUNGEONS & DRAGONS® rules created by **E. Gary Gygax** and **Dave Arneson**, and the later editions by **David "Zeb" Cook** (2nd Edition); **Jonathan Tweet, Monte Cook, Skip Williams, Richard Baker,** and **Peter Adkison** (3rd Edition); and **Rob Heinsoo, Andy Collins,** and **James Wyatt** (4th Edition).

620-21790720-001 EN
9 8 7 6 5 4 3 2 1
First Printing: July 2009
ISBN: 978-0-7869-4982-3

U.S., CANADA, ASIA, PACIFIC, & LATIN AMERICA
Wizards of the Coast LLC
P.O. Box 707
Renton WA 98057-0707
+1-800-324-6496

EUROPEAN HEADQUARTERS
Hasbro UK Ltd
Caswell Way
Newport, Gwent NP9 0YH
GREAT BRITAIN
Please keep this address for your records

WIZARDS OF THE COAST, BELGIUM
Industrialaan 1
1702 Groot-Bijgaarden
Belgium
+32.070.233.277

VISIT OUR WEBSITE AT WWW.WIZARDS.COM/DND

Introduction

Staunch protector, saver of lives, formidable foe, and worldly representative of the gods—all of these are roles filled by divine characters. Their special connections with the deities and other forces of the cosmos give them a suite of powers and abilities—as well as responsibilities—that make them indispensable in the continual struggle to advance the causes of righteousness and justice. Those who attain the highest levels of accomplishment literally do ascend, becoming entities not unlike the deities they worship and emulate.

Divine Power™ is a tome that broadens the choices available to those who follow the dictates of a deity. In its pages are new ways to build a divine character, along with new options to fill out your role as an avenger, a cleric, an invoker, or a paladin.

Using This Book

As you can see by the table of contents, *Divine Power* is organized by class. Whether you have a character of a particular class or you want to make a character of that class, all you have to do is consult the proper chapter for new class features, builds, powers, and paragon paths. The final chapter of the book contains a large section on divine domains, dozens of new feats, ten divine-themed epic destinies, several new rituals, and information on deities and divine backgrounds that will deepen your roleplaying experience.

D&D Insider: Some of the material in this book was originally featured in articles in *Dragon*™ magazine, part of D&D™ Insider. It's compiled here, along with plenty of new information, for easy reference at your game table. When you subscribe to D&D Insider, you get access to hundreds of pages of content like this—new powers, feats, and inspiration to make your D&D® game more fun, and to make you a better player. Your D&D Insider subscription also gives you tools like the D&D Character Builder, the easiest way to create and maintain your character at any level. Visit www.dndinsider.com to learn more.

Reimagining Your Character

It happens. You've played your divine character a while, and suddenly *Divine Power* shows up, offering many new possibilities—options you might have picked if you had known about them earlier.

Don't despair; you have a few choices. Retraining rules (see page 28 of the *Player's Handbook*®) make tapping into *Divine Power* easy. If retraining won't do the trick quickly enough, talk to your DM about reworking your character along the lines *Divine Power* provides. Chances are you can overhaul your PC to match your desires without doing any harm to the campaign. Your DM might even have a way to make the change a part of the story. If doing that ultimately proves too difficult, a dramatic exit for the older character could make way for a new one.

Contents

CHAPTER 1

Avenger

"Messenger, enforcer, assassin—in time I might walk each of these paths. I go as I am called, and let the wicked tremble at the sound of my footsteps."

YOU ARE an agent of divine justice. It is your task to guard the innocent, to stand watch in the shadows, to censure your deity's foes with sacred power, and to lay them low with your weapon no matter where they hide. The enemies of your god reign unchecked throughout the world; there is much to be done.

Avengers rely on their zealous piety to see them through their battles, employing *oath of enmity* and Avenger's Censure to destroy their foes. The Censure of Pursuit and the Censure of Retribution are described in *Player's Handbook 2*. This chapter introduces the Censure of Unity. If you choose this version of Avenger's Censure, you don't focus on chasing after your enemies or driving them away from your chosen foe. Instead, you specialize in powers that bring enemies to meet judgment at your hand one at a time. Through the Censure of Unity, your attacks against your chosen foe gain strength when your allies are nearby, giving you the ability to dispatch foes quickly who arouse your wrath.

This chapter includes material for avengers who choose the Censure of Unity, as well as for other avengers.

- **New Class Feature:** The Censure of Unity, a new version of Avenger's Censure, rewards you for cooperating with your allies.
- **New Build:** As a commanding avenger, bring the power of your friends to bear against your sworn enemy.
- **New Avenger Powers:** Almost a hundred new avenger powers for you to choose from, including powers suitable for the Censure of Pursuit, the Censure of Retribution, and the Censure of Unity.
- **New Paragon Paths:** New avenger paragon paths are introduced, including the favored soul, the relentless slayer, and the watchful shepherd.

WILLIAM O'CONNOR

NEW CLASS FEATURE

When you choose your Avenger's Censure, you can choose the Censure of Unity instead of another option, such as the ones in *Player's Handbook* 2.

Censure of Unity: You gain a +1 bonus to damage rolls against your *oath of enmity* target for each ally adjacent to that target. The bonus increases to +2 at 11th level and +3 at 21st level.

NEW BUILD

Player's Handbook 2 features the isolating avenger and the pursuing avenger. This chapter adds the commanding avenger, who becomes even more formidable when allies enter the fray against his or her foe.

Commanding Avenger

The commanding avenger build is based on the Censure of Unity. Once you have sworn your *oath of enmity*, you hope to surround your *oath of enmity* target with as many of your allies as possible. If the enemy seeks to flee, your powers enable you to compel it to face you. Alone you are powerful, but fighting alongside your comrades you are vengeance incarnate. Like other avengers, you should make Wisdom your highest ability score. Intelligence should be your second highest, followed by Dexterity.

Suggested Class Feature: Censure of Unity*

Suggested Feat: Weapon Focus

Suggested Skills: Athletics, Perception, Religion, Stealth

Suggested At-Will Powers: *bond of censure,* overwhelming strike*

Suggested Encounter Power: *pass at arms**

Suggested Daily Power: *strength of many**

*New option presented in this book

NEW AVENGER POWERS

The new powers presented in this chapter supplement those already available to avengers. Many of the powers support the Censure of Unity, but the broad range of powers here provides useful options for any avenger.

Level 1 At-Will Prayers

Bond of Censure — Avenger Attack 1

You compel your enemy to come forward and face judgment.

At-Will ✦ Charm, Divine, Implement, Radiant
Standard Action **Ranged** 5
Target: One creature
Attack: Wisdom vs. Will. If the target is your *oath of enmity* target and no enemies are adjacent to you, you can make two attack rolls and use either result.
Hit: You pull the target a number of squares equal to your Intelligence modifier. If the target ends this movement adjacent to you, it takes 1d10 radiant damage.
Level 21: 2d10 radiant damage.

Leading Strike — Avenger Attack 1

You show an ally how to hit your foe where it hurts.

At-Will ✦ Divine, Weapon
Standard Action **Melee** weapon
Target: One creature
Attack: Wisdom vs. AC
Hit: 1[W] + Wisdom modifier damage. One ally adjacent to you or to the target gains a bonus to his or her next damage roll against the target equal to your Intelligence modifier.
Level 21: 2[W] + Wisdom modifier damage.

Level 1 Encounter Prayers

Compelling Blade — Avenger Attack 1

Your weapon weaves a subtle trap, locking your enemy's steps to yours.

Encounter ✦ Divine, Weapon
Standard Action **Melee** weapon
Target: One creature
Attack: Wisdom vs. AC
Hit: 1[W] + Wisdom modifier damage. Until the end of your next turn, the first time an enemy enters a square adjacent to you on its turn, you can shift 1 square as a free action and then slide the target 1 square into the space you left.
Censure of Retribution: The distance of the shift and the slide equals your Intelligence modifier, but after the slide, you must be adjacent to the target.

Avenger Origins

The avenger class describes an origin for members of the class outside the normal expectations of a god's worshipers. What's true for your avenger? Did you learn your skills from a recognized religious organization, a breakaway sect of heretics, or a version of the religion thought to be extinct? How do leaders of the faith view you? Are you a hero to them, a trusted servant, a misguided fool, or a dangerous free thinker? What do you think of other faithful? Are they like family to you, or do they seem like blind sheep deaf to the truth? How do you see your own actions? Is your killing a necessary evil, a grim but righteous duty of the faithful, or a tribute to your deity?

Day's First Light — Avenger Attack 1

You envelop your foe in a burning shroud of light. If the foe moves, the brilliance scorches it.

Encounter ✦ Divine, Implement, Radiant
Standard Action **Melee** touch
Attack: Wisdom vs. Reflex
Hit: 1d8 + Wisdom modifier radiant damage. If the target willingly moves before the start of your next turn, it takes 5 + your Wisdom modifier radiant damage.

Pass at Arms — Avenger Attack 1

Your strike creates an opening that you or a nearby ally can use to change position. If you take advantage of the opening, you can force your foe to move.

Encounter ✦ Divine, Weapon
Standard Action **Melee** weapon
Target: One creature
Attack: Wisdom vs. AC
Hit: 2[W] + Wisdom modifier damage. You or an ally adjacent to the target can then shift 1 square as a free action.
Censure of Unity: If you shift, rather than your ally, you can slide the target into the space you left.

Relentless Attack — Avenger Attack 1

Your attacks drive the enemy away, and no matter where it goes, you are not far behind.

Encounter ✦ Divine, Weapon
Standard Action **Melee** weapon
Target: One creature
Attack: Wisdom vs. AC
Hit: 2[W] + Wisdom modifier damage. You push the target 2 squares and then shift 3 squares to a square adjacent to it.

Shielded by Faith — Avenger Attack 1

The words of your prayer lend power to your strike while shielding you from the interference of your enemies.

Encounter ✦ Divine, Weapon
Standard Action **Melee** weapon
Target: One creature
Attack: Wisdom vs. AC
Hit: 2[W] + Wisdom modifier damage. Until the end of your next turn, you gain a +2 power bonus to all defenses against attacks made by creatures other than the target.

Speed and Stillness — Avenger Attack 1

You move in a blur, and your strike places a glowing sigil above your enemy. The sigil's strength flows back to you if that enemy moves.

Encounter ✦ Divine, Radiant, Weapon
Standard Action **Melee** weapon
Effect: Before the attack, you shift 1 square.
Censure of Pursuit: The number of squares you shift equals your Dexterity modifier.
Target: One creature
Attack: Wisdom vs. AC
Hit: 1[W] + Wisdom modifier radiant damage. If the target moves on its turn before the end of your next turn, you gain 5 temporary hit points.

LAYNE JOHNSON

Level 1 Daily Prayers

Argent Mantle — Avenger Attack 1

You channel divine light and thunder through your holy symbol, smiting enemies nearby. For the rest of the battle, a mantle of silver light clings to your shoulders, a sign of divine favor.

Daily ✦ Divine, Implement, Radiant, Thunder
Standard Action **Close** burst 1
Effect: Until the end of the encounter, you can reroll the damage roll for any avenger attack power you use, including this one, and you must use the second result.
Target: Each enemy in burst
Attack: Wisdom vs. Fortitude
Hit: 2d10 + Wisdom modifier radiant and thunder damage.
Miss: Half damage.

Celestial Fist — Avenger Attack 1

A great fist of light smashes down at your enemy, and then holds the foe fast in its grip.

Daily ✦ Divine, Implement, Radiant
Standard Action **Ranged** 5
Target: One creature
Attack: Wisdom vs. Reflex
Hit: 2d10 + Wisdom modifier radiant damage, and the target is immobilized (save ends).
Each Failed Saving Throw: The target takes 5 radiant damage.
Aftereffect: The target is slowed (save ends).
Miss: Half damage, and the target is immobilized until the end of your next turn.

Strength of Many — Avenger Attack 1

You call on the loyalty and courage of your allies to strike a mighty blow.

Daily ✦ Divine, Weapon
Standard Action **Melee** weapon
Effect: Whenever you make a damage roll before the end of your next turn, you gain a +2 bonus for each ally within 2 squares of you.
Target: One creature
Attack: Wisdom vs. AC
Hit: 3[W] + Wisdom modifier damage.
Miss: Half damage.

Thunder and Echo — Avenger Attack 1

Thunder rides your weapon and then reverberates around you.

Daily ✦ Divine, Thunder, Weapon
Standard Action **Melee** weapon
Primary Target: One creature
Primary Attack: Wisdom vs. AC
Hit: 1[W] + Wisdom modifier damage plus 1d10 thunder damage.
Miss: Half damage.
Effect: Make a secondary attack that is a close burst 2.
Secondary Target: Each enemy in burst other than the primary target
Secondary Attack: Wisdom vs. Fortitude
Hit: 1d6 + Wisdom modifier thunder damage, and you push the secondary target 2 squares.

Wings of Light — Avenger Attack 1

Shining wings sprout from your shoulders for a moment, carrying you swiftly to your sworn foe.

Daily ✦ Divine, Weapon
Standard Action **Melee** weapon
Effect: Before the attack, you can fly 6 squares and must land in a square adjacent to your *oath of enmity* target. This movement does not provoke opportunity attacks.
Target: Your *oath of enmity* target
Attack: Wisdom vs. AC
Hit: 3[W] + Wisdom modifier damage.
Miss: Half damage.

Level 2 Utility Prayers

Avenger's Resolve — Avenger Utility 2

For a few moments, your faith infuses you with supernatural toughness.

Encounter ✦ Divine
Immediate Interrupt **Personal**
Trigger: An enemy other than your *oath of enmity* target hits you
Effect: You gain resist 5 to all damage until the end of your next turn.

Enduring Spirit — Avenger Utility 2

The strength of your spirit shines most brightly in adversity.

Encounter ✦ Divine
Minor Action **Personal**
Requirement: You must be bloodied.
Effect: You gain a +4 bonus to all defenses until the end of your next turn.

Loyal Sanction — Avenger Utility 2

You bless your comrade's efforts to aid you in the defeat of your chosen foe.

Encounter ✦ Divine
Minor Action **Close** burst 5
Target: One ally in burst
Effect: Until the end of your next turn, the target gains a power bonus to damage rolls against your *oath of enmity* target equal to your Wisdom modifier.

Righteous Pursuit — Avenger Utility 2

Try as your enemy might, there's no escaping your wrath.

Encounter ✦ Divine
Immediate Reaction **Personal**
Trigger: Your *oath of enmity* target ends its turn in a square not adjacent to you
Effect: You shift a number of squares equal to your Wisdom modifier and must end this movement as close to your *oath of enmity* target as possible.

Silver Shadow — Avenger Utility 2

You cloak yourself in astral mist, which guards you from harm.

Daily ✦ Divine
Minor Action **Personal**
Effect: You gain temporary hit points equal to 5 + your level. You also gain concealment, which lasts until you have no temporary hit points.

Level 3 Encounter Prayers

Bound by Fate — Avenger Attack 3

You strike your foe and then share your pain with it.

Encounter ✦ Divine, Weapon
Standard Action **Melee** weapon
Target: One creature
Attack: Wisdom vs. AC
Hit: 2[W] + Wisdom modifier damage. Until the end of your next turn, the target is immobilized, and the first time an enemy other than the target hits and damages you while you are adjacent to the target, you take half of the damage and the target takes the other half.

Deadly Stride — Avenger Attack 3

No obstacle can stop you from visiting righteous fury on your foe.

Encounter ✦ Divine, Weapon
Standard Action **Melee** weapon
Effect: Before the attack, you shift a number of squares equal to one-half your speed. You gain phasing during this movement.
Target: One creature
Attack: Wisdom vs. AC
Hit: 2[W] + Wisdom modifier damage.

Fury's Advance — Avenger Attack 3

A quick flick of your weapon forces the enemy to stumble backward.

Encounter ✦ Divine, Weapon
Minor Action **Melee** weapon
Target: One creature
Attack: Wisdom vs. AC
Hit: 1[W] damage. You push the target 1 square, and it takes 3 damage for each of your allies adjacent to it after the push. You then shift 1 square to a square adjacent to the target.
Censure of Unity: The number of squares you push and shift equals your Intelligence modifier. You still must end the shift adjacent to the target.

Intervening Blades — Avenger Attack 3

Mystic echoes of your weapon weave around your target after your blow strikes home, interfering with your foe's attacks.

Encounter ✦ Divine, Weapon
Standard Action **Melee** weapon
Target: One creature
Attack: Wisdom vs. AC
Hit: 2[W] + Wisdom modifier damage, and the target takes a -2 penalty to attack rolls until the end of your next turn.
Censure of Pursuit: You can use this power as an opportunity attack against your *oath of enmity* target.

Sparking Wounds — Avenger Attack 3

The sparks after your strike warn off your enemy's companions.

Encounter ✦ Divine, Fire, Lightning, Weapon
Standard Action **Melee** weapon
Target: One creature
Attack: Wisdom vs. AC
Hit: 1[W] + Wisdom modifier damage. At the end of the target's next turn, each enemy adjacent to the target takes 5 fire and lightning damage, and if no enemies are adjacent to it, the target takes 5 fire and lightning damage.
Censure of Retribution: If no other creatures are adjacent to the target when the attack hits, you gain a bonus to the damage roll equal to your Intelligence modifier.

Level 5 Daily Prayers

Dance of Flame — Avenger Attack 5

Multicolored flames dance across your weapon and ignite your enemy, erupting onto other enemies the longer the flames dance.

Daily ✦ Divine, Fire, Weapon
Standard Action **Melee** weapon
Target: One creature
Attack: Wisdom vs. AC
Hit: 2[W] + Wisdom modifier damage.
Effect: The target takes ongoing 5 fire damage (save ends).
Each Failed Saving Throw: An enemy of your choice within 5 squares of the target takes ongoing 5 fire damage (save ends).

Light of Truth — Avenger Attack 5

A brilliant shaft of light streaks down from above and fixes on the enemy you touch. In the merciless light, your enemy suffers pain commensurate with the number of your friends near it.

Daily ✦ Divine, Implement, Radiant
Standard Action **Melee** touch
Target: One creature
Attack: Wisdom vs. Fortitude
Hit: 1d10 + Wisdom modifier radiant damage, and ongoing 10 radiant damage (save ends).
Miss: Half damage, and ongoing 5 radiant damage (save ends).
Effect: When the target rolls any saving throw before the ongoing damage ends, the target takes a penalty to the saving throw equal to the number of your allies adjacent to it.

Menacing Presence — Avenger Attack 5

You attack and then emanate divine menace, weakening the resolve of nearby foes.

Daily ✦ Divine, Fear, Weapon
Standard Action **Melee** weapon
Target: One creature
Attack: Wisdom vs. AC
Hit: 3[W] + Wisdom modifier damage.
Miss: Half damage.
Effect: Until the end of the encounter, any enemy that starts its turn adjacent to you takes a -2 penalty to AC until the end of its next turn.

Nine Souls of Wrath — Avenger Attack 5

As you strike your enemy, you call forth souls to protect you. Streaming around you, they lash out at enemies nearby, weakening them.

Daily ✦ Divine, Weapon
Standard Action **Melee** weapon
Target: One creature
Attack: Wisdom vs. AC
Hit: 2[W] + Wisdom modifier damage.
Miss: Half damage.
Effect: Until the end of the encounter, any enemy other than your *oath of enmity* target that ends its turn adjacent to you gains vulnerable 5 to all damage until the end of your next turn.

Oath of Righteous Fury — Avenger Attack 5

You swear an oath to reduce your enemies to ruin. Each slain foe renews your zeal.

Daily ✦ Divine, Weapon
Standard Action **Melee** weapon
Target: One creature
Attack: Wisdom vs. AC
Hit: 3[W] + Wisdom modifier damage.
Miss: Half damage.
Effect: Until the end of the encounter, whenever your *oath of enmity* target drops to 0 hit points, you can shift a number of squares equal to your Dexterity modifier as a free action.

Level 6 Utility Prayers

Aspect of Majesty — Avenger Utility 6

Your faith fills you with courage and mystically extends the reach of your attacks.

Daily ✦ Divine, Stance
Minor Action **Personal**
Effect: Until the stance ends, you gain a +1 bonus to Will, and your melee reach increases by 1.

Fortifying Chant — Avenger Utility 6

You recite holy verses, armoring yourself with the strength of your faith.

Daily ✦ Divine, Stance
Minor Action **Personal**
Effect: Until the stance ends, you gain a +1 bonus to AC and Fortitude. In addition, whenever you reduce your *oath of enmity* target to 0 hit points, this bonus increases to +4 until the end of your next turn.

Harsh Lesson — Avenger Utility 6

You seek penance in the hope that your faults might be corrected.

Encounter ✦ Divine
Free Action **Personal**
Trigger: You miss every target with an avenger attack power
Effect: You take 5 damage, and you gain a +2 power bonus to attack rolls until the end of your next turn.

Step of Fate — Avenger Utility 6

Your world is in motion with your sworn enemy as its center.

Daily ✦ Divine, Stance
Minor Action **Personal**
Effect: Until the stance ends, you can use a free action to shift 1 square as the first action on each of your turns. You can't end this movement farther away from your *oath of enmity* target than you started.

Level 7 Encounter Prayers

Celestia Endures — Avenger Attack 7

This prayer comes from a battle hymn of the War of Creation. Its uplifting words lend you strength.

Encounter ✦ Divine, Healing, Weapon
Standard Action **Melee** weapon
Target: One creature
Attack: Wisdom vs. AC
Hit: 1[W] + Wisdom modifier damage. If this attack reduces the target to 0 hit points or if you have reduced your *oath of enmity* target to 0 hit points during this encounter, you can spend a healing surge. In addition, you gain a bonus to the damage rolls of your next attack before the end of your next turn equal to your Wisdom modifier.

CONCEPT ART HOUSE LLC

Chains of Censure — Avenger Attack 7

As you deliver a punishing blow with your weapon, your prayer invokes spectral chains to immobilize a foe.

Encounter ✦ Divine, Weapon
Standard Action **Melee** weapon
Target: One creature
Attack: Wisdom vs. AC
Hit: 2[W] + Wisdom modifier damage. You choose to immobilize either the target or an enemy within 5 squares of it until the end of your next turn.
Censure of Pursuit: If no other creatures are adjacent to you or to the target, the attack deals extra damage equal to your Dexterity modifier.

Dismiss the Unworthy — Avenger Attack 7

You deal a stinging blow to your target and then speak a prayer of contemptuous dismissal, sending it away from you.

Encounter ✦ Charm, Divine, Weapon
Standard Action **Melee** weapon
Target: One creature
Attack: Wisdom vs. AC
Hit: 2[W] + Wisdom modifier damage, and you push the target 1 square to a square adjacent to at least one of your allies.
Censure of Unity: The number of squares you push the target equals 1 + your Intelligence modifier. The target still must end this movement adjacent to at least one of your allies.

Excoriating Call — Avenger Attack 7

Your holy symbol flashes as you utter a mighty rebuke, which drives creatures away from you but draws your chosen foe closer.

Encounter ✦ Divine, Implement, Radiant
Standard Action **Close** burst 3
Target: Each creature in burst
Attack: Wisdom vs. Will
Hit: You push the target 3 squares. If the target is your *oath of enmity* target, it instead takes 2d10 + your Wisdom modifier radiant damage, and you pull it to a square adjacent to you.

Inexorable Summons — Avenger Attack 7

When you call, your adversary must answer.

Encounter ✦ Divine, Implement, Radiant, Teleportation
Standard Action **Ranged** 5
Target: One creature
Attack: Wisdom vs. Reflex
Hit: 2d8 + Wisdom modifier radiant damage, and you teleport the target to a square adjacent to you.
Effect: When any enemy enters a square adjacent to you before the end of your next turn, the target takes 5 radiant damage.
Censure of Retribution: The radiant damage the target takes when any enemy enters a square adjacent to you equals 5 + your Intelligence modifier.

Level 9 Daily Prayers

Blade of Guilt — Avenger Attack 9

At the touch of your weapon, your foe relives its misdeeds. Only by standing still can it keep the painful visions at bay.

Daily ✦ Divine, Psychic, Weapon
Standard Action **Melee** weapon
Target: One creature
Attack: Wisdom vs. AC
Hit: 2[W] + Wisdom modifier damage. The target takes 5 psychic damage for each square it enters willingly (save ends).
Miss: Half damage. Until the end of your next turn, the target takes 5 psychic damage for each square it enters willingly.

Glyph of Agony — Avenger Attack 9

Crimson runes flare into being above your enemies, flashing when they draw near.

Daily ✦ Divine, Implement, Radiant
Standard Action **Close** burst 2
Target: Each enemy in burst
Attack: Wisdom vs. Will
Hit: 1d10 + Wisdom modifier radiant damage, and you pull the target 1 square. The target takes 10 radiant damage if it starts its turn adjacent to you (save ends).
Aftereffect: If the target is adjacent to you, you push it 2 squares.
Miss: Half damage.

Holy Ardor — Avenger Attack 9

Your battle prayer transports you into a rapturous state, eyes blazing with fire. Your exaltation increases as your foe's life slips away.

Daily ✦ Divine, Weapon
Standard Action **Melee** weapon
Target: One creature
Attack: Wisdom vs. AC
Hit: 2[W] + Wisdom modifier damage.
Effect: The target takes ongoing 5 damage (save ends). Whenever the target takes this ongoing damage, you gain a power bonus to your next damage roll made before the end of your next turn against your *oath of enmity* target. The bonus equals your Wisdom modifier.

Winds of Woe — Avenger Attack 9

After you hit your foe, a dread wind whips around you, tossing aside your enemies.

Daily ✦ Divine, Weapon
Standard Action **Melee** weapon
Primary Target: One creature
Primary Attack: Wisdom vs. AC
Hit: 3[W] + Wisdom modifier damage.
Miss: Half damage.
Effect: You make a secondary attack that is a close burst 1.
Secondary Target: Each enemy in burst other than the primary target
Secondary Attack: Wisdom vs. Fortitude
Hit: You push the secondary target 1d4 squares.

Zealot's Call — Avenger Attack 9

Your prayer wrenches your foe from where it stands and makes it appear beside you.

Daily ✦ Divine, Implement, Psychic, Teleportation
Standard Action **Ranged** 5
Target: One creature
Attack: Wisdom vs. Will
Hit: 2d10 + Wisdom modifier psychic damage, and you teleport the target to a square adjacent to you. The target is dazed (save ends).
Miss: Half damage, and you teleport the target to a square adjacent to you.
Effect: Whenever you hit the target with a melee attack before the end of the encounter, you can shift 1 square and then slide the target to a square adjacent to you as a free action.

Level 10 Utility Prayers

Ever Onward — Avenger Utility 10

You breathe the words of a restorative prayer. New vigor and swiftness course through you.

Daily ✦ Divine, Healing
Minor Action **Personal**
Effect: You can spend a healing surge. In addition, you gain a +2 power bonus to speed until the end of the encounter.

Leading Step — Avenger Utility 10

After your enemy strikes, you teleport away. An instant later, you bring the enemy after you.

Encounter ✦ Divine, Teleportation
Immediate Reaction **Melee** 1
Trigger: An enemy adjacent to you damages you
Target: The triggering enemy
Effect: You teleport 5 squares and then teleport the target to a square adjacent to you.

Shielding Symbol — Avenger Utility 10

You channel divine power through your holy symbol to shield yourself.

Encounter ✦ Divine, Implement
Immediate Interrupt **Personal**
Trigger: You are hit by an attack
Effect: Make a Wisdom attack using your implement. The result is your defense against the triggering attack.

Wings of Vengeance — Avenger Utility 10

Ephemeral wings carry you across the battlefield to strike where you are most needed.

Encounter ✦ Divine
Move Action **Personal**
Effect: Until the end of your next turn, you gain a fly speed of 7, and you can hover.

Level 13 Encounter Prayers

Avenger's Demand — Avenger Attack 13

Your beckoning gesture compels the enemy to face swift justice.

Encounter ✦ Charm, Divine, Weapon
Standard Action **Ranged** 5
Target: One creature
Effect: You pull the target to a square adjacent to you, then make the following melee attack against it.
Attack: Wisdom vs. AC
Hit: 2[W] + Wisdom modifier damage, and you push the target 2 squares and knock it prone.
Censure of Pursuit: After you knock the target prone, you can shift 2 squares to a square adjacent to it.

Crimson Stride — Avenger Attack 13

You stride through nothingness, appearing at your enemy's side to make a deadly attack. Then you stride away, carrying your foe with you.

Encounter ✦ Divine, Teleportation, Weapon
Standard Action **Melee** 1
Effect: Before the attack, you teleport 5 squares to a square adjacent to an enemy.
Target: One enemy
Attack: Wisdom vs. AC
Hit: 2[W] + Wisdom modifier damage. You teleport 5 squares and then teleport the target to a square adjacent to you.
Censure of Retribution: If no creatures are adjacent to either you or the target after you teleport it, the target takes damage equal to your Intelligence modifier.
Censure of Unity: If you teleport the target at least 2 squares, it takes 2 damage for each of your allies adjacent to it after the movement.

Dervish Strike — Avenger Attack 13

Spinning gracefully, you aim a deft strike that sends your enemy sprawling into its companions.

Encounter ✦ Divine, Weapon
Standard Action **Melee** weapon
Primary Target: One enemy
Primary Attack: Wisdom vs. AC
Hit: 3[W] + Wisdom modifier damage, and you push the primary target 5 squares. When you push it through any square occupied by an enemy, make a secondary attack.
Secondary Target: Each enemy in the square
Secondary Attack: Wisdom vs. Fortitude
Hit: The secondary target is knocked prone.

Wages of Sin — Avenger Attack 13

Your prayer channels the anger, the fear, and the wickedness of your enemy's comrades to harm it.

Encounter ✦ Divine, Implement, Psychic
Standard Action **Ranged** 5
Target: One creature
Attack: Wisdom vs. Will
Hit: 2d10 + Wisdom modifier psychic damage. The attack deals 3 extra psychic damage for each enemy adjacent to the target.

Weaving Blades — Avenger Attack 13

You flourish your weapon in a dazzling display, striking your foe and any other that dares approach.

Encounter ✦ Divine, Weapon
Standard Action **Melee** weapon
Target: One creature
Attack: Wisdom vs. Reflex
Hit: 2[W] + Wisdom modifier damage. Until the end of your next turn, any enemy other than the target that enters a square adjacent to you or starts its turn there is affected by your weaving blades: As a free action, you can deal 5 damage to it and push it 1 square.

Level 15 Daily Prayers

Forceful Call — Avenger Attack 15

Channeled through your weapon, astral winds propel your enemies toward you and then spirit you away when you deliver an attack.

Daily ✦ Divine, Teleportation, Weapon
Standard Action **Close** burst 2
Primary Target: Each enemy in burst
Primary Attack: Wisdom vs. Will
Hit: You pull the primary target 2 squares.
Effect: Make a melee secondary attack.
Secondary Target: One adjacent enemy
Secondary Attack: Wisdom vs. AC
Hit: 3[W] + Wisdom modifier damage, plus 2 damage for each enemy adjacent to you.
Effect: You teleport 1 square for each enemy adjacent to you after the secondary attack.

KEREM BEYIT

Ghostly Chains — Avenger Attack 15

At the touch of your weapon, phantasmal fetters appear around your enemy, hindering its steps.

Daily ✦ Divine, Weapon
Standard Action **Melee** weapon
Target: One creature
Attack: Wisdom vs. AC
Hit: 3[W] + Wisdom modifier damage, and the target is slowed (save ends).
Miss: Half damage, and the target is slowed until the end of your next turn.
Special: If two or more of your allies are adjacent to the target, it is immobilized instead of slowed.

Inescapable Justice — Avenger Attack 15

No matter where your quarry goes, you are there.

Daily ✦ Divine, Teleportation, Weapon
Standard Action **Melee** weapon
Effect: Before the attack, you shift 2 squares.
Target: One creature
Attack: Wisdom vs. AC
Hit: 3[W] + Wisdom modifier damage.
Miss: Half damage.
Effect: Until the end of the encounter or until you or the target drops to 0 hit points, whenever you start your turn 3 or more squares away from the target, you can teleport to a square within 3 squares of it as a free action.

Soul Lightning — Avenger Attack 15

Your prayer sends lightning crackling through your enemy's body and mind, and it arcs to nearby foes.

Daily ✦ Divine, Implement, Lightning, Psychic
Standard Action **Ranged** 5
Target: One creature
Attack: Wisdom vs. Will
Hit: 3d10 + Wisdom modifier psychic damage, and ongoing 10 lightning damage (save ends).
Miss: Half damage, and ongoing 5 lightning damage (save ends).
Effect: Whenever the target takes this ongoing damage, each enemy within 2 squares of the target takes the same amount of lightning damage.

Temple of Brilliance — Avenger Attack 15

Your touch scours your foe with light, which lingers as a dazzling edifice over it.

Daily ✦ Divine, Implement, Radiant, Zone
Standard Action **Melee** touch
Target: One creature
Attack: Wisdom vs. Fortitude
Hit: 2d6 + Wisdom modifier radiant damage.
Miss: Half damage.
Effect: The attack creates a zone of radiant energy in a burst 2 centered on the target. The zone lasts until the end of your next turn. When the target moves, the zone moves with it, remaining centered on it. Any enemy that ends its turn within the zone is blinded until the end of its next turn.
Sustain Minor: The zone persists.

Tether of Light — Avenger Attack 15

As you swing your weapon, you forge a thin strand of light between you and your adversary, and then leap through the brilliant void to another spot. Compelled by the tether, your enemy follows.

Daily ✦ Divine, Teleportation, Weapon
Standard Action **Melee** weapon
Target: One creature
Attack: Wisdom vs. AC
Hit: 2[W] + Wisdom modifier damage. You teleport 5 squares and then teleport the target to a square adjacent to you.
Miss: Half damage.
Effect: When you hit the target with any melee attack before the end of the encounter, you can teleport a number of squares equal to your Intelligence modifier and then teleport the target to a square adjacent to you.

Zealous Onslaught — Avenger Attack 15

Trusting in your deity to guide your steps, you dash forward to smite your foe, sending it staggering away.

Daily ✦ Divine, Teleportation, Weapon
Standard Action **Melee** weapon
Effect: Before the attack, you shift 5 squares.
Target: One creature
Attack: Wisdom vs. AC
Hit: 2[W] + Wisdom modifier damage, and you push the target 3 squares. The target grants combat advantage (save ends).
Aftereffect: As a free action, you can teleport to a square adjacent to the target and make a melee basic attack.
Miss: Half damage, and the target grants combat advantage until the end of your next turn.

Level 16 Utility Prayers

Battle Blessing — Avenger Utility 16

You have sworn that your enemy shall fall—and it will, by your or your ally's hand.

Encounter ✦ Divine
Immediate Interrupt **Close** burst 5
Trigger: You or an ally within 5 squares of you makes an opportunity attack against your *oath of enmity* target
Effect: The opportunity attack deals 1[W] extra damage.

Pillar of Chernoggar — Avenger Utility 16

You summon strength from the oppressive dominion of Chernoggar, slowing your enemies.

Daily ✦ Divine, Stance
Minor Action **Personal**
Effect: Until the stance ends, any enemy that starts its turn adjacent to you is slowed until the end of your next turn.

Strength in Unity — Avenger Utility 16

The ties that join you and your friends become visible for a moment and serve as wards that shield you from harm.

Encounter ✦ Divine
Immediate Interrupt **Personal**
Trigger: An enemy attack damages you
Effect: The damage of the triggering attack is reduced against you by an amount equal to your Intelligence modifier × the number of allies within 2 squares of you.

Summons to Duty — Avenger Utility 16

Your ally is propelled toward your foe in a burst of wind and light.

Encounter ✦ Divine
Minor Action **Close** burst 5
Target: One ally in burst
Effect: You slide the target to a square adjacent to an enemy adjacent to you.

Temple of Seclusion — Avenger Utility 16

Fiery blue runes appear in the air around you, forming a pattern that scatters approaching creatures.

Daily ✦ Divine, Stance, Teleportation
Minor Action **Personal**
Effect: Until the stance ends, when any creature ends its turn adjacent to you, you can teleport that creature 3 squares as a free action.

For the DM: Avengers in the Campaign

You might want to have the avenger represent more than just a class in your campaign setting. With no great stretch of the imagination, you could create an organization made up of, or led by, avengers. Then, depending on the classes, alignments, and deities the PCs choose, the characters could be friends or foes of that group.

Your avenger organization might be made up of knights fighting to reclaim their holy land or a territory that they believe is rightfully theirs. With such a motivation, avengers could come across as heroes or villains. The avengers could also be a clandestine group working behind the scenes, undermining governments or working against greater evils and trappings than the typical political rivalries of nations.

You might encourage a PC to incorporate his or her background into this organization. Perhaps the character is an agent working to keep an eye on the other PCs or to guide them toward certain paths. Or maybe she is trying to recruit the other PCs for the organization's purposes. Or, perhaps the character is trying to escape the organization, hoping to start a new life free of duty or expectations.

Level 17 Encounter Prayers

Accept No Defeat — Avenger Attack 17

Single-minded pursuit is usually your strength, but prayers, like plans, can be phrased with fallback maneuvers.

Encounter ✦ Divine, Weapon
Standard Action **Melee** weapon
Target: One creature
Attack: Wisdom vs. AC
Hit: 3[W] + Wisdom modifier damage.
Miss: You shift 1 square and make a melee basic attack against a different creature, with a +4 bonus to the damage roll.

Lethal Intercession — Avenger Attack 17

Spiritual echoes of your weapon surround your foe, confounding its attacks.

Encounter ✦ Divine, Weapon
Standard Action **Melee** weapon
Target: One creature
Attack: Wisdom vs. AC
Hit: 3[W] + Wisdom modifier damage, and the target takes a -2 penalty to attack rolls until the end of your next turn.
Censure of Pursuit: When you use this power against your *oath of enmity* target, the power is reliable.
Special: This power can be used as an opportunity attack against your *oath of enmity* target.

Punishing Blow — Avenger Attack 17

Your sworn enemy and all who stand with it must answer to you now.

Encounter ✦ Divine, Weapon
Standard Action **Melee** weapon
Target: One creature
Attack: Wisdom vs. AC
Hit: 3[W] + Wisdom modifier damage. If the target is your *oath of enmity* target, each enemy adjacent to the target also counts as a target of your *oath of enmity* until the end of your next turn.

Vengeful Parry — Avenger Attack 17

You parry your enemy's attack and make a riposte infused with holy power.

Encounter ✦ Divine, Weapon
Immediate Interrupt **Melee** 1
Trigger: An enemy adjacent to you hits or misses you
Target: The triggering enemy
Effect: The target takes a -2 penalty to the attack roll. Make the following attack against the target.
Censure of Unity: The penalty to the target's attack roll equals your Intelligence modifier.
Attack: Wisdom vs. AC
Hit: 2[W] + Wisdom modifier damage. You shift 1 square and then slide the target 2 squares to a square adjacent to you.

Wrathful Charge — Avenger Attack 17

You dash across the battlefield, gaining momentum from each attack against you, until you slam into your enemy with your weapon.

Encounter ✦ Divine, Weapon
Standard Action **Melee** 1
Effect: You gain phasing and a +4 bonus to AC against opportunity attacks until the end of your turn. You then charge and make the following attack in place of a melee basic attack.
Target: One creature
Attack: Wisdom vs. AC
Hit: 2[W] + Wisdom modifier damage. The attack deals 2 extra damage for each opportunity attack made against you during the charge movement.
Censure of Retribution: The extra damage for each opportunity attack equals your Intelligence modifier.

Level 19 Daily Prayers

Blade of Astral Hosts — Avenger Attack 19

You stride into the midst of your enemies, laying about with your weapon. For each foe you strike, a celestial blade forms alongside your own, lending might to your final attack.

Daily ✦ Divine, Teleportation, Weapon
Standard Action **Close** burst 1
Effect: Before the primary attack, you teleport 5 squares.
Primary Target: Each enemy in burst
Primary Attack: Wisdom vs. AC
Hit: 1[W] + Wisdom modifier damage.
Effect: You teleport 5 squares and make a melee secondary attack.
Secondary Target: One creature adjacent to you
Secondary Attack: Wisdom vs. AC
Hit: 3[W] + Wisdom modifier damage, plus 2 damage for each enemy hit by the primary attack.
Miss: Half damage.

Bonded by Blood — Avenger Attack 19

Your attack forges a bond between you and your enemy.

Daily ✦ Divine, Teleportation, Weapon
Standard Action **Melee** weapon
Target: One creature
Attack: Wisdom vs. Fortitude
Hit: 4[W] + Wisdom modifier damage.
Miss: Half damage.
Effect: Whenever the target moves, you can teleport to a square adjacent to it as a free action after its movement is complete. This effect lasts until the end of the encounter or until you end your turn not adjacent to the target.

Flame Unquenchable — Avenger Attack 19

Your prayer sets your weapon ablaze with blue fire. A single thrust transfers the flames to your foe.

Daily ✦ Divine, Fire, Weapon
Standard Action **Melee** weapon
Target: One creature
Attack: Wisdom vs. AC
Hit: 3[W] + Wisdom modifier damage, and ongoing 10 fire damage (save ends).
Miss: Half damage, and ongoing 5 fire damage (save ends).
Effect: Until the end of the encounter, the target takes a -1 penalty to saving throws against ongoing damage. The penalty worsens by -1 for each creature taking ongoing damage within 10 squares of the target.

SERVING MULTIPLE MASTERS

You can choose one god for your avenger to follow, but there's no reason why your character must champion only a single deity. You might serve the whole pantheon as a weapon against the primordials and others who oppose the immortals, or you could worship a particular pairing or group of gods based upon common cause.

Perhaps you despise slavery and tyrants, and as such you pray to Avandra for luck and Sehanine for stealth as you seek to bring your foes down. You might see yourself as the hand of fate and look to both Ioun and the Raven Queen for what the future should hold. Maybe you strike out in the dark parts of the world, hoping to bring the triune light of civilization, craft, and knowledge, serving Erathis, Ioun, and Moradin. Perhaps your dragonborn avenger puts faith in the might of dragons and pays homage to both Bahamut and Tiamat. You might believe in protecting others from dangerous knowledge and pray to both Sehanine and Vecna, believing that some secrets are better left kept. Your righteous wrath might be directed against undead with the blessings of both Pelor and the Raven Queen. It could be that you take strength from the pristine wilderness, and thus you follow Melora and Kord.

Serving more than one deity gives you more roleplaying options. You have more sources for made-up adages, more imagined religious rites you might perform, and more than one lens through which to view the world and express your perspectives. Having multiple deities also increases your opportunities to make a personal mark on the story of the campaign. If your avenger has more than one deity's cause to care about, you'll have more chances to bring those different causes into focus during adventures.

Stroke of Doom — Avenger Attack 19

You brandish your weapon, seeking to drag your foe toward you with divine force. Failing that, you leap to the foe. Either way, your weapon is charged with lethal power.

Daily ✦ Divine, Weapon
Standard Action **Ranged** 5
Target: One creature
Primary Attack: Wisdom vs. Fortitude
Hit: You pull the target to a square adjacent to you.
Miss: You shift 5 squares to a square adjacent to the target.
Effect: Make a melee secondary attack against the target if it is adjacent to you.
Secondary Attack: Wisdom vs. AC
Hit: 5[W] + Wisdom modifier damage.
Miss: Half damage.

LEVEL 22 UTILITY PRAYERS

Refuge of Piety — Avenger Utility 22

You clear your mind and magically slough off impediments.

Encounter ✦ Divine
Move Action **Personal**
Effect: You make a saving throw against each effect on you that a save can end. You shift 1 square for each save.

Seeker's Step — Avenger Utility 22

They might hit you once, but you'll be damned if they'll do it twice.

Daily ✦ Divine, Stance, Teleportation
Minor Action **Personal**
Effect: Until the stance ends, whenever you are hit by an enemy's melee or ranged attack, you can teleport 10 squares to a square adjacent to your *oath of enmity* target as an immediate reaction.

Shield of Providence — Avenger Utility 22

Uttering a quick prayer, you partially leave the physical realm for a moment and channel the power of your foe's attack into your own.

Encounter ✦ Divine
Immediate Interrupt **Personal**
Trigger: An enemy hits you with an area or a close attack
Effect: You become insubstantial until the end of your next turn. In addition, your next attack before the end of your next turn deals 2d10 extra damage.

LEVEL 23 ENCOUNTER PRAYERS

Chains of Fate — Avenger Attack 23

As you attack, you mystically bind your sworn enemy's fate to yours, causing it to share your injuries.

Encounter ✦ Divine, Weapon
Standard Action **Melee** weapon
Target: One creature
Attack: Wisdom vs. AC
Hit: 3[W] + Wisdom modifier damage. Until the start of your next turn, you take half damage from any source and your *oath of enmity* target takes the other half.

Excoriating Challenge — Avenger Attack 23

Your holy symbol glows red as you curse your foes. The might of your rebuke hurls away nearby creatures but brings your chosen foe before you for judgment.

Encounter ✦ Divine, Implement, Radiant, Teleportation
Standard Action **Close** burst 3
Target: Each creature in burst
Attack: Wisdom vs. Will
Hit: You teleport the target 5 squares to a square that is farther away from you. If the target is your *oath of enmity* target, it instead takes 4d10 + your Wisdom modifier radiant damage, and you teleport it to a square adjacent to you.

Fearsome Fury — Avenger Attack 23

Nothing clarifies your objective better than the terror in your enemies' eyes.

Encounter ✦ Divine, Fear, Weapon
Standard Action **Melee** weapon
Target: One creature
Attack: Wisdom vs. AC
Hit: 4[W] + Wisdom modifier damage. Until the end of your next turn, when the target makes any attack roll, it takes a penalty to that attack roll equal to the number of your allies adjacent to it.
Censure of Unity: The penalty equals the number of your allies adjacent to the target + your Intelligence modifier.

Threatening Strike — Avenger Attack 23

Your strike knocks your foe aside, and any hope it has of escaping is dashed when it finds your weapon in its face.

Encounter ✦ Divine, Teleportation, Weapon
Standard Action **Melee** weapon
Target: One creature
Attack: Wisdom vs. Fortitude
Hit: 3[W] + Wisdom modifier damage, and you slide the target 2 squares. If the target moves before the start of your next turn, you can teleport to a square adjacent to it and make a melee basic attack against it.
Censure of Retribution: Until the end of your next turn, you gain a bonus to your basic attacks' damage rolls equal to your Intelligence modifier.

Vengeful Apparition — Avenger Attack 23

The touch of your weapon sends your foe reeling in terror, and you become ghostly, able to walk through walls and soar through the air.

Encounter ✦ Divine, Fear, Weapon
Standard Action **Melee** weapon
Target: One creature
Attack: Wisdom vs. Fortitude
Hit: 3[W] + Wisdom modifier damage, and you push the target a number of squares equal to your Wisdom modifier and knock it prone.
Effect: You gain phasing and a fly speed of 6 until the end of your next turn.
Censure of Pursuit: The fly speed equals 6 + your Dexterity modifier.

Victory Hymn — Avenger Attack 23

You hum a hymn about a time when war will not be needed. But for now, you seek to end the fight as the victorious survivor.

Encounter ✦ Divine, Healing, Weapon
Standard Action **Melee** weapon
Target: One creature
Attack: Wisdom vs. AC
Hit: 3[W] + Wisdom modifier damage. Before the end of your next turn, you gain a bonus to your next attack's damage rolls equal to your Wisdom modifier.
Effect: If this attack reduces the target to 0 hit points or if you have reduced your *oath of enmity* target to 0 hit points during this encounter, you can spend a healing surge and make a saving throw.

Level 25 Daily Prayers

Amber Prisons — Avenger Attack 25

When you pull your hand away from your enemy, it leaves behind an amber sigil from which shines an eerie light. Those touched by its glow become encased in amber sarcophagi.

Daily ✦ Divine, Implement, Radiant
Standard Action **Melee** touch
Primary Target: One creature
Primary Attack: Wisdom vs. Fortitude
Hit: 5d8 + Wisdom modifier radiant damage, and the primary target is immobilized (save ends).
Miss: Half damage, and the primary target is immobilized until the end of your next turn.
Effect: Make a secondary attack that is a close burst 1, using the primary target's space as the origin square.
Secondary Target: Each enemy in burst other than the primary target
Secondary Attack: Wisdom vs. Fortitude
Hit: You slide the secondary target 3 squares, and it is immobilized until the end of your next turn.
Miss: The secondary target is slowed until the end of your next turn.

Drawn by Fate — Avenger Attack 25

Two shimmering portals appear, drawing you or your enemy to find your fate.

Daily ✦ Divine, Implement, Teleportation
Standard Action **Ranged** 10
Target: One creature
Primary Attack: Wisdom vs. Will
Hit: You teleport the target to a square adjacent to you.
Miss: You teleport to a square adjacent to the target.
Effect: Make a melee secondary attack against the target using your weapon. In addition, the target is drawn by fate (save ends). Until this effect ends, you can teleport the target to a square adjacent to you as a minor action.
Secondary Attack: Wisdom vs. AC
Hit: 4[W] + Wisdom modifier damage.
Miss: Half damage.

Mantle of the Astral Champion — Avenger Attack 25

As you attack, your prayer bestows on you the mantle of the astral champion, allowing you to fly like an angelic being.

Daily ✦ Divine, Weapon
Standard Action **Melee** weapon
Target: One creature
Attack: Wisdom vs. AC
Hit: 4[W] + Wisdom modifier damage.
Effect: Until the end of the encounter, you gain phasing and a fly speed of 6, and you can hover.

WHOM TO HUNT?

The avenger walks a dark path of retribution and punishment. Yet with some deities it might be difficult to figure out whom the avenger seeks to censure. When the deity is as fair-minded as Bahamut or as kind as Pelor, what role does your avenger fill? Below are some suggestions for the types of individuals or groups that an avenger devoted to a certain deity might obsess about.

Avandra: Asmodeus worshipers, cheaters, people complacent in the face of evil, slavers, Torog worshipers

Bahamut: Bullies, chromatic dragons, liars, Tiamat worshipers, unjust leaders

Corellon: Drow, fomorians, Lolth worshipers, those who destroy beauty, those who destroy magic

Erathis: Demons, Gruumsh worshipers, overzealous worshipers of Melora, revolutionaries, those who destroy the works of civilization, uncivilized peoples

Ioun: Those who destroy knowledge, those who destroy magic, those who promote ignorant ideas, Vecna worshipers

Kord: Cowards, those who possess strength but fail to use it, those who dissemble or employ subterfuge instead of direct confrontations, those who gain strength by making others weak

Melora: Aberrants, overzealous worshipers of Erathis, Gruumsh worshipers, cultists of Yeenoghu

Moradin: Cultists of primordials, "deviant" dwarves such as azers or duergar, those who leech off others' labors, traitors

Pelor: Shadar-kai, those who cause undue suffering, the causes of famine and disease, undead, Vecna worshipers

The Raven Queen: Cultists of Orcus, those who seek to prolong life beyond its natural end, undead, Vecna worshipers

Sehanine: Asmodeus worshipers, zealots of any kind, those who destroy love, Zehir worshipers

Thunderhead Smite — Avenger Attack 25

You present your holy symbol with a shouted prayer, causing a shock wave to scatter your foes, and thunder crashes over an enemy that remains behind.

Daily ✦ Divine, Implement, Thunder
Standard Action **Close** burst 3
Target: Each enemy in burst
Attack: Wisdom vs. Reflex
Hit: You push the target 3 squares.
Effect: One enemy adjacent to you takes 10 thunder damage for each target hit. If no enemy is adjacent to you, you regain the use of this power.

Level 27 Encounter Prayers

Anvil of Faith — Avenger Attack 27

Summoning strength from your comrades' courage, you deliver a mighty blow that tosses your enemy across the battlefield.

Encounter ✦ Divine, Weapon
Standard Action **Melee** weapon
Target: One creature
Attack: Wisdom vs. AC
Hit: 3[W] + Wisdom modifier damage, and you push the target a number of squares equal to the number of your allies adjacent to it. The target takes 5 damage for each square it enters during the forced movement.
Censure of Unity: The target is knocked prone at the end of the forced movement.

Brilliant Halo — Avenger Attack 27

As you hurl divine light at your enemy, a scintillating halo appears above you. Any enemy that approaches is burned in its glow.

Encounter ✦ Divine, Healing, Implement, Radiant
Standard Action **Ranged** 5
Target: One creature
Attack: Wisdom vs. Fortitude
Hit: 4d6 + Wisdom modifier radiant damage. Until the end of your next turn, any enemy that ends its turn within 5 squares of you takes 5 radiant damage, and you regain 5 hit points.
Censure of Retribution: Your Intelligence modifier is added to the damage and healing caused when an enemy ends its turn within 5 squares of you.

Hand of Silver — Avenger Attack 27

Your hand shines with a silvery light as you touch your enemy, preventing its escape.

Encounter ✦ Divine, Implement, Radiant
Standard Action **Melee** touch
Target: One creature
Attack: Wisdom vs. Reflex
Hit: 2d12 + Wisdom modifier radiant damage, and the target is restrained until the end of your next turn.
Censure of Pursuit: The attack deals extra radiant damage equal to your Dexterity modifier.

Spark of Hatred — Avenger Attack 27

There is a spark of hatred in every foul creature, and in many fair ones. The power of your oath fans that spark, quick and lethal.

Encounter ✦ Charm, Divine, Implement
Minor Action **Ranged** 5
Target: One enemy that is not your *oath of enmity* target
Attack: Wisdom vs. Will
Hit: The target is dominated until the start of your next turn. Until this domination ends, the target can attack only your *oath of enmity* target.

Level 29 Daily Prayers

Cataclysmic Duel — Avenger Attack 29

Mighty shock waves resound around you and your enemy. Each exchange of blows sends roiling tendrils of destruction across the battlefield.

Daily ✦ Divine, Thunder, Weapon
Standard Action **Melee** weapon
Target: One creature
Attack: Wisdom vs. AC
Hit: 7[W] + Wisdom modifier thunder damage, and the target takes a -2 penalty to attack rolls against you (save ends).
Miss: Half damage.
Effect: Until the end of the encounter, whenever the target hits you, it chooses one of your allies within 5 squares of you or within 5 squares of the target. That ally is knocked prone. In addition, whenever you hit the target, you choose an enemy other than the target within 5 squares of you or within 5 squares of the target. That enemy is dazed (save ends).

Divide and Condemn — Avenger Attack 29

You stride instantly to your enemy and set your hand upon it, speaking a prayer of condemnation. Nearby enemies are scattered by your power.

Daily ✦ Divine, Implement, Radiant, Teleportation
Standard Action **Melee** touch
Effect: Before the attack, you teleport 10 squares.
Target: One creature
Attack: Wisdom vs. Will
Hit: 7d8 + Wisdom modifier radiant damage.
Miss: Half damage.
Effect: You teleport each enemy adjacent to the target 10 squares.

Eye of the Hurricane — Avenger Attack 29

You inhale and draw your enemies close, using their energy to deliver a thunderous attack against the object of your malice.

Daily ✦ Divine, Implement, Thunder
Standard Action **Close** burst 3
Primary Target: Each enemy in burst
Primary Attack: Wisdom vs. Fortitude
Hit: You pull the primary target 3 squares, and it is deafened (save ends).
Effect: Make a melee secondary attack using your weapon.
Secondary Target: One adjacent creature
Secondary Attack: Wisdom vs. AC
Hit: 6[W] + Wisdom modifier damage, plus 5 thunder damage for each enemy adjacent to you.

Impaling Summons — Avenger Attack 29

Channeling the fury of the gods, you compel an enemy to fling itself onto your weapon.

Daily ✦ Charm, Divine, Weapon
Standard Action **Ranged** 10
Target: One creature
Effect: You pull the target to a square adjacent to you, then make the following melee attack against it.
Attack: Wisdom vs. AC
Hit: 6[W] + Wisdom modifier damage.
Miss: Half damage.

March of Doom — Avenger Attack 29

You command your foe to march to the place where you intend for it to die, and then send your allies to slay it there.

Daily ✦ Charm, Divine, Teleportation, Weapon
Standard Action **Close** burst 5
Target: One creature in burst
Effect: You slide the target 5 squares and teleport to a square adjacent to it. You then slide each ally in the burst 5 squares to a square adjacent to the target. Then you make the following melee attack against it.
Attack: Wisdom vs. AC
Hit: 5[W] + Wisdom modifier damage, and you knock the target prone.

Merciless Nemesis — Avenger Attack 29

As you attack, you appoint yourself the nemesis of your chosen foe. Where you go, it must follow.

Daily ✦ Divine, Teleportation, Weapon
Standard Action **Melee** weapon
Target: One creature
Attack: Wisdom vs. AC
Hit: 5[W] + Wisdom modifier damage.
Miss: Half damage.
Effect: Until the end of the encounter, whenever you hit your *oath of enmity* target with an avenger attack power, you can teleport 5 squares and then teleport your *oath of enmity* target to a square adjacent to you.

Ardent Champion

"The fires of heaven inflame my soul. I am a sword in the hand of my god. Death means nothing to me!"

Prerequisite: Avenger, Censure of Pursuit class feature, *oath of enmity* power

Most avengers undergo training in secret temples or monasteries to prepare for their service and receive their powers through rites of initiation, but some are endowed with divine power simply through raw devotion to their god. Such avengers dig deep within themselves to find unmatched reserves of faith, making up for their lack of formal training with holy passion. These are ardent champions.

As an ardent champion, you are an outsider, your spirit touched directly by the hand of your deity. You are most likely unlearned in the esoteric lore of your faith, and you have little connection to any hierarchies associated with it. In fact, others who lack your passion might see you as a threat to the established ways. Where cynics and pragmatists see despair or uncertainty, you see only your divine patron's will, and you set out to accomplish it regardless of obstacles. If you are meant to triumph, you will. If you are not, you are confident that you will soon be shown another way to serve your god.

Ardent Champion Path Features

Holy Ardor (11th level): Whenever you make two attack rolls because of your *oath of enmity*, you score a critical hit if both dice have the same roll, except if both rolls are 1.

Ardent Action (11th level): When you spend an action point to take an extra action, you can also make a saving throw or shift a number of squares equal to your Dexterity modifier.

Ardent Fury (16th level): Once per round when you score a critical hit against your *oath of enmity* target, you can shift 1 square and make a basic attack against that target as a free action.

Ardent Champion Prayers

Fanatical Flurry — Ardent Champion Attack 11

You launch a reckless attack against your chosen enemy and all foes nearby, ignoring your own safety.

Encounter ✦ Divine, Weapon
Standard Action **Close** burst 2
Target: Your *oath of enmity* target and each enemy in burst
Attack: Wisdom vs. AC
Hit: 2[W] + Wisdom modifier damage.
Effect: You take a -2 penalty to all defenses until the end of your next turn.

Battle Rapture — Ardent Champion Utility 12

You enter a state of zealous passion, consumed by the power of your faith. Defeating your sworn enemy is a test of faith for you.

Daily ✦ Divine, Stance
Minor Action **Personal**
Effect: Until the stance ends, your attacks deal extra damage against your *oath of enmity* target equal to 1d10 + one-half your level. In addition, when any ally deals damage (not ongoing damage) to your *oath of enmity* target, you take 3d6 damage.

Irresistible Ardor — Ardent Champion Attack 20

Your spirit blazes with devotion, lending holy power to your strike. Your sworn enemy's attacks are as nothing to you.

Daily ✦ Divine, Weapon
Standard Action **Melee** weapon
Target: One creature
Attack: Wisdom vs. AC
Hit: 4[W] + Wisdom modifier damage. You regain the use of an encounter power that you have already used during this encounter.
Miss: Half damage.
Effect: Until you attack a creature other than your *oath of enmity* target or until the end of the encounter, you gain a +2 power bonus to all defenses against the attacks of your *oath of enmity* target.

KEREM BEYIT

Dervish of Dawn

"In the turnings of the dance, the divine purpose is made clear."

Prerequisite: Avenger

You are among a small number of avengers who seek enlightenment through the study of desert dervish traditions. In the tireless turns of the dervish dance, the cares and distractions of the mortal world fall away, allowing you to perceive divine truths.

There are a number of dervish traditions, and not all dervishes are avengers; most are priests and scholars of desert peoples. Dervishes of the dawn represent a tradition celebrating the mystic power of the sunrise and venerating gods of hope and enlightenment. As a dervish of dawn, you are an agent of hope, a wandering mystic given the sacred task of fighting oppression and despair and setting an example of piety wherever you travel.

Dervish of Dawn Path Features

Celerity of Morning (11th level): When you spend an action point to take an extra action, you can also make a saving throw with a bonus equal to your Wisdom modifier.

Radiant Blessing (11th level): When you use an encounter or a daily attack power that has the radiant keyword, you gain a +2 bonus to all defenses until the end of your next turn.

Dervish Ecstasy (16th level): If you are bloodied during an encounter, you can use a second Channel Divinity power in that encounter.

Dervish of Dawn Prayers

Whirling Assault — Dervish of Dawn Attack 11

You launch into a graceful, spinning dance as you close on your enemy. In the mesmerizing form of your dance, you free yourself from an enemy's power and inspire your comrade as well.

Encounter ✦ Divine, Radiant, Weapon
Standard Action **Melee** weapon
Effect: Before the attack, you shift 3 squares.
Target: One creature
Attack: Wisdom vs. AC
Hit: 2[W] + Wisdom modifier radiant damage. You and one ally within 10 squares of you can each choose to do one of the following things:
- ✦ Make an escape attempt against a grab as a free action.
- ✦ Make a saving throw against an effect that a save can end and that dazes, immobilizes, slows, or stuns.

Wild Hope — Dervish of Dawn Utility 12

Your dance inspires you to wild ecstasy. Mortals cannot long endure such joy, but each time you strike your foe, new vigor flows into you.

Daily ✦ Divine, Healing, Stance
Minor Action **Personal**
Effect: Until the stance ends, whenever you hit one or more enemies with an attack, you regain hit points equal to your Wisdom modifier. In addition, whenever you miss every target with an attack, you take 3 damage.

Dance of Sunrise — Dervish of Dawn Attack 20

As you gracefully carry yourself across the battlefield, your weapon begins to gleam. For the rest of the fight, you glow with the hues of dawn, which scorch your foe with light.

Daily ✦ Divine, Radiant, Weapon
Standard Action **Melee** weapon
Effect: Before the attack, you shift 3 squares.
Target: One creature
Attack: Wisdom vs. AC
Hit: 3[W] + Wisdom modifier radiant damage.
Miss: Half damage.
Effect: Until the end of the encounter, your at-will attack powers against the target deal 1d8 extra radiant damage to it.

KIERAN YANNER

Dread Imperator

"When the gods command, I make sure you obey."

Prerequisite: Avenger, Censure of Unity class feature, *oath of enmity* power

In the days of the human empire of Nerath, many temples and faiths were wealthy and widespread enough to give rise to powerful hierarchies, kingdom-spanning organizations that often wielded both religious and secular power. These empires of faith lapsed into disorder when Nerath fell. Temples lost touch with each other, local leaders split from their distant masters, and disaffected people abandoned the great temples for generations. But in a few places, the titles and trappings of the old hierarchies survive. Imperators are among these surviving traditions, a reminder of the days when archpriests maintained temple armies led by imperators, ruled over estates, and sponsored vigilant orders of inquisitors to ferret out dissent and disloyalty.

As a dread imperator, you have been invested in accordance with the old ways. Even though your deity's faith is only a shadow of its former kingdom-spanning glory, you still wield divine authority against your deity's enemies. You have the power to compel obedience from your foes and inspire loyalty in your allies. You are a guardian of what you consider the right path, tirelessly seeking out foes both hidden and open. The day will come when the faith is restored throughout the lands, and you mean to be there to see it.

Dread Imperator Path Features

Deceptive Control (11th level): When your *oath of enmity* target misses you with an attack, your allies gain combat advantage against that target until the end of its next turn.

Imperious Action (11th level): When you spend an action point to take an extra action, you also slide an enemy within 5 squares of you 1 square or slide an ally within 5 squares of you 3 squares.

Templar Reaction (16th level): When any ally scores a critical hit against your *oath of enmity* target, you can make an opportunity attack against that target if it is within your reach. You gain a bonus to the damage roll equal to your Intelligence modifier.

Dread Imperator Prayers

Soul Stab — Dread Imperator Attack 11

A twist of your blade is a twist in your enemy's soul, wrenching it sideways to strike its companion.

Encounter ✦ Charm, Divine, Weapon
Standard Action **Melee** weapon
Target: One creature
Attack: Wisdom vs. AC
Hit: 2[W] + Wisdom modifier damage, and you slide the target 2 squares. The target then makes a basic attack against a creature of your choice.

Crown of Souls — Dread Imperator Utility 12

The radiant crown settling on your brow symbolizes your mastery. Shadows of the crown flash above your companions.

Daily ✦ Divine, Stance
Minor Action **Personal**
Effect: Until the stance ends, whenever you make multiple attack rolls at one time against your *oath of enmity* target and they would all hit, choose an ally within 5 squares of you. That ally gains a +1 power bonus to attack rolls and all defenses until the end of your next turn.

Imperator's Judgment — Dread Imperator Attack 20

You deliver a punishing blow to your foe while pronouncing judgment against it. For a moment, your divine authority compels it to obey you.

Daily ✦ Charm, Divine, Weapon
Standard Action **Melee** weapon
Target: One creature
Attack: Wisdom vs. AC
Hit: 3[W] + Wisdom modifier damage, and the target is dominated until the end of your next turn.
Effect: You gain another use of your *soul stab* power for this encounter.

CONCEPT ART HOUSE LLC

Favored Soul

"Who am I? I am the sword of heaven, forged on the anvil of the world, and you have angered my master."

Prerequisite: Avenger

You have long harbored a divine spark within yourself, a subtle shard of your god's essence. Long has it lain dormant, but as you dispatch your enemies and see your oaths through, the essence awakens and infuses your body with astral brilliance until your mortal shell transmutes into something greater than what it once was. Your deeds are the catalyst for your transformation into a favored soul. Once you set foot on this glorious path, you ever after carry with you the blessings of your god.

Becoming a favored soul triggers several physical changes, specifically the appearance of feathery wings that grow, almost overnight, from your back. These wings have strength enough to bear your weight. Your feathers can be any color you like. As you continue down this path, your body lightens, your bones becoming hollow and strong so you can fly more easily without sacrificing your durability. By the time you complete this path, your lower body trails off into mist when you fly, thus marking you as one of the heavenly host, kin to angels, and a special servant of your god.

EMRAH ELMASLI

Favored Soul Path Features

Favored Action (11th level): When you spend an action point to take an extra action, you or an ally adjacent to you can also spend a healing surge.

Heaven's Shield (11th level): While you have maximum hit points, you gain a +1 bonus to all defenses.

Heaven's Boon (16th level): A pair of feathery wings unfolds from your back, and you gain a fly speed of 6. You can use this speed only if you are wearing no armor or light armor.

Favored Soul Prayers

Radiant Rush — Favored Soul Attack 11

You blur into action, speeding across the battlefield to smash into your enemy in a halo of radiance. If your blow misses, the light conceals you.

Encounter ✦ Divine, Radiant, Weapon
Standard Action **Melee** weapon
Target: Your *oath of enmity* target
Attack: Wisdom vs. AC
Hit: 2[W] + Wisdom modifier radiant damage, you push the target 2 squares, and the target is dazed until the end of your next turn.
Miss: You gain concealment until the end of your next turn.
Special: When charging, you can use this power in place of a melee basic attack.

Wings of Angels — Favored Soul Utility 12

Your lower body fades into swirling mist as you gain mastery of your airborne movement.

Daily ✦ Divine, Healing, Stance
Minor Action **Personal**
Effect: Until the stance ends, your fly speed increases by 4, and you can hover. In addition, while you aren't bloodied, you gain regeneration equal to your Wisdom modifier.

Celestial Skirmish — Favored Soul Attack 20

You take to the sky, your weapon aglow. You swoop and strike repeatedly as you dart past your foes.

Daily ✦ Divine, Radiant, Weapon
Standard Action **Melee** weapon
Effect: You fly your speed + 2. During this movement, you gain a +6 bonus to AC against opportunity attacks. At any point during the movement, you can make the following attack three times, each time against a different target.
Target: One creature
Attack: Wisdom vs. AC
Hit: 2[W] + Wisdom modifier radiant damage. If you hit two creatures, the second is dazed (save ends). If you hit three creatures, the third is stunned (save ends).

Relentless Slayer

"I am the bane of your kind."

Prerequisite: Avenger, *oath of enmity* power

Many avengers find themselves confronting some great threat, such as a group of drow seeking to enslave a surface kingdom, an incursion of demons, a cult of Tharizdun worshipers, or an empire of vampires secretly ruling over human cities. Whatever the threat might be, it is dire enough to drive you to an old and powerful rite of sacred commitment. Through prayerful vigils, you have invested your *oath of enmity* with tremendous potency. All avengers rely on *oath of enmity*, but you draw on yours to perform exceptional feats in battle.

As a relentless slayer, you are always alert for signs that your enemies are at work. Your adventures often lead you away from a longtime adversary for weeks or months at a time, but you know that you have a sacred duty to which you must eventually return.

Choosing a Slayer's Enemy

Consult with your Dungeon Master about an appropriate enemy for your character. It should be a kind of monster you've faced before, and one that the DM plans to feature occasionally in upcoming adventures. A slayer's enemy is a specific group of monsters—for example, demons, devils, drow, fire giants, minotaurs, or vampires.

Relentless Slayer Path Features

Slayer's Oath (11th level): Whenever you use *oath of enmity*, you can target a second enemy with it if that enemy is your slayer's enemy (see the sidebar). In addition, when you make an attack and could make two attack rolls because of *oath of enmity*, you can choose to forgo making the second roll to cause the attack to deal 2d6 extra damage instead. You make this choice before making the first attack roll.

Lethal Action (11th level): If you spend an action point to make an attack against your *oath of enmity* target, the attack can score a critical hit on a roll of 18–20.

Relentless Determination (16th level): When you fail a saving throw against an effect caused by an enemy, your divine attack powers deal 5 extra damage until the end of your next turn.

Relentless Slayer Prayers

Slayer's Gambit — Relentless Slayer Attack 11

You recklessly bull your way through the press of enemies to meet your destiny near your chosen foe.

Encounter ✦ Divine, Weapon
Standard Action — **Melee** weapon
Effect: You move your speed to a square where your *oath of enmity* target is within your reach. During this movement, you can move through enemies' squares. Then you make the following attack.
Target: Your *oath of enmity* target
Attack: Wisdom vs. AC
Hit: 2[W] + Wisdom modifier damage. The attack deals 5 extra damage for each opportunity attack made against you during the movement that is part of this power.

Relentless Fervor — Relentless Slayer Utility 12

Success against your chosen foe creates opportunities against nearby enemies.

Daily ✦ Divine, Stance
Minor Action — **Personal**
Effect: Until the stance ends, when you make two attack rolls because of your *oath of enmity*, make the rolls one at a time. If the first attack roll hits, you can choose to use the second attack roll as a melee basic attack against another enemy within reach.

Slayer's Ascendancy — Relentless Slayer Attack 20

Through the power of your god, you see the battle as if everyone else was moving at half speed.

Daily ✦ Divine, Stance, Weapon
Standard Action — **Melee** weapon
Target: One enemy
Attack: Wisdom vs. AC
Hit: 4[W] + Wisdom modifier damage.
Miss: Half damage.
Effect: You assume the slayer's stance. Until the stance ends, you can make a melee basic attack once per round as a minor action.

LUCIO PARRILLO

Serene Initiate

"Only when the mind is calm and the passions stilled can the divine purpose be understood. Never do I wield my sword in anger—only in necessity."

Prerequisite: Avenger, *oath of enmity* power

AMELIA STONER

You have chosen to follow a path of contemplation and calm. Some heroes are ruled by their passions, but you seek a disciplined approach to your quests. You are not emotionless, but you believe that you should rule your emotions instead of being ruled by them. Anger, despair, fear—all turn the mortal heart away from the divine will. Likewise, you must remain vigilant against excesses of mirth, desire, or pride. You believe that powerful emotions and worldly attachments entangle the spirit with the mortal realm and keep you from paying attention to what is most important.

Although you are slow to anger and careful in your actions, you are no pacifist. The world is full of dangers that must be met with force, and you are a warrior sworn to the service of the divine. When violent action is necessary—as it all too often is—you battle your enemies with dispassionate efficiency. You see no reason to waste words on those who can't or won't listen, or to extend mercy to those who would try to exploit it.

Between adventures, you strive to set an example of moderation and piety. Many serene initiates are cloistered monks who pass their days in monasteries, leading lives of self-discipline and prayer until they are needed to confront darkness again.

Serene Initiate Path Features

Calm Eye (11th level): When you spend an action point to use an at-will attack power, that attack deals 2d10 extra damage.

Serene Edge (11th level): When you miss your *oath of enmity* target with an encounter attack power, the attack deals damage to the target equal to your Dexterity modifier.

Certain Cut (16th level): When you miss your *oath of enmity* target with an at-will attack power, the attack deals damage to the target equal to your Dexterity modifier.

Serene Initiate Prayers

Defining Cut — Serene Initiate Attack 11

Your deadly calm shapes the battle.

Encounter ✦ Divine, Weapon
Standard Action — **Melee** weapon
Target: One or two creatures
Attack: Wisdom vs. AC. If one of the targets is your *oath of enmity* target, both targets are treated as your *oath of enmity* target for this attack.
Hit: 3[W] + Wisdom modifier damage. Until the end of your next turn, the target takes 10 damage the first time it uses an attack other than a basic attack.

Deadly Calm — Serene Initiate Utility 12

Without malice, without anger, each blow is delivered as smoothly and perfectly as a one-word prayer.

Daily ✦ Divine, Stance
Minor Action — **Personal**
Effect: Until the stance ends, when you make two attack rolls because of *oath of enmity* and both would hit, the target takes extra damage equal to one-half your level.

Heaven's Edge — Serene Initiate Attack 20

Your strike wins the favor of your deity, which in turn guides your weapon against your sworn foe.

Daily ✦ Divine, Weapon
Standard Action — **Melee** weapon
Target: One creature
Attack: Wisdom vs. AC
Hit: 3[W] + Wisdom modifier damage. Before the end of the encounter, when you are next able to make two attack rolls because of your *oath of enmity*, you can instead make three attack rolls and use the result you prefer.
Special: If you have no encounter attack powers available when you use this power, it is reliable.

Watchful Shepherd

"Sometimes it falls to me to keep the wolves away from the flock. I do what I can."

Prerequisite: Avenger

Hidden orders and secret ceremonies of initiation are the way for many avengers, but you have come to embrace a simpler tradition. You are a protector of the common folk who hides in plain sight. With a quiet manner and thoughtful devotion, you are a steward of the gods' teachings, and between adventures you pay as much attention to the spiritual well-being of the common folk as you pay to your avenger prayers.

Many of the people you guard think you are nothing more than a rustic village priest or a wandering friar—unusually wise and compassionate, perhaps, but certainly no monster-slaying hero. They're mistaken, of course, but that suits you just fine. While you tend to their spiritual needs, you remain vigilant for trouble; brigands, marauders, hungry monsters, and villains all seek to prey on the weak and defenseless, so you stand guard over your flock to keep these threats at bay.

You prefer to avoid fame and glory, since that way leads to pride and an inevitable fall. To you it's far better to allow your fellow adventurers to bask in the triumphs of the day and downplay your own contributions. After all, you believe that your reward lies in the next world, not in this one.

Watchful Shepherd Path Features

Stronger and Stronger (11th level): When you spend an action point to take an extra action, you also regain hit points equal to 1d6 + one-half your level.

Shepherd's Guard (11th level): When you spend a healing surge, each ally adjacent to you regains hit points equal to your Intelligence modifier.

Humble Determination (16th level): While you are bloodied, when your *oath of enmity* target damages you (not with ongoing damage), your attacks deal 1d6 extra damage until the end of your next turn.

Watchful Shepherd Prayers

Shepherd's Aegis — Watchful Shepherd Attack 11

The brilliance of your holy symbol warns your enemy against hate and reckless wrath.

Encounter ✦ Divine, Implement, Radiant
Standard Action **Melee** touch
Target: One creature
Attack: Wisdom vs. Reflex
Hit: 2d8 + Wisdom modifier radiant damage. Until the end of your next turn, the target takes 2d10 radiant damage the first time it attacks you or an ally within 2 squares of you.

Hidden Strength — Watchful Shepherd Utility 12

Your devotion provides you with a reservoir of hidden strength, which your enemies do not suspect.

Daily ✦ Divine, Stance
Minor Action **Personal**
Effect: Until the stance ends, you gain a +1 power bonus to attack rolls and all defenses. If you have reached at least one milestone today, you instead gain a +2 power bonus.

Quell the Hateful — Watchful Shepherd Attack 20

Your prayer quells your foe's will to harm you and your allies. The anger you take from your foe becomes healing power in your hands.

Daily ✦ Divine, Healing, Implement, Psychic
Standard Action **Melee** touch
Target: One creature
Attack: Wisdom vs. Will
Hit: 3d8 + Wisdom modifier psychic damage, and the target takes a -4 penalty to attack rolls (save ends).
Miss: Half damage.
Effect: You and each bloodied ally within 5 squares of you can spend a healing surge.

MAZIN KASSIS

Weapon of Fortune

"Everything comes down to chance: whether I live and whether you die."

Prerequisite: Avenger, *oath of enmity* power

You are a servant of a deity of luck, and you completely trust your own good fortune. As a symbol of your devotion to chance, you always carry a set of dice with you. When in doubt, you trust the dice to determine your actions. Just like the wind, you can be gentle and complacent or a dangerous storm capable of destroying those who stand in your way. Although you are always unpredictable, you can be a brave and loyal companion; fortune brought your company together, after all, and you know better than most that great deeds often flow from unlikely friendships or chance meetings.

You are probably a worshiper of Avandra or a similar deity. Your purpose is to inspire people to be daring, to take chances and seize opportunities, for those who take no risks never realize their full potential. In battle, you have learned to rely on chance. You are a potent combatant when luck favors you.

Although you might not represent the typical image of a divine servant, you are nonetheless a faithful devotee of your deity and your beliefs. You have little regard for the strictures of formal worship—you're more likely to be found gambling in a tavern than praying in a temple. But when chance leads you to down the path to adventure or into a situation that demands action, you don't hesitate to join the fight. After all, that's what's the dice told you to do.

AMELIA STONER

Weapon of Fortune Path Features

Fortune Favors the Fortunate (11th level): When you spend an action point to take an extra action, roll a d6. If the result is 6, you take the extra action but keep the action point, and you can use another action point during the same encounter.

I'll Take that Bet (11th level): When you take a critical hit or when your *oath of enmity* target scores a critical hit, you can roll a d6 as a free action. If the result is 1, you take 2d6 damage. If the result is 5 or 6, the critical hit becomes a normal hit.

Luck Is on My Side (16th level): When you roll a 20 on a saving throw, you end two effects on yourself that a save can end.

Weapon of Fortune Prayers

Luck, Not Skill — Weapon of Fortune Attack 11

It's better to be lucky than skillful. You swing wildly, hoping that your enemy fails to get out of the way.

Encounter ✦ Divine, Weapon
Standard Action **Melee** weapon
Target: One creature
Attack: Wisdom vs. AC. You can choose to take a -4 penalty to the attack roll. If you do so, the attack deals 2[W] extra damage if it hits.
Hit: 2[W] + Wisdom modifier damage.

Signs of Favor — Weapon of Fortune Utility 12

Your prayer invokes divine favor or disfavor on your efforts. Your successful strikes against your sworn foe lend you new strength, but each miss weakens you with doubt.

Daily ✦ Divine, Healing, Stance
Minor Action **Personal**
Effect: Until the stance ends, whenever you hit your *oath of enmity* target, you regain hit points equal to your Wisdom modifier, but whenever you miss that target, you take 5 damage.

Gambler's Flourish — Weapon of Fortune Attack 20

Your weapon swings true, but sometimes a bit of extra risk is worth the payoff.

Daily ✦ Divine, Weapon
Standard Action **Melee** weapon
Target: One creature
Attack: Wisdom vs. AC. You can choose to take a -5 penalty to the attack roll. If you take the penalty and the attack hits, the target is stunned instead of dazed and takes a -2 penalty to saving throws (save ends both). If you take the penalty and the attack misses, you grant combat advantage until the end of your next turn.
Hit: 4[W] + Wisdom modifier damage, and the target is dazed (save ends).
Miss: Half damage, and the target is dazed until the end of its next turn.

CHAPTER 2

Cleric

"The powers of darkness do not deter me, foul demon! Pelor is my shield and strength!"

Wielding power sanctioned by the gods, you are the center of your adventuring party. You guard your comrades and heal them when they are hurt, and you direct the course of the battle by weakening chosen enemies.

Some clerics prefer to deal with foes directly, wading into hand-to-hand combat or scouring enemies with radiant blasts and pillars of flame. Others follow the path of the shielding cleric (a build introduced in this chapter) to defeat opponents by supporting stouthearted companions. In this role, you do not fear battle, but you understand that your divine power does the most good by blunting the attacks of your enemies and bolstering the efforts of your allies. Through your prayers, you share your own unshakable confidence and determination with your companions, heartening them for the challenges ahead.

Whether you're a skull-thumping battler, a devoted protector, or a charismatic source of inspiration, this chapter offers numerous ways to lead your comrades in your deity's cause.

- **New Class Feature:** A new Channel Divinity power, *healer's mercy*, lets you further focus on healing your comrades, though at the expense of your own strength.
- **New Build:** The shielding cleric is an expert at weakening and hindering enemies. In addition, you excel at helping your allies to help themselves by rewarding them for striking the foes you designate.
- **New Cleric Powers:** Almost a hundred new powers expand the possibilities for battle clerics and devoted clerics as well as shielding clerics.
- **New Paragon Paths:** Choose from among ten new paragon paths, such as the battle chaplain, the compassionate healer, and the miracle worker.

LUCIO PARRILLO

NEW CLASS FEATURE

When you make your cleric, you can select the Channel Divinity power *healer's mercy* in place of *turn undead*.

Channel Divinity: Healer's Mercy Cleric Feature

Strength flows out from you to your injured comrades, rekindling their resolve to see the battle to its end.

Encounter ✦ Divine, Healing
Standard Action **Close** burst 5
Target: Each bloodied ally in burst
Effect: Each target can spend a healing surge. You are weakened until the end of your next turn.

NEW BUILD

The *Player's Handbook* features the battle cleric and the devoted cleric. This chapter adds the shielding cleric, who leads the party through subtle prayers that aid and support other heroes.

SHIELDING CLERIC

As a shielding cleric, you believe that your place is not to take the fight to the enemy directly, but to bolster allies with your presence. Your prayers lend additional resources to your friends and create opportunities for them to defeat their foes. Yours is a life of leadership through self-sacrifice, ongoing support, and inspiration. You do not seek personal glory, and you take comfort in knowing that your allies couldn't have succeeded without you.

Wisdom is your most important ability, since the prayers that support your tactics rely on it. Charisma is a vital secondary ability, making many of your prayers more effective. A good Strength is important if you intend to take melee powers. You should select powers that emphasize your role as healer and facilitator.

Suggested Class Feature: Channel Divinity (*healer's mercy*)*

Suggested Feat: Defensive Grace*

Suggested Skills: Diplomacy, Heal, Insight, Religion

Suggested At-Will Powers: *astral seal,* sacred flame*

Suggested Encounter Power: *bane**

Suggested Daily Power: *font of tears**

*New option presented in this book

NEW CLERIC POWERS

Many of the powers described below benefit the shielding cleric, though any cleric interested in more of a support role can benefit from them. In addition, new powers expand options for the two cleric builds described in the *Player's Handbook*.

Level 1 At-Will Prayers

Astral Seal — Cleric Attack 1

You outline your enemy with the silver glow of the Astral Sea, and its healing light bathes your friend.

At-Will ✦ Divine, Healing, Implement
Standard Action **Ranged** 5
Target: One creature
Attack: Wisdom +2 vs. Reflex
Hit: Until the end of your next turn, the target takes a -2 penalty to all defenses. The next ally who hits it before the end of your next turn regains hit points equal to 2 + your Charisma modifier.

Recovery Strike — Cleric Attack 1

Your attack heals a companion who strikes at the foe you condemn.

At-Will ✦ Divine, Healing, Weapon
Standard Action **Melee** weapon
Target: One creature
Attack: Strength vs. AC
Hit: 1[W] + Strength modifier damage, and the next ally who hits the target before the end of your next turn regains hit points equal to your Charisma modifier.
Level 21: 2[W] + Strength modifier damage.

Level 1 Encounter Prayers

Bane — Cleric Attack 1

You lay a divine curse upon your foe that shrouds it in enervating shadows.

Encounter ✦ Divine, Implement
Standard Action **Ranged** 10
Target: One creature
Attack: Wisdom vs. Will
Hit: Until the end of your next turn, the target takes a penalty to attack rolls and all defenses equal to 1 + your Charisma modifier.

Exacting Utterance — Cleric Attack 1

The suffering of your enemy instills your comrades with righteous vigor.

Encounter ✦ Divine, Implement
Standard Action **Ranged** 5
Target: One creature
Attack: Wisdom vs. Will
Hit: Until the end of your next turn, the target gains vulnerability to all damage equal to your Wisdom modifier, and any ally who attacks the target gains temporary hit points equal to your Wisdom modifier.

Numinous Shield — Cleric Attack 1

Divine radiance blazes from your holy symbol as you strike your foe, forming a halo of protection about you.

Encounter ✦ Divine, Radiant, Weapon, Zone
Standard Action **Melee** weapon
Target: One creature
Attack: Strength vs. AC
Hit: 1[W] + Strength modifier radiant damage. The attack creates a zone of shielding light in a close burst 2. The zone lasts until the end of your next turn. You and your allies gain a +2 power bonus to AC while within the zone.

Shield Bearer — Cleric Attack 1

A shimmering warrior steps from between the worlds to defend your allies.

Encounter ✦ Conjuration, Divine, Implement, Radiant
Standard Action **Ranged** 10
Target: One creature
Attack: Wisdom vs. Reflex
Hit: 2d8 + Wisdom modifier radiant damage. You conjure a shield bearer in an unoccupied square adjacent to the target. The shield bearer lasts until the end of your next turn. The shield bearer occupies 1 square, and allies can move through it as if it were an ally. While adjacent to the shield bearer, any ally gains a +2 power bonus to all defenses.

War Priest's Strike — Cleric Attack 1

You smite your foe, crushing its armor and leaving a glowing rune that guides your allies' attacks.

Encounter ✦ Divine, Radiant, Weapon
Standard Action **Melee** weapon
Target: One creature
Attack: Strength vs. AC
Hit: 2[W] + Strength modifier radiant damage. Until the end of your next turn, you and your allies have combat advantage against the target.

Level 1 Daily Prayers

Astral Condemnation — Cleric Attack 1

You brand a foe with your god's glowing symbol to drain power from its attacks.

Daily ✦ Divine, Implement, Radiant
Standard Action **Ranged** 5
Target: One creature
Attack: Wisdom vs. Reflex
Hit: 3d6 + Wisdom modifier radiant damage.
Effect: Until the end of your next turn, the target takes a penalty to damage rolls equal to 5 + your Charisma modifier.
Sustain Minor: The effect persists.

Font of Tears — Cleric Attack 1

A glimmering rain showers enemies around you and saps their will.

Daily ✦ Divine, Implement, Zone
Standard Action **Close** burst 3
Target: Each enemy in burst
Attack: Wisdom vs. Will
Hit: The target is dazed (save ends).
Effect: The burst creates a zone of shimmering energy that lasts until the end of your next turn. Any enemy that starts its turn within the zone takes a -2 penalty to attack rolls until the end of its next turn.
Sustain Minor: The zone persists.

Moment of Glory — Cleric Attack 1

You call down a brilliant column of light that drives your enemies to the ground and bolsters your allies against harm.

Daily ✦ Divine, Fear, Implement
Standard Action **Close** blast 5
Target: Each enemy in blast
Attack: Wisdom vs. Will
Hit: You push the target 3 squares and knock it prone.
Effect: You and each ally in the blast gain resist 5 to all damage until the end of your next turn.
Sustain Minor: The effect persists.

Shield of the Gods — Cleric Attack 1

Slamming your weapon into the ground, you create a blast of force that bowls over your foes. The energy then coalesces into a glowing shield.

Daily ✦ Divine, Force, Weapon
Standard Action **Close** blast 3
Target: Each enemy in blast
Attack: Strength vs. Reflex
Hit: 1[W] + Strength modifier force damage, and you knock the target prone.
Miss: Half damage.
Effect: You or an ally within 5 squares of you gains a +3 shield bonus to AC and Reflex until the end of the encounter. As a minor action, you can transfer the bonus to yourself or a different ally within 5 squares of you.

Weapon of Astral Flame — Cleric Attack 1

You conjure a weapon of divine flame that duplicates the one you wield.

Daily ✦ Conjuration, Divine, Fire, Weapon
Standard Action **Melee** weapon
Effect: You conjure a weapon of astral flame in your space. The weapon lasts until the end of your next turn. When you move, the weapon moves with you, remaining in your space. The weapon makes the following primary attack when it appears.
Primary Target: One creature
Primary Attack: Strength vs. Reflex
Hit: 1[W] + Strength modifier fire damage, and the primary target takes a -2 penalty to attack rolls until the end of your next turn.
Sustain Minor: The weapon persists and makes a secondary attack.
Secondary Target: One creature
Secondary Attack: Strength vs. Reflex
Hit: 1[W] fire damage.

WILLIAM O'CONNOR

Level 2 Utility Prayers

Armor of Faith — Cleric Utility 2

You clothe your ally in shining golden armor created from the essence of the Astral Sea.

Daily ✦ Divine
Standard Action **Close** burst 5
Target: One ally in burst
Effect: The target gains a +4 power bonus to a defense of your choice until the end of the encounter.

Divine Skill — Cleric Utility 2

You grant divine grace to bolster your ally's prowess in a skill at a crucial moment.

Encounter ✦ Divine
Minor Action **Close** burst 5
Target: One ally in burst
Effect: The target gains a power bonus to his or her next skill check before the end of the encounter. The bonus equals your Charisma modifier.

Holy Vestments — Cleric Utility 2

Glowing sigils blossom over your armor, forming a protective web.

Daily ✦ Divine
Standard Action **Personal**
Effect: Choose acid, cold, fire, lightning, poison, or thunder. Until the end of the encounter, you gain resist 5 to that damage type, and any ally who ends a move adjacent to you gains resist 5 to that damage type until the start of his or her next turn.

Life Transference — Cleric Utility 2

Bruises and lacerations appear on your body as they vanish from your patient.

Encounter ✦ Divine, Healing
Standard Action **Melee** touch
Target: One creature
Effect: You take damage equal to your healing surge value, which can't be reduced in any way. The target regains hit points equal to twice that value.

Return from Death's Door — Cleric Utility 2

You snatch an ally from the brink of death.

Daily ✦ Divine, Healing
Immediate Interrupt **Ranged** 20
Trigger: An ally within 20 squares of you fails a death saving throw
Target: The triggering ally
Effect: The target succeeds on the death saving throw and can spend a healing surge.

Level 3 Encounter Prayers

Astral Flare — Cleric Attack 3

You brandish your holy symbol and invoke the power of the gods to dazzle your foes.

Encounter ✦ Divine, Implement
Standard Action **Close** burst 3
Target: Each enemy in burst
Attack: Wisdom vs. Will
Hit: The target is dazed until the end of your next turn.

Hammer of the Gods — Cleric Attack 3

Your inspired onslaught batters a foe, and your companions strike it with equal zeal.

Encounter ✦ Divine, Radiant, Weapon
Standard Action **Melee** weapon
Target: One creature
Attack: Strength vs. AC
Hit: 1[W] + Strength modifier radiant damage. When any ally hits the target before the start of your next turn, the target takes 1d6 extra radiant damage.

Hymn of Resurgence — Cleric Attack 3

Your foes' resolve crumbles as your hymn bestows divine vigor on your allies.

Encounter ✦ Divine, Implement
Standard Action **Close** blast 5
Target: Each enemy in blast
Attack: Wisdom vs. Fortitude
Hit: The target takes a -2 penalty to all defenses. When any ally hits the target before the end of your next turn, the target is knocked prone.
Effect: Each ally in the burst can choose either to gain 5 temporary hit points or to make a saving throw.

Light of Arvandor — Cleric Attack 3

A web of gleaming strands cuts into your foes and defends your allies.

Encounter ✦ Divine, Implement, Radiant
Standard Action **Area** burst 1 within 5 squares
Target: Each enemy in burst
Attack: Wisdom vs. Will
Hit: 1d8 + Wisdom modifier radiant damage, and each ally in the burst gains a +2 power bonus to AC until the end of your next turn.

Sacred Shielding — Cleric Attack 3

Your weapon is limned in holy light, and a mantle of equal brilliance springs into existence around you.

Encounter ✦ Divine, Radiant, Weapon
Standard Action **Melee** weapon
Target: One creature
Attack: Strength vs. AC
Hit: 2[W] + Strength modifier radiant damage. Until the end of your next turn, each ally adjacent to you or to the target gains resistance to all damage equal to your Charisma modifier.

Level 5 Daily Prayers

Hallowed Advance — Cleric Attack 5

The power of your god draws an ally to your side, eager to share in victory.

Daily ✦ Divine, Healing, Teleportation, Weapon
Standard Action **Melee** weapon
Target: One creature
Attack: Strength vs. AC
Hit: 2[W] + Strength modifier damage.
Miss: Half damage.
Effect: One ally within 5 squares of you can teleport adjacent to the target and make a melee basic attack against it as a free action. In addition, that ally can spend a healing surge.

Halo of Consequence — Cleric Attack 5

A ring of faint light surrounds your enemy and punishes it for attacking you or your allies.

Daily ✦ Divine, Implement, Reliable
Standard Action **Ranged** 10
Target: One creature
Attack: Wisdom vs. Reflex
Hit: The target is affected by your halo of consequence (save ends). Until the halo ends, the target takes a -4 penalty to attack rolls, and after the target attacks you or any ally, it is dazed until the end of its next turn. The target takes a -2 penalty to saving throws against the halo.

Hold Foe — Cleric Attack 5

With an impassioned prayer, you transfix your enemy to the spot.

Daily ✦ Divine, Implement
Standard Action **Ranged** 10
Target: One creature
Attack: Wisdom vs. Will
Hit: 2d6 + Wisdom modifier damage. The target is dazed and immobilized (save ends both).
Miss: Half damage, and the target is slowed until the end of your next turn.

Iron to Glass — Cleric Attack 5

Tracing runes of denial in the air, you cause your foe's weapons to become as brittle as glass.

Daily ✦ Divine, Implement
Standard Action **Ranged** 10
Target: One creature
Attack: Wisdom vs. Reflex
Hit: Until the end of the encounter, the target takes a -4 penalty to melee damage rolls. Whenever the target hits with a melee attack, the penalty worsens by 2 to a maximum of -10.
Miss: Until the end of the encounter, the target takes a -2 penalty to melee damage rolls. Whenever the target hits with a melee attack, the penalty worsens by 1 to a maximum of -5.

Revealing Light — Cleric Attack 5

A narrow beam of brilliant blue-white light lances down to illuminate a foe that seeks the shadows.

Daily ✦ Divine, Implement, Radiant
Standard Action **Ranged** 10
Target: One creature
Attack: Wisdom vs. Reflex. The attack ignores concealment and cover.
Hit: 3d6 + Wisdom modifier radiant damage.
Effect: The target takes ongoing 5 radiant damage and cannot become hidden (save ends both).

Level 6 Utility Prayers

Blades of Holy Fire — Cleric Utility 6

Your allies' implements and weapons blaze with white-hot, consecrated flames.

Daily ✦ Divine, Fire, Radiant
Minor Action **Close** burst 5
Target: Each ally in burst
Effect: The next time the target hits before the end of the encounter, that attack deals 1d6 extra fire and radiant damage.

Divine Favor — Cleric Utility 6

Sacred light suffuses your comrade, bestowing your god's blessing in battle.

Daily ✦ Divine, Healing
Standard Action **Melee** touch
Target: You or one ally
Effect: Until the end of the encounter, the target gains a +2 power bonus to attack rolls and damage rolls, and when the target is first bloodied, he or she can spend a healing surge.

Holy Celerity — Cleric Utility 6

You imbue an ally with the confidence to advance against all impediments.

Encounter ✦ Divine
Minor Action **Ranged** 10
Target: You or one ally
Effect: Until the end of your next turn, the target ignores the effects of the immobilized, restrained, and slowed conditions.

Spirit of Healing — Cleric Utility 6

A glowing figure appears at your command, casting an aura of health over your allies.

Daily ✦ Conjuration, Divine, Healing
Minor Action **Ranged** 10
Effect: You conjure a spirit of healing in 1 square within range. The spirit lasts until the end of your next turn. When an ally in the spirit's square or adjacent to it hits an enemy, that ally regains hit points equal to twice your Wisdom modifier. As a move action, you can move the spirit 4 squares.
Sustain Minor: The spirit persists.

Stream of Life — Cleric Utility 6

Your life energy flows into a companion and grants your friend the vigor to fight on.

Daily ✦ Divine, Healing
Minor Action **Personal**
Effect: You take ongoing 5 damage (save ends). This damage can't be reduced in any way. At the end of your turn, you can choose not to make a saving throw against this ongoing damage. Whenever you take the ongoing damage, an ally within 5 squares of you regains 15 hit points.

Level 7 Encounter Prayers

Bolts of Warding — Cleric Attack 7

Your weapon crackles with divine lightning that arcs out to strike any who threaten your allies.

Encounter ✦ Divine, Lightning, Weapon
Standard Action **Melee** weapon
Target: One creature
Attack: Strength vs. AC
Hit: 2[W] + Strength modifier lightning damage. Until the end of your next turn, any enemy takes 5 lightning damage if it ends its turn adjacent to any ally within 5 squares of you.

Denunciation — Cleric Attack 7

You pronounce a divine curse, and motes of darkness swirl around your enemy to hinder it.

Encounter ✦ Divine, Implement
Standard Action **Ranged** 5
Target: One creature
Attack: Wisdom vs. Will
Hit: Until the end of your next turn, the target is dazed and takes a penalty to attack rolls and all defenses equal to your Charisma modifier.

Price of Violence — Cleric Attack 7

Your enemy claws at its sightless eyes after daring to attack.

Encounter ✦ Divine, Implement
Immediate Reaction **Ranged** 5
Trigger: An enemy within 5 squares of you hits you or your ally
Target: The triggering enemy
Attack: Wisdom vs. Fortitude
Hit: The target is blinded until the end of your next turn.

Strike of Judgment — Cleric Attack 7

Your attack visits pain upon your foe and ensures that you and your allies will be compensated if that foe dares to retaliate.

Encounter ✦ Divine, Healing, Weapon
Standard Action **Melee** weapon
Target: One creature
Attack: Strength vs. Will
Hit: 2[W] + Strength modifier damage.
Effect: The next time the target hits or misses an ally before the end of your next turn, one ally of your choice within 5 squares of the target regains 10 hit points.

GEORGI "CALADER" SIMEONOV

Zealous Sanction — Cleric Attack 7

You name your foe an enemy of your god. Divine power sears it and heals any who strike it.

Encounter ✦ Divine, Healing, Implement, Radiant
Standard Action **Ranged** 10
Target: One creature
Attack: Wisdom vs. Will
Hit: 2d8 + Wisdom modifier radiant damage. The first time any ally hits the target before the end of your next turn, that ally can spend a healing surge.

Level 9 Daily Prayers

Crucial Resurgence — Cleric Attack 9

The pain of your wounds only inspires you to greater heights.

Daily ✦ Divine, Healing, Weapon
Standard Action **Melee** weapon
Requirement: You must be bloodied.
Target: One creature
Attack: Strength vs. AC
Hit: 2[W] + Strength modifier damage.
Effect: You and each ally within 5 squares of you can spend a healing surge.

Dismissal — Cleric Attack 9

You utter a mighty shout and cast your enemy out of the world.

Daily ✦ Divine, Implement, Teleportation
Standard Action **Ranged** 10
Target: One creature
Attack: Wisdom vs. Will
Hit: The target disappears into an extraplanar prison (save ends). The target takes a -2 penalty to saving throws against this effect, or a -5 penalty if it is an aberrant, elemental, fey, immortal, or shadow creature. When the target saves against this effect, it reappears in its original space. If that space is occupied, the target returns to the nearest unoccupied space.
Aftereffect: The target is dazed until the end of its next turn.
Miss: The target disappears into an extraplanar prison until the end of your next turn. The target then reappears in its original space. If that space is occupied, the target returns to the nearest unoccupied space.

Divine Fury — Cleric Attack 9

Your patron's servants take notice of your struggle and reward companions while punishing your enemies.

Daily ✦ Divine, Healing, Radiant, Weapon, Zone
Standard Action **Close** burst 1
Target: Each enemy in burst
Attack: Strength vs. Fortitude
Hit: 2[W] + Strength modifier radiant damage.
Miss: Half damage.
Effect: The burst creates a zone of divine fury that lasts until the end of your next turn. When any ally within the zone hits an enemy, that ally regains 10 hit points.
Sustain Minor: The zone persists.

Dwarves Who Don't Worship Moradin

Many dwarves revere Moradin first among the gods, but they also recognize that different deities hold sway over different aspects of life. Like other folk, the great majority of dwarves venerate various deities at appropriate times. Dwarves whose interests go beyond the typical values of industry, stoicism, and artisanship are just as likely to give homage to the deity of their vocation as to Moradin. The Soul Forger shaped them in body and soul long ago, but they have lived under the influence of many gods—both beneficial and malevolent—ever since.

For example, a dwarf soldier makes offerings in Moradin's name most of the time, but when marching off to war she might call upon Kord for strength, Bane for victory, or Bahamut for honor. A dwarf tomb-keeper might take the Raven Queen as his patron, while a dwarf rogue who travels in search of adventure is likely to honor Avandra. Likewise, dwarves know that their hearts are touched by Sehanine, their minds shaped by Erathis and Ioun, and their fates overseen by the Raven Queen. They thank Pelor for the warmth of the sun and Corellon for the inspiration to create works of beauty.

Rebuke Violence — Cleric Attack 9

With a fervent prayer, you purge all thoughts of battle from your enemy's mind.

Daily ✦ Divine, Implement
Standard Action **Ranged** 10
Target: One creature
Attack: Wisdom vs. Will
Hit: The target cannot attack (save ends). Until you or any ally attacks the target, it takes a -5 penalty to saving throws against this effect.
Miss: The target cannot attack until the end of your next turn.

Level 10 Utility Prayers

Godsight — Cleric Utility 10

You bestow the ability to see through deception.

Daily ✦ Divine
Minor Action **Ranged** 5
Target: You or one ally
Effect: The target gains truesight 5 until the end of the encounter.

Healer's Balm — Cleric Utility 10

You lay a hand on your comrade's brow, taking on his or her pain and suffering.

Encounter ✦ Divine
Standard Action **Melee** touch
Target: One ally
Effect: You transfer to yourself all effects on the target that a save can end. You gain a +4 bonus to saving throws against those effects.

Recall Ally — Cleric Utility 10

You summon a comrade to your side.

Encounter ✦ Divine, Teleportation
Move Action **Ranged** 20
Target: One ally
Effect: You teleport the target to a square adjacent to you.

Sacred Beneficence — Cleric Utility 10

As long as you stand firm against the enemy, your companion draws on your strength to remain unbowed.

Daily ✦ Divine, Healing
Standard Action **Melee** touch
Requirement: You must not be bloodied.
Target: One ally
Effect: The target gains regeneration 10 until you are bloodied or until the end of the encounter.

Word of Vigor — Cleric Utility 10

Your ringing prayer inspires all nearby to draw on inner reserves.

Encounter ✦ Divine, Healing
Minor Action **Close** burst 1
Target: You and each ally in burst
Effect: Each target can spend a healing surge and regain 2d6 additional hit points.

Level 13 Encounter Prayers

Angel's Rescue Cleric Attack 13

You invoke an angel's name to lend strength to your attack and carry your ally out of danger.

Encounter ✦ Divine, Weapon
Standard Action **Melee** weapon
Target: One creature
Attack: Wisdom vs. AC
Hit: 3[W] + Strength modifier damage.
Effect: You slide an ally who is adjacent to you or to the target 2 squares.
Special: When charging, you can use this power in place of a melee basic attack.

Crown of Light Cleric Attack 13

Blazing light coalesces over your ally to form a crown whose radiance pierces surrounding foes.

Encounter ✦ Divine, Implement, Radiant
Standard Action **Ranged** 10
Primary Target: One ally
Effect: Until the end of your next turn, the primary target gains a power bonus to all defenses equal to your Charisma modifier. Make a secondary attack that is an area burst 1 centered on the primary target.
Secondary Target: Each enemy in burst
Attack: Wisdom vs. Reflex
Hit: 3d6 + Wisdom modifier radiant damage.

Deadly Lure Cleric Attack 13

Your imperious gesture drags an enemy toward you, compelling it to lower its defenses.

Encounter ✦ Charm, Divine, Implement
Standard Action **Ranged** 5
Target: One creature
Attack: Wisdom vs. Will
Hit: The target gains vulnerability to all damage equal to 2 + your Wisdom modifier until the end of your next turn. The target then moves its speed toward you, taking the safest path possible.

Promise of Victory Cleric Attack 13

With a flurry of devastating strikes, you show your enemies how close they are to defeat.

Encounter ✦ Divine, Weapon
Standard Action **Close** burst 1
Target: Each enemy in burst
Attack: Strength vs. AC
Hit: 2[W] + Strength modifier damage, and the target takes a -2 penalty to all defenses until the end of your next turn.

Remorse Cleric Attack 13

Your words of reproach cause your foes to hesitate as they regret their violent acts.

Encounter ✦ Divine, Healing, Implement
Standard Action **Area** burst 1 within 5 squares
Target: Each enemy in burst
Attack: Wisdom vs. Will
Hit: Until the end of your next turn, the target gains vulnerable 10 to all damage and is dazed.
Effect: Each ally in the burst can spend a healing surge.

Level 15 Daily Prayers

Brilliant Censure Cleric Attack 15

Awful brilliance flashes from your eyes, blinding foes and inspiring allies.

Daily ✦ Divine, Implement, Radiant, Zone
Standard Action **Close** burst 3
Target: Each enemy in burst
Attack: Wisdom vs. Fortitude
Hit: The target is blinded (save ends).
Effect: The burst creates a zone of bright light that lasts until the end of the encounter. When you move, the zone moves with you, remaining centered on you. Any ally who begins his or her turn within the zone deals 2d6 extra radiant damage with melee or ranged attacks until the start of his or her next turn.

Divine Reprisal Cleric Attack 15

You utter a prayer to heal an ally's injury and exact punishment against the attacker.

Daily ✦ Divine, Healing, Implement, Radiant
Immediate Reaction **Ranged** 10
Trigger: An enemy within 10 squares of you hits your ally
Target: The triggering enemy
Attack: Wisdom vs. Will
Hit: 3d8 + Wisdom modifier radiant damage.
Effect: The ally can make a saving throw and can spend a healing surge.

Ivory Rampart Cleric Attack 15

As your weapon strikes your foe, divine power flows from you to form a barrier that protects your allies.

Daily ✦ Conjuration, Divine, Weapon
Standard Action **Melee** weapon
Target: One creature
Attack: Strength vs. AC
Hit: 2[W] + Strength modifier damage.
Miss: Half damage.
Effect: You conjure a wall of gleaming energy that originates in your space and can be up to 8 squares long and up to 2 squares high. The wall lasts until the end of your next turn. Any ally within the wall or adjacent to it gains cover. Any enemy that enters the wall is immobilized until the end of its turn.
Sustain Minor: The wall persists.

Penance of Blood Cleric Attack 15

Divine displeasure visits even more pain on your enemies.

Daily ✦ Divine, Implement
Standard Action **Close** burst 3
Target: Each enemy in burst
Attack: Wisdom vs. Fortitude
Hit: The target gains vulnerable 5 to all damage until the end of the encounter.
Effect: Until the end of the encounter, any vulnerability you cause your enemies is increased by your Wisdom modifier.

Wrath of the Faithful — Cleric Attack 15

You draw resolve from your allies to strike down the enemy they face.

Daily ✦ Divine, Reliable, Weapon
Standard Action **Melee** weapon
Target: One creature
Attack: Strength vs. AC. You gain a +1 bonus to the attack roll for each ally adjacent to the target.
Hit: 4[W] + Strength modifier damage.

Level 16 Utility Prayers

Air Walk — Cleric Utility 16

With deliberate steps, you stride upward on luminous clouds.

Daily ✦ Divine
Minor Action **Personal**
Effect: Until the end of the encounter, you gain the ability to move on air as if it were a solid surface. If you end your turn more than 2 squares above a solid surface, you descend gently until you are 2 squares above one.

Cloak of Courage — Cleric Utility 16

Your prayer bolsters your companions' will and fills them with hope.

Encounter ✦ Divine
Standard Action **Close** burst 2
Target: Each ally in burst
Effect: Each target gains temporary hit points equal to his or her healing surge value. Until the end of your next turn, each target gains a +4 power bonus to all defenses against fear effects.

Cure Critical Wounds — Cleric Utility 16

Intoning the name of your god, you heal your friend's injuries with a soothing touch.

Daily ✦ Divine, Healing
Standard Action **Melee** touch
Target: You or one creature
Effect: The target regains hit points as if it had spent three healing surges.

Radiant Beams — Cleric Utility 16

A halo of brilliance springs from your brow, defending your comrades from the foulness of the undead.

Daily ✦ Divine, Radiant
Standard Action **Close** burst 5
Target: You and each ally in burst
Effect: Until the end of your next turn, each target gains resist 20 necrotic and deals 1 radiant damage to any enemy that attacks him or her.
Sustain Minor: The effect persists.

Unexpected Return — Cleric Utility 16

A swift chant gives your ally a second chance at life.

Encounter ✦ Divine, Healing
Immediate Reaction **Ranged** 5
Trigger: An ally within 5 squares of you drops to 0 hit points or fewer
Target: The triggering ally
Effect: The target can spend a healing surge.

Level 17 Encounter Prayers

Divine Phalanx — Cleric Attack 17

As you attack, divine trumpets sound, and your allies rally to your side. Together, you are all stronger.

Encounter ✦ Divine, Radiant, Teleportation, Weapon
Standard Action **Melee** weapon
Target: One creature
Attack: Strength vs. AC
Hit: 2[W] + Strength modifier radiant damage.
Effect: You teleport each ally within 10 squares of you to a square adjacent to you. Each ally you teleport gains a +2 power bonus to AC and to attack rolls until the end of your next turn.

Halo of Peace — Cleric Attack 17

You slam your weapon into your foe and enfold it in brilliant energy that hampers its attacks.

Encounter ✦ Divine, Radiant, Weapon
Standard Action **Melee** weapon
Target: One creature
Attack: Strength vs. AC
Hit: 2[W] + Strength modifier radiant damage. Until the end of your next turn, the target takes a -4 penalty to attack rolls and cannot make opportunity attacks.

Malediction — Cleric Attack 17

Your enemy is crippled by the terrible curse you pronounce against it.

Encounter ✦ Divine, Implement
Standard Action **Ranged** 5
Target: One creature
Attack: Wisdom vs. Will
Hit: The target is weakened and dazed until the end of your next turn.

Sever the Source — Cleric Attack 17

A gleaming rune of anathema appears on your enemy, cutting it off from divine blessings.

Encounter ✦ Divine
Standard Action **Ranged** 5
Target: One creature
Effect: Until the end of your next turn, the target gains vulnerability to all damage equal to 10 + your Wisdom modifier and cannot regain hit points.

Starry Snare — Cleric Attack 17

You weave a net of astral light, which imprisons your foe in glittering strands.

Encounter ✦ Divine, Implement, Radiant
Standard Action **Ranged** 10
Target: One creature
Attack: Wisdom vs. Fortitude
Hit: 3d8 + Wisdom modifier radiant damage. Until the end of your next turn, the target is immobilized, cannot teleport, and does not benefit from being insubstantial.

Level 19 Daily Prayers

Beacon of Doom — Cleric Attack 19

With a resounding strike, you denounce your enemy. It crumples under a flurry of attacks from your friends.

Daily ✦ Divine, Weapon
Standard Action **Melee** weapon
Target: One creature
Attack: Strength vs. AC
Hit: 2[W] + Strength modifier damage.
Miss: Half damage.
Effect: The target takes a -4 penalty to all defenses (save ends).
Each Failed Saving Throw: One ally within 10 squares of the target can make a basic attack against it as a free action.
Aftereffect: Each ally within 5 squares of the target can make a basic attack against it as a free action.

Miraculous Intervention — Cleric Attack 19

Your ally is overcome, but you buy time to restore that companion's health.

Daily ✦ Divine, Healing, Implement
Immediate Reaction **Ranged** 5
Trigger: An ally within 5 squares of you drops to 0 hit points or fewer
Primary Target: The triggering ally
Effect: The primary target regains hit points as if he or she had spent a healing surge. Make a secondary attack that is an area burst 2 centered on the primary target.
Secondary Target: Each enemy in burst
Attack: Wisdom vs. Will
Hit: The secondary target is stunned (save ends).

Moment of Peace — Cleric Attack 19

A wave of tranquility washes over your foes, rendering them harmless for a critical moment.

Daily ✦ Divine, Implement
Standard Action **Close** blast 5
Target: Each enemy in blast
Attack: Wisdom vs. Will
Hit: The target's attacks deal no damage (save ends).
Miss: The target's attacks deal no damage until the end of your next turn.

Realm of Battle — Cleric Attack 19

You sweep your weapon through the air and call out for divine aid. A flock of angels soars through the sky to surround you, driving back the enemy.

Daily ✦ Divine, Radiant, Weapon, Zone
Standard Action **Melee** weapon
Target: One creature
Attack: Strength vs. AC
Hit: 3[W] + Strength modifier radiant damage.
Miss: Half damage.
Effect: The attack creates a zone of angelic soldiers in a close burst 3. The zone lasts until the end of the encounter. While within the zone, you and your allies gain a +1 power bonus to AC and attack rolls. While within the zone, any enemy takes 5 radiant damage at the start of its turn and provokes opportunity attacks when it shifts.

MATIAS TAPIA

Small Devotions

Many practices common among the people of the world have their origin in various minor devotions to the gods.

For example, someone telling a lie might splay wide the fingers of the left hand under a table or behind his or her back. Whether that person knows it or not, the gesture is meant to represent the holy symbol of Lolth, god of lies, and to ask her help in making sure the untruth is not discovered.

Another such gesture is to place the weapon of a fallen warrior in the corpse's hand. This act is believed to arm the warrior for the next world and to show Bane, the god of war, that he or she died fighting and therefore deserves honor.

Travelers setting out on journeys often scoop up a handful of dirt or dust from the road and let it fall from their hands. Most people regard this tradition as simply checking the strength and direction of the wind, but it is meant to honor Avandra. The god is said to show a sign of the fortune awaiting the journey by blowing the dust away (which favors departure) or back toward the traveler (indicating difficulty ahead).

Supernal Radiance — Cleric Attack 19

You create a pulse of light that gleams with divine clarity. No foe can hide within its brilliance.

Daily ✦ Divine, Implement, Radiant
Standard Action **Area** burst 1 within 5 squares
Target: Each enemy in burst
Attack: Wisdom vs. Will
Hit: 2d10 + Wisdom modifier radiant damage.
Effect: The target takes ongoing 10 radiant damage, cannot benefit from invisibility or concealment, and cannot become hidden (save ends all).

Level 22 Utility Prayers

Adjure the Chosen — Cleric Utility 22

With a ringing voice, you urge your companions to direct your god's fury against your foes.

Encounter ✦ Divine
Standard Action **Close** burst 5
Target: You and each ally in burst
Effect: Until the end of your next turn, each target gains a +2 power bonus to speed, attack rolls, and damage rolls, and can score a critical hit on a roll of 18–20.

Heal — Cleric Utility 22

Bowing your head in prayer, you restore a desperately injured comrade to complete health.

Daily ✦ Divine, Healing
Standard Action **Melee** touch
Target: One ally
Effect: The target regains all his or her hit points.

Mass Cure Serious Wounds — Cleric Utility 22

Glimmering blue motes envelop you and your companions, staunching wounds.

Daily ✦ Divine, Healing
Standard Action **Close** burst 5
Target: You and each ally in burst
Effect: Each target regains hit points as if he or she had spent two healing surges.

Ramparts of Light — Cleric Utility 22

Divine light encases you or your ally to thwart even the deadliest attacks.

Encounter ✦ Divine
Minor Action **Close** burst 20
Target: You or one ally in burst
Effect: The target gains resist 25 to all damage until the end of your next turn.

Dead Gods

Gods cannot die of old age or mortal ailments and infirmities, but they can still be slain. Few beings have the power to kill a god: primordials, rival gods, and great entities of the Far Realm, several demon lords or archdevils working in concert—and sometimes a group of the mightiest mortals. Gods also have been known to simply fade away, forgotten by the mortal world. They slip into ever deeper slumber and linger dreaming through the ages, until finally they dream of nothing at all and cease to be.

Some of the dead gods known to have once existed include the following.

Amoth: Many centuries ago, Amoth was a god of justice and mercy who ruled over the astral dominion of Kalandurren. The demon lords Orcus, Demogorgon, and Rimmon conspired against him and launched an overwhelming attack against Kalandurren. Although Amoth destroyed Rimmon and nearly slew Demogorgon as well, Orcus struck him down, and the demons overthrew his realm. Kalandurren is now a ruined dominion, abandoned by all but a few demons who still prowl its shattered castles and gray hills.

He Who Was: Once among the mightiest of the gods, the lord of the great dominion Baathion presided over kingship, wisdom, and the sky. The archangel Asmodeus rebelled against him, and with the *Ruby Rod* struck down his lord. The dying god pronounced a curse against Asmodeus and his followers, transforming the idyllic realm of Baathion into Baator, a cruel prison of black rock and unending fire. Asmodeus has worked for ages to erase the knowledge of his defeated master's name, so only a handful of mortal scholars still know it; most refer to this being as He Who Was. It is whispered that Asmodeus dispatches powerful devils to slay any mortal who speaks the forbidden name, and that he fears the name to this day.

Io: The creator of dragons, Io was beset by mighty primordials and destroyed in the War of Creation. From his shattered body two new gods sprang—Bahamut, the Platinum Dragon, and Tiamat, the Queen of Evil Dragons. Some stories say that the god was betrayed to the primordials by Zehir, who envied Io his mighty children.

Khala: The original god of winter was a cruel, malicious being who schemed against the other gods and sought to extend her grip over all the mortal world. Her glaciers and blizzards threatened to destroy the fragile races of mortals as her son Kord ran wild, bringing storms and calamity to all. Khala and her allies—Gruumsh, Tiamat, Zehir, and several powerful primordials—grew strong enough to assault the dominions of the gods who stood against her. But Kord came to regret the harm he had done and turned against Khala. Pelor and the assembled gods who stood with him destroyed Khala and drove off Gruumsh; the Raven Queen later claimed dominion over winter.

Nerull: Formerly the god of the dead, Nerull ruled over the grim dominion of Pluton, where he held all the souls of mortals as powerless, miserable shades. In time the Raven Queen overthrew him and became goddess of death. See the "Rise of the Raven Queen" sidebar (page 43).

Tuern: A god of conquest and fire, Tuern was overthrown by a mortal king. Bane was the greatest of mortal tyrants in the dawn of the world, and he became so powerful that he dared to give battle to the war god. He launched an invasion of the war god's realm, defeated Tuern, and seized the dominion for his own.

Revive — Cleric Utility 22

You call back an ally from the clutches of death.

Daily ✦ Divine, Healing
Standard Action **Melee** touch
Target: One bloodied or dying ally or a dead ally who died during this encounter
Effect: The target regains enough hit points to bring his or her current hit point total to his or her bloodied value. If the target is dead, he or she revives, then regains the hit points, and is considered not to have failed any death saving throws during this encounter.

Level 23 Encounter Prayers

Divine Fervor — Cleric Attack 23

Your god's power flares from your weapon to bless you and a companion as you batter down an enemy.

Encounter ✦ Divine, Healing, Radiant, Weapon
Standard Action **Melee** weapon
Target: One creature
Attack: Strength vs. AC
Hit: 4[W] + Strength modifier radiant damage.
Effect: You and an ally within 10 squares of you can each spend a healing surge.

Mortal Terror — Cleric Attack 23

You smash your foe and overwhelm it with fear of imminent death.

Encounter ✦ Divine, Fear, Weapon
Standard Action **Melee** weapon
Target: One creature
Attack: Strength vs. AC
Hit: 3[W] + Strength modifier damage, and the target moves its speed away from you, taking the safest path possible.

Rebuke the Wrathful — Cleric Attack 23

You reproach your foe, and your allies brutally punish its violence.

Encounter ✦ Divine, Implement
Standard Action **Ranged** 10
Target: One creature
Attack: Wisdom vs. Will
Hit: The first time the target makes an attack before the end of your next turn, each ally within 10 squares of you can make a basic attack against the target as an opportunity action.

Spirit Flame — Cleric Attack 23

Raising your holy symbol high, you call down a great pulse of divine fire against your foes and restore yourself and your friends.

Encounter ✦ Divine, Fire, Implement
Standard Action **Close** blast 5
Target: Each enemy in blast
Attack: Wisdom vs. Reflex
Hit: 3d10 + Wisdom modifier fire damage.
Effect: You end the following conditions on yourself: blinded, dazed, immobilized, slowed, stunned, and weakened. In addition, each ally in the blast can choose to have one of these conditions ended on himself or herself.

Word of Deterrence — Cleric Attack 23

You drive back the foe who injured your ally and dissuade it from further aggression.

Encounter ✦ Divine, Implement, Radiant
Immediate Reaction **Ranged** 5
Trigger: An enemy within 5 squares of you hits your ally
Target: The triggering enemy
Attack: Wisdom vs. Will
Hit: You push the target 3 squares. If the target makes an attack roll before the end of your next turn, it takes radiant damage equal to 20 + your Wisdom modifier.

Level 25 Daily Prayers

Divine Intervention — Cleric Attack 25

You pull your friend out of the way, taking the brunt of the attack onto yourself. Your furious rebuke steals the sight from your foes.

Daily ✦ Divine, Implement, Teleportation
Immediate Interrupt **Close** burst 5
Trigger: An enemy makes an attack roll against your ally within 5 squares of you, and you are not a target of that attack
Primary Target: The triggering ally
Effect: You teleport yourself and the primary target, swapping positions with him or her, and the triggering enemy makes the attack roll against you instead. If you take damage from the attack, the primary target gains temporary hit points equal to that damage. You then make the following secondary attack.
Secondary Target: Each enemy adjacent to you
Attack: Wisdom vs. Fortitude
Hit: The secondary target is blinded (save ends).

Flames of Torment — Cleric Attack 25

You smite your enemy with wrathful fire that feeds on its soul.

Daily ✦ Divine, Fire, Weapon
Standard Action **Melee** weapon
Target: One creature
Attack: Strength vs. Reflex
Hit: 4[W] + Strength modifier fire damage. The target takes ongoing 10 fire damage and a penalty to all defenses equal to 1 + your Charisma modifier (save ends both).
Miss: Half damage. The target takes ongoing 5 fire damage and a -2 penalty to all defenses (save ends both).

Life Lanterns — Cleric Attack 25

Tiny lanterns appear next to your foes and bedazzle them with divine light, which can heal your friends' wounds.

Daily ✦ Conjuration, Divine, Healing, Implement
Standard Action **Ranged** 5
Target: One, two, or three creatures
Attack: Wisdom vs. Will
Hit: The target is weakened (save ends).
Effect: For each target, you conjure a life lantern, which appears in 1 square occupied by that target and lasts until the end of the encounter. Any enemy that starts its turn in a life lantern's square is dazed until the start of its next turn. Any ally who starts or ends his or her turn in a life lantern's square can regain hit points as if he or she had spent a healing surge. Doing so destroys that lantern.

Prayer of Victory — Cleric Attack 25

You declaim an inspirational prayer as you march among your foes, leading your allies to strike true.

Daily ✦ Divine, Radiant, Weapon
Standard Action **Melee** weapon
Target: One creature
Attack: Strength vs. AC
Hit: 3[W] + Strength modifier radiant damage.
Miss: Half damage.
Effect: Until the end of the encounter, whenever you hit an enemy with a melee attack, one ally adjacent to that enemy gains a +3 power bonus to his or her next melee attack roll against that enemy. In addition, whenever you move on your turn, one ally within 5 squares of you can shift 2 squares as a free action.

Righteous Might — Cleric Attack 25

Divine power wells up within you, and you seem to tower over your god's enemies.

Daily ✦ Divine, Weapon
Standard Action **Melee** weapon
Effect: Until the end of the encounter, your reach increases by 1, your melee attacks deal 1d6 extra damage, and you gain a +1 power bonus to speed and a +2 power bonus to AC. Then make the following attack.
Target: One creature
Attack: Strength vs. AC
Hit: 4[W] + Strength modifier damage.

Level 27 Encounter Prayers

Divine Contempt — Cleric Attack 27

You utter a scathing curse that crushes your enemy's spirit with despair.

Encounter ✦ Divine, Implement, Psychic
Standard Action **Ranged** 10
Target: One creature
Attack: Wisdom vs. Will
Hit: 2d6 + Wisdom modifier psychic damage, and the target is stunned until the end of your next turn.
Aftereffect: Until the end of your next turn, the target is dazed and takes a penalty to attack rolls equal to 1 + your Charisma modifier.

Healer's Reproof — Cleric Attack 27

Your shout confounds your enemies and fills your ally with renewed strength.

Encounter ✦ Divine, Healing, Implement
Standard Action **Close** burst 1
Target: Each enemy in burst
Attack: Wisdom vs. Will
Hit: The target is stunned until the end of your next turn.
Effect: One ally in the burst can spend a healing surge and regain additional hit points equal to 3d6 + your Wisdom modifier.

Scouring Smite — Cleric Attack 27

The shining power of your faith consumes your foe as you attack and lances out to assail others who threaten you.

Encounter ✦ Divine, Radiant, Weapon
Standard Action **Melee** weapon
Target: One creature
Attack: Strength vs. Fortitude
Hit: 3[W] + Strength modifier radiant damage, and the target and each enemy within 2 squares of it gain vulnerable 5 to all damage until the end of your next turn.

Stroke of Ruin — Cleric Attack 27

Your weapon opens a tear in the fabric of the cosmos that consumes the strength of the enemy you strike.

Encounter ✦ Divine, Necrotic, Weapon
Standard Action **Melee** weapon
Target: One creature
Attack: Strength vs. AC
Hit: 3[W] + Strength modifier necrotic damage, and the target is weakened until the end of your next turn. If the target has resistance or immunity to necrotic damage, it takes no damage and is stunned instead of weakened.

Sublime Light — Cleric Attack 27

Your holy symbol blazes brightly, restoring your allies and blinding your foes with its irresistible glare.

Encounter ✦ Divine, Implement, Radiant
Standard Action **Close** blast 5
Target: Each enemy in blast
Attack: Wisdom vs. Reflex
Hit: 2d10 + Wisdom modifier radiant damage, and the target is blinded until the end of your next turn.
Effect: You and each ally in the blast make a saving throw. Also, each enemy in the blast cannot benefit from invisibility until the end of your next turn.

Level 29 Daily Prayers

Astral Exile — Cleric Attack 29

Your strike hurls your enemy deep into the Astral Sea.

Daily ✦ Divine, Radiant, Teleportation, Weapon
Standard Action **Melee** weapon
Target: One creature
Attack: Strength vs. AC
Hit: 4[W] + Strength modifier radiant damage, and the target disappears into the Astral Sea (save ends). When this effect ends, the target reappears in a space of your choice within 5 squares of its original space.
Aftereffect: The target is dazed (save ends).
Miss: Half damage, and the target is dazed (save ends).

Breath of the Stars — Cleric Attack 29

You exhale the cold, pale light of the Astral Sea, driving back your enemies and healing your friends.

Daily ✦ Cold, Divine, Healing, Implement, Radiant
Standard Action **Close** blast 5
Target: Each enemy in blast
Attack: Wisdom vs. Fortitude
Hit: 4d8 + Wisdom modifier cold and radiant damage, and you push the target 5 squares. The target is dazed (save ends).
Effect: Each ally in the blast regains hit points as if he or she had spent a healing surge. Each dying ally in the blast instead regains hit points equal to his or her bloodied value.

Chains of the Peacemaker — Cleric Attack 29

Glowing chains enwrap your foe and interfere with its attacks.

Daily ✦ Divine, Implement
Standard Action **Ranged** 20
Target: One creature
Attack: Wisdom vs. Will
Hit: The target takes a -5 penalty to attack rolls and is weakened (save ends both).
Aftereffect: The target takes a -5 penalty to attack rolls until it hits with an attack.
Miss: The target takes a -5 penalty to attack rolls and is weakened until the end of your next turn.

Enforced Surrender — Cleric Attack 29

Divine will echoes in your voice as you command your enemy to lay down its arms.

Daily ✦ Charm, Divine, Implement
Standard Action **Ranged** 10
Target: One creature
Attack: Wisdom vs. Will
Hit: The target is dominated (save ends).
Aftereffect: Each ally within your line of sight gains a +5 power bonus to attack rolls and damage rolls against the target until the end of its next turn.
Miss: Each ally within your line of sight gains a +5 power bonus to attack rolls and damage rolls against the target until the end of your next turn.

Stern Judgment — Cleric Attack 29

Your weapon imposes blinding pain on a foe, cursing it and its fellows with your god's disfavor.

Daily ✦ Divine, Reliable, Weapon
Standard Action **Melee** weapon
Target: One creature
Attack: Strength vs. Will
Hit: 3[W] + Strength modifier damage, and ongoing 10 damage (save ends). Whenever the target takes the ongoing damage, it and each enemy adjacent to it are blinded until the end of the target's next turn.
Aftereffect: Ongoing 5 damage (save ends).

Rise of the Raven Queen

In the early ages of the world, the souls of mortals unclaimed by the gods were not free to pass to the great beyond after death. Instead Nerull, the god of the dead, held them in his gray, cheerless dominion of Pluton. There they would spend eternity as powerless shades, haunted by the memory of life's rich sensation and vigor. Nerull's dominion grew ever greater, as each day myriad souls came to his realm, never to depart. The god of the dead set his sights on making himself king over all the gods, and began to send blights and plagues into the world to speed the passage of mortals into his realm.

Then an especially powerful mortal died and came to Nerull's domain, a beautiful and proud sorcerer-queen. Unique among the gray shades held in Pluton, her ghostly form glowed with her fierce will and ambition. Nerull deemed her a worthy consort, and he gave her form and substance so that she could rule at his side. Her name in life is forgotten now, but some knew her as Nera, which was the name that Nerull bestowed on her. She proved to be Nerull's doom, for the sorcerer-queen refused to be second to any being, god or mortal.

Nera discovered the means by which Nerull held mortal shades in thrall and seized that power for herself. Strengthened by countless souls, she challenged the god of death and strove with him for mastery of Pluton. Although she was mighty indeed, Nerull was an old and formidable god, and even shorn of his dead legions he was too strong for her. In order to defeat him, she had to release the souls she held: Each one freed gave up a tiny surge of strength as it passed from bondage. By freeing almost all the souls imprisoned in Pluton, she grew strong enough to destroy Nerull and seize his dominion over death.

After her victory, the sorcerer-queen thought to take Nerull's place—but the other gods intervened. Rather than rising as the new deity of the dead, she instead presides over death itself. Mortal souls are no longer bound to eternal imprisonment but instead pass into the infinite, beyond the power or knowledge of the gods.

Ever since those events, the death goddess has sought to escape the strictures limiting her power. Soon after her ascension, she expunged her true name from the knowledge of all creatures and took to calling herself the Raven Queen. In this way she hoped to void the restrictions on her role. She abandoned Pluton, founding a realm of her own in the mountains of Letherna in the Shadowfell.

In the long centuries since the Raven Queen overthrew Nerull, she has slowly increased her power, adding dominion over fate and winter to her rule over death. She sorely resents the gods who denied her the full power Nerull once wielded, and she jealously guards her domain. She has no power over souls who do not bind themselves to gods or devils in life, but the Raven Queen claims all who place themselves in her power, and they are enslaved within her cold realm forever.

NEW PARAGON PATHS

In addition to the paragon paths in this chapter, the hammer of Moradin paragon path (page 100) is open to clerics.

Anointed Champion

"Ancient blessings have I spoken over my armaments. I do not fear any power that stands against me."

Prerequisite: Cleric

In times long past, when the gods warred with the primordials, the divine armies were arrayed in majestic regalia blessed by angelic armorers with powerful wards against their foes. By long study of holy texts, you have learned those ancient prayers and rites.

As an anointed champion, you ward yourself against your foes by sanctifying the arms and armor you bear into battle with sacred oil and special ceremonies. You speak prayers that have not been heard by mortals for centuries, conferring the ancient blessings upon your companions as well. As you perform your holy tasks, you can feel the pull of history urging you on to the same glory the armies of the gods knew as they bested their enemies in ages past.

Anointed Champion Path Features

Anointed Regalia (11th level): You can choose to anoint one item you wear or carry. Doing so confers a benefit based on the item. Only one item can be anointed at a time, and the benefit lasts until you anoint a new item. As a free action, you can anoint a different item or choose a different benefit (if the anointed item is a weapon) during a short rest or after you use an anointed champion power.

Anointed Armor: You gain a +1 bonus to AC.

Anointed Weapon: You gain resistance equal to your Charisma modifier against a damage type of your choice: fire, necrotic, radiant, or thunder.

Anointed Amulet: You gain a +1 bonus to Fortitude, Reflex, and Will.

Anointed Action (11th level): When you spend an action point to take an extra action, you also gain a bonus to attack rolls and damage rolls equal to your Charisma modifier. The bonus lasts until the end of your turn.

Additional Anointed Regalia (16th level): Your Anointed Regalia path feature includes two additional types of items.

Anointed Holy Symbol: When you hit with a divine attack, you grant temporary hit points equal to your Charisma modifier to yourself or to an ally within your line of sight.

Anointed Helm: You gain a +2 bonus to saving throws.

Anointed Champion Prayers

Blessed Blade — Anointed Champion Attack 11

You smite your foe with a spectral sword, and you speak a blessing for your allies to match that of your own armaments.

Encounter ✦ Divine, Force, Implement
Standard Action **Ranged** 10
Target: One creature
Attack: Wisdom vs. Reflex
Hit: 2d8 + Wisdom modifier force damage, and each ally within 5 squares of you gains your current Anointed Regalia benefit until the end of your next turn.

Exaltation — Anointed Champion Utility 12

Fired by your ancient blessing, your ally's armaments and armor glow with supernatural power.

Encounter ✦ Divine, Healing
Minor Action **Close** burst 5
Target: One ally in burst
Effect: The target can make a saving throw or spend a healing surge. Until the end of your next turn, the target gains a +2 power bonus to his or her next attack roll and all defenses.

Anointed Army — Anointed Champion Attack 20

Divine brilliance burns your foes and grants your companions blessings that once warded the armies of the gods.

Daily ✦ Divine, Implement, Radiant
Standard Action **Close** burst 5
Target: Each enemy in burst
Attack: Wisdom vs. Will
Hit: 2d10 + Wisdom modifier radiant damage.
Miss: Half damage.
Effect: Until the end of the encounter, each ally in the burst gains a +4 power bonus to all defenses and a +2 power bonus to attack rolls and damage rolls.

RON SPENCER

Astral Savant

"Beyond the world you know, higher powers dwell. There lies the font of my strength, and the source of your doom."

Prerequisite: Cleric

You are a theologian, and you have devoted yourself to learning the nature of the gods and their dominions. Through years of study, you have developed a philosophy that grants you a deep understanding of higher realities and the properties of divine power.

As an astral savant, you use your uncanny insights to tap into the raw power of the forces that shape the Astral Sea, creating a wide range of effects with your prayers. You wield divine energy in ways that other clerics cannot, warding and sustaining your allies against their foes.

Astral Savant Path Features

Astral Mask (11th level): You are considered an immortal creature for the purpose of effects that relate to creature origin.

Savant's Action (11th level): When you spend an action point to take an extra action, one ally within your line of sight can also spend a healing surge.

Radiant Healing (11th level): Whenever you use the *healing word* power, each enemy adjacent to the power's target takes radiant damage equal to your Charisma modifier.

Divine Resurgence (16th level): When an enemy scores a critical hit against you or an ally within your line of sight, you regain the use of a Channel Divinity power you have used during this encounter. If you haven't used a Channel Divinity power during this encounter, you gain a +2 bonus to all defenses until the end of your next turn.

Astral Savant Prayers

Astral Flood — Astral Savant Attack 11

A wave of raw energy drawn from the Astral Sea flows through you and lashes out at your enemies.

Encounter ✦ Divine, Implement; Cold or **Radiant**
Standard Action **Close** blast 5
Target: Each enemy in blast
Attack: Wisdom vs. Reflex
Hit: 2d8 + Wisdom modifier cold or radiant damage (choose one for all targets). The attack has an additional effect based on the damage type.
✦ *Cold:* The target takes a -2 penalty to attack rolls until the end of your next turn.
✦ *Radiant:* The target cannot see creatures more than 5 squares away from it.

Swim the Astral Sea — Astral Savant Utility 12

You and your companion move effortlessly through astral currents, bypassing mundane impediments.

Daily ✦ Divine
Minor Action **Close** burst 10
Target: You and one ally in burst
Effect: Each target can shift a number of squares equal to his or her speed, ignoring difficult terrain. Each target is unaffected by the immobilized, restrained, and slowed conditions during this movement.

Astral Terrain — Astral Savant Attack 20

You assail your enemies with the raw stuff of the Astral Sea, creating a temporary echo of that plane.

Daily ✦ Divine, Implement; Cold or **Radiant**
Standard Action **Area** burst 2 within 10 squares
Target: Each enemy in burst
Attack: Wisdom vs. Reflex
Hit: 3d8 + Wisdom modifier cold or radiant damage (choose one for all targets).
Miss: Half damage.
Effect: The burst creates a zone of shimmering substance that lasts until the end of your next turn. The zone's effect depends on the attack's damage type.
✦ *Cold:* Any enemy that starts its turn within the zone takes a -2 penalty to all defenses until the end of your next turn.
✦ *Radiant:* Any ally within the zone who spends a healing surge regains 2d6 additional hit points.
Sustain Minor: The zone persists.

KIERAN YANNER

Battle Chaplain

"Fear not, friends, for we do the work of the gods."

Prerequisite: Cleric

When evil bubbles up from the Abyss and spills into the world, when insane hordes raid and plunder civilized lands, or when lawlessness threatens society, you fight back to preserve the world. You shoulder this burden willingly, but you can lighten the load by uniting your companions behind your holy mission. You lead through your inspiring presence, wise words, and brave deeds, with the goal of one day ushering your allies to the glory that awaits bold champions of your faith.

You are a soldier of your god, but not a proselytizer. All deities and their servants have a place in the world. Your role is to unite disparate beliefs and achieve a common victory. Your tolerance, however, does not extend to those agents of ruin who would subvert your harmonious message with their ambition and greed.

When you sing hymns and recite scripture in battle, a silver halo appears above your head as a symbol of your belief and divine blessing. Its light fills your comrades with hope and purpose, helping them to rise above the mundane and seize their destinies.

Battle Chaplain Path Features

Battle Chant (11th level): Whenever an ally hits an enemy that is adjacent to you, you can mark that enemy. The mark lasts until the end of your next turn. If the enemy marked by you makes an attack that does not include you as a target, you can shift 1 square as a free action.

Shielded Priest (11th level): You gain proficiency with light and heavy shields.

Stirring Action (11th level): When you spend an action point to make an attack, one ally adjacent to you or to the target of your attack can also make a melee basic attack as a free action, with a bonus to the attack roll equal to your Strength modifier.

Deeds not Words (16th level): When you bloody an enemy, reduce an enemy to 0 hit points, or score a critical hit with a melee attack, an ally adjacent to you gains a bonus to damage rolls equal to your Strength modifier until the start of your next turn.

Battle Chaplain Prayers

Revelation of Battle — Battle Chaplain Attack 11

A ringing impact from your favored weapon instructs your allies in the more direct matters of faith.

Encounter ✦ Divine, Weapon
Standard Action **Melee** weapon
Target: One creature
Attack: Strength vs. Reflex
Hit: 2[W] + Strength modifier damage.
Effect: Each ally within 10 squares of you gains a +2 power bonus to attack rolls and damage rolls until the start of your next turn.

Battle Hymn — Battle Chaplain Utility 12

You raise your voice in song, and your companions carry its power into battle.

Daily ✦ Divine
Standard Action **Close** burst 5
Target: You and each ally in burst
Effect: Until the end of the encounter, each target deals 1d8 extra damage when making a melee basic attack as part of a charge.

Deny Defeat — Battle Chaplain Attack 20

You refuse to let your allies fall—their desperation drives you to heroic effort.

Daily ✦ Divine, Healing, Weapon
Standard Action **Melee** weapon
Target: One creature
Attack: Strength vs. AC. You gain a +2 bonus to the attack roll for each dying ally within your line of sight.
Hit: 4[W] + Strength modifier damage.
Miss: Half damage.
Effect: Each dying ally within your line of sight can spend a healing surge.

AMELIA STONER

Compassionate Healer

"To alleviate the suffering of the just, the innocent, and the valiant is the highest of callings."

Prerequisite: Cleric

Swords and spells can hold off enemies for a time, but still the best and bravest heroes fall to opposing forces. Thus, you have dedicated all your spirit to healing heroes' injuries and sustaining their efforts. You are a master of healing, and you are not afraid to give freely of your own strength and life to aid your companions.

Even more than your fellow heroes, you willingly risk yourself so that others might live, inspiring your comrades to daring acts of courage. You are not suicidal; you're just committed to your cause. Every wound you suffer spares another champion to fight on in the name of your god and beliefs. Death elicits no fear in you; your reward waits in the hereafter.

Compassionate Healer Path Features

Compassionate Blessing (11th level): When you restore hit points with a healing power, you can choose to take 5 damage. If you do, the power's target regains 2d6 additional hit points, and you gain a +2 power bonus to all defenses until the end of your next turn.

Selfless Action (11th level): When you spend an action point to take an extra action, an ally within 5 squares of you can also spend a healing surge.

Healer's Sacrifice (16th level): When you grant an ally the opportunity to spend one or more healing surges and that ally has no more than one healing surge left, you can spend one or more healing surges but regain no hit points. Each healing surge you spend reduces the number that ally spends by one. The ally regains hit points as if he or she had spent the healing surges.

Compassionate Healer Prayers

So Others Might Live — Compassionate Healer Attack 11

Your prayer saps your enemy's strength. You then take its attack onto yourself to protect your ally, who is healed by your sacrifice.

Encounter ✦ Divine, Healing, Implement
Standard Action **Ranged** 5
Target: One creature
Attack: Wisdom vs. Fortitude
Hit: The target is weakened until the end of your next turn. The first time the target damages one of your allies with an attack before the end of your next turn, you take the damage instead, and that ally can spend a healing surge.

Bear the Wounds — Compassionate Healer Utility 12

Your ally's injuries fade, only to reappear on your body.

Daily ✦ Divine, Healing
Standard Action **Melee** touch
Target: One ally
Effect: Choose a number up to your bloodied value. The target regains that number of hit points, and you take the same amount of damage. You can then transfer to yourself any effect on the target that a save can end.

Martyr's Cry — Compassionate Healer Attack 20

The wounds you suffer weaken your enemy.

Daily ✦ Divine, Implement
Immediate Reaction **Close** burst 5
Trigger: An enemy within 5 squares of you bloodies you or damages you while you're bloodied
Target: The triggering enemy in burst
Attack: Wisdom vs. Fortitude
Hit: The target is weakened (save ends).
Aftereffect: The target is weakened (save ends).
Miss: The target is weakened (save ends).

EMRAH ELMASLI

Holy Emissary

"I bring a message from my god—and you will hear it, on pain of death."

Prerequisite: Cleric

You are a herald of the gods, imbued with divine will. Wherever you travel, you announce the intentions and desires of your patron. Your actions, words, and beliefs are windows into the gods' dominions, and through them shines the divine presence.

Although you serve a single deity, you enjoy a special connection with all divine powers, allowing them to subtly influence you and those around you. You might even be moved to prophesy from time to time. Some devotees of your faith might distrust this relationship; although they too honor all the gods, they take pride in their service to a single deity.

Whenever you speak in Supernal or utter your prayers, a tongue of fire appears over your head. The flame does not burn and sheds only the faintest light, but it does identify your special status.

Holy Emissary Path Features

Holy Tongue (11th level): You are fluent in Supernal.

Gift of Hope (11th level): Any ally who ends his or her turn adjacent to you gains a bonus to saving throws equal to your Wisdom modifier until the start of his or her next turn.

Gift of Grace Action (11th level): When you spend an action point to take an extra action, each ally adjacent to you also gains a bonus to all defenses equal to your Wisdom modifier until the end of your next turn.

Gift of Life (16th level): When you restore hit points to a bloodied target by using a divine healing power, the target regains 1d6 additional hit points.

Holy Emissary Prayers

Trumpet of Awe — Holy Emissary Attack 11

Astral trumpets announce your god. Your allies take heart and your enemies quail before the divine presence.

Encounter ✦ Divine, Implement, Thunder
Standard Action **Close** blast 3
Target: Each enemy in blast
Attack: Wisdom vs. Will
Hit: 1d8 + Wisdom modifier thunder damage, and the target grants combat advantage until the end of your next turn.
Effect: Each ally in the blast can make a saving throw with a bonus equal to your Charisma modifier.

Call Home the Weary — Holy Emissary Utility 12

Your ally has fought well, but now must withdraw to rest and recover.

Encounter ✦ Divine, Healing, Teleportation
Standard Action **Ranged** 10
Target: One bloodied ally
Effect: The target teleports to a square adjacent to you and can spend a healing surge, adding your Charisma modifier to the hit points regained.

Message of War — Holy Emissary Attack 20

You raise your voice in song, joining your music with an angelic choir to urge your comrades to victory.

Daily ✦ Divine, Implement, Radiant
Standard Action **Ranged** 10
Target: One enemy
Attack: Wisdom vs. Reflex
Hit: 3d8 + Wisdom modifier radiant damage.
Effect: Each ally adjacent to the target can make a melee basic attack against it as a free action, with a bonus to the attack roll and the damage roll equal to your Charisma modifier.

Messenger of Peace

"Violence should be the last resort."

Prerequisite: Cleric, trained in Diplomacy

You grieve for the so-called civilized races, too many of whom are locked in useless, never-ending strife. Unless some brave soul steps forward to set a better example, constant warfare can only create more conflict. Thus you have laid down your weapons and spoken vows of nonviolence, hoping to find a civilized solution to the problems of mortals.

As a messenger of peace, you always work to find a way around combat when battle is avoidable. Diplomacy is your principal weapon: Through carefully chosen words and accurate assessments of your opponent's desires, you might be able to circumvent conflict altogether. Not all enemies are willing to set aside their anger, though. Should battle erupt despite your best efforts, you are an eye of calm in war's hurricane. The weak, the weary, and the sorely wounded find succor in your presence.

Messenger of Peace Path Features

Vow of Nonviolence (11th level): When you hit with an attack that doesn't deal damage, you gain a +2 bonus to all defenses until the start of your next turn.

Peacemaker's Action (11th level): When you spend an action point to make an attack, you gain a +4 bonus to attack rolls with attacks that don't deal damage. The bonus lasts until the end of your turn.

Aura of Peace (16th level): Enemies within 2 squares of you take a -2 penalty to attack rolls.

Peace, Not Pacifism

Your commitment to nonviolence applies chiefly to thinking mortals who can be reasoned with. It doesn't make sense when you deal with monsters trying to eat you, creatures such as demons or evil dragons that are destructive by their very nature, or even intelligent beings that have an unslakable thirst for violence, such as gnolls and orcs. You can fight to defend yourself and your allies, although you should use as little violence as possible against foes who might someday choose a different path. If your enemies are capable of learning from your example, urge your companions to refrain from dealing killing blows, instead taking prisoners and showing mercy to the defeated.

KIERAN YANNER

Messenger of Peace Prayers

Pacify — Messenger of Peace Attack 11

Your words make your foe think twice before resorting to violence.

Encounter ✦ Divine, Implement
Standard Action **Ranged** 5
Target: One creature
Attack: Wisdom vs. Will
Hit: If the target hits or misses with an attack before the start of your next turn, it is stunned until the end of its next turn.

Peacemaker's Pronouncement — Messenger of Peace Utility 12

At your word, an enemy's punishment or a friend's blessing continues.

Encounter ✦ Divine
Minor Action **Close** burst 5
Target: One creature in burst
Effect: One effect on the target that would otherwise end at the end of your current turn instead lasts until the end of your next turn.

End to Strife — Messenger of Peace Attack 20

You utter a stern command, and your enemies lose their will to fight.

Daily ✦ Divine, Implement
Standard Action **Area** burst 2 within 5 squares
Target: Each enemy in burst
Attack: Wisdom vs. Will
Hit: The target cannot attack until it is attacked or until the end of the encounter.
Miss: The target takes a -5 penalty to attack rolls until it is attacked or until the end of the encounter.

Miracle Worker

"These hands have cured the sick, healed the injured, and forestalled death's cruel touch."

Prerequisite: Cleric, trained in Heal

You've always had a knack for the healing arts. People just seem to recover more quickly under your care: Bones knit and cuts mend quickly, and even sickness flees your touch. As your mastery of divine power has strengthened, so too have your skills at tending the sick and injured. Now life energy flows through your fingertips to anyone you attend.

More than other clerics, you commit your life to alleviating suffering in any form. When you are not adventuring, you might work in the temples of any god and lend your talents to help the community, whether supplying food to the hungry or removing sickness from the afflicted. You bring these same sensibilities to an adventuring group. You move across the battlefield to shore up weakness and patch up the wounded so they can get back into the fight. You might not directly share in the glory enjoyed by your companions, but you take heart in knowing that they couldn't have done it without you.

Miracle Worker Path Features

Word of Life (11th level): When you use your *healing word* power, you roll d8s instead of d6s for the additional hit points restored.

Healing Action (11th level): When you spend an action point to use a divine healing power, each ally adjacent to you regains hit points equal to 1d6 + your Wisdom modifier. The hit points regained increase to 2d6 + your Wisdom modifier at 21st level.

Aura of Health (16th level): When an ally within 5 squares of you uses his or her second wind, that ally regains 3d6 additional hit points.

Miracle Worker Prayers

Reversal of Fortunes — Miracle Worker Attack 11

A whispered benediction heals the injuries of an ally and gives the attacker a taste of the pain it inflicted.

Encounter ✦ Divine, Healing, Implement
Immediate Reaction **Ranged** 5
Trigger: An enemy within 5 squares of you hits your ally adjacent to it
Target: The triggering enemy
Attack: Wisdom vs. Fortitude
Hit: 2d10 + Wisdom modifier damage. The ally hit by the triggering enemy's attack can spend a healing surge and regain 2d10 additional hit points.

Miraculous Grace — Miracle Worker Utility 12

Your timely prayer enables your ally to escape certain doom.

Daily ✦ Divine, Healing
Immediate Reaction **Ranged** 5
Trigger: An ally within 5 squares of you drops to 0 hit points or fewer
Target: The triggering ally
Effect: The target regains hit points as if he or she had spent a healing surge and regains 2d6 additional hit points. In addition, the target makes a saving throw against each effect on him or her that a save can end.

Reap What You Sow — Miracle Worker Attack 20

You denounce a foe, making it suffer all the pains dealt to your friends.

Daily ✦ Divine, Implement
Standard Action **Close** burst 5
Target: One enemy in burst
Attack: Wisdom vs. Will
Hit: You transfer all effects that a save can end from each ally within the burst to the target.
Miss: You transfer one effect that a save can end from each ally within the burst to the target.

AMELIA STONER

Seldarine Dedicate

"Corellon guide my heart, Sehanine my arrow."

Prerequisite: Elf or eladrin, cleric, proficiency with longbow or shortbow

The Seldarine, the fellowship of brothers and sisters of the woods, comprises Corellon, Sehanine, and the other gods and exarchs who dwell in the dominion of Arvandor. Revered by elves and eladrin alike, these gods watch over and protect their favored scions. Elf and eladrin clerics often worship one or another of the Seldarine, but a few pay homage to the whole, drawing their power from Arvandor's combined wisdom.

As a Seldarine dedicate, you occupy a high position within your temples. You and the few others like you enjoy a broader connection to the gods of Arvandor than other clerics do, and you know methods for communing with them. You draw a bow as readily as you raise your holy symbol to focus your prayers.

Your weapon is inscribed with sigils and runes, which flare with emerald light when you fire a shot with a whispered prayer.

HOWARD LYON

Seldarine Dedicate Path Features

Honor the Bow (11th level): You can use a longbow or a shortbow as an implement for your cleric or Seldarine dedicate implement powers. When you use an implement power through a longbow or a shortbow, you add the weapon's enhancement bonus, if any, to the power's attack rolls and damage rolls, but you don't use the weapon's proficiency bonus. If you score a critical hit with a magic longbow or shortbow when using it as an implement, you use the weapon's critical hit effect.

Renewing Action (11th level): When you spend an action point to take an extra action, you also gain an extra use of your *healing word* power for this encounter.

Footsteps of the Gods (16th level): When you use a cleric or a Seldarine dedicate implement power, you can use a free action to shift 1 square before or after using that power.

Seldarine Dedicate Prayers

Moonbeam — Seldarine Dedicate Attack 11

A ray of frosty light streaks from your bow to slow the limbs of your prey.

Encounter ✦ Cold, Divine, Implement
Standard Action **Ranged** 20
Requirement: You must be wielding a longbow or a shortbow.
Target: One creature
Attack: Wisdom vs. Reflex
Hit: 2d10 + Wisdom modifier cold damage. Until the end of your next turn, the target grants combat advantage to anyone that makes a ranged attack against it.

Shroud of Stars — Seldarine Dedicate Utility 12

Myriad specks of light swirl about you, hiding you from enemies.

Daily ✦ Divine, Stance
Minor Action **Personal**
Effect: Until the stance ends, whenever you shift, you gain concealment until the start of your next turn.

Seldarine Wrath — Seldarine Dedicate Attack 20

You launch a fiery bolt from your bow that erupts into white-hot flame where it hits.

Daily ✦ Divine, Fire, Implement
Standard Action **Ranged** 20
Requirement: You must be wielding a longbow or a shortbow.
Target: One creature
Attack: Wisdom vs. Reflex
Hit: 3d10 + Wisdom modifier fire damage, and the target takes ongoing 10 fire damage and is dazed (save ends both).
Miss: Half damage, and ongoing 10 fire damage (save ends).

Stone Keeper

"Memory, like stone, lasts forever."

Prerequisite: Dwarf, cleric, trained in History

Dwarves have long memories. They strengthen their recollections by retelling stories passed down since the dark days of their enslavement to giants. Preserving these tales is the responsibility of the stone keepers, dwarves chosen for their wisdom and commitment to history. These stone fathers and mothers, as they are sometimes called, chisel stories into shrine walls and temple domes to give their history a physical presence, making them part of the architecture and wonder of dwarven cities.

As a stone keeper, you concern yourself with the past, but you are not simply a scholar. You are a holy champion who draws strength from your fury over all the wrongs ever committed against your people, bringing it to bear against foes who still threaten your race. When dwarven strongholds are in danger, you are the first to unite the clans against the enemy. You also travel widely, visiting ruined dwarven kingdoms and city-states to learn their fates and to exact vengeance when it is deserved.

Your views and beliefs encompass all of history and the place your people occupy in it. You harbor a deep-seated, smoldering anger born of ancient wrongs and long centuries of grief. Your prayers focus this anger into your attacks.

Stone Keeper Path Features

None So Great (11th level): When you score a critical hit against a target that is larger than you, the target is knocked prone after the attack's other effects are resolved.

Memorable Action (11th level): When you spend an action point to make an attack, your weapon attacks deal 1[W] extra damage until the end of your next turn.

Unfailing Fortune (16th level): When you use your *divine fortune* power, you gain a +3 bonus instead of a +1 bonus. If you apply this bonus to an attack and miss, you gain another use of *divine fortune* for this encounter.

Stone Keeper Prayers

Rancorous Smite — Stone Keeper Attack 11

Enraged by the harm done to your companions, you force your enemy to repay the debt in blood.

Encounter ✦ Divine, Weapon
Standard Action — **Melee** weapon
Target: One creature
Attack: Strength vs. AC. You gain a +1 bonus to the attack roll for each bloodied ally within your line of sight.
Hit: 3[W] + Wisdom modifier damage.

Scrape the Sky — Stone Keeper Utility 12

Fury fills you, and you tower over your enemies.

Daily ✦ Divine
Standard Action — **Personal**
Effect: Until the end of the encounter, your reach and speed both increase by 1, and your melee attacks deal 2d6 extra damage.

Every Wrong Righted — Stone Keeper Attack 20

You channel your smoldering resentment into a savage strike and inspire your allies to finish the job.

Daily ✦ Divine, Healing, Weapon
Standard Action — **Melee** weapon
Target: One creature
Attack: Strength vs. AC
Hit: 5[W] + Strength modifier damage.
Miss: Half damage, and each ally adjacent to you gains a +3 power bonus to attack rolls against the target until the start of your next turn.
Effect: You and each ally adjacent to you can spend a healing surge.

TRUTHSEEKER

"The light of truth reveals all secrets and denies all falsehoods."

Prerequisite: Cleric

Deception worms its way through the world, corroding morals and subverting ideals. Only through constant vigilance can this welling corruption be checked. Many divine servants battle obvious foes—undead, demons, and other foul creatures—but the enemies you face are far more insidious. You explore realms of shadow and deception, leading the fight against enemies who use guile instead of brutality.

To combat such forces, you armor yourself in the truth, using its radiance to burn away the lies and falsehoods your foes employ. In your presence, the enemy cannot hide or use its tricks, and it stands exposed before you.

Facing the worst sort of villains leaves its mark on you. You age prematurely, lines creasing your face, but such ravages of the body do not extend to your spirit. Each victory only firms your resolve. When you wield your truthseeker powers in the name of your god, your voice sounds like thunder and your enemies quail before your righteous presence.

TRUTHSEEKER PATH FEATURES

Censuring Action (11th level): When you spend an action point to use a divine attack power, until the end of your next turn, any enemy that ends its turn adjacent to you takes a -2 penalty to all defenses (save ends).

Healing Truth (11th level): Each target of your *healing word* power gains a +2 power bonus to all defenses against fear, illusion, and polymorph effects until the end of the encounter.

Unequaled Clarity (16th level): When you make an Insight check, you can roll twice and use either result. In addition, you gain a +4 bonus to passive Insight checks.

TRUTHSEEKER PRAYERS

Corruption Unveiled — Truthseeker Attack 11

You brandish your symbol, whose irresistible glow reveals your enemy's secrets.

Encounter ✦ Divine, Implement, Radiant
Standard Action **Ranged** 5
Target: One creature
Attack: Wisdom vs. Will
Hit: 2d10 + Wisdom modifier radiant damage, and the target cannot use fear, illusion, or polymorph powers until the end of your next turn.

Shrine of Clarity — Truthseeker Utility 12

Tracing a circle of binding power, you force your enemies to stand and face you.

Encounter ✦ Divine, Zone
Standard Action **Close** burst 5
Effect: The burst creates a zone of planar interference that lasts until the end of your next turn. Enemies cannot teleport into the zone. While within the zone, enemies cannot teleport and cannot benefit from phasing or being insubstantial.

Moment of Truth — Truthseeker Attack 20

Your holy symbol flashes, confounding a foe.

Daily ✦ Divine, Implement
Standard Action **Ranged** 5
Target: One creature
Attack: Wisdom vs. Will
Hit: The target is stunned and helpless until the end of your next turn.
Aftereffect: The target is dazed (save ends).
Miss: The target is dazed (save ends).

LUCAS GRACIANO

CHAPTER 3

INVOKER

"Do not look to me for forgiveness. Do not implore me to be merciful. I am a truth unendurable and a reckoning of wrongs, and I am here to call you to account."

YOU ARE a speaker of truth and a shouter of defiance. Through your hand, your staff, and your voice the power of the gods is loosed against your foes. You scour enemies by the half-dozen with divine power: blinding them with radiance, hammering them with thunder, burning them with holy flame, driving them to the ground, and binding them in chains of light. Your words of judgment are the last the gods' enemies hear.

Unlike divine characters who gain their powers through rites of investiture, invokers gain their powers through covenants made directly with the gods. The Covenant of Preservation and the Covenant of Wrath are presented in *Player's Handbook 2*; the Covenant of Malediction is described here. All invokers rely on fragments of the words of creation to some extent, but as a malediction invoker, you master more of these ancient syllables and wield their power against your foes. Like the Covenant of Wrath, the Covenant of Malediction is an offensively oriented path. Many of its powers cripple enemies' defenses and prove unusually difficult to shake off.

Regardless of your choice of covenant, this chapter offers you new options for wielding divine power against your foes. The chapter includes the following material.

- **New Class Feature:** The Covenant of Malediction includes a new Channel Divinity power, which hinders your foes.
- **New Build:** As a malediction invoker, make your enemies quail at the sound of your very words.
- **New Invoker Powers:** Nearly a hundred new powers for you to choose from, including ones suitable for the Covenant of Preservation, the Covenant of Malediction, and the Covenant of Wrath.
- **New Paragon Paths:** A variety of new invoker paragon paths, including the adept of whispers, the Keeper of the Nine, and the stonecaller.

HOWARD LYON

NEW CLASS FEATURE

When you choose your Divine Covenant, you can select the Covenant of Malediction instead of another option, such as the ones in *Player's Handbook 2*.

Covenant of Malediction

The gods entrust you with the invocations of destruction used in their war against the primordials, so you can carry forward their sacred cause and ensure that the world's enemies never rise again.

Channel Divinity: You gain the Channel Divinity power *maledictor's doom*.

Covenant Manifestation: When you use a divine encounter or daily attack power on your turn, you can push one target hit by the power 1 square after the power's effect is resolved.

Channel Divinity: Maledictor's Doom — Invoker Feature

Foes who hear your solemn vow are shaken by its weighty promise.

Encounter ✦ Divine, Fear
Minor Action **Close** blast 5
Target: Each enemy in blast
Effect: Each target takes a -1 penalty to attack rolls and saving throws until the end of your next turn. In addition, whenever the target is hit by a fear attack before the end of your next turn, you push the target 1 square as a free action.

NEW BUILD

Player's Handbook 2 introduced the preserving invoker and the wrathful invoker. This chapter adds the malediction invoker, whose pronouncements on the battlefield bring ruin to those that would stand in opposition.

Malediction Invoker

The malediction invoker build is based on the Covenant of Malediction. The malediction invoker employs dread words of power to eradicate the gods' foes. These words of power come from the gods' lexicon, the very words of creation. The words are frequently too potent for mortals, imperiling the health and sanity of those who speak them. Malediction invokers need a high Wisdom score to intone the words properly and to piece together the inflections and holy grammar required to use the words in battle. Words of power bear a physical price, so malediction invokers should consider making Constitution their second highest ability, followed closely by Intelligence.

Suggested Class Feature: Covenant of Malediction*
Suggested Feat: Baleful Malediction
Suggested Skills: Arcana, Endurance, Insight, Religion
Suggested At-Will Powers: *grasping shards, visions of blood**
Suggested Encounter Power: *summons of justice**
Suggested Daily Power: *execration**
*New option presented in this book

NEW INVOKER POWERS

The invoker is the hand of divine will, a champion of the gods who brings to bear terrible prayers in the name of his or her holy cause. This section expands the power options for all invokers, as well as presenting powers tailored for the Covenant of Malediction.

Level 1 At-Will Prayers

Hand of Radiance — Invoker Attack 1

Tendrils of radiance streak from your fingertips across the battlefield. The beams strike your enemies, raining sparks of light on impact.

At-Will ✦ Divine, Implement, Radiant
Standard Action **Ranged** 10
Target: One, two, or three creatures
Level 21: Target an additional creature.
Attack: Wisdom vs. Reflex
Hit: 1d4 + Wisdom modifier radiant damage.

Mantle of the Infidel — Invoker Attack 1

Holding your implement high, you conjure a radiant mantle that sears a foe and marks it as an enemy of the faith.

At-Will ✦ Divine, Implement, Radiant
Standard Action **Ranged** 20
Target: One creature
Attack: Wisdom vs. Will
Hit: 1d6 + Wisdom modifier radiant damage. If the target is marked, the penalty to attack rolls it takes from the marked condition is -4 instead of -2.
Level 21: 2d6 + Wisdom modifier radiant damage.

Visions of Blood — Invoker Attack 1

The images of carnage and death that you invoke sow doubt in your enemies.

At-Will ✦ Divine, Fear, Implement, Psychic
Standard Action **Close** blast 3
Target: Each creature in blast
Attack: Wisdom vs. Will
Hit: 1d6 + Wisdom modifier psychic damage, and the target takes a -1 penalty to all defenses until the start of your next turn.
Level 21: 2d6 + Wisdom modifier psychic damage.

Level 1 Encounter Prayers

Forceful Denunciation — Invoker Attack 1

It is as if your god brushes aside your foes, such is the forcefulness of your denunciation.

Encounter ✦ Divine, Implement, Thunder
Standard Action **Close** blast 3
Target: Each enemy in blast
Attack: Wisdom vs. Fortitude
Hit: 2d6 + Wisdom modifier thunder damage, and you push the target 1 square.
Covenant of Preservation: The number of squares you push the target equals your Intelligence modifier.

Lightning's Revelation — Invoker Attack 1

Lightning splits the air, striking your foes and exposing their frailty.

Encounter ✦ Divine, Implement, Lightning
Standard Action **Area** burst 1 within 10 squares
Target: Each creature in burst
Attack: Wisdom vs. Reflex
Hit: 2d6 + Wisdom modifier lightning damage, and the target takes a -1 penalty to all defenses until the end of your next turn.
Covenant of Wrath: The penalty to all defenses equals your Constitution modifier.

Summons of Justice — Invoker Attack 1

Justice will be served no matter the cost. You draw from your own vitality to hurl a brilliant ray that compels your enemies to come forward.

Encounter ✦ Charm, Divine, Implement, Radiant
Standard Action **Close** burst 5
Target: One or two creatures in burst
Attack: Wisdom vs. Will
Hit: 2d8 + Wisdom modifier radiant damage, and you pull the target 3 squares.
Covenant of Malediction: You also knock the target prone.
Effect: You are dazed until the end of your next turn.

Whispers of Defeat — Invoker Attack 1

Your words assume a life of their own, worming into your enemies' minds and creating a feeling that defeat is inevitable.

Encounter ✦ Divine, Fear, Implement, Psychic
Standard Action **Close** burst 5
Target: Each enemy in burst
Attack: Wisdom vs. Will
Hit: Until the end of your next turn, the target takes a -2 penalty to attack rolls, and whenever the target misses with an attack, it takes 5 psychic damage.
Covenant of Malediction: Add your Wisdom modifier to the psychic damage.

MATIAS TAPIA

Level 1 Daily Prayers

Crown of Retaliation — Invoker Attack 1

You point at a foe and form a circle with your hands. A translucent crown then appears over that foe's head, searing it with each injury your companions suffer.

Daily ✦ Divine, Implement, Radiant
Standard Action **Ranged** 10
Target: One creature
Attack: Wisdom vs. Will
Hit: 2d6 + Wisdom modifier radiant damage.
Effect: The target is affected by your crown of retaliation (save ends). Until the crown ends, the target takes 5 radiant damage when any ally within 5 squares of it takes damage.

Execration — Invoker Attack 1

You spit a dread curse, which punishes your enemies and causes you to feel an echo of their pain.

Daily ✦ Divine, Implement
Standard Action **Close** burst 5
Target: One or two creatures in burst
Attack: Wisdom vs. Will
Hit: 1d8 + Wisdom modifier damage, or 2d8 + Wisdom modifier damage if you target only one creature. The target takes ongoing 10 damage (save ends).
Miss: Half damage, and ongoing 5 damage (save ends).
Effect: You take ongoing 5 damage (save ends).

Invocation of Ice and Fire — Invoker Attack 1

Flaming hail bludgeons your opponents.

Daily ✦ Cold, Divine, Fire, Implement, Zone
Standard Action **Close** blast 5
Target: Each creature in blast
Attack: Wisdom vs. Reflex
Hit: 2d6 + Wisdom modifier cold and fire damage.
Effect: The blast creates a zone of flaming hail that lasts until the end of your next turn. Any creature that starts its turn within the zone takes 5 cold and fire damage.
Sustain Minor: The zone persists.

Silent Malediction — Invoker Attack 1

You enter a trance as your lips move. Your enemies don't hear what you're saying because of the thunder rumbling around them.

Daily ✦ Divine, Implement, Thunder
Standard Action **Close** blast 3
Target: Each creature in blast
Attack: Wisdom vs. Fortitude
Hit: 2d6 + Wisdom modifier thunder damage, and the target is stunned (save ends).
Miss: Half damage, and the target is dazed until the end of your next turn.
Effect: You are dazed until the end of your next turn.

Storm Call — Invoker Attack 1

Filled with the wrath of the gods, you call down thunder and lightning on your enemy.

Daily ✦ Divine, Implement, Lightning, Thunder
Standard Action **Ranged** 10
Target: One creature
Attack: Wisdom vs. Reflex
Hit: 1d8 + Wisdom modifier thunder damage. The target takes ongoing 5 lightning damage and is dazed (save ends both).
Miss: Half damage, and the target is slowed (save ends).

Level 2 Utility Prayers

Divine Protection — Invoker Utility 2

You act knowing that your god will save you from harm.

Encounter ✦ Divine
Minor Action **Personal**
Effect: Until the end of your next turn, you don't provoke opportunity attacks.

Encouraging Chant — Invoker Utility 2

You shout a word of hope to restore your allies' confidence.

Encounter ✦ Divine, Zone
Minor Action **Close** burst 2
Effect: The burst creates a zone of hope that lasts until the end of your next turn. While within the zone, you and any allies gain a power bonus to saving throws equal to your Intelligence modifier.

AMELIA STONER

Know Weakness — Invoker Utility 2

You utter words of power that are also words of knowledge.

Encounter ✦ Divine
Minor Action **Personal**
Effect: Choose a creature within 10 squares of you. You know that creature's current resistances and vulnerabilities, if any.

Lore of Shom — Invoker Utility 2

You invoke the vast knowledge of the lost civilization of Shom, gaining access to esoteric lore that might otherwise escape you.

Daily ✦ Divine
Free Action **Personal**
Trigger: You make an Arcana check, a History check, or a Religion check and dislike the result
Effect: You reroll the skill check with a power bonus equal to your Intelligence modifier and use either result.

Miraculous Fortune — Invoker Utility 2

Though the attack strikes you, your timely prayer reduces the worst of the injury and inspires a nearby ally.

Encounter ✦ Divine
Immediate Interrupt **Personal**
Trigger: You are damaged by an enemy's attack
Effect: The damage is reduced by 5. One ally within 5 squares of you gains a +1 power bonus to attack rolls until the start of your next turn.

Level 3 Encounter Prayers

Knives of the Soul — Invoker Attack 3

Two translucent blades burst out of your body and streak toward your enemies. You stagger from the unleashed power.

Encounter ✦ Divine, Force, Implement
Standard Action **Ranged** 5
Target: One or two creatures
Attack: Wisdom vs. Reflex
Hit: 2d10 + Wisdom modifier force damage, or 2d12 + Wisdom modifier force damage if you target only one creature. You push the target 1 square.
Covenant of Malediction: The number of squares you push the target equals your Constitution modifier.
Effect: You take 5 damage.

Penance Compelled — Invoker Attack 3

Someone will pay for these crimes; you guarantee it.

Encounter ✦ Divine, Implement, Radiant
Standard Action **Ranged** 10
Target: One creature
Attack: Wisdom vs. Will
Hit: 2d6 + Wisdom modifier radiant damage. The next time the target deals damage before the end of your next turn, choose another enemy within 10 squares of you. That enemy takes 5 radiant damage.
Covenant of Wrath: The radiant damage that the chosen enemy takes equals 5 + your Constitution modifier.

Symbol of the Broken Sword — Invoker Attack 3

You place a symbol of pacification on your enemy, partly subduing it.

Encounter ✦ Charm, Divine, Implement
Standard Action **Ranged** 10
Target: One creature
Attack: Wisdom vs. Will
Hit: Until the end of your next turn, the target cannot use any attack power that requires a standard action, other than basic attacks.
Covenant of Preservation: Until the end of your next turn, the target also takes a penalty to attack rolls equal to your Intelligence modifier.

Word of Ruin — Invoker Attack 3

You utter syllables of damnation, which attack the minds of creatures around you and cloud your own.

Encounter ✦ Divine, Implement, Psychic
Standard Action **Close** burst 2
Target: Each creature in burst
Attack: Wisdom vs. Will
Hit: 1d8 + Wisdom modifier psychic damage, and the target is dazed and slowed until the end of your next turn.
Effect: You are dazed until the end of your next turn.

Level 5 Daily Prayers

Deluge of Blood — Invoker Attack 5

Fresh blood streams from the wounds of your enemy as it is dazed by wracking pain. You must endure some of the pain too and are momentarily dazed.

Daily ✦ Divine, Implement
Immediate Reaction **Close** burst 5
Trigger: An enemy within 5 squares of you is damaged by a melee or a ranged attack
Target: The triggering enemy in burst
Attack: Wisdom vs. Fortitude
Hit: The target is dazed and takes ongoing 10 damage (save ends both).
Miss: Ongoing 5 damage (save ends).
Effect: You are dazed until the end of your next turn.

Lamentation of the Wicked — Invoker Attack 5

You speak an ancient curse. Your enemies gnash their teeth and wail at the doom you promise, distracted from their own defense. Your and your allies' attacks take advantage of this distraction.

Daily ✦ Divine, Implement, Psychic
Standard Action **Close** burst 2
Target: Each enemy in burst
Attack: Wisdom vs. Will
Hit: 2d8 + Wisdom modifier psychic damage, and the target grants combat advantage and cannot shift (save ends both).
Effect: Until the end of the encounter, when you or any ally within 5 squares of you attacks an enemy and has combat advantage against it, the attack deals extra damage equal to your Constitution modifier.

Malediction of Blindness — Invoker Attack 5

At your command, your foes lose their sight. The power of this prayer leaves you barely able to defend yourself for a moment.

Daily ✦ Divine, Implement
Standard Action **Close** blast 3
Target: Each creature in blast
Attack: Wisdom vs. Fortitude
Hit: 2d8 + Wisdom modifier damage, and the target is blinded (save ends).
Miss: Half damage, and the target takes a -2 penalty to attack rolls until the end of your next turn.
Effect: You grant combat advantage until the start of your next turn.

Sun Shard — Invoker Attack 5

You call down a fragment of solar essence on your enemies.

Daily ✦ Divine, Implement, Radiant
Standard Action **Area** burst 1 within 10 squares
Target: Each creature in burst
Attack: Wisdom vs. Reflex
Hit: 2d6 + Wisdom modifier radiant damage, and the target is dazed until the end of its next turn. If this power targets only one creature, the target is dazed (save ends).
Miss: Half damage.

CRAFTING A COVENANT

Invokers take an oath to oppose the gods' enemies when they gain their powers, but your invoker's covenant need not be so simple. Consider adding other promises or special taboos to make your connection to your deity more distinct.

Maybe you agreed to bear the gods' power in order to avenge some wrong, and as repayment for the power they granted toward this end, you must complete a particular quest. Perhaps you have sworn not to kill members of some race or organization favored by the god you serve. You covenant might drive you to take seemingly inconsequential events or concepts as seriously as life and death. For example, you might have sworn to protect love as a follower of Sehanine, thus forcing you to break battle lines as you seek to reunite two young lovers drawn apart by war.

Your worship might include rites unknown to other faithful, or you might adhere to prohibitions that seem odd. You can simply do strange things for the humor of it, or you can craft these taboos or ceremonies so that they have meaning based on the deity you follow. Perhaps, as a follower of Melora, you can't cross running water without first throwing something in. Maybe Moradin demands that you say a blessing over every forge you see. Kord might call upon you to engage in all contests of strength that you encounter. As an adherent of the Raven Queen, you might speak a small prayer for the souls of the dead bodies you discover, and you might even breathe a well-wishing in the midst of battle for the souls you send on their way.

Trumpet the Star's Fall — Invoker Attack 5

A brilliant orb appears overhead and then smashes into your enemies in a storm of light and fire.

Daily ✦ Divine, Fire, Implement, Radiant, Zone
Standard Action **Area** burst 2 within 10 squares
Target: Each creature in burst
Attack: Wisdom vs. Reflex
Hit: 2d6 + Wisdom modifier fire and radiant damage, and you knock the target prone.
Miss: Half damage, and you push the target 1 square.
Effect: The burst creates a zone of smoke that lasts until the end of the encounter. The zone is heavily obscured.

Level 6 Utility Prayers

Brilliant Cloak — Invoker Utility 6

Your clothing comes to life with a dazzling display of color.

Daily ✦ Divine
Standard Action **Personal**
Effect: Until the end of your next turn, you and any allies adjacent to you gain a +2 bonus to AC and Reflex.
Sustain Minor: The effect persists.

Guardian Angel — Invoker Utility 6

A prayer to the gods summons a fearsome, winged angel to protect your comrades.

Daily ✦ Conjuration, Divine
Standard Action **Ranged** 10
Effect: You conjure a guardian angel in 1 square within range. The angel lasts until the end of your next turn. Any ally in the angel's space or adjacent to it gains a +2 power bonus to AC. In addition, when you or an ally is hit by an attack while in the angel's space or adjacent to it, you can dismiss the angel as an immediate interrupt and reduce the damage by half.
Sustain Minor: The angel persists, and you can move it 5 squares.

Prayer for Victory — Invoker Utility 6

Seeing the danger, you whisper a prayer to bolster your courage in the face of harm.

Daily ✦ Divine
Immediate Interrupt **Personal**
Trigger: An enemy makes a melee or a ranged attack roll against you
Effect: You gain temporary hit points equal to 5 + your Wisdom modifier, and you gain a +2 power bonus to AC until the end of your next turn.

Solid Fog — Invoker Utility 6

Each word spoken carries thick fog until dense mist covers the battlefield.

Daily ✦ Divine, Zone
Minor Action **Close** blast 3
Effect: The burst creates a zone of dense fog that lasts until the end of your next turn. The zone is difficult terrain and heavily obscured.
Sustain Minor: The zone persists, and you can increase its size by 1 to a maximum of blast 5.

Level 7 Encounter Prayers

Rain of Blood — Invoker Attack 7

Blood rains down from the sky, pelting your enemies.

Encounter ✦ Divine, Implement
Standard Action **Area** burst 2 within 10 squares
Target: Each enemy in burst
Attack: Wisdom vs. Fortitude
Hit: 2d6 + Wisdom modifier damage, and the target gains vulnerable 5 to all damage until the end of your next turn.
Covenant of Wrath: Until the end of your next turn, each ally in the burst gains a power bonus to attack rolls equal to your Constitution modifier.

Tide of the First Storm — Invoker Attack 7

You call on the first storm that rolled over the world, using its power to blow your allies away from harm while buffeting your enemies.

Encounter ✦ Divine, Implement
Standard Action **Area** burst 2 within 10 squares
Target: Each enemy in burst
Attack: Wisdom vs. Reflex
Hit: 1d6 + Wisdom modifier damage, and the target is slowed until the end of your next turn.
Effect: You slide each ally in the burst a number of squares equal to 1 + your Intelligence modifier.

Trumpets of Celestia — Invoker Attack 7

You invoke the divine dominion of Celestia, calling on the trumpets of the immortals there to blast your enemies and shatter their resolve.

Encounter ✦ Divine, Fear, Implement, Thunder
Standard Action **Close** blast 3
Target: Each creature in blast
Attack: Wisdom vs. Fortitude
Hit: 2d6 + Wisdom modifier thunder damage, and the target takes a -2 penalty to attack rolls until the end of your next turn.
Covenant of Preservation: The penalty to attack rolls equals your Intelligence modifier.

Word of Fiery Condemnation — Invoker Attack 7

Your words ignite creatures before you with fire from the heavens. The blaze of glory demands all your attention, dazing you for a short time.

Encounter ✦ Divine, Fire, Implement, Radiant
Standard Action **Close** blast 5
Target: Each creature in blast
Attack: Wisdom vs. Reflex
Hit: 2d6 + Wisdom modifier radiant damage, and ongoing 5 fire damage (save ends).
Covenant of Malediction: The target takes a -2 penalty to saving throws against the ongoing damage.
Effect: You are dazed until the end of your next turn.

Written in Fire — Invoker Attack 7

Fiery letters flicker in the air and sear nearby enemies.

Encounter ✦ Conjuration, Divine, Fire, Implement
Standard Action **Ranged** 10
Effect: You conjure fiery symbols in 1 square within range. The symbols last until the end of your next turn. Any enemy that starts its turn within 5 squares of the symbols and does not end its turn at least 6 squares away from them takes fire damage equal to 10 + your Wisdom modifier.

Level 9 Daily Prayers

Baleful Admonishment — Invoker Attack 9

Your damning words wrack your body at the same time that they doom your foes to defeat.

Daily ✦ Divine, Implement
Standard Action **Ranged** 10
Target: One, two, or three creatures
Attack: Wisdom vs. Will
Hit: 1d10 + Wisdom modifier damage, and the target is affected by your baleful admonishment (save ends). Whenever the target hits with an attack before the baleful admonishment ends, you can take 5 damage as a free action to force the target to reroll the attack and use the second result. If the rerolled attack misses, the target takes 5 + your Constitution modifier damage.
Miss: Half damage, and the target is dazed until the end of your next turn.

Hall of Thunderous Battle — Invoker Attack 9

You evoke a vision of a divine hall of battle. Your allies are emboldened by the brave shouts within it, while the sounds of battle thunder over your enemies, pushing them back.

Daily ✦ Divine, Implement, Thunder, Zone
Standard Action **Close** burst 2
Target: Each enemy in burst
Attack: Wisdom vs. Fortitude
Hit: 2d6 + Wisdom modifier thunder damage, and you push the target a number of squares equal to your Intelligence modifier.
Miss: Half damage, and you push the target 1 square.
Effect: The burst creates a thundering zone that lasts until the end of your next turn. When you move, the zone moves with you, remaining centered on you. While within the zone, any ally gains a +2 power bonus to AC and Fortitude.
Sustain Minor: The zone persists, and you push each enemy within it 1 square.

Herald the Storm Unleashed — Invoker Attack 9

From a mote of flashing light, a savage storm is born, scourging enemies with lightning and thunder.

Daily ✦ Divine, Implement, Lightning, Thunder, Zone
Standard Action **Area** burst 1 within 10 squares
Target: Each creature in burst
Attack: Wisdom vs. Fortitude
Hit: 3d6 + Wisdom modifier lightning and thunder damage, and you slide the target 2 squares.
Miss: Half damage.
Effect: The burst creates a zone of lightning and thunder that lasts until the end of your next turn. Any creature that begins its turn within the zone takes 5 lightning damage. Any creature that leaves the zone takes 5 thunder damage. As a move action, you can move the zone 5 squares.
Sustain Minor: The zone persists.

Malediction of Rigidity — Invoker Attack 9

Those arrayed around you are reluctant to move lest you blister them again with your punishing words, which stiffen your own limbs.

Daily ✦ Divine, Fear, Implement
Minor Action **Close** blast 5
Target: Each creature in blast
Attack: Wisdom vs. Will
Hit: 1d8 + Wisdom modifier damage. The target takes ongoing 10 damage and is immobilized (save ends both).
Miss: Half damage. The target takes ongoing 5 damage and is slowed (save ends both).
Covenant of Malediction: The target takes a -2 penalty to saving throws against these effects.
Effect: You are immobilized until the end of your next turn.

Twist of Fate — Invoker Attack 9

You assault your enemies' minds and invoke destiny to alter the course of events, limiting the attacks the enemies can make.

Daily ✦ Charm, Divine, Implement, Psychic
Standard Action **Area** burst 1 within 10 squares
Target: Each enemy in burst
Attack: Wisdom vs. Will
Hit: 2d6 + Wisdom modifier psychic damage. The only attacks the target can make during its next turn are basic attacks. If your attack hits only one enemy, the only attacks it can make during its turn are basic attacks (save ends).
Covenant of Preservation: Until the end of your next turn, the target also takes a penalty to attack rolls equal to your Intelligence modifier.
Miss: Half damage.

Level 10 Utility Prayers

Call of the Vanguard — Invoker Utility 10

Divine inspiration turns an ambush to your advantage.

Daily ✦ Divine
No Action **Ranged** 10
Trigger: You roll initiative
Target: You and one ally
Effect: Each target gains a bonus to his or her initiative check equal to your Intelligence modifier. In addition, neither target is surprised.

Enunciation — Invoker Utility 10

Your voice raised, you extend the reach of your prayers.

Daily ✦ Divine
Minor Action **Personal**
Effect: Until the end of your next turn, you can increase the size of your close blast or close burst attacks by 1.

Prayer of Vengeance — Invoker Utility 10

You recite the ancient declaration of war against the primordials. Friends who hear it are filled with righteous indignation against their attackers.

Daily ✦ Divine, Zone
Minor Action **Close** burst 3
Effect: The burst creates a zone of retribution that lasts until the end of your next turn. When any ally within the zone takes damage from an attack, that ally gains a +2 power bonus to attack rolls against the attacker until the start of the ally's next turn.
Sustain Minor: The zone persists.

Word of Urgency — Invoker Utility 10

You exclaim with authority, inspiring your friend to leap away from harm.

Encounter ✦ Divine
Free Action **Close** burst 10
Trigger: You use an area or a close attack power and an ally within 10 squares of you is in the area of effect
Target: The triggering ally in burst
Effect: The target can shift a number of squares equal to your Intelligence modifier as a free action.

Level 13 Encounter Prayers

Brilliant Revelation Invoker Attack 13

You blast nearby creatures' minds with a dizzying vision of divine dominions.

Encounter ✦ Divine, Implement, Psychic
Standard Action **Close** blast 5
Target: Each creature in blast
Attack: Wisdom vs. Will
Hit: 1d10 + Wisdom modifier psychic damage, and the target is dazed and slowed until the end of your next turn. The first time the target attacks before the end of your next turn, it takes 10 psychic damage.
Covenant of Malediction: The psychic damage the target takes when it attacks equals 10 + your Constitution modifier.

Deadly Doubt Invoker Attack 13

Your words assail your foes' minds with self-doubt strong enough to wound them. Any further attack dazes the victims too.

Encounter ✦ Divine, Implement, Psychic
Standard Action **Close** blast 5
Target: Each enemy in blast
Attack: Wisdom vs. Will
Hit: 2d8 + Wisdom modifier psychic damage. If the target is hit again before the end of your next turn, it is dazed until the end of its next turn.
Covenant of Wrath: The first creature to attack the target before the end of your next turn gains a power bonus to its attack roll equal to your Constitution modifier.

Earthen Reversal Invoker Attack 13

You utter a nearly forgotten word dedicated to the earth, and it heaves in response, lifting allies and upturning enemies.

Encounter ✦ Divine, Implement
Standard Action **Area** burst 2 within 10 squares
Target: Each enemy in burst
Attack: Wisdom vs. Fortitude
Hit: 1d8 + Wisdom modifier damage, and you knock the target prone.
Effect: You and each ally in the burst can stand up as a free action.
Covenant of Preservation: Each ally in the burst can also shift 1 square as a free action.

Destined for Greatness

As an invoker, you have been personally chosen by the gods to serve their ends. How does that make you feel?

Do you envy those who are able to pursue their own destinies, or do you take great pride in your contact with the divine? Others, even other divine characters, lack your direct, moment-by-moment connection to the gods. They have faith, but you *know*. Do you feel pity for them, or are you awed by their greater devotion?

Is your covenant a burden imposed upon you, or did you seek it? Do you revel in your power, or do you regret the oath you made? Do you seek the gods' approval with your deeds, or are you confident that the choices you make represent their desires?

Thunderous Rebuke Invoker Attack 13

You blast your enemies away in a wave of thunder and destruction.

Encounter ✦ Divine, Implement, Thunder
Immediate Reaction **Close** blast 5
Trigger: You are hit by an enemy attack
Target: Each creature in blast
Attack: Wisdom vs. Fortitude
Hit: 2d6 + Wisdom modifier thunder damage, and the target is pushed 1 square and deafened until the end of your next turn.

Word of Blindness Invoker Attack 13

At your command, creatures around you lose their sight. The power of this prayer leaves you dazed for a short time.

Encounter ✦ Divine, Implement, Radiant
Standard Action **Close** burst 1
Target: Each creature in burst
Attack: Wisdom vs. Will
Hit: 2d8 + Wisdom modifier radiant damage, and the target is blinded until the end of your next turn.
Effect: You are dazed until the end of your next turn.
Covenant of Malediction: The size of the burst increases by 1.

Level 15 Daily Prayers

Deific Imprecation Invoker Attack 15

You are a conduit for your god's wrath. You feel its sting as it smites your enemies.

Daily ✦ Divine, Implement
Standard Action **Ranged** 10
Target: One creature
Attack: Wisdom vs. Fortitude
Hit: 2d8 + Wisdom modifier damage, and ongoing 10 damage (save ends).
Aftereffect: Each enemy within 3 squares of the target takes 10 damage.
Miss: Half damage, and ongoing 5 damage (save ends).
Effect: You take ongoing 5 damage (save ends). Whenever you take this ongoing damage, choose an enemy within 5 squares of you. That enemy also takes 5 damage.

Dire Banishment Invoker Attack 15

You temporarily banish your enemy from this world, using your life force to prevent the enemy from returning.

Daily ✦ Divine, Implement, Necrotic, Teleportation
Standard Action **Ranged** 5
Target: One creature
Attack: Wisdom vs. Will
Hit: 4d10 + Wisdom modifier necrotic damage, and the target vanishes from this world (save ends). You can end the effect as a minor action. When the effect ends, the target reappears in the space it last occupied or in the nearest unoccupied space.
Each Failed Saving Throw: You take 5 damage.
Miss: Half damage, and you teleport the target 5 squares.

Shadowdark Invocation — Invoker Attack 15

You call forth a chill darkness, which deepens until light is but a dim memory.

Daily ✦ Cold, Divine, Implement, Zone
Standard Action **Close** burst 3
Target: Each creature in burst
Attack: Wisdom vs. Fortitude
Hit: 2d8 + Wisdom modifier cold damage.
Miss: Half damage.
Effect: The burst creates a zone of shadow that lasts until the end of your next turn. The zone is heavily obscured. When any creature starts its turn within the zone, that creature takes 10 cold damage, and you can slide it 3 squares as a free action. You are immune to the zone's effects. As a move action, you can move the zone 3 squares.
Sustain Minor: The zone persists.

Storm of Punishment — Invoker Attack 15

Raising your implement, you invoke the gods and create a hole in the sky through which thunder and lightning cascade onto your foes.

Daily ✦ Divine, Implement, Lightning, Thunder
Standard Action **Area** burst 1 within 10 squares
Target: Each creature in burst
Attack: Wisdom vs. Fortitude
Hit: 2d8 + Wisdom modifier lightning and thunder damage, and the target is blinded and deafened (save ends both).
Miss: Half damage, and the target is blinded and deafened until the end of your next turn.

Level 16 Utility Prayers

Confounding Utterance — Invoker Utility 16

You speak a word of seeming gibberish and then take shelter behind the confusion it creates.

Daily ✦ Divine
Minor Action **Personal**
Effect: Until the end of the encounter, when any enemy makes a melee attack roll against you, it must roll twice and use the lower result.

Words of Creation

You character uses the words the gods spoke to command the substance of the world and bring about life. What do those words sound like? Does your invoker speak bold sounds or mumble eerie chants?

Since you have a relatively small number of powers, you can easily devise unique words of phrases for each. Your words of creation might be nonsense sounds or peculiar sayings. If you're familiar with the movie *Dune* or with the Klingon language from *Star Trek*, you can probably think of some nonsense words that sound cool. Below are some other suggestions to get your creative juices flowing.

"The Maimed Lord seeks truth in the darkness."
"Time is a door that cannot be closed."
"I pass beyond to arrive within."
"This fire already burns in all souls."

Pennant of Heaven's Armies — Invoker Utility 16

A tattered white flag appears. Those who behold it find the courage they need to win the day.

Daily ✦ Conjuration, Divine
Standard Action **Ranged** 10
Effect: You conjure a shining banner in 1 square within range. The banner lasts until the end of your next turn. Any ally who has line of sight to the banner gains a bonus to all defenses, saving throws against fear effects, and damage rolls. The bonus equals your Wisdom modifier.
Sustain Minor: The banner persists.

Serene Visage — Invoker Utility 16

Your god's visage overlays your own and draws the attention of your foes, buying your allies a needed reprieve.

Encounter ✦ Divine
Minor Action **Close** burst 2
Target: Each ally in burst
Effect: The target doesn't provoke opportunity attacks until the end of your next turn.

Walls of Hestavar — Invoker Utility 16

You trace your implement through the air and conjure a simulacrum of the Bright City's walls.

Daily ✦ Conjuration, Divine
Minor Action **Area** wall 10 within 10 squares
Effect: You conjure a wall of divine energy. The wall can be up to 2 squares high, and it lasts until the end of your next turn. The wall is a solid obstacle, and it blocks line of sight. It can be climbed with an Athletics check (DC 20 + one-half your level).
Sustain Minor: The wall persists.

Word of Refuge — Invoker Utility 16

With a word, you escape an attack, but at a price.

Encounter ✦ Divine, Teleportation
Immediate Interrupt **Personal**
Trigger: An enemy makes an attack against you
Effect: You negate the triggering enemy's attack against you and teleport 10 squares. You are dazed until the end of your next turn. If you were the only target of the triggering enemy's attack, the attacker can take a different action.

Level 17 Encounter Prayers

Astral Dust — Invoker Attack 17

Motes of silvery dust rain from above, burning whatever enemy they land on.

Encounter ✦ Divine, Fire, Implement, Radiant
Standard Action **Close** burst 3
Target: Each enemy in burst
Attack: Wisdom vs. Reflex
Hit: 2d8 + Wisdom modifier fire and radiant damage. If the target doesn't move away from you before the end of its next turn, it takes 5 fire and radiant damage and a -2 penalty to all defenses until the end of your next turn.

Chainfire — Invoker Attack 17

You ignite a foe in a column of holy flames, from which fire streams to nearby enemies.

Encounter ✦ Divine, Fire, Implement
Standard Action **Ranged** 10
Primary Target: One creature
Primary Attack: Wisdom vs. Reflex
Hit: 3d6 + Wisdom modifier fire damage. Make a secondary attack that is an area burst 2 centered on the primary target.
Secondary Target: Each enemy in burst other than the primary target
Secondary Attack: Wisdom vs. Reflex
Hit: 2d6 + Wisdom modifier fire damage.

Daunting Blasphemy — Invoker Attack 17

The vile words you speak darken your soul as they eat away at your enemies, who dare not move.

Encounter ✦ Divine, Implement, Necrotic
Standard Action **Close** burst 3
Target: Each enemy in burst
Attack: Wisdom vs. Fortitude
Hit: 2d10 + Wisdom modifier necrotic damage. The first time the target moves before the start of your next turn, it takes 5 necrotic damage.
Effect: You take 5 damage.

Sound of the Golden Clarion — Invoker Attack 17

Heavenly trumpets sound, blasting your foes with a perfect note.

Encounter ✦ Divine, Implement, Thunder
Standard Action **Close** blast 5
Target: Each creature in blast
Attack: Wisdom vs. Fortitude
Hit: 3d6 + Wisdom modifier thunder damage, and the target is pushed 1 square and deafened until the end of its next turn.

SERVING EVIL GODS

As an invoker, you can't dedicate yourself to an evil deity without matching the god's alignment, but that doesn't mean the dark gods can't ask for some return on the immortals' divine investment. Perhaps you hear Tiamat's whispers amid the clinking of coins. Maybe snakes occasionally raise their heads and hiss Zehir's wishes. When you battle Bane's followers, they might salute you and not raise their hands against you unless you first attack them.

If you're interested in roleplaying through this gray area, talk about it with your DM and discuss some of the ways that the evil gods might call in their debts. You don't want to derail the game by betraying the other PCs or committing disruptive acts, but a character who occasionally walks the narrow path between right and wrong can give the DM story ideas and be great fun for everyone. Then, when an envoy of Vecna gives you the information you need to do some great service for the gods and the world, surely you can do some small favor in return. . . .

Word of Pain — Invoker Attack 17

At your word, agony lances through the minds of the creatures around you. You are momentarily distracted by their mental screams.

Encounter ✦ Divine, Implement, Psychic
Standard Action **Close** burst 1
Target: Each creature in burst
Attack: Wisdom vs. Will
Hit: 2d10 + Wisdom modifier psychic damage, and the target is weakened until the end of your next turn.
Effect: You are dazed until the end of your next turn.
Covenant of Malediction: The size of the burst increases by 1.

Level 19 Daily Prayers

Forced Submission — Invoker Attack 19

Your enemy bends to the divine will expressed through you. You cease focusing on your own defense while you harness it.

Daily ✦ Charm, Divine, Implement, Psychic, Reliable
Standard Action **Ranged** 10
Target: One creature
Attack: Wisdom vs. Will
Hit: 2d10 + Wisdom modifier psychic damage, and the target is dominated (save ends). Until this domination ends, you grant combat advantage.
Covenant of Malediction: The target takes a -2 penalty to saving throws against this domination.

Mark of Forbearance — Invoker Attack 19

You superimpose a divine glyph on your foe. The ancient mark sears your foe with radiant damage and interferes with its attacks.

Daily ✦ Divine, Implement, Radiant
Standard Action **Ranged** 10
Target: One creature
Attack: Wisdom vs. Will
Hit: 4d8 + Wisdom modifier radiant damage.
Miss: Half damage.
Effect: The target takes a -5 penalty to attack rolls against your bloodied allies (save ends). On each of the target's turns, it can make a saving throw against this effect only if it does not attack during that turn.

Thunderous Shout — Invoker Attack 19

Intoning a word of creation, you split the air with a cacophonous blast. Your ears bleed as the word hurls your foes away.

Daily ✦ Divine, Implement, Thunder
Standard Action **Close** blast 5
Target: Each creature in blast
Attack: Wisdom vs. Fortitude
Hit: 3d10 + Wisdom modifier thunder damage, and you push the target 5 squares and knock it prone. In addition, the target is deafened (save ends).
Miss: Half damage, and you push the target 2 squares.
Effect: You take 10 damage.
Covenant of Malediction: You instead take 5 damage.

Wrath of the Fallen God — Invoker Attack 19

The memory of a fallen god's anger and agony fills nearby creatures' minds.

Daily ✦ Divine, Implement, Psychic, Zone
Standard Action **Area** burst 2 within 10 squares
Target: Each creature in burst
Attack: Wisdom vs. Fortitude
Hit: 4d6 + Wisdom modifier psychic damage, and ongoing 10 psychic damage (save ends).
Miss: Half damage, and ongoing 5 psychic damage (save ends).
Effect: The burst creates a zone of agony that lasts until the end of your next turn. Any creature that starts its turn within the zone is slowed and takes a -2 penalty to attack rolls until the end of your next turn.

Level 22 Utility Prayers

Call Angelic Shield — Invoker Utility 22

You summon angelic energy to shield you from harm.

Daily ✦ Divine
Minor Action **Personal**
Effect: You gain a bonus to all defenses equal to your Intelligence modifier. Each time an attack misses you, the bonus is reduced by 1. This effect lasts until the end of the encounter or until the bonus is 0.

Herald of God — Invoker Utility 22

Your voice resonates with divine might.

Daily ✦ Divine
Minor Action **Personal**
Effect: Until the end of the encounter, you gain a +10 power bonus to Bluff checks, Diplomacy checks, and Intimidate checks.

Invoke Sight — Invoker Utility 22

Calling on the gods, you bestow the ability to see the unseen.

Daily ✦ Divine
Minor Action **Melee** touch
Target: You or one ally
Effect: The target gains truesight until the end of your next turn. If the target is blinded, that condition ends.
Sustain Minor: The truesight persists.

Invoker Origins

As an invoker, you make a covenant with one or more gods to carry a fraction of their power and use it in their names. How did that promise come about? Did you have a fateful meeting with a strange mystic? Did the gods speak to you in a dream or through a waking vision? Have you met an angel, an exarch, or even the deity embodied? Perhaps you sealed the deal on another plane, miraculously transported there by the power that desired your service. It could be that you were born with your gifts and grew up knowing that your destiny was to use them in a deity's service. For a darker twist, maybe an evil deity gave you your powers, but you seek to use them in a righteous way and to serve another deity in the hopes that your deeds can overcome the oaths you swore.

Level 23 Encounter Prayers

Fateful Foresight — Invoker Attack 23

Prophetic forces showed you this moment long ago. With this foresight, you invoke fate to alter the course of events.

Encounter ✦ Divine, Implement, Psychic
Immediate Interrupt **Ranged** 10
Trigger: An enemy within 10 squares of you makes an attack on its turn
Target: The triggering enemy
Attack: Wisdom vs. Will
Hit: 2d8 + Wisdom modifier psychic damage. The target's attack is negated and is not expended, and the target can't use that attack until the start of its next turn, unless that attack is a basic attack. The target can immediately make a different attack.
Covenant of Preservation: The target takes a penalty to its next attack roll before the end of your next turn equal to your Intelligence modifier.

Fetters of Darkness — Invoker Attack 23

You tether your enemies with shadowy manacles.

Encounter ✦ Divine, Implement, Necrotic, Teleportation
Standard Action **Ranged** 10
Target: One or two creatures
Attack: Wisdom vs. Reflex
Hit: 2d8 + Wisdom modifier necrotic damage. You teleport the target 5 squares, and it is immobilized until the end of your next turn. If you target only one creature, the attack deals 1d8 extra necrotic damage, and you teleport the target 10 squares instead of 5.

Final Reproach — Invoker Attack 23

You warned them, but they wouldn't listen.

Encounter ✦ Divine, Force, Implement
Standard Action **Close** burst 3
Target: Each enemy in burst
Attack: Wisdom vs. Will
Hit: Whenever the target deals damage with an attack before the end of your next turn, it takes 15 force damage and is dazed until the end of your next turn.

Plague of Poison — Invoker Attack 23

The gods answered the blasphemies of the city Sazarus with six vicious plagues. You call down the poisonous plague on your enemies.

Encounter ✦ Divine, Implement, Poison, Zone
Standard Action **Close** blast 5
Target: Each creature in blast
Attack: Wisdom vs. Fortitude
Hit: 4d6 + Wisdom modifier poison damage. The target's space becomes a zone of poison gas that lasts until the end of your next turn. Any creature that starts its turn within the zone or adjacent to it takes 5 poison damage.
Covenant of Wrath: The zone deals extra poison damage equal to your Wisdom modifier.

THE WAR OF WINTER

Over the ages, the gods have battled one another on many occasions. Battles between Tiamat and Bahamut and between Bane and Gruumsh are still being fought. But most deities do not come into direct conflict with each other. The gods are bound by alliances forged during the Dawn War and by other mythic events. One of those events was a clash in the waning moments of the Dawn War when Khala, the god of winter, tried to make herself queen over all the deities.

Khala aimed to establish supremacy over the world and over the gods who had survived the nearly completed war with the primordials. Khala relied on her son Kord and her consort Zehir, and on Gruumsh and Tiamat, who preferred Khala's vision of a winter-bound world of savagery and darkness to Avandra's ancient compromise that also offered days of light and seasons of hope.

The forces of winter attacked the dominions of the strongest gods most likely to object to Khala's reign—Pelor, Erathis, Moradin, Amoth, and Bahamut—and scored early victories. Amoth's defenses were devastated on Kalandurren, the lower slopes of Celestia fell, and Hestavar was besieged. But Khala's success was temporary, for the remaining gods leagued against her. Bane joined the war against winter to preserve the world for conquest and tyranny, rather than abandon it to unceasing savagery. Sehanine intervened alongside Pelor to protect the ancient compromises of night and day from being overthrown. Even Lolth worked secretly against Khala, unwilling to allow a single deity to subjugate the rest.

The turning point came when Kord and Moradin battled in the mountains of Celestia. Despite Kord's irresistible fury, Moradin refused to yield; Kord's storms battered Moradin's mountains in vain. After a long battle, Kord drew back. Moradin showed Kord the destruction their battle had wrought in the mortal world, and Kord regretted his actions. He abandoned the cause of winter and turned against his mother.

With the aid of Kord, Bane, and others, the forces standing against Khala rallied. They broke the siege of Hestavar and destroyed or imprisoned the primordials and abominations Khala had released. Tiamat retreated to her lair, and Gruumsh abandoned Khala's cause as well. But Khala refused to yield and sought to destroy the mortal world under never-ending winter rather than admit defeat. Pelor, Bane, and Moradin defeated her in her great castle of ice, and the Raven Queen was called on to expel Khala into death. The Raven Queen agreed, but only if she was given power over winter. So the War of Winter ended with Khala's death, Kord's transformation, and the Raven Queen's dominion over winter.

The gods are not quick to admit it, but the War of Winter had another huge consequence, convincing the great primal spirits that the world needed to be protected from the gods as much as it needed to be protected from the primordials. That story is in *Player's Handbook 2* and the upcoming *Primal Power* supplement.

Word of Bewilderment — Invoker Attack 23

One word is all it takes to strip your enemies of their faculties. Yours are also temporarily dimmed.

Encounter ✦ Divine, Implement, Psychic
Standard Action **Close** burst 2
Target: Each creature in burst
Attack: Wisdom vs. Will
Hit: 1d10 + Wisdom modifier psychic damage, and the target is stunned until the end of your next turn.
Effect: You are dazed until the end of your next turn.
Covenant of Malediction: You can choose to become stunned until the end of your next turn to increase the size of the burst by as much as 3.

Level 25 Daily Prayers

Despised of the Gods — Invoker Attack 25

Your words strip away your enemy's defenses, exposing the soul of your foe before the ominous eye of your god.

Daily ✦ Divine, Implement
Standard Action **Ranged** 10
Target: One creature
Attack: Wisdom vs. Fortitude
Hit: 2d10 + Wisdom modifier damage. The target loses all resistances and gains vulnerable 20 to all damage (save ends both).
Miss: Half damage, and the target gains vulnerable 10 to all damage until the end of your next turn.
Covenant of Malediction: You can choose to gain vulnerable 20 to all damage until the end of your next turn. If you do so, the target takes a penalty to saving throws equal to your Constitution modifier until the end of your next turn.

Eye of the Sun — Invoker Attack 25

You conjure a glimmering ball of radiant energy, which expands into a diminutive sun. It can sear enemies and protect allies.

Daily ✦ Conjuration, Divine, Implement, Radiant
Standard Action **Ranged** 10
Effect: You conjure a radiant sphere in an unoccupied square within range. The sphere occupies 1 square, and it lasts until the end of your next turn. Any enemy that starts its turn adjacent to the sphere takes 1d8 + your Wisdom modifier radiant damage. While adjacent to the sphere, any ally gains a +2 power bonus to all defenses. As a move action, you can move the sphere 8 squares. When the sphere appears, it makes the following attack.
Target: One creature adjacent to the sphere
Attack: Wisdom vs. Reflex
Hit: 4d8 + Wisdom modifier radiant damage, and the target cannot attack bloodied creatures until the end of its next turn.
Sustain Minor: The sphere persists, and you can make another attack with it as a standard action.

Shackles of the Chained God — Invoker Attack 25

The Unspeakable One sought power and for his greed found chains and suffering. Those chains wrap around your foe and lash out at its allies.

Daily ✦ Divine, Force, Implement
Standard Action **Ranged** 10
Target: One creature
Attack: Wisdom vs. Fortitude
Hit: 4d6 + Wisdom modifier force damage, and the target takes ongoing 20 force damage and is immobilized (save ends both).
Miss: Half damage, and the target takes ongoing 10 force damage and is slowed (save ends both).
Effect: Whenever the target takes this power's ongoing damage, each enemy within 5 squares of it is pulled 1 square toward it, and then each enemy adjacent to it takes 10 force damage.

Trumpet the Eight Dooms — Invoker Attack 25

Angels blew eight trumpets, each sounding a doom more terrible than the last. Your invocation calls one of those dooms onto your enemies.

Daily ✦ Divine, Implement, Thunder
Standard Action **Close** blast 5
Target: Each creature in blast
Attack: Wisdom vs. Fortitude
Hit: 4d8 + Wisdom modifier thunder damage. Roll a d8 to determine an effect.
1. The target takes ongoing 10 damage (save ends).
2. You push the target 1 square, and it takes ongoing 10 damage (save ends).
3. You push the target 2 squares, and it takes ongoing 10 damage (save ends).
4. You push the target 3 squares, and it takes ongoing 10 damage (save ends).
5. You push the target 3 squares, and it takes ongoing 10 damage and is slowed (save ends both).
6. You push the target 3 squares and knock it prone, and it takes ongoing 10 damage (save ends).
7. You push the target 3 squares, and it takes ongoing 10 damage and is dazed (save ends both).
8. The target takes 2d8 extra thunder damage.

Miss: 6d6 + Wisdom modifier thunder damage.

Word of Cessation — Invoker Attack 25

You utter a word so potent that it can snuff out your enemy's life. Even if the foe survives, its ability to fight is reduced for a time. The price you pay is momentary defenselessness.

Daily ✦ Divine, Implement, Psychic
Standard Action **Ranged** 10
Target: One target
Attack: Wisdom vs. Will
Hit: 8d6 + Wisdom modifier psychic damage. The only attacks the target can make are basic attacks (save ends).
Miss: Half damage, and the target takes a -2 penalty to attack rolls until the end of your next turn.
Effect: You grant combat advantage until the start of your next turn.

Level 27 Encounter Prayers

Brand of Fire — Invoker Attack 27

Your solemn curse causes fire to leap at your enemies to brand them.

Encounter ✦ Divine, Fire, Implement
Standard Action **Ranged** 10
Target: One, two, or three creatures
Attack: Wisdom vs. Reflex
Hit: 4d6 + Wisdom modifier fire damage. The first time the target is hit by a melee or a close attack before the end of your next turn, it takes 10 fire damage.
Covenant of Wrath: The first time the target is hit by any attack (not just a melee or a close attack) before the end of your next turn, it takes 10 fire damage.

Compel Action — Invoker Attack 27

You force your enemies to act as you command for a moment. Controlling them requires much of your attention.

Encounter ✦ Charm, Divine, Implement
Standard Action **Close** blast 5
Target: Each creature in blast
Attack: Wisdom vs. Will
Hit: The target is dominated until the end of your next turn.
Covenant of Preservation: The target gains a +2 bonus to attack rolls until the domination ends.
Effect: You grant combat advantage until the start of your next turn.

Pall of the Shadowfell — Invoker Attack 27

A shadowy shroud of chill descends on two foes, dooming them together.

Encounter ✦ Cold, Divine, Implement
Standard Action **Ranged** 10
Target: Two creatures
Attack: Wisdom vs. Fortitude
Hit: 3d8 + Wisdom modifier cold damage. Whenever the target deals damage before the end of your next turn, the other target of this power takes 15 cold damage.

Word of Death — Invoker Attack 27

You enter a trance and make an ancient utterance, inviting creatures around you to enter the realm of death.

Encounter ✦ Divine, Implement, Necrotic
Standard Action **Close** burst 1
Target: Each creature in burst
Attack: Wisdom vs. Will
Hit: 4d10 + Wisdom modifier necrotic damage.
Covenant of Malediction: If the target is already bloodied, it takes extra necrotic damage equal to your Constitution modifier.
Effect: You are dazed until the end of your next turn.

Level 29 Daily Prayers

Apocalypse from the Sky — Invoker Attack 29

You invoke a gigantic, ghostly fist of magical force that smashes down from overhead and blasts out a great pit in one titanic blow.

Daily ✦ Divine, Force, Implement
Standard Action **Area** burst 2 within 10 squares
Target: Each creature in burst
Attack: Wisdom vs. Reflex
Hit: 4d8 + Wisdom modifier force damage, and the target is dazed (save ends).
Miss: Half damage, and you knock the target prone. You must slide the target to the nearest unoccupied space outside the burst.
Effect: A pit fills the area of the burst and is 10 feet deep. Any creature fully within the area of the pit descends 10 feet, taking no falling damage for descending that distance.

Invoked Devastation — Invoker Attack 29

In ancient days, invokers spoke the word of ending to annihilate their enemies, but at such a dreadful cost that it nearly erased their own civilization.

Daily ✦ Divine, Implement, Zone; Varies
Standard Action **Area** burst 3 within 20 squares
Target: Each creature in burst
Attack: Wisdom vs. Fortitude, Reflex, Will. You make one attack roll per target, comparing the result against all three defenses. A target might be hit up to three times, depending on which defenses are hit.
Hit (Fortitude): 1d8 + Wisdom modifier force damage, and ongoing 5 cold damage (save ends).
Hit (Reflex): 1d8 + Wisdom modifier lightning damage, and ongoing 5 fire damage (save ends).
Hit (Will): 1d8 + Wisdom modifier radiant damage, and ongoing 5 psychic damage (save ends).
Effect: The zone creates an area of devastation that lasts until the end of the encounter. The zone is difficult terrain. Any creature that enters the zone or starts its turn there takes 10 damage.

Malediction of the Eternal Pyre — Invoker Attack 29

Flames roar out of you as you consign your enemies to a fiery death.

Daily ✦ Divine, Fire, Implement
Standard Action **Close** blast 5
Target: Each creature in blast
Attack: Wisdom vs. Reflex
Hit: 3d10 + Wisdom modifier fire damage, and ongoing 20 fire damage (save ends).
Miss: 1d10 + Wisdom modifier fire damage, and ongoing 10 fire damage (save ends).
Effect: You take ongoing 10 fire damage (save ends).

Storm of Creation — Invoker Attack 29

You tap into the power of creation itself and use it to pound your foes with a force that disrupts their very existence.

Daily ✦ Divine, Force, Implement
Standard Action **Area** burst 2 within 10 squares
Target: Each creature in burst
Attack: Wisdom vs. Fortitude
Hit: 4d8 + Wisdom modifier force damage, and the target is stunned (save ends).
Aftereffect: The target is dazed (save ends). This aftereffect applies only if you target a single creature.
Miss: Half damage, and the target is dazed until the end of your next turn.

Avandra and the First Doppelganger

When the world was young, Avandra was deeply involved in the lives of its creatures. She delighted in making their lives better. One mortal who was the object of Avandra's favor was a beautiful woman who was pursued by a cruel suitor. This suitor set his servants on her like hunting dogs. Two times Avandra helped the woman to flee or fight by changing her luck, and each time the woman praised Avandra after her escape.

The third time the woman was threatened, Avandra gifted her with the power to change her form so that she could save herself from any future threat. The woman used her power to become an assassin, killing her suitor and all who served him. When Avandra sought her out to rebuke her, the woman used her power to hide from the goddess. By the time Avandra found the woman, her children's children had given birth to many more offspring, all having the power to change shape. The goddess's gift, once given, could not be taken away. Thus the race of doppelgangers, or changelings, was born.

From that episode Avandra learned a bitter lesson about being overly generous to mortals. Ever since then, she has been careful to help mortals only in small ways, often hiding her hand. By allowing mortals to face their own problems, Avandra provides them with the chance to discover their full potential.

KIERAN YANNER

NEW PARAGON PATHS

ADEPT OF WHISPERS

"The wise know that one cannot speak and listen at the same time."

Prerequisite: Invoker

The words of creation can bend the elements to your desires, but the words of mortal speech also have power to create or destroy. Far better to listen instead of speak, to seek the wisdom that comes with quiet understanding. You speak sparingly and softly, and you choose your words with great care. By husbanding the power of your voice for the words of creation, you ensure that your mind and soul are focused on the powerful prayers you utter.

ADEPT OF WHISPERS PATH FEATURES

Adept's Action (11th level): When you spend an action point to take an extra action, you also gain a +2 bonus to attack rolls with divine powers, and you can increase the size of your divine blasts or bursts by 1. These benefits last until the start of your next turn.

Silent Presence (11th level): You gain a +2 bonus to Stealth checks, Insight checks, and Intimidate checks, and creatures cannot perceive you with blindsight or tremorsense. You take a -2 penalty to Bluff checks and Diplomacy checks.

Raised Voice (16th level): When you use a divine attack power, you can choose to raise your voice before you make any attack rolls for it. For that attack, you can score a critical hit on a roll of 19-20, and enemies take a -2 penalty to saving throws against the attack's effects. However, you are dazed until the end of your next turn.

ADEPT OF WHISPERS PRAYERS

Admonishing Whisper Adept of Whispers Attack 11

You whisper a single word of power, and your enemies reel back from its might, deafened by it and admonished to do no more harm to your friends.

Encounter ✦ Divine, Implement
Standard Action **Close** burst 2
Target: Each enemy in burst
Attack: Wisdom vs. Will
Hit: 3d6 + Wisdom modifier damage, and you push the target 2 squares. The target is deafened until the end of your next turn. If the target is then adjacent to a bloodied ally, the target is also dazed until the end of your next turn.

Restorative Word Adept of Whispers Utility 12

You softly call your comrade's name and whisper a word of healing power.

Daily ✦ Divine, Healing
Standard Action **Melee** touch
Target: One ally
Effect: The target can spend two healing surges and make a saving throw.

Whisper of Doom Adept of Whispers Attack 20

You whisper an ancient curse of dire potency against your enemies.

Daily ✦ Divine, Implement
Standard Action **Close** burst 3
Target: Each enemy in burst
Attack: Wisdom vs. Fortitude
Hit: 3d8 + Wisdom modifier damage. The target takes ongoing 10 damage and is weakened (save ends both).
Miss: Half damage.

VOW OF SILENCE

Your adept of whispers might have taken a vow of silence. If so, you can still talk to the DM to tell him what your character is doing. You can also take part in normal table discussions and repartee with other players; you can assume that your character uses a basic sign language or a chalk and slate to contribute to party decisions. When your character addresses a PC or another character, you can roleplay your character's taciturn nature by describing nods, hard looks, head shakes, or hand gestures. Finally, your character can speak in times of great need, since the adept's vow is voluntary.

DAN SCOTT

Crimson Arbiter

"You have transgressed, and restitution must be made. Drink deep of your misfortune."

Prerequisite: Invoker

You are an agent of justice to your deity's enemies. You are judge, jury, and executioner, although you are more than an inflicter of punishment. You are also a redresser of wrongs and a giver of absolution, enjoined to aid those who have been unfairly treated and to set injustices aright. According to longstanding tradition, you conceal your features beneath a crimson mask or hood while you perform your duties. By this sign the condemned and the forgiven alike know that you are acting not from your mortal passions or preferences, but as your divine master instructs. Crimson arbiters are most likely to serve deities concerned with law or justice, such as Erathis, Bahamut, Pelor, or Bane.

You carry small strips of paper marked with sacred glyphs that lend strength to your prayers for justice. Each holds the name of a power epitomizing mercy, perception, balance, or punishment, guiding you in your judgments.

Crimson Arbiter Path Features

Arbiter's Action (11th level): When you spend an action point to make an attack, any enemy you hit with that attack takes a -2 penalty to attack rolls (save ends).

Just Presence (11th level): When you score a critical hit with an invoker power, you gain a +2 power bonus to attack rolls against any enemy within 2 squares of you. This bonus lasts until the end of the encounter.

Justice's Wrath (16th level): The first enemy that damages you in an encounter is subject to your wrath. Until the end of the encounter, you can reroll any damage die that comes up as a 1 when you make a damage roll that includes that enemy as a target.

Crimson Arbiter Prayers

Sign of Guilt — Crimson Arbiter Attack 11

You trace a magical glyph in the air. Your enemy cannot bear the sight of it as the magic evokes deep guilt, causing the enemy to waver in its attacks.

Encounter ✦ Divine, Fear, Implement, Psychic
Standard Action **Ranged** 10
Target: One enemy
Attack: Wisdom vs. Will
Hit: 1d10 + Wisdom modifier psychic damage. Until the end of your next turn, the target takes a -5 penalty to attack rolls, and if the target attacks and misses, it must make a melee basic attack against an enemy adjacent to it as a free action.

AMELIA STONER

No Rest for the Wicked — Crimson Arbiter Utility 12

You call forth souls from the Shadowfell. As foes strike you, the souls distract them with wailing.

Daily ✦ Divine
Minor Action **Personal**
Effect: When any enemy hits you before the end of your next turn, that enemy takes a -2 penalty to all defenses (save ends).
Sustain Minor: The effect persists.

Sign of Penance — Crimson Arbiter Attack 20

A glyph of penance appears before you and ignites. Divine fire leaps from it to enemies of weak will.

Daily ✦ Divine, Fire, Implement, Radiant
Standard Action **Ranged** 10
Primary Target: One target
Primary Attack: Wisdom vs. Will
Hit: 3d6 + Wisdom modifier fire and radiant damage.
Miss: Half damage.
Effect: Make a secondary attack that is an area burst 1 centered on the primary target.
  Secondary Target: Each creature in burst other than the primary target
  Secondary Attack: Wisdom vs. Reflex
  Hit: 2d6 + Wisdom modifier fire and radiant damage, and the secondary target is slowed (save ends).
  Effect: If the primary attack reduces the primary target to 0 hit points, the burst creates an area of difficult terrain that lasts until the end of the encounter.

Devoted Orator

"Take heed! My words are those of the gods, and they are to be feared."

Prerequisite: Invoker

You are a messenger of the gods and a preacher of divine virtues. Your speech evokes devotion in the faithful and fear in the irreligious. You are an authority for anyone wishing to know the desires of your deity, and you are renowned for your power to enhance and amplify your voice and for your ability to speak in ominous, multilayered tones.

A few devoted orators are trained at temples, but most arise through private devotion. You might have communed directly with a deity and been forever moved by the experience, or you could be one whose faith is strong enough to bridge the mortal and immortal. People who dislike your message might regard you as a scolder, a rabble-rouser, or a threat to the established order, but you have little concern for how they react to you; you speak what the gods put in your heart, and you trust that they will deal harshly with those who ignore you or hinder you in your mission. If you serve a temple, you often prove to be difficult for your superiors to deal with, since your pronouncements chastise the great and the powerful as well as the rest of the people. Consequently, you rarely stay in one place for long. A few theocracies have devoted orators at their head or in close service to the ruler, for few dare to refute the power of one such as you.

HOWARD LYON

Devoted Orator Path Features

Brilliant Rhetoric (11th level): You can use your Intelligence modifier instead of your Charisma modifier when making Diplomacy checks.

Fearsome Oration (11th level): When you spend an action point to take an extra action, you either pull or push each enemy within 5 squares of you a number of squares equal to your Intelligence modifier.

Thundering Prayer (16th level): When you use a close attack power, you can choose to deal extra thunder damage equal to one-half your Intelligence modifier, and you can push a target you hit 1 square. If you do so, the power gains the thunder keyword.

Devoted Orator Prayers

Legion Rebuke — Devoted Orator Attack 11

You chastise nearby enemies with divine displeasure. Your voice sounds as if many people are speaking at once.

Encounter ✦ Divine, Fear, Implement, Thunder
Standard Action **Close** blast 3
Target: Each enemy in blast
Attack: Wisdom vs. Will
Hit: 1d8 + Wisdom modifier thunder damage. The target moves its speed + your Intelligence modifier away from you by the safest path possible.

Chastisement — Devoted Orator Utility 12

Your thunderous rebuke weakens an enemy's resolve.

Encounter ✦ Divine
Immediate Reaction **Close** burst 5
Trigger: An enemy within 5 squares of you makes an attack
Target: The triggering enemy in burst
Effect: The target gains vulnerable 10 thunder until the end of your next turn.

Thunderous Oration — Devoted Orator Attack 20

Your enemies reel upon hearing your thunderous voice.

Daily ✦ Divine, Implement, Thunder
Standard Action **Close** blast 5
Target: Each enemy in blast
Attack: Wisdom vs. Fortitude
Hit: 3d8 + Wisdom modifier thunder damage, and the target is dazed and deafened until the end of your next turn.
Miss: Half damage.
Effect: As the first action of your next turn, you can make the attack again as a free action.

Divine Hand

"I am the hand of my god. Through my actions, my god's touch is felt, whether it be a tender caress or a crushing fist."

Prerequisite: Invoker

Through faithful devotion, you have attracted the attention of your deity, who has elevated you as a divine hand. A mortal representative of your deity, you have a divine mission, such as to construct a great monument in your god's image, to subdue a tyrant, or to create a temple in a distant land. Your actions sometimes seem without purpose, but they are part of your deity's grand design. Many divine hands are marked physically by their god in the form of unusual eye or hair color or a blemish on the skin.

As a divine hand, you wield powerful invocations for smiting the enemies of your deity. You are a dauntless soldier for your cause, because your fervor fills your heart with limitless courage. Your great faith strikes fear into your enemies and blazes a bright path across the world.

Divine Hand Path Features

Inspire Terror (11th level): When you spend an action point to take an extra action, you also end any slowed or immobilized conditions on you. In addition, if you make an attack with your extra action, each enemy you hit with that attack is immobilized until the end of your next turn. This attack is a fear effect.

Undaunted (11th level): You gain a +2 bonus to saving throws and to all defenses against fear effects.

Quell the Fearful (16th level): When you hit an enemy with a fear power, that enemy takes a -2 penalty to attack rolls against you until the end of your next turn.

Divine Hand Prayers

Harvest the Craven — Divine Hand Attack 11

You call terror down on your foes. They fear to remain alone.

Encounter ✦ Divine, Fear, Implement, Psychic
Standard Action — **Area** burst 2 within 10 squares
Target: Each enemy in burst
Attack: Wisdom vs. Will
Hit: 2d6 + Wisdom modifier psychic damage. Until the end of your next turn, the target is slowed, and it takes a -2 penalty to all defenses when it is not adjacent to another enemy.

Tenor of Wrath — Divine Hand Utility 12

The sky darkens and the ground trembles as you manifest your god's terrifying presence.

Daily ✦ Divine, Fear, Zone
Minor Action — **Close** burst 5
Effect: The burst creates a zone of fear that lasts until the end of your next turn. When you move, the zone moves with you, remaining centered on you. If willingly entering a square within the zone would bring an enemy closer to you, entering that square costs the enemy 1 extra square of movement.
Sustain Minor: The zone persists.

Cascade of Fear — Divine Hand Attack 20

You raise your implement high and speak words of portent, assuring your foes of your god's wrath and sending them sprawling in fear.

Daily ✦ Divine, Fear, Implement, Psychic
Standard Action — **Close** blast 5
Target: Each enemy in blast
Attack: Wisdom vs. Will
Hit: 2d8 + Wisdom modifier psychic damage, and the target is knocked prone and dazed (save ends). The target takes a penalty to saving throws against this effect equal to your Constitution modifier.
Miss: Half damage, and the target is knocked prone.

Divine Philosopher

"Knowledge is my weapon, for it cuts truer than any sword."

Prerequisite: Invoker

A paragon of scholarship, you wield the power of knowledge. You believe that the gods are the ultimate vessels of wisdom in the universe, and through devotion to them and careful study of their words, you seek to understand and shape reality itself.

Divine philosophers generally arise from remote monasteries where the words of the gods are studied and debated amid daily chants and meditations. A rare few divine philosophers are self-taught savants, who learn through careful study of divine texts and personal devotion to the gods. Whatever their origins, divine philosophers seek knowledge throughout the world, in temple archives, hidden vaults, and ancient libraries.

As a divine philosopher, you call on your deep understanding of the gods to aid you in your adventures. Your tireless pursuit of knowledge leads you across the planes to ancient civilizations and hostile lands. Although you might serve a particular deity, you seek the wisdom of all the gods, wherever it can be found.

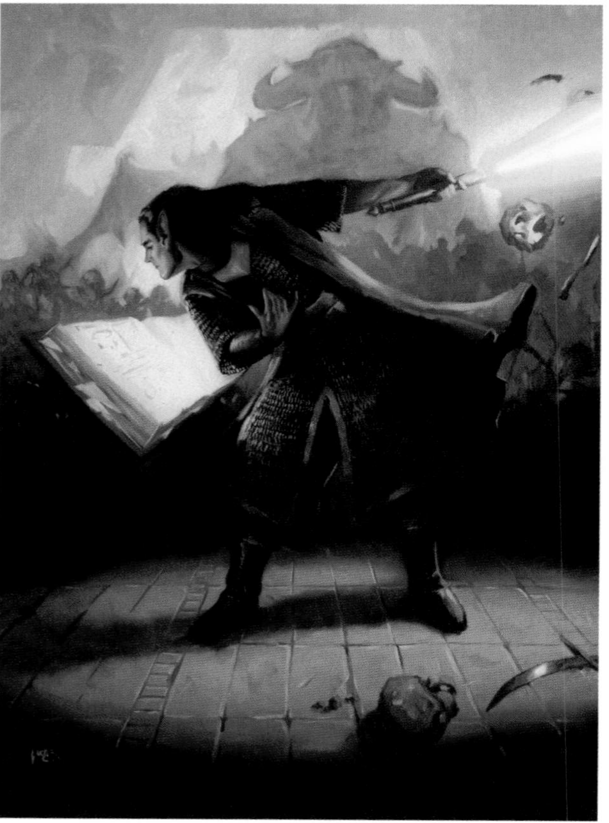

Divine Philosopher Path Features

Insight of the Ancients (11th level): When you spend an action point to make an attack, you can reroll one attack roll you make as part of that attack. You must use the second result.

Student of the Gods (11th level): You gain one divine at-will attack power from a class other than your own as an encounter power.

Knowledge Is Power (16th level): When you succeed on a DC 20 monster knowledge check about a particular creature (DC 25 for a paragon tier creature or DC 30 for an epic tier creature), you gain a +1 bonus to attack rolls and a +2 bonus to damage rolls against that creature until the end of the encounter. If your check result is 25 (30 for a paragon tier creature or 35 for an epic tier creature), you instead gain a +2 bonus to attack rolls and a +4 bonus to damage rolls. You can use this path feature once per day.

Divine Philosopher Prayers

Hit the Weak Spot — Divine Philosopher Attack 11

You invoke the knowledge of the gods and send out a beam of radiance that lowers your foe's resistances.

Encounter ✦ Divine, Implement, Radiant
Standard Action **Ranged** 10
Target: One creature
Attack: Wisdom vs. Reflex
Hit: 2d8 + Wisdom modifier radiant damage. Until the end of your next turn, the target's resistances are reduced by 5 + your Intelligence modifier, and its vulnerabilities are increased by your Intelligence modifier.

Uncanny Insight — Divine Philosopher Utility 12

You foresee your foe's next course of action and act, taking advantage of that knowledge.

Encounter ✦ Divine
Immediate Interrupt **Personal**
Trigger: An enemy within your line of sight takes a standard action, and you are trained in the skill related to that creature's origin
Effect: You take a standard action.

Word of Anathema — Divine Philosopher Attack 20

You speak one of the sacred words handed down to you from the gods. The word is anathema to your enemies, enfeebling them.

Daily ✦ Divine, Fear, Implement
Standard Action **Close** burst 5
Target: Each enemy in burst that has a creature origin related to a skill you're trained in
Attack: Wisdom vs. Will
Hit: 1d10 + Wisdom modifier damage, and the target is weakened and gains vulnerable 5 + your Intelligence modifier to all damage (save ends both).
Miss: The target is slowed and gains vulnerable 5 to all damage until the end of your next turn.

LUCAS GRACIANO

Keeper of the Nine

"You brought this onto yourself."

Prerequisite: Invoker, trained in History

Ancient scrolls speak of the world's last days, foretelling a time of violence and destruction that will consume everything. You have studied these scrolls and know the disasters destined to befall the world: nine terrible catastrophes that will one day cause its doom. These supernatural disasters were sown in the world's foundations during the first days and now lie buried beneath mighty seals in its far corners. It is your task to ensure that these seals remain intact, for each time some evil power breaks one, the end of all things draws closer. Those who meddle with the seals flirt with the destruction of all and risk upsetting the great purpose of the cosmos.

To safeguard the ancient seals, you are initiated into a secretive order: the Keepers of the Nine. You learn powerful prayers of warding and destruction so that you can deal with those who meddle with forces they do not understand. Keepers are drawn from many races and include servants of different gods, but most are dedicated to Erathis, Ioun, or Moradin. Old disagreements and jealousies are common among the Keepers, but all agree that the Nine Seals must remain hidden and unbroken.

Keeper of the Nine Path Features

Dooming Action (11th level): When you spend an action point to make an attack, one target hit by that attack gains vulnerable 5 to all damage (save ends).

Ruining Prayer (11th level): When you use any invoker power that is a close attack, you can turn the ground around you into rubble; each square adjacent to you becomes difficult terrain until the rubble is cleared.

Keeper's Vengeance (16th level): When you are bloodied and use an invoker power that creates a burst, you can increase the size of the burst by 1.

Keeper of the Nine Prayers

Glyph of Warning — Keeper of the Nine Attack 11

A complex glyph appears in the air above you, repelling your enemies.

Encounter ✦ Divine, Fear
Standard Action **Close** burst 10
Target: Each enemy in burst
Effect: Each target moves its speed away from you as a free action. Any ally who makes an opportunity attack provoked by this movement gains a power bonus to the attack roll and the damage roll equal to 2 + your Intelligence modifier.

WILLIAM O'CONNOR

Keeper's Mantle — Keeper of the Nine Utility 12

A shimmering blue aura of energy settles over your shoulders, whisking you away from your enemies' attacks and distracting foes standing too close to you.

Daily ✦ Divine, Teleportation
Immediate Reaction **Personal**
Trigger: You take damage from an enemy's attack while you are bloodied
Effect: You teleport 5 squares. Each enemy adjacent to you when you teleport grants combat advantage until the end of your next turn.

The Tenth Seal — Keeper of the Nine Attack 20

You conjure a glyph that unleashes the magic of the Tenth Seal, known only to the most powerful Keepers of the Nine. Your enemies are stunned by its thunder.

Daily ✦ Conjuration, Divine, Implement, Thunder
Standard Action **Ranged** 10
Effect: You conjure a glyph of the Tenth Seal in an unoccupied square within range. The glyph lasts until the end of your next turn. When the glyph appears, it makes an attack that is a close burst 3.
Primary Target: Each enemy in burst
Primary Attack: Wisdom vs. Will
Hit: 2d8 + Wisdom modifier thunder damage, and the primary target is stunned (save ends).
Sustain Minor: The glyph persists and makes a secondary attack that is a close burst 3.
Secondary Target: Each enemy in burst
Secondary Attack: Wisdom vs. Will
Hit: 1d8 + Wisdom modifier thunder damage, and the secondary target is dazed (save ends).

Speaker of the Word

"It is simple to speak the Word. Knowing how and when to use the Word—and how to ease your conscience after you unleash its power—is more complex."

Prerequisite: Invoker

You are an initiate in a rare tradition, one that embraces a unified religious concept summed up in one word of power. The Word was crafted by the gods to be a great weapon. Only the most trustworthy and compassionate invokers are taught the syllables of the Word, and even they seldom use its power. Each syllable, when spoken in the proper pitch and cadence, is a powerful prayer in its own right, and those brief tones are the most powerful weapons of your faith.

It is not enough simply to repeat the syllables that comprise the Word; to unleash its power you must desire to do so, speaking it exactly and framing the philosophical significance of each syllable in your mind as you say it. Uttering the Word unleashes dangerous divine energy, and even speakers of the Word dare not utter it in a voice louder than a whisper.

Speaker of the Word Path Features

Speaker's Action (11th level): When you spend an action point to take an extra action, you can also reroll one die you roll during the same turn for an attack roll, a damage roll, a skill check, or a saving throw and use either result.

Influencing Syllable (11th level): You gain a +2 bonus to Charisma-based skill checks.

Empowering Syllable (16th level): After you use a speaker of the Word power, you gain a +2 power bonus to attack rolls until the end of your next turn.

Speaker of the Word Prayers

Syllable of Light — Speaker of the Word Attack 11

You whisper an otherworldly tone, and lights swirl around you, blinding your foes and surrounding your allies in cloaks of radiance.

Encounter ✦ Divine, Implement, Radiant
Standard Action — **Close** burst 2
Target: Each enemy in burst
Attack: Wisdom vs. Will
Hit: 1d8 + Wisdom modifier radiant damage, and the target is blinded and deafened until the end of your next turn.
Effect: Each ally in the burst gains a +2 power bonus to all defenses and resist 5 radiant until the end of your next turn.

Guiding Syllable — Speaker of the Word Utility 12

A syllable of the Word is enough to guide others' steps.

Encounter ✦ Divine
Minor Action — **Close** burst 5
Target: You and each ally in burst
Effect: You slide the target a number of squares equal to your Intelligence modifier. The next time the target hits with an attack before the end of your next turn, you can slide the hit creature 1 square as a free action.

The Word Spoken — Speaker of the Word Attack 20

In a soft voice, you intone the complete Word, unleashing sublime destruction.

Daily ✦ Divine, Implement, Psychic
Standard Action — **Area** burst 3 within 10 squares
Target: Each creature in burst
Attack: Wisdom vs. Will
Hit: 3d8 + Wisdom modifier psychic damage, and ongoing 10 psychic damage (save ends). In addition, the target fails its next saving throw before the end of the encounter.
Miss: Half damage, and ongoing 5 psychic damage (save ends).

RALPH BEISNER

Stonecaller

"The wrongs of old are remembered in the very rocks of the world. Secret wrath lies sleeping in stone."

Prerequisite: Invoker

The ancient language of creation lies locked within the bones of the earth. You have mastered some of the oldest and most fundamental syllables of this language, syllables so sonorous that they almost defy being uttered by mortals. With your words and your will, you can wake the very stone of the world to lend you its strength or lash out at your enemies.

Dwarves were the first mortal stonecallers, but the tradition has since spread to other races, especially goliaths, shifters, and barbaric humans—people who live close to the elements. Throughout the world, mountain folk know the power of the stonecaller's voice.

Stonecaller Path Features

Stonecaller's Action (11th level): When you spend an action point to take an extra action, you also create an earthquake in a close burst 2, 5, or 10 (your choice). Until the start of your next turn, all creatures other than you treat the area of the burst as difficult terrain, and any creature you hit while it is in the burst is knocked prone after the attack's effects are resolved.

Strong Footing (11th level): When any attack would knock you prone, you can make a saving throw. If you save, you don't fall prone. In addition, you ignore difficult terrain if it is the result of rubble, uneven stone, or an earthen construction.

Stonesight (16th level): You gain tremorsense 5 as long as you are in contact with the ground.

Stonecaller Prayers

Earthbolt — Stonecaller Attack 11

At your command, the ground beneath your enemies erupts in jagged fangs of stone.

Encounter ✦ Divine, Implement, Zone
Standard Action **Area** burst 2 within 10 squares
Target: Each creature in burst
Attack: Wisdom vs. Fortitude
Hit: 3d6 + Wisdom modifier damage, and the target is knocked prone.
Effect: The burst creates a zone of uneven stone that lasts until the end of your next turn. The zone is difficult terrain.

Rooted to the Earth — Stonecaller Utility 12

The earth grants you or your friend its immovable mass and deep power.

Encounter ✦ Divine
Immediate Interrupt **Close** burst 2
Trigger: You or an ally within 2 squares of you is bloodied, pulled, pushed, or slid by an enemy attack
Target: The triggering character
Effect: The target can use his or her second wind and isn't subject to the forced movement, if any.

Black Obelisk of Doom — Stonecaller Attack 20

You call forth a great pillar of rock. An ancient rune of destruction is carved on it. Enemies that behold it are drawn to their doom.

Daily ✦ Conjuration, Divine, Implement, Necrotic
Standard Action **Ranged** 20
Effect: You conjure a black obelisk that fills an unoccupied square within range. The obelisk must be on a solid surface and is a 10-foot-high solid obstacle. It lasts until the end of your next turn. Any enemy that starts its turn adjacent to the obelisk is weakened until the start of its next turn. When the obelisk appears, it makes an attack that is a close burst 4.
Target: One creature in burst
Attack: Wisdom vs. Will
Hit: 3d8 + Wisdom modifier necrotic damage, and the target is pulled 3 squares toward the obelisk and immobilized (save ends).
Sustain Minor: The obelisk persists. As a standard action, you can make its attack again.

KIERAN YANNER

Theurge of the Compact

"I will not bow."

Prerequisite: Invoker, Covenant of Wrath class feature

You walk a perilous path, for you study the rare and dangerous fragments of the Compact Infernal. Through your understanding of this dark lore, you have harnessed the power of the Nine Hells. You hold mastery over infernal conflagrations and can conjure fiendish servants. With such power at your command, you run the risk of becoming consumed by pride and being seduced by fell whispers. You must use your powers with great care—if you falter, the fiends that serve you might become your masters.

Theurge of the Compact Path Features

Incendiary Action (11th level): When you spend an action point to make an attack, each target hit by that attack gains vulnerable 5 fire until the end of your next turn.

Bringer of Despair (11th level): When you score a critical hit with an invoker attack power, you can take 5 damage. If you do so, the target of the critical hit takes a -2 penalty to attack rolls (save ends).

Fiery Wrath (16th level): The bonus damage of your Covenant Manifestation is fire and is 2 instead of 1 for each enemy.

GORAN JOSIC

Theurge of the Compact Prayers

Hellfire Unleashed — Theurge of the Compact Attack 11

Hellish fire erupts within your enemy, while black smoke poisons the air around it.

Encounter ✦ Divine, Fire, Implement, Poison
Standard Action — **Ranged** 10
Target: One creature
Attack: Wisdom vs. Fortitude
Hit: 2d10 + Wisdom modifier fire and poison damage. Each creature adjacent to the target takes 5 poison damage and grants combat advantage until the end of your next turn.

Infernal Guardian — Theurge of the Compact Utility 12

A sinister figure formed from hellfire appears beside you to protect you from harm.

Encounter ✦ Conjuration, Divine
Minor Action — **Melee** 1
Effect: You conjure an infernal guardian in an unoccupied square adjacent to you. The guardian lasts until the end of your next turn. While you are adjacent to the guardian, you are immune to charm effects and fear effects, and you gain resist 10 fire.
Sustain Minor: The guardian persists.

Fiery Companions — Theurge of the Compact Attack 20

Fire erupts across your body as you scream the word to rip open reality and call forth fiends to aid you.

Daily ✦ Conjuration, Divine, Fire, Implement
Standard Action — **Close** burst 10
Effect: You conjure four fiery fiends in four unoccupied squares in the burst. The fiends occupy their squares, and they last until the end of your next turn. Any creature that leaves a square adjacent to a fiend on its turn takes ongoing 10 fire damage (save ends). When the fiends appear, they each make the following melee attack (determine line of sight from each fiend). A fiend attacks an ally if no enemies are adjacent to it.
  Target: One adjacent creature
  Attack: Wisdom vs. Reflex
  Hit: 2d8 + Wisdom modifier fire damage, and ongoing 5 fire damage (save ends).
Sustain Minor: The fiends persist. As a standard action, you can cause each of the fiends to make its attack again. As before, a fiend attacks an ally if no enemies are adjacent to it.

Vessel of Ichor

"I am more than mortal, for I have tasted the blood of the gods."

Prerequisite: Invoker, Covenant of Wrath class feature

To strengthen you for the hardships that lie ahead, you have been given a rare blessing: You have drunk a single drop of ichor, the blood of the gods. The potency of ichor is more than the mortal frame was meant to bear, and the effect of consuming even a drop was almost enough to kill you. But you survived, and now a tiny portion of immortal blood flows through your veins.

Ichor is exceedingly rare in the world. Secretive religious orders carefully hoard vials containing the silvery substance, concealing it in well-defended temples, remote monasteries, or hidden shrines. You might have discovered the drop you consumed in a long-forgotten vault years ago and carried the vial until you grew powerful enough to drink its contents and live. Or emissaries of those who first schooled you in the invoker's way might have arrived when you were ready to take this path, bringing you the drop of ichor. In any event, your goal as a vessel of ichor is to defend the great and noble things the gods have created against those who would tear them down. Whenever a servant of the gods is murdered, whenever something sacred is defiled, it is an affront to divine sovereignty.

GEORGI "CALADER" SIMEONOV

Vessel of Ichor Path Features

Vessel's Action (11th level): When you spend an action point to take an extra standard action, you also gain an extra minor action you can use before the end of your next turn. If you are bloodied when you spend the action point, you gain an extra move action instead.

Invoker's Blood (11th level): When you use your *armor of wrath* power, you deal 2d6 extra damage if you are bloodied.

Vessel's Resistance (16th level): You gain resist 5 to all damage while you are bloodied.

Vessel of Ichor Prayers

Fiery Glance — Vessel of Ichor Attack 11

You summon the divine power in your blood. Your eyes blaze with silver fire as you fix your gaze on your foe.

Encounter ✦ Divine, Implement, Radiant
Standard Action **Ranged** 20
Primary Target: One creature
Primary Attack: Wisdom vs. Reflex
Hit: 1d10 + Wisdom modifier radiant damage, and the target is dazed until the end of your next turn. Make a secondary attack that is an area burst 2 centered on the primary target.
Secondary Target: Each enemy in burst other than the primary target
Secondary Attack: Wisdom vs. Reflex
Hit: 1d10 + Wisdom modifier radiant damage.

Holy Vigor — Vessel of Ichor Utility 12

You call on the divine potency in your blood. In a flash, you and your friend are emboldened to strike back at your foe.

Daily ✦ Divine, Healing
Immediate Reaction **Close** burst 10
Trigger: An enemy hits your ally within 10 squares of you
Target: The triggering ally in burst
Effect: You and the target gain a +2 power bonus to the next attack roll each of you makes against the triggering enemy before the end of the encounter. If the target was bloodied by the triggering enemy's attack, he or she can spend a healing surge.

Silver Rain — Vessel of Ichor Attack 20

A rain of silver droplets showers your friends and foes with the power of divine ichor.

Daily ✦ Divine, Healing, Implement, Radiant, Zone
Standard Action **Area** burst 3 within 20 squares
Target: Each enemy in burst
Attack: Wisdom vs. Fortitude. You gain a bonus to the attack roll and the damage roll equal to the number of bloodied allies in the burst and an additional +1 if you are bloodied.
Hit: 4d8 + Wisdom modifier radiant damage, and ongoing 5 radiant damage (save ends).
Miss: Half damage.
Effect: The burst creates a zone of ichor that lasts until the end of your next turn. Any bloodied ally who starts his or her turn within the zone regains hit points equal to your Constitution modifier. Any enemy that isn't bloodied that starts its turn within the zone takes radiant damage equal to your Constitution modifier.
Sustain Minor: The zone persists.

CHAPTER 4

Paladin

My good blade carves the casques of men,
My tough lance thrusteth sure,
My strength is as the strength of ten,
Because my heart is pure.
—Tennyson, "Sir Galahad"

A LIVING rampart of steel and courage, you stand against all enemies. You anchor the front line of the adventuring party, first to throw yourself in harm's way. With bold challenges, you defy the most fearsome of enemies and force them to reckon with you. Your place is in the middle of the fray, testing your mettle in hand-to-hand combat.

Different deities have varying expectations of their paladins. Some deities favor those who excel in shielding their comrades from harm, while others demand vengeance from their champions. But you might instead be an ardent paladin, one who sacrifices your own defense and even your health for greater offensive power. Or you are a virtuous paladin, a warrior of pure heart who can withstand the wiles and blights of your gods' enemies. You might follow one of these paths exclusively, or you might forge a course of your own.

However you choose to serve your divine patron, this chapter provides you with many new options.

- **New Class Features:** In place of your *lay on hands* power, you can select one of two new powers to better focus on dealing damage or overcoming harmful conditions. These are best suited to the paladin builds presented in this chapter, though any paladin can choose them.
- **New Builds:** The ardent paladin takes the battle to the enemy, heedless of personal risk. The virtuous paladin excels in resisting conditions imposed by enemies.
- **New Paladin Powers:** Almost one hundred new paladin powers include prayers for ardent and virtuous paladins, as well as prayers suited to avenging and protecting paladins.
- **New Paragon Paths:** New paragon paths focus your paladin's service, including the champion of Corellon, the demonslayer, and the holy conqueror.

NEW CLASS FEATURES

When you make your paladin, you can select one of these powers in place of *lay on hands.*

Ardent Vow — Paladin Feature

You draw on unwavering faith and inner strength to strike with divine fury.

Daily (Special) ✦ Divine
Minor Action **Melee** touch
Target: One creature
Effect: The next time you attack the target before the end of your next turn, you gain a bonus to the damage roll equal to 5 + your Wisdom modifier. In addition, whenever you attack the target before the end of the encounter, it is subject to your divine sanction until the end of your next turn.
Special: You can use this power a number of times per day equal to your Wisdom modifier (minimum 1), but only once per round.

Virtue's Touch — Paladin Feature

Your gentle touch removes affliction.

Daily (Special) ✦ Divine
Minor Action **Melee** touch
Target: One creature
Effect: You remove one condition from the target: blinded, dazed, deafened, slowed, stunned, or weakened.
Special: You can use this power a number of times per day equal to your Wisdom modifier (minimum 1), but only once per round.

NEW BUILDS

The avenging paladin and the protecting paladin are described in the *Player's Handbook.* This chapter introduces two paladin builds: the ardent paladin, who specializes in offense, and the virtuous paladin, who focuses on resisting harmful effects.

Ardent Paladin

Your brutal assaults demonstrate the power of your god's wrath. You're more like a striker than other paladins are. You willingly sacrifice your own health and defense to strike down your foes, even giving up some healing ability to be a more powerful attacker. The *ardent vow* power allows you to focus on a specific opponent, dealing additional damage with attacks and keeping that foe's attention on you. This power also enhances powers that work better against enemies marked by you.

Take Strength as your highest ability score, since you use it for many attacks and damage. Wisdom should be your second-highest score, to maximize the number of uses you get of *ardent vow.* A good Constitution score can help soothe the sting of powers that require you to spend some of your own hit points for best effect. Because of this build's focus on dealing damage, choose a weapon with the best possible damage capacity, typically a two-handed weapon.

Suggested Class Feature: *ardent vow**
Suggested Feat: Mighty Challenge
Suggested Skills: Heal, Insight, Intimidate, Religion
Suggested At-Will Powers: *ardent strike,* valiant strike*
Suggested Encounter Power: *divine pursuit**
Suggested Daily Power: *blood of the mighty**
*New option presented in this book

Virtuous Paladin

You are a tower of faith; enchantments and dreadful powers wielded by your foes can find little purchase in your devoted heart. Like the protecting paladin, you shield your companions, but you do so while protecting yourself so that you can stay in the fight. No matter how your enemies attack you, you excel at resisting conditions that would impede others. As a warrior of exceptional piety, you also make more use of your holy symbol than other paladins do. You have several options for engaging enemies at range, so that even foes beyond your weapon's reach cannot escape your challenge.

Your highest ability score should be Charisma. Choose Wisdom for your second-best score, since a good Wisdom enhances the effects of many of your powers. Strength should be your third-best score. First choose powers that let you make extra saving throws or use healing surges, then powers that bolster your allies or deal high damage. You should wield a shield and a one-handed weapon, since having high defenses is a goal of this build.

DIVINE SANCTION

Many new paladin powers and some of the new feats in this book subject a target to your divine sanction. Being subject to it means the target is marked by you for a duration specified in the description of the power or feat. Unless otherwise noted, the mark ends before the specified duration if someone else marks the target.

Until the mark ends, the target takes radiant damage equal to 3 + your Charisma modifier the first time each round it makes an attack that doesn't include you as a target. The damage increases to 6 + your Charisma modifier at 11th level and 9 + your Charisma modifier at 21st level.

Divine sanction is meant to complement *divine challenge.* You can use *divine challenge* to mark one creature and use divine sanction to mark others. Divine sanction has fewer restrictions than *divine challenge* so that you can easily use the two in concert.

Suggested Class Feature: *virtue's touch**
Suggested Feat: Virtuous Recovery
Suggested Skills: Endurance, Heal, Insight, Religion
Suggested At-Will Powers: *bolstering strike, virtuous strike**
Suggested Encounter Power: *valorous smite**
Suggested Daily Power: *majestic halo**
*New option presented in this book

NEW PALADIN POWERS

Paladins excel at calling out foes, and a number of the new powers presented here reinforce that ability using divine sanction. Ardent paladin powers represent zealous devotion to deity and cause, dealing tremendous damage at a cost to yourself, and virtuous paladin powers reflect devotion and strength of spirit to guard you from enemy attacks. Avenging paladins might choose a few ardent paladin powers for a boost to damage, and protecting paladins can make good use of many virtuous paladin powers.

Level 1 At-Will Prayers

Ardent Strike Paladin Attack 1

You attack your enemy and make it the focus of your god's anger.

At-Will ✦ Divine, Weapon
Standard Action **Melee** weapon
Target: One creature
Attack: Strength or Charisma vs. AC
Hit: 1[W] + Strength or Charisma modifier damage, and the target is subject to your divine sanction until the end of your next turn.
Level 21: 2[W] + Strength or Charisma modifier damage.
Special: When charging, you can use this power in place of a melee basic attack.

Virtuous Strike Paladin Attack 1

The clean light of your weapon pierces your enemies and fills you with resolve.

At-Will ✦ Divine, Radiant, Weapon
Standard Action **Melee** weapon
Target: One creature
Attack: Charisma vs. AC
Hit: 1[W] + Charisma modifier radiant damage, and you gain a +2 bonus to saving throws until the start of your next turn.
Level 21: 2[W] + Charisma modifier radiant damage.
Special: This power can be used as a melee basic attack.

EMRAH ELMASLI

Level 1 Encounter Prayers

Dazzling Flare — Paladin Attack 1

Painfully bright light flashes from your holy symbol.

Encounter ✦ Divine, Implement, Radiant
Standard Action **Ranged** 5
Target: One creature
Attack: Charisma vs. Reflex
Hit: 2d8 + Charisma modifier radiant damage, and the target takes a -2 penalty to attack rolls until the end of your next turn.

Divine Pursuit — Paladin Attack 1

You drive your foe back with a mighty attack and follow it to prevent its escape.

Encounter ✦ Divine, Weapon
Standard Action **Melee** weapon
Target: One creature
Attack: Strength vs. Fortitude
Hit: 2[W] + Strength modifier damage, and you push the target a number of squares equal to your Wisdom modifier. You then shift to the nearest square adjacent to the target.

Guardian Light — Paladin Attack 1

As you attack, a faint glow envelops your weapon and bolsters your defenses for a time.

Encounter ✦ Divine, Radiant, Weapon
Standard Action **Melee** weapon
Target: One creature
Attack: Strength or Charisma vs. AC
Hit: 1[W] + Strength or Charisma modifier radiant damage. Until the end of your next turn, you gain a bonus to Fortitude, Reflex, and Will equal to your Wisdom modifier.

Heedless Fury — Paladin Attack 1

You lay into your foe without regard to your own safety.

Encounter ✦ Divine, Weapon
Standard Action **Melee** weapon
Target: One creature
Attack: Strength vs. AC
Hit: 3[W] + Strength modifier damage, and you take a -5 penalty to all defenses until the end of your next turn.

Valorous Smite — Paladin Attack 1

You cry out as you strike, daring all your enemies to face you.

Encounter ✦ Divine, Weapon
Standard Action **Melee** weapon
Target: One creature
Attack: Charisma vs. AC
Hit: 2[W] + Charisma modifier damage. Each enemy within 3 squares of you is subject to your divine sanction until the end of your next turn.

Level 1 Daily Prayers

Blood of the Mighty — Paladin Attack 1

You draw on your own life force to deal a decisive blow.

Daily ✦ Divine, Reliable, Weapon
Standard Action **Melee** weapon
Target: One creature
Attack: Strength vs. AC
Hit: 4[W] + Strength modifier damage.
Effect: You take 5 damage, which can't be reduced in any way.

Blazing Brand — Paladin Attack 1

Your strike burns your god's symbol onto the enemy, a beacon to your companions.

Daily ✦ Divine, Fire, Reliable, Weapon
Standard Action **Melee** weapon
Target: One creature
Attack: Strength vs. Fortitude
Hit: 2[W] + Strength modifier fire damage. The target takes ongoing 5 fire damage and grants combat advantage to any ally adjacent to it (save ends both).

Glorious Charge — Paladin Attack 1

You wade into battle and urge your allies to greater heights.

Daily ✦ Divine, Healing, Weapon
Standard Action **Melee** weapon
Target: One creature
Attack: Charisma vs. AC
Hit: 2[W] + Charisma modifier damage.
Effect: After the attack, each ally within 2 squares of you regains hit points equal to one-half your level + your Wisdom modifier.
Special: When charging, you can use this power in place of a melee basic attack.

Majestic Halo — Paladin Attack 1

You shine with divine radiance that sears your enemies as you attack and commands their respect.

Daily ✦ Divine, Radiant, Weapon
Standard Action **Melee** weapon
Target: One creature
Attack: Charisma vs. AC
Hit: 3[W] + Charisma modifier radiant damage.
Miss: Half damage.
Effect: Until the end of the encounter, any enemy that starts its turn adjacent to you is subject to your divine sanction until the end of its turn.

Level 2 Utility Prayers

Bless Weapon Paladin Utility 2

You recite an ancient prayer to imbue your weapon with the power of pure faith.

Daily ✦ Divine, Radiant
Minor Action **Personal**
Effect: Choose one weapon you are wielding. Until the end of the encounter, you gain a +1 power bonus to attack rolls with that weapon, and it deals 1d6 extra radiant damage on a hit. In addition, you can score a critical hit with the weapon on a roll of 18–20 against creatures vulnerable to radiant damage.

Call of Challenge Paladin Utility 2

You brandish your weapon and demand that all foes nearby face you in battle.

Encounter ✦ Divine
Minor Action **Close** burst 3
Target: Each enemy in burst
Effect: Each target is subject to your divine sanction until the end of your next turn.

Divine Counter Paladin Utility 2

The power of your god deflects part of an attack against you, and you call out the attacker.

Encounter ✦ Divine
Immediate Interrupt **Personal**
Trigger: An enemy hits your Fortitude, Reflex, or Will
Effect: You take only half damage from the triggering enemy's attack, and the triggering enemy is subject to your divine sanction until the end of its next turn.

Touch of Grace Paladin Utility 2

You take onto yourself the suffering of your ally.

Encounter ✦ Divine
Minor Action **Melee** touch
Target: One ally
Effect: You transfer to yourself one effect on the target that a save can end.

Virtue Paladin Utility 2

You gird yourself in your high ideals and face the enemy with renewed determination.

Encounter ✦ Divine
Minor Action **Personal**
Effect: You spend a healing surge but regain no hit points. You instead gain temporary hit points equal to your healing surge value.

Level 3 Encounter Prayers

Avenging Smite Paladin Attack 3

Your steel transfixes an enemy that harms your friend.

Encounter ✦ Divine, Weapon
Immediate Reaction **Melee** 1
Trigger: An enemy adjacent to you hits your ally
Target: The triggering enemy
Attack: Charisma vs. AC
Hit: 2[W] + Charisma modifier damage, and the target is immobilized until the end of your next turn.

Call to Arms Paladin Attack 3

You lead your foe to the ground where you want to fight.

Encounter ✦ Divine, Implement
Standard Action **Close** burst 5
Target: One creature marked by you
Primary Attack: Charisma vs. Will
Hit: You pull the target to a square adjacent to you. Then make a melee secondary attack against it using your weapon.
Secondary Attack: Charisma + 2 vs. AC
Hit: 2[W] + Charisma modifier damage.

Hold Fast Paladin Attack 3

You engage your foe and prevent it from advancing on your allies.

Encounter ✦ Divine, Weapon
Standard Action **Melee** weapon
Target: One creature
Attack: Strength or Charisma vs. AC
Hit: 2[W] + Strength or Charisma modifier damage, and the target is immobilized until the end of your next turn.
Special: You can use this power in place of a melee basic attack.

Strength from Valor Paladin Attack 3

As foes encircle you, you fight all the harder.

Encounter ✦ Divine, Weapon
Standard Action **Close** burst 1
Target: Each enemy in burst
Attack: Strength vs. Fortitude
Hit: 1[W] + Strength modifier damage. You gain 5 temporary hit points for each target hit by the attack.

Trial of Strength Paladin Attack 3

You shake off affliction to strike true and hard.

Encounter ✦ Divine, Weapon
Standard Action **Melee** weapon
Target: One creature
Effect: Before the attack, you make a saving throw with a bonus equal to your Wisdom modifier.
Attack: Charisma vs. AC
Hit: 2[W] + Charisma modifier damage.

Level 5 Daily Prayers

Arc of Vengeance — Paladin Attack 5

Your flashing weapon promises a swift end to your foes.

Daily ✦ Divine, Radiant, Weapon
Standard Action **Close** burst 1
Target: Each enemy in burst
Attack: Strength vs. AC
Hit: 2[W] + Strength modifier radiant damage.
Miss: Half damage.
Effect: The target is subject to your divine sanction until the end of your next turn. If the target was already marked by you, it also takes radiant damage equal to your Wisdom modifier whenever it deals damage to you or any ally (save ends).

Name of Might — Paladin Attack 5

You shout an ancient angelic name of thunderous power that slows your foes.

Daily ✦ Divine, Implement, Thunder
Standard Action **Close** blast 3
Target: Each enemy in blast
Attack: Charisma vs. Fortitude
Hit: 3d8 + Charisma modifier thunder damage, and the target is slowed (save ends).
Miss: Half damage, and the target is slowed until the end of its next turn.

Prayer of Two Paths — Paladin Attack 5

As you strike one enemy, you direct a beam of holy radiance against another.

Daily ✦ Divine, Healing, Radiant, Weapon
Standard Action **Melee** weapon
Primary Target: One creature
Primary Attack: Strength vs. AC
Hit: 2[W] + Strength modifier damage.
Effect: Make a ranged secondary attack using your implement. Doing so doesn't provoke opportunity attacks.
Secondary Target: One creature other than the primary target within 5 squares of you
Secondary Attack: Charisma vs. Will
Hit: 2d8 + Charisma modifier radiant damage, and you regain hit points equal to 1d6 + your Charisma modifier.

Unrelenting Punishment — Paladin Attack 5

After your initial attack, divine power continues to assault your foe, and you grow stronger all the while.

Daily ✦ Divine, Healing, Weapon
Standard Action **Melee** weapon
Target: One creature
Attack: Strength vs. AC
Hit: 2[W] + Strength modifier damage.
Effect: The target takes ongoing 5 damage (save ends). Whenever the target takes this ongoing damage, you regain hit points equal to your Wisdom modifier.

Unyielding Faith — Paladin Attack 5

You let faith alone guide your weapon. No enemy can distract you from your sacred task.

Daily ✦ Divine, Weapon
Standard Action **Melee** weapon
Target: One creature
Attack: Charisma vs. AC
Hit: 3[W] + Charisma modifier damage, and the target is subject to your divine sanction until the end of the encounter.
Miss: Half damage.
Effect: You gain a +5 power bonus to all defenses against charm effects until the end of the encounter.

Level 6 Utility Prayers

Fear Not — Paladin Utility 6

You reassure your ally, conferring divine power to throw off ill effects.

Encounter ✦ Divine
Minor Action **Melee** touch
Target: One creature
Effect: The target can make a saving throw. Against a fear effect, the target gains a bonus to the saving throw equal to your Wisdom modifier.

Pure Devotion — Paladin Utility 6

The intensity of your faith protects you from your enemy's insidious power.

Encounter ✦ Divine
Immediate Interrupt **Personal**
Trigger: An enemy attacks you
Effect: You gain a +4 power bonus to Fortitude and Will until the end of your next turn.

Shield of Discipline — Paladin Utility 6

Toughness hard won through years of rigorous self-control blunts your enemies' attacks.

Encounter ✦ Divine
Minor Action **Personal**
Effect: Until the end of your next turn, you gain resistance to all damage equal to your Strength modifier.

Shield the Virtuous — Paladin Utility 6

You speak a prayer of protection for an ally, who is surrounded by a shining halo.

Daily ✦ Divine, Radiant
Minor Action **Close** burst 10
Target: One ally in burst
Effect: Until the end of the encounter, any enemy that hits or misses the target takes 3 + your Charisma modifier radiant damage, unless that enemy is marked by the target.
Level 11: 6 + your Charisma modifier radiant damage.
Level 21: 9 + your Charisma modifier radiant damage.

Valiant Rush Paladin Utility 6

You plunge into battle with divine speed.

Encounter ✦ Divine
Move Action **Personal**
Effect: You move twice your speed to a square adjacent to an enemy that is within your line of sight at the start of this movement.

Level 7 Encounter Prayers

Astral Thunder Paladin Attack 7

The power of your god's dominion thunders through your holy symbol to pummel nearby foes.

Encounter ✦ Divine, Implement, Thunder
Standard Action **Close** burst 3
Target: Each enemy in burst
Attack: Charisma vs. Fortitude
Hit: 2d8 + Charisma modifier thunder damage. Until the end of your next turn, the target takes a penalty to attack rolls equal to your Wisdom modifier.

Blade of Light Paladin Attack 7

As you charge, a golden light envelops your weapon and fortifies you against the powers of darkness and fear.

Encounter ✦ Divine, Radiant, Weapon
Standard Action **Melee** weapon
Target: One creature
Attack: Charisma vs. AC
Hit: 3[W] + Charisma modifier radiant damage. Until the end of your next turn, you gain a +2 bonus to all defenses against fear or necrotic effects.
Special: When charging, you can use this power in place of a melee basic attack.

Comeback Smite Paladin Attack 7

You shrug off the effects of your enemies' attacks and strike back with even greater purpose.

Encounter ✦ Divine, Weapon
Standard Action **Melee** weapon
Effect: Before the attack, you make a saving throw against each effect on you that a save can end. You gain a bonus to the attack roll and the damage roll equal to the number of effects you save against.
Target: One creature
Attack: Strength vs. AC
Hit: 2[W] + Strength modifier damage.

Force of Arms Paladin Attack 7

You channel your entire spirit into a powerful attack.

Encounter ✦ Divine, Weapon
Standard Action **Melee** weapon
Target: One creature
Attack: Strength vs. AC. If you have used the Channel Divinity power *divine strength* during this turn, you gain a bonus to the attack roll equal to your Wisdom modifier.
Hit: 2[W] + Strength modifier damage.

Price of Cowardice Paladin Attack 7

A searing flash of light punishes a foe who refuses to face you in battle.

Encounter ✦ Divine, Implement, Radiant
Immediate Interrupt **Close** burst 5
Trigger: An enemy marked by you makes an attack that does not include you as a target
Target: The triggering enemy
Attack: Charisma vs. Will
Hit: 2d10 + Charisma modifier radiant damage, and the target is blinded until the end of your next turn.

LUCIO PARRILLO

Resurgent Smite — Paladin Attack 7

Your inspiring attack bestows health on your ally.

Encounter ✦ Divine, Healing, Weapon
Standard Action **Melee** weapon
Target: One creature
Attack: Strength or Charisma vs. AC
Hit: 2[W] + Strength or Charisma modifier damage, and an ally within 5 squares of you can spend a healing surge. If the attack deals at least 20 damage, the ally gains additional hit points equal to twice your Wisdom modifier.

Level 9 Daily Prayers

Final Rebuke — Paladin Attack 9

You roar with outrage, and your furious strike hurls your foe away.

Daily ✦ Divine, Reliable, Weapon
Standard Action **Melee** weapon
Target: One creature
Attack: Strength vs. Fortitude
Hit: 2[W] + Strength modifier damage, and you push the target 5 squares. If the target ends this movement in a square adjacent to a solid obstacle, the target takes 1[W] extra damage.

Knightly Intercession — Paladin Attack 9

You command a foe to attack you instead of your companion.

Daily ✦ Divine, Weapon
Immediate Interrupt **Close** burst 10
Trigger: An enemy within 10 squares of you hits your ally with a melee or a ranged attack
Target: The triggering enemy
Effect: The triggering attack hits you instead of the ally. You pull the target to a square adjacent to you and then make the following attack against it.
Attack: Strength vs. AC
Hit: 2[W] + Strength modifier damage, and the target is subject to your divine sanction until the end of the encounter.

Ray of Reprisal — Paladin Attack 9

You direct a beam of fierce radiance against an enemy and force it to feel the pain of the wounds it inflicted on your comrade.

Daily ✦ Divine, Implement, Radiant
Immediate Interrupt **Close** burst 5
Trigger: An enemy within 5 squares of you hits your ally
Target: The triggering enemy
Attack: Charisma vs. Fortitude
Hit: 3d6 + Charisma radiant damage.
Miss: Half damage.
Effect: The ally hit takes half damage from the triggering enemy's attack.

Shackles of Justice — Paladin Attack 9

Consecrated light enfolds the enemy you smite, exacting a price whenever that foe causes harm.

Daily ✦ Divine, Radiant, Weapon
Standard Action **Melee** weapon
Target: One creature
Attack: Charisma vs. AC
Hit: 2[W] + Charisma modifier damage.
Effect: Whenever the target deals damage, it takes 2d6 radiant damage (save ends).

Shout of Condemnation — Paladin Attack 9

Your thunderous words consign your foes to continual pain.

Daily ✦ Divine, Implement, Thunder
Standard Action **Close** blast 5
Target: Each creature in blast
Attack: Strength vs. Will
Hit: 2d6 + Strength modifier thunder damage, and the target takes ongoing 5 thunder damage and is subject to your divine sanction (save ends both).
Miss: Half damage, and the target is subject to your divine sanction until the end of your next turn.

Level 10 Utility Prayers

Benediction — Paladin Utility 10

A quick prayer grants vigor and strength to a comrade in battle.

Encounter ✦ Divine, Healing
Immediate Reaction **Close** burst 5
Trigger: An ally within 5 squares of you hits with a melee attack
Target: The triggering ally
Effect: The target can either spend a healing surge or make two damage rolls for the attack and use either result.

Font of Healing — Paladin Utility 10

Divine beneficence heals you and your companion.

Daily ✦ Divine, Healing
Minor Action **Close** burst 5
Target: You and one ally in burst
Effect: You spend a healing surge, and each target regains hit points equal to your healing surge value.

Guiding Verse — Paladin Utility 10

In the sacred words of a prayer, you find the resolve to shake off a deleterious condition.

Encounter ✦ Divine
Minor Action **Personal**
Effect: You make a saving throw with a bonus equal to 1 + your Wisdom modifier.

Righteous Indignation — Paladin Utility 10

Seeing your ally harmed enrages you.

Daily ✦ Divine
Immediate Reaction **Personal**
Trigger: An enemy hits your ally within your line of sight
Effect: The next time you attack before the end of your next turn, you gain a +2 power bonus to the attack roll and deal extra damage equal to 2 + your Strength modifier.

Level 13 Encounter Prayers

Castigating Strike — Paladin Attack 13

As you attack, you chide your foes for neglecting you and compel their attention.

Encounter ✦ Divine, Weapon
Standard Action **Melee** weapon
Target: One creature
Attack: Strength or Charisma vs. AC
Hit: 1[W] + Strength or Charisma modifier damage, and each enemy within 3 squares of you is subject to your divine sanction until the end of your next turn.

Compel Obedience — Paladin Attack 13

You lead an enemy away from those under your protection.

Encounter ✦ Divine, Weapon
Standard Action **Melee** weapon
Target: One creature
Attack: Charisma vs. Will
Hit: 3[W] + Charisma modifier damage, and you shift 3 squares. You then pull the target 5 squares to a square adjacent to you.

Eye for an Eye — Paladin Attack 13

You raise your holy symbol and shout an imprecation to blind a foe that dares to assault your comrade.

Encounter ✦ Divine, Implement
Immediate Reaction **Close** burst 5
Trigger: An enemy within 5 squares of you hits your ally
Target: The triggering enemy in burst
Attack: Charisma vs. Will
Hit: 2d8 + Charisma modifier damage, and the target is blinded until the end of your next turn.

Fervent Strike — Paladin Attack 13

Still burning with your ardent vow, you launch a mighty attack.

Encounter ✦ Divine, Weapon
Standard Action **Melee** weapon
Target: One creature
Attack: Strength vs. AC. If the target is marked by you, you gain a +2 bonus to the attack roll, and you can score a critical hit on a roll of 18–20.
Hit: 2[W] + Strength modifier damage. If you have used *ardent vow* during this encounter, the attack deals extra damage equal to your Wisdom modifier.

Zealous Smite — Paladin Attack 13

Being wounded in battle only makes you strike the harder.

Encounter ✦ Divine, Weapon
Standard Action **Melee** weapon
Target: One creature
Attack: Strength vs. AC
Hit: 3[W] + Strength modifier damage, and the target is subject to your divine sanction until the end of your next turn. The attack deals 1[W] extra damage if the target has hit you since your last turn.

Level 15 Daily Prayers

Divine Vengeance — Paladin Attack 15

Brilliance flares from you to dispense pain to attacking enemies.

Daily ✦ Divine, Radiant, Stance
Minor Action **Personal**
Effect: Until the stance ends, whenever an enemy hits you or an ally adjacent to you with a melee attack, that enemy takes radiant damage equal to 5 + your Wisdom modifier.

Flames of Devotion — Paladin Attack 15

Divine fire ignites your consecrated weapon.

Daily ✦ Divine, Fire, Weapon
Standard Action **Melee** weapon
Target: One creature
Attack: Strength vs. AC
Hit: 2[W] + Strength modifier fire damage.
Effect: Until the end of your next turn, your weapon attacks deal 2d6 extra fire damage.
Sustain Minor: The effect persists.

Knight's Defiance — Paladin Attack 15

You demand that your foes meet you in battle, then strike fiercely against one of them.

Daily ✦ Divine, Weapon
Standard Action **Close** burst 5
Primary Target: Each enemy in burst
Effect: Before the attack, you pull each primary target to a square adjacent to you, and each target is subject to your divine sanction (save ends). Make a melee secondary attack.
Secondary Target: One primary target adjacent to you
Attack: Charisma vs. AC
Hit: 3[W] + Charisma modifier damage.

Pyre of Judgment — Paladin Attack 15

You consign a foe to the flames. The blaze consumes enemies that stay by its side.

Daily ✦ Divine, Fire, Reliable, Weapon
Standard Action **Melee** weapon
Target: One creature
Attack: Strength vs. AC
Hit: 2[W] + Strength modifier fire damage, and ongoing 10 fire damage (save ends). Whenever the target takes this ongoing damage, each enemy adjacent to it takes fire damage equal to 5 + your Wisdom modifier.

Tower of Faith — Paladin Attack 15

As you swing your weapon, a surge of divine confidence buoys the spirits of allies nearby.

Daily ✦ Divine, Weapon
Standard Action **Melee** weapon
Target: One creature
Attack: Charisma vs. AC
Hit: 3[W] + Charisma modifier damage.
Miss: Half damage.
Effect: Until the end of the encounter, you and any allies within 5 squares of you gain a +2 power bonus to saving throws. The bonus increases to +5 against charm or fear effects.

Level 16 Utility Prayers

Devotion — Paladin Utility 16

Your enemy seeks to overwhelm your resolve, but your calm certainty shields you and your comrades.

Daily ✦ Divine
Immediate Interrupt **Close** burst 5
Trigger: An enemy hits you or your ally within 5 squares of you
Target: You and each ally in burst
Effect: Each target gains a +4 power bonus to Fortitude and Will until the end of your next turn.

Divine Aegis — Paladin Utility 16

Your god shelters you and your allies from harm.

Daily ✦ Divine, Stance
Minor Action **Personal**
Effect: Until the stance ends, you and any allies within 2 squares of you gain a +2 bonus to all defenses.

Higher Cause — Paladin Utility 16

When your body falters, your faith takes over to let you keep up the fight.

Daily ✦ Divine, Healing, Stance
Minor Action **Personal**
Requirement: You must be bloodied.
Effect: Until the stance ends, you gain a +2 power bonus to saving throws. In addition, you gain regeneration 5 while bloodied.

Liberation — Paladin Utility 16

Hearing your call, your embattled comrade falls back to safety.

Encounter ✦ Divine, Healing
Move Action **Close** burst 5
Target: One ally in burst
Effect: You pull the target a number of squares equal to your Charisma modifier. At the end of this movement, the target can spend a healing surge.

Prayer for the Valiant — Paladin Utility 16

You seek aid for your beleaguered companions. A warm light shines down, bringing relief.

Daily ✦ Divine
Minor Action **Close** burst 5
Target: Each ally in burst
Effect: Each target can make a saving throw with a power bonus equal to your Charisma modifier.

Level 17 Encounter Prayers

Mark of Terror — Paladin Attack 17

As you strike, your god's presence fills the enemy with dread.

Encounter ✦ Divine, Fear, Weapon
Standard Action **Melee** weapon
Target: One creature marked by you
Attack: Strength vs. AC
Hit: 1[W] + Strength modifier damage, and the target is stunned until the end of your next turn.

Reassuring Strike — Paladin Attack 17

You land a solid blow and are rewarded with renewed vitality.

Encounter ✦ Divine, Healing, Weapon
Standard Action **Melee** weapon
Target: One creature
Attack: Strength or Charisma vs. AC
Hit: 3[W] + Strength or Charisma modifier damage. You can spend a healing surge and add your Wisdom modifier to the hit points regained.

Sanctified Light — Paladin Attack 17

A flash from your holy symbol sears your foes, particularly those bearing your mark.

Encounter ✦ Divine, Implement, Radiant
Standard Action **Area** burst 1 within 10 squares
Target: Each creature in burst
Attack: Charisma vs. Reflex
Hit: 1d8 radiant damage. If the target is marked by you, the attack instead deals 2d8 + your Charisma modifier radiant damage.

Shattering Smite — Paladin Attack 17

A well-placed strike punches through your opponent's defenses.

Encounter ✦ Divine, Weapon
Standard Action **Melee** weapon
Target: One creature
Attack: Strength vs. AC
Hit: 3[W] + Strength modifier damage, and the target loses all resistances until the end of your next turn.

Wrathful Smite — Paladin Attack 17

With a burst of whirling steel, you batter down foes who surround you.

Encounter ✦ Divine, Weapon
Standard Action **Close** burst 1
Target: Each enemy in burst
Attack: Charisma vs. Reflex
Hit: 2[W] + Charisma modifier damage, and the target takes a -2 penalty to attack rolls until the end of your next turn. If the target is marked by you, the attack deals 1[W] extra damage.

Hymn to Corellon

Lord of the wood, lord of the stars,
Maker of songs and teacher of arts—
Great Corellon, as your servant I stand.
Open my eyes to the works of your hand.

Lord of the wood, lighten my heart;
Maker of songs, your wisdom impart.
Great Corellon, grant me a dream
Of the twilight courts of the Seldarine!

Lord of magic, lord of starlight,
Lover of beauty and poet of night—
Long lies the path through mists and through moor
But home I will come to Arvandor.

Level 19 Daily Prayers

Name of Potency — Paladin Attack 19

In a resounding voice, you speak an ancient angelic name that stops your enemies in their tracks.

Daily ✦ Divine, Implement, Thunder
Standard Action **Close** burst 2
Target: Each enemy in burst
Attack: Charisma vs. Fortitude
Hit: 3d8 + Charisma modifier thunder damage, and the target is immobilized (save ends).
Miss: Half damage, and the target is slowed (save ends).

Overwhelming Fervor — Paladin Attack 19

You name your enemy a foe of the faith and press the attack relentlessly.

Daily ✦ Divine, Weapon
Standard Action **Melee** weapon
Target: One creature
Attack: Strength vs. AC
Hit: 5[W] + Strength modifier damage, and the target is subject to your divine sanction until the end of your next turn. Whenever you attack the target until the end of the encounter, the target is subject to your divine sanction until the end of your next turn.
Miss: Half damage.

Righteous Resolve — Paladin Attack 19

Each blow struck by your foe only heightens your resistance.

Daily ✦ Divine, Weapon
Standard Action **Melee** weapon
Target: One creature
Attack: Charisma vs. AC
Hit: 4[W] + Charisma modifier damage.
Miss: Half damage.
Effect: Until the end of the encounter, whenever the target deals damage to you or an ally, you gain temporary hit points equal to 5 + your Wisdom modifier.

Smite the Soul — Paladin Attack 19

Your wrathful strike drives deep, incapacitating your foe.

Daily ✦ Divine, Weapon
Standard Action **Melee** weapon
Target: One creature
Attack: Strength vs. AC
Hit: 2[W] + Strength modifier damage, and the target is stunned (save ends).
Aftereffect: The target is dazed until the end of its next turn.
Miss: Half damage, and the target is dazed until the end of your next turn.

Wheel of Fate — Paladin Attack 19

You unleash a flurry of attacks against all nearby enemies, drawing greater strength from their pain.

Daily ✦ Divine, Healing, Weapon
Standard Action **Close** burst 1
Target: Each enemy in burst
Attack: Strength vs. AC
Hit: 3[W] + Strength modifier damage. If the attack hits two or more targets, you regain hit points equal to your healing surge value.
Effect: Until the end of the encounter, you gain regeneration equal to your Wisdom modifier while bloodied.

Level 22 Utility Prayers

Failure Is No Option — Paladin Utility 22

Your battle cry renews the determination of flagging allies.

Daily ✦ Divine, Healing, Teleportation
Standard Action **Close** burst 3
Target: Each ally in burst
Effect: You teleport each target a number of squares equal to your Charisma modifier. The target must end this movement adjacent to an enemy. The target then regains hit points equal to 15 + your Charisma modifier.

MAZIN KASSIS

Holy Wings — Paladin Utility 22

Majestic silver wings carry you past obstacles.

Encounter ✦ Divine
Minor Action **Personal**
Effect: Until the end of your next turn, you gain a fly speed equal to your speed and a +4 bonus to AC against opportunity attacks.

Inspiring Hymn — Paladin Utility 22

You recite an ancient verse to avert ill fortune in battle.

Encounter ✦ Divine
Immediate Interrupt **Close** burst 5
Trigger: An enemy scores a critical hit against your ally within 5 squares of you
Target: The triggering enemy in burst
Effect: The target rerolls the attack and uses the second result.

Return to the Living — Paladin Utility 22

Your tenacity defies even death.

Daily ✦ Divine, Healing
No Action **Personal**
Trigger: You drop to 0 hit points or fewer and do not die
Effect: You regain 1 hit point and can spend four healing surges.

The Divine Compromises

When the immortals had won the war against the primordials, they fought among themselves for dominion over various aspects of the natural world. Zehir contested with Pelor over mastery of the sky, for the sun banished darkness. Pelor in turn fought with Khala, whose icy mists and snows blocked the life-giving rays of the sun. Each of Pelor's opponents gathered allies, and Pelor had allies of his own. On one side stood Corellon, Khala, Zehir, and Sehanine, while on the other stood Pelor, Erathis, Moradin, and Melora. The two forces argued for ages to no avail, leaving hurts and grudges that linger still.

At last Avandra parlayed between the two factions. To settle the argument between Pelor and Zehir, she offered day and night. As a compromise between Khala and Pelor, she proposed alternating seasons of summer and winter. The gods, weary of their quarrels, agreed. Pelor abides faithfully by his agreement with Zehir, but from time to time Zehir seeks to shadow the sun during daytime with an eclipse. Khala is no more, but the Raven Queen—who holds sway over winter now—honors the ancient pact. Yet she also tests Pelor's resolve, seeking to end summers early and delaying springs as long as she can. In this way, autumn snows and spring thaws can come early or late.

Level 23 Encounter Prayers

Censuring Radiance — Paladin Attack 23

Your weapon sears a sigil into your foe that hinders its attacks against your companions.

Encounter ✦ Divine, Radiant, Weapon
Standard Action **Melee** weapon
Target: One creature
Attack: Charisma vs. Fortitude
Hit: 3[W] + Strength modifier radiant damage. Until the end of your next turn, whenever the target makes an attack that doesn't include you as a target, the target is weakened for that attack.

Champion's Call — Paladin Attack 23

You funnel your devotion into a mighty yell that drags your foes to you and leaves them reeling.

Encounter ✦ Divine, Implement, Thunder
Standard Action **Close** burst 5
Primary Target: Each enemy in burst
Effect: You pull each primary target 5 squares and then make the following attack.
Secondary Target: Each enemy adjacent to you
Attack: Strength vs. Will
Hit: 2d8 + Strength modifier thunder damage. If the secondary target is marked by you, it is also immobilized until the end of your next turn.

Demand Respect — Paladin Attack 23

You visit divine punishment on a foe that attacks your friends, bowing it beneath your god's displeasure.

Encounter ✦ Divine, Implement, Radiant
Immediate Interrupt **Close** burst 10
Trigger: An enemy makes an attack that does not include you as a target
Target: The triggering enemy in burst
Attack: Charisma vs. Will
Hit: 2d10 + Charisma modifier radiant damage, and you knock the target prone. The target is also blinded until the end of your next turn.

Resurgent Wrath — Paladin Attack 23

Your furious attack unleashes divine might that revitalizes you and an ally.

Encounter ✦ Divine, Healing, Weapon
Standard Action **Melee** weapon
Target: One creature
Attack: Charisma vs. AC
Hit: 3[W] + Charisma modifier damage. You and one ally adjacent to you can each choose to do one of the following things:
- ✦ Spend a healing surge (and regain additional hit points equal to twice your Wisdom modifier if the attack deals at least 30 damage).
- ✦ Make a saving throw (with a bonus equal to your Wisdom modifier if the attack deals at least 30 damage).

Trial of Adversity — Paladin Attack 23

You confer determination and discipline on your allies, drawing on their strength to steady your hand.

Encounter ✦ Divine, Weapon
Standard Action **Melee** weapon
Target: One creature
Effect: Before the attack, you and each ally within 5 squares of you make a saving throw. You gain a +1 bonus to the attack roll and the damage roll for each ally who saves against an effect.
Attack: Strength or Charisma vs. AC
Hit: 4[W] + Strength or Charisma modifier damage.

Level 25 Daily Prayers

Discipline the Unruly — Paladin Attack 25

Blinding radiance explodes from your weapon as you strike, searing foes who dare to attack your comrades.

Daily ✦ Divine, Radiant, Weapon
Standard Action **Melee** weapon
Target: One creature
Attack: Charisma vs. AC
Hit: 3[W] + Charisma modifier radiant damage.
Effect: Until the end of your next turn, any enemy within 5 squares of you that hits or misses any ally takes 4d6 radiant damage and is blinded until the end of your next turn.
Sustain Minor: The effect persists.

Harsh Verdict — Paladin Attack 25

You judge one of your enemies in the name of your god, and none of its companions can hide from your wrath.

Daily ✦ Divine, Radiant, Weapon
Standard Action **Melee** weapon
Primary Target: One creature
Primary Attack: Charisma vs. Will
Hit: 3[W] + Strength modifier damage.
Miss: Half damage.
Effect: Make a secondary attack that is a close burst 1 centered on the primary target.
Secondary Target: The primary target and each enemy in burst
Secondary Attack: Charisma vs. Will
Hit: The secondary target takes ongoing 10 radiant damage and cannot benefit from concealment or total concealment (save ends both).

Mark of Weakness — Paladin Attack 25

Your divinely inspired attack enfeebles your foe.

Daily ✦ Divine, Weapon
Standard Action **Melee** weapon
Target: One creature
Attack: Strength vs. AC
Hit: 3[W] + Strength modifier damage, and the target is weakened and subject to your divine sanction (save ends both).
Miss: Half damage, and the target is weakened until the end of your next turn.

Spurn the Unworthy — Paladin Attack 25

You slap down a foe that keeps you from greater enemies.

Daily ✦ Divine, Weapon
Standard Action **Melee** weapon
Target: One creature
Attack: Strength vs. AC
Hit: 3[W] + Strength modifier damage, and you knock the target prone.
Miss: Half damage.
Effect: You and the target swap places. Until the end of the encounter, your melee basic attacks deal 1[W] extra damage.

Level 27 Encounter Prayers

Ardent Judgment — Paladin Attack 27

As you strike your foe, the power of your sacred vow shatters its resilience.

Encounter ✦ Divine, Weapon
Standard Action **Melee** weapon
Target: One creature
Attack: Strength vs. AC. If the target is marked by you, you gain a +2 bonus to the attack roll, and you can score a critical hit on a roll of 18-20.
Hit: 2[W] + Strength modifier damage. If you have used *ardent vow* during this encounter, the target also gains vulnerable 10 to all damage until the end of your next turn.

Astral Thunderbolt — Paladin Attack 27

The power of the dominions rings through your strike, and you raise your symbol to hurl divine thunder at a nearby foe.

Encounter ✦ Divine, Thunder, Weapon
Standard Action **Melee** weapon
Primary Target: One creature
Primary Attack: Charisma vs. Fortitude
Hit: 4[W] + Charisma modifier thunder damage. The primary target is slowed and takes a -2 penalty to attack rolls until the end of your next turn. Make a secondary attack that is a close burst 10 using your implement.
Secondary Target: One creature in burst
Secondary Attack: Charisma vs. Fortitude
Hit: 3d8 + Charisma modifier thunder damage, and the secondary target takes a -2 penalty to attack rolls until the end of your next turn.

Overwhelming Smite — Paladin Attack 27

The shining hand of the divine guides your weapon, and none can ignore you.

Encounter ✦ Divine, Radiant, Weapon
Standard Action **Melee** weapon
Target: One creature
Attack: Strength vs. AC
Hit: 4[W] + Strength modifier radiant damage, and each enemy adjacent to you is subject to your divine sanction until the end of your next turn.

Terrible Charge — Paladin Attack 27

Your fervor drives you into the fray and strikes terror into your enemy.

Encounter ✦ Divine, Fear, Weapon
Standard Action **Melee** 1
Effect: You charge and make the following attack in place of a melee basic attack.
Target: One creature
Attack: Strength vs. AC
Hit: 3[W] + Strength modifier damage, and the target is stunned until the end of your next turn.

Wrathful Flame — Paladin Attack 27

Pure blue fire blazes from your holy symbol to devastate foes around you.

Encounter ✦ Divine, Fire, Implement
Standard Action **Close** burst 5
Target: Each enemy in burst
Attack: Charisma vs. Reflex
Hit: 4d8 + Charisma modifier fire damage. If the target is marked by you, it is also dazed until the end of your next turn.

Level 29 Daily Prayers

Day of Reckoning — Paladin Attack 29

Like an agent of vengeance, you appear beside your foe to deliver the killing blow.

Daily ✦ Divine, Teleportation, Weapon
Standard Action **Melee** 1
Effect: You teleport 10 squares to a square adjacent to a creature marked by you.
Target: One creature marked by you
Attack: Strength vs. AC
Hit: 6[W] + Strength modifier damage.
Miss: Half damage.

Devastating Surge — Paladin Attack 29

You give of your own vitality to heal an ally and wound an enemy.

Daily ✦ Divine, Healing, Weapon
Standard Action **Melee** weapon
Requirement: You must have at least one healing surge remaining.
Effect: You spend a healing surge but do not regain hit points. Choose an ally within 10 squares of you. That ally regains hit points equal to your healing surge value. Then make the following attack.
Target: One creature
Attack: Strength vs. AC
Hit: The target takes damage equal to your healing surge value + your Strength modifier.
Miss: Half damage.

Name of Awe — Paladin Attack 29

You utter an ancient name of such power that your enemies are rooted to the spot, unable to escape.

Daily ✦ Divine, Implement, Thunder
Standard Action **Close** blast 5
Target: Each enemy in blast
Attack: Charisma vs. Fortitude
Hit: 5d8 + Charisma modifier thunder damage, and the target is immobilized and weakened (save ends both).
Miss: Half damage, and the target is slowed (save ends).
Effect: Each target is subject to your divine sanction until the end of your next turn.

Prostration — Paladin Attack 29

In a resounding voice, you command the respect of your enemies.

Daily ✦ Divine, Lightning, Thunder, Weapon
Standard Action **Close** burst 1
Target: Each enemy in burst
Attack: Strength vs. Reflex
Hit: 4[W] + Strength modifier lightning and thunder damage.
Miss: Half damage.
Effect: You knock each target prone.

Sanctioned Slaughter — Paladin Attack 29

Your god demands your enemy's blood, and your weapon draws it.

Daily ✦ Divine, Weapon
Standard Action **Melee** weapon
Target: One creature
Attack: Strength vs. AC
Hit: 4[W] + Strength modifier damage, and ongoing 10 damage (save ends).
Miss: Half damage, and ongoing 5 damage (save ends).

Champion of Corellon

"With Corellon's grace I fear no foe in reach of my sword."

Prerequisite: Paladin, must worship Corellon

A knight of the eladrin courts, you are pledged to the service of the lords of the fey. Along with valor and martial skill, you have shown exceptional patience, grace, and compassion—qualities admired in eladrin and elven realms alike. You follow a personal code that resembles the chivalric traditions of the mortal world, but you bring a fey perspective to the concepts of honor, valor, and fidelity. Most knights are obligated to prove their bravery by declining advantages that reduce risk in battle, but you do not scorn the bow, the spell, or the ruse of war when such tactics are effective. You have learned techniques for making the best use of agility and quickness even while wearing the heaviest armor.

Among the eladrin, those who follow this path are known as the *Aelavellin Seldarine*—the Sword Knights of the Seldarine. Most such champions are eladrin, elves, or half-elves, for Corellon is the patron of these peoples. However, any noble warrior devoted to the lord of the Seldarine can become a champion of Corellon. Those champions of Corellon who are of other races find a warm welcome in most eladrin and elven communities and are usually regarded as *ruathar* ("star-friends"), honored allies.

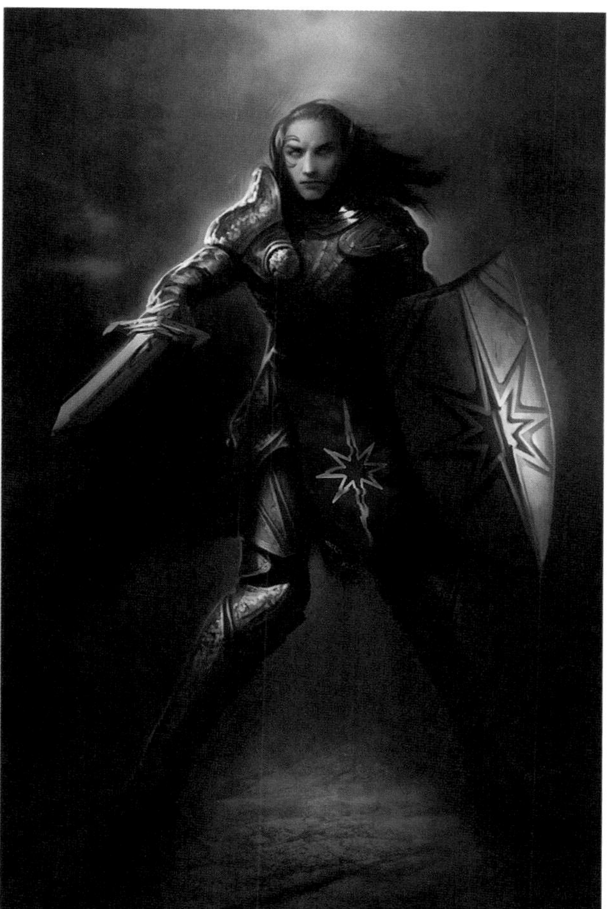

MAZIN KASSIS

Champion of Corellon Path Features

Restorative Action (11th level): When you spend an action point to take an extra action, you can also spend a healing surge.

Superior Defense (11th level): If your Dexterity score is 13 or higher, you gain a +1 bonus to AC while wearing heavy armor. If your Dexterity score is 15 or higher, the bonus is +2.

Light-Footed Warrior (16th level): You ignore the speed penalty for wearing heavy armor. In addition, when you bloody an enemy or reduce it to 0 hit points on your turn, you can shift 1 square as a free action.

Champion of Corellon Prayers

Elegant Strike — Champion of Corellon Attack 11

You move and strike with a dancer's grace, confounding your foe.

Encounter ✦ Divine, Weapon
Standard Action **Melee** weapon
Target: One creature
Attack: Charisma vs. AC
Hit: 3[W] + Charisma modifier damage, and the target is slowed and cannot shift until the end of your next turn.
Weapon: If you are wielding a light blade or a heavy blade, you gain a bonus to the damage roll equal to your Dexterity modifier.

Graceful Step — Champion of Corellon Utility 12

You maneuver with speed and balance that few warriors can match.

Encounter ✦ Divine
Move Action **Personal**
Effect: You shift your speed. During this movement, you ignore difficult terrain and gain a +5 bonus to Acrobatics checks and Athletics checks.

Corellon's Wrath — Champion of Corellon Attack 20

Just as Corellon's blade once took the eye of Gruumsh, so too does your weapon seek your enemy's eyes.

Daily ✦ Divine, Radiant, Weapon
Standard Action **Melee** weapon
Target: One creature
Attack: Charisma vs. Reflex
Hit: 4[W] + Charisma modifier radiant damage, and the target is blinded (save ends).
Miss: Half damage.
Effect: Your opportunity attacks deal 1d10 extra radiant damage until the end of the encounter.

Demonslayer

"Run back to the Abyss and tell them I'm coming. Let them prepare their defenses and raise their armies. I look forward to obliterating them all!"

Prerequisite: Paladin

Embodiments of chaos and cruelty, demons are an affront to your faith, and you seek to destroy them at every opportunity. You have received special blessings and learned battle prayers that are anathema to the denizens of the Abyss. Your attacks pierce their unholy defenses, and simply being near you causes them pain. You won't rest until every demon is dead.

All but the darkest and most vile of gods regard demons as a blight upon the cosmos and urge their followers to root out demonic threats wherever they appear. Most well-organized faiths support orders devoted to confronting demons; some anoint demonslayers from among the ranks of the faithful using ancient rituals.

Demonslayer Path Features

Demonslayer's Presence (11th level): Any demon that starts its turn adjacent to you takes damage equal to your Wisdom modifier. While any demon is adjacent to you, it can't shift.

Demonslayer's Action (11th level): When you spend an action point to make an attack, the attack deals extra damage equal to one-half your level and ignores resistances.

Suppress Resistance (16th level): When you hit a creature that has variable resistance with a melee attack, you negate the resistance until the end of the creature's next turn.

Demonslayer Prayers

Demonslayer's Smite — Demonslayer Attack 11

You intone a prayer over your weapon, empowering it to overwhelm demonic defenses.

Encounter ✦ Divine, Weapon
Standard Action **Melee** weapon
Target: One creature
Attack: Strength vs. AC. If the target is a demon, you gain a +2 bonus to the attack roll.
Hit: 3[W] + Strength modifier damage, and the target loses its resistances until the end of your next turn.
Special: Whenever a demon within 10 squares of you scores a critical hit or spends an action point, you regain the use of this power.

Demonslayer's Resistance — Demonslayer Utility 12

A gleaming halo surrounds you and blunts the attacks of your demonic foes.

Daily ✦ Divine
Immediate Interrupt **Personal**
Trigger: An enemy hits you
Effect: You gain resist 5 against damage dealt by the triggering enemy until the end of the encounter. If the triggering enemy is a demon, the resistance increases to 10, and the enemy is subject to your divine sanction until the end of the encounter.
Level 21: Resist 10, or resist 15 if the triggering enemy is a demon.

Edict of Destruction — Demonslayer Attack 20

You recite words of divine law as you attack, twisting your prey's very being.

Daily ✦ Divine, Weapon
Standard Action **Melee** weapon
Target: One creature
Attack: Strength vs. AC
Hit: 3[W] + Strength modifier damage, and the target is affected by your edict of destruction (save ends). Until the edict ends, roll a d4 at the start of each of the target's turns to determine the edict's effect at that time. If the target is a demon, roll two times and apply both results (if you roll the same number twice, roll again).
1. The target and each enemy adjacent to it take 1d10 + your Strength modifier damage.
2. The target gains vulnerable 5 to all damage until the end of your next turn.
3. The target is blinded until the end of your next turn.
4. The target takes a -2 penalty to attack rolls until the end of your next turn.
Miss: Half damage. At the start of the target's next turn, roll a d4 to determine the effect, as above.

AMELIA STONER

Dragonslayer

"My sword, my shield, and my faith are all I need to confront the most terrifying monsters."

Prerequisite: Paladin

A champion must fight many monsters, and the most savage and ferocious of these are dragons. They sport a daunting arsenal of claws, fangs, stings, roars, and breath weapons, and they are protected by iron-hard scales and supernatural vitality. Many also have a wicked, calculating intelligence. Few warriors stand a chance against such foes, but you have made it your duty to protect defenseless folk against their depredations. You seek out all destructive monsters–including other fantastic beasts such as manticores, wyverns, and sphinxes–and put an end to their reigns of terror.

You might be a hunter of some skill, but you do not rely on patient stalking, trap-setting, or sudden ambush to defeat your sworn enemies. You meet monsters openly in chivalrous combat, pitting your skill and courage against fiery breath and flashing fang. It's a fair fight.

Dragonslayer Path Features

Dragonslayer's Action (11th level): When you spend an action point to take an extra action, you also gain a +2 bonus to all defenses against creatures marked by you. This bonus lasts until the end of your next turn.

Dragonslayer's Challenge (11th level): The first time you mark a target during an encounter, you gain a +2 bonus to damage rolls against that target until that mark ends. The bonus increases to +4 at 21st level.

True Heart (16th level): You gain a +2 bonus to Will against fear effects.

Dragonslayer Prayers

Challenging Smite — Dragonslayer Attack 11

Your strike demands the attention of your chosen enemy, and that enemy ignores you at its peril.

Encounter ✦ Divine, Weapon
Standard Action **Melee** weapon
Target: One creature marked by you
Attack: Charisma vs. AC
Hit: 3[W] + Charisma modifier damage. Until the start of your next turn, your divine sanction and *divine challenge* deal 10 extra radiant damage.

Deflect the Blast — Dragonslayer Utility 12

You take shelter behind your trusty shield, protecting a nearby friend as well.

Encounter ✦ Divine
Immediate Interrupt **Melee** 1
Trigger: A close or an area attack against AC or Reflex damages you
Requirement: You must be using a shield.
Effect: You take only half damage from the triggering attack. The damage is also halved against one adjacent ally who took damage from the triggering attack.

Ground the Foe — Dragonslayer Attack 20

The power of your prayer hurls your foe to the ground.

Daily ✦ Divine, Force, Implement
Standard Action **Ranged** 10
Target: One creature
Attack: Charisma + 2 vs. Reflex
Hit: 5d6 + Charisma modifier force damage, and the target is knocked prone and immobilized (save ends).
Aftereffect: The target is slowed and cannot fly (save ends both).
Miss: Half damage. The target is slowed and is clumsy while flying (save ends both).

Faithful Shield

"Behind me, friends! They shall not touch you."

Prerequisite: Paladin

You are a living bulwark, protecting the defenseless. You are the shelter in the storm. As a faithful shield, you place your companions' well-being above your own.

Faithful shields are supreme examples of devout warriors, found in most of the world's faiths. Such warriors safeguard holy sites and divine servants. Others set out into the world to lend their talents to those who need it most, whether the folk of a frontier town surrounded by enemies or a band of adventurers working to thwart a dire threat.

Rather than focusing on dealing damage, you give your companions the time they need to win through. You might partner with another defender, forming an impregnable wall, or work with a trusted striker, blocking enemy attacks and creating openings for your ally. When your group is hard pressed, you might cover the retreat, slowly giving ground while your friends flee to safety.

Faithful Shield Path Features

Sheltering Hands (11th level): Whenever you use your *lay on hands* power, the power's target gains a +2 power bonus to all defenses until the start of his or her next turn.

Shielding Action (11th level): When you spend an action point to take an extra action, you and each ally within 5 squares of you also gain a +2 bonus to AC and Reflex until the start of your next turn.

Defensive Presence (16th level): When any ally within 5 squares of you takes the second wind or the total defense action, any enemy that hits that ally before the end of his or her next turn takes radiant damage equal to 5 + your Wisdom modifier.

Faithful Shield Prayers

Protecting Smite — Faithful Shield Attack 11

A decisive strike against your enemy gives your allies a chance to see to their own defense.

Encounter ✦ Divine, Weapon
Standard Action **Melee** weapon
Target: One creature
Attack: Charisma vs. AC
Hit: 2[W] + Charisma modifier damage, and each ally within 5 squares of you gains a +2 power bonus to all defenses until the start of your next turn.

Constant Shield — Faithful Shield Utility 12

You channel divine might through your shield to defend yourself and your charges.

Daily ✦ Divine, Stance
Minor Action **Personal**
Requirement: You must be using a shield.
Effect: Until the stance ends, you and any allies adjacent to you gain a +2 power bonus to AC and Reflex. In addition, when you or any ally adjacent to you is pulled, pushed, or slid, you can reduce the forced movement by 1 square.

Rampart of Strength — Faithful Shield Attack 20

You raise your shield, and from it bursts scintillating astral radiance that drives back your foes.

Daily ✦ Divine, Implement, Radiant
Standard Action **Close** burst 5
Requirement: You must be using a shield.
Target: Each enemy in burst
Attack: Charisma vs. Fortitude
Hit: 3d8 + Charisma modifier radiant damage, and you push the target 3 squares.
Miss: Half damage, and you push the target 1 square.
Effect: Until the end of the encounter, at the start of each of your turns, if you have not moved since the start of your last turn, you can use a free action to grant yourself and each ally adjacent to you a +4 power bonus to all defenses until the start of your next turn.

KIERAN YANNER

Gray Guard

"Do whatever it takes to get the job done, and worry about the moral questions later."

Prerequisite: Paladin, trained in Insight and Intimidate

As a paladin, you cleave to principles that guide you through life, shaping your worldview and forming your moral foundation. Even if you don't follow a code of behavior, you follow the precepts of your god and work to live up to your faith's expectations. Yet the enemy never plays fair. Sometimes rules must be bent, or even broken, for the greater good.

No one knows this better than you, a gray guard. You have made a career of defying expectations and making the tough choices that your peers avoid. For you, the ends justify the means—even stealing, lying, or brutal interrogation. You do what you must to defeat the enemy. Your tactics don't make you popular with others in service to your god. Many see you as dangerous, almost as much of a threat as your enemies. Let them say what they will. You know that, deep down, they fear you and might even respect you.

WILLIAM O'CONNOR

As you continue down this path, you might feel estranged from your god, a disappointment to the one for whom you have sacrificed so much. The blood staining your hands has somehow darkened your soul, although your abilities are unaffected. But you do what you must.

Gray Guard Path Features

Gray Guard Action (11th level): When you spend an action point to take an extra action, you can also shift 3 squares as a free action. In addition, you gain a +2 bonus to attack rolls until the start of your next turn.

Gray Guard Vigilance (11th level): You are trained in Perception and Streetwise. In addition, enemies marked by you cannot benefit from concealment or total concealment against your attacks.

Demoralizing Critical (16th level): When you score a critical hit, the enemy nearest to the target takes a -2 penalty to attack rolls and all defenses until the end of your next turn.

Gray Guard Prayers

Debilitating Smite — Gray Guard Attack 11

So painful is the injury to your enemy that it can barely continue to fight.

Encounter ✦ Divine, Weapon
Standard Action — **Melee** weapon
Target: One creature
Attack: Strength vs. AC
Hit: 2[W] + Strength modifier damage, and the target is dazed and slowed until the end of your next turn. If the target makes an attack before then, it is dazed until the end of its next turn.

Relentless Justice — Gray Guard Utility 12

You persevere in your attacks until you make an enemy pay.

Encounter ✦ Divine
Free Action — **Personal**
Trigger: You do not hit with a paladin encounter attack power
Effect: You regain the use of one paladin encounter attack power that you have used during this encounter.

Devastating Smite — Gray Guard Attack 20

Divine power charges your strike, tearing through your foe and opening it to your ally's attack.

Daily ✦ Divine, Reliable, Weapon
Standard Action — **Melee** weapon
Target: One creature
Attack: Strength vs. AC
Hit: 4[W] + Strength modifier damage. You can expend a use of your *lay on hands* power (or a power that you took in place of it) to cause the attack to deal extra damage equal to your healing surge value. Until the end of your next turn, the target grants combat advantage to one ally within 5 squares of you.

Hammer of Moradin

"I strike in the name of the Soul Forger. Let my enemies taste Moradin's wrath!"

Prerequisite: Cleric or paladin, proficiency with warhammer or throwing hammer, must worship Moradin

As a devotee of Moradin, you have dedicated yourself to the destruction of your god's traditional enemies and the protection of his faith. In return for your dedication, Moradin lends strength to your hand and shields you with his power. In some lands, hammers of Moradin form an elite knightly order of clerics and paladins who defend dwarven citadels. Others are solitary agents of order who use their powers to protect the weak and confront injustice wherever they encounter it.

Although many hammers of Moradin are dwarves, any hero who wields Moradin's divine power is free to choose this path. Champions of many races turn to Moradin for the strength to hold back evil and defeat the wicked. Human knights, eladrin swordsmiths, and dragonborn battle-priests are all numbered among the hammers of Moradin.

Hammer of Moradin Path Features

Hammer Bond (11th level): You gain a +1 bonus to attack rolls with hammers.

Powerful Action (11th level): When you spend an action point to make an attack, each target hit by the attack is knocked prone or dazed until the end of your next turn. You choose the effect for each target after the attack's other effects are resolved.

Champion's Aura (16th level): You and any allies within 3 squares of you gain a +4 bonus to all defenses against fear effects.

Hammer of Moradin Prayers

Hammer Throw — Hammer of Moradin Attack 11

You hurl your hammer. It bashes one foe and spins through the air to knock another to the ground before returning to your hand.

Encounter ✦ Divine, Weapon
Standard Action **Ranged** 10
Requirement: You must be wielding a hammer.
Primary Target: One creature
Primary Attack: Strength vs. Fortitude
Hit: 2[W] + Strength modifier damage, and the target is dazed until the end of your next turn. Make a secondary attack.
Secondary Target: One creature within 3 squares of the primary target
Secondary Attack: Strength vs. Fortitude
Hit: 1[W] + Strength modifier damage, and you knock the secondary target prone.
Special: When you use this power, you can make the attacks as if your hammer was a heavy thrown weapon. The hammer returns to your hand after the attacks are resolved.

Stalwart Defense — Hammer of Moradin Utility 12

Moradin's power shields you from the onslaught of your foes.

Daily ✦ Divine, Stance
Minor Action **Personal**
Effect: Until the stance ends, you gain resist 5 to all damage and a +2 bonus to Fortitude.

Quake Strike — Hammer of Moradin Attack 20

You slam your hammer to the ground, unleashing an earthquake that represents Moradin's wrath.

Daily ✦ Divine, Thunder, Weapon, Zone
Standard Action **Close** blast 5
Requirement: You must be wielding a hammer.
Target: Each creature in blast
Attack: Strength vs. Fortitude
Hit: 2[W] + Strength modifier thunder damage, and you knock the target prone.
Effect: The burst creates a zone of difficult terrain that lasts until the end of the encounter.

RALPH BEISNER

Holy Conqueror

"No wall is too high and no moat too wide to protect a villain from my wrath. Bastions of evil cannot stand before me."

Prerequisite: Paladin, *ardent vow* power

WILLIAM O'CONNOR

You are a divine warrior in service to a deity of order and righteousness, looking beyond the immediate threat of evil to its source. You set mighty goals of triumph, such as the overthrow of a terrible tyrant or the fall of a nation of villains, to tear power from your deity's enemies and give it to the deserving. You have no interest in possessing a territory and seek to preserve governance by virtuous rulers.

You are single-minded in your pursuit of a goal and go to almost any length to achieve it, and you are better suited to the role of a frontline soldier than a leader. You prefer to charge into battle, using *ardent vow* to smite your foes. You have little patience for negotiation and can be impulsive to a fault.

Holy conquerors often worship Bahamut, Kord, or Pelor, glorifying their god with each victory in battle. Many have strong connections to specific locations that were seized in battle or that hold particular religious significance.

Holy Conqueror Path Features

Holy Rebuke (11th level): When you deal extra damage with your *ardent vow,* you also push the target 1 square. As a free action, you can shift 1 square closer to the target.

Divine Fortification (11th level): When you spend an action point to take an extra action, each enemy adjacent to you is subject to your divine sanction until the end of your next turn.

Hold the Line (16th level): When you or any ally adjacent to you is pulled, pushed, or slid, you can use a free action to reduce the forced movement by a number of squares equal to one-half your Strength modifier.

Holy Conqueror Prayers

Charge of the Conqueror — Holy Conqueror Attack 11

As an enemy launches an attack at your comrade, you give a defiant yell and charge across the battlefield at the foe.

Encounter ✦ Divine, Weapon
Immediate Interrupt **Melee weapon**
Trigger: An enemy makes an attack roll against your ally within 5 squares of you
Effect: You charge the triggering enemy and make the following attack in place of a melee basic attack.
Target: The triggering enemy
Attack: Strength vs. AC
Hit: 2[W] + Strength modifier damage.
Effect: The target is subject to your divine sanction until the start of your next turn.

Sacrificial Intervention — Holy Conqueror Utility 12

You appeal to your god and leap to take the wound meant for an ally, condemning the foe for its insolence.

Encounter ✦ Divine, Teleportation
Immediate Interrupt **Close burst 5**
Trigger: An enemy hits your ally within 5 squares of you with a melee or a ranged attack
Target: The ally hit by the triggering enemy's attack
Effect: You and the target teleport, swapping positions. The triggering enemy's attack hits you instead. Until the end of the encounter, whenever you end your turn adjacent to the triggering enemy, it is subject to your divine sanction until the end of your next turn.

Take the Keep — Holy Conqueror Attack 20

You cry out, urging your foes to attack you. Your shout encourages your allies to seize enemy ground.

Daily ✦ Divine, Weapon
Standard Action **Close** burst 3
Target: Each enemy in burst
Effect: You pull each target to a square adjacent to you, and each target is subject to your divine sanction until the end of your next turn. Each ally in the burst can shift a number of squares equal to your Wisdom modifier as a free action but cannot end this movement closer to you. You then make the following melee attack.
Target: Each enemy adjacent to you
Attack: Strength vs. AC
Hit: 3[W] + Strength modifier damage.
Miss: Half damage.

Knight of the Chalice

"Begone, devils! You have no power here!"

Prerequisite: Paladin

Devils scheme amid the layers of the Nine Hells and infest the world with evil. You are sworn to protect innocents from their infernal machinations. To this end, you have joined an order of like-minded warriors.

The Knights of the Chalice take their order's name from an artifact belonging to the deity slain by Asmodeus when he ascended to godhood. It is rumored that with a single draught of water from the chalice of that deity, the drinker can atone for any wrong and completely purify his or her soul. Some say that drinking from the cup can turn any being, even Asmodeus himself, from evil to good. Whether or not these tales of these legendary properties are true, the chalice is undoubtedly a powerful artifact for good, and many Knights of the Chalice seek it. Some pursue a loftier goal still: to resurrect the chalice's divine owner and restore him to his throne.

As a Knight of the Chalice, you remain vigilant for any signs of infernal activity. You aid all of good heart who stand in the path of devilish influence, and you answer the call of your fellow knights when the powers of the Nine Hells gather in force.

Knight of the Chalice Path Features

Censure Devils (11th level): You gain the Channel Divinity power *censure devils*.

Saving Action (11th level): When you spend an action point to take an extra action, you also make a saving throw against each effect on you that a save can end. If an effect was caused by a devil, you gain a +2 bonus to the saving throw against that effect.

Aura Suppression (16th level): When you hit any creature marked by you that has an aura, the aura is deactivated. The creature cannot reactivate the aura before the end of your next turn.

Knight of the Chalice Prayers

Channel Divinity: Censure Devils — Knight of the Chalice Feature

The power of your faith pains your diabolical enemies.

Encounter ✦ Divine, Implement
Minor Action — **Close** burst 5
Target: Each devil in burst
Attack: Charisma vs. Will
Hit: The target is weakened until the end of your next turn.

Ensnaring Smite — Knight of the Chalice Attack 11

You bind your foe with ancient magic used to imprison devils.

Encounter ✦ Divine, Weapon
Standard Action — **Melee** weapon
Target: One creature
Attack: Charisma vs. AC
Hit: 1[W] + Charisma modifier damage, and the target is restrained until the end of your next turn. If the target is a devil marked by you, it takes 1[W] extra damage and can't teleport (save ends).

Heavenly Courage — Knight of the Chalice Utility 12

Honeyed words and malicious threats have no effect on you but bring punishment to your foes.

Encounter ✦ Divine, Radiant
No Action — **Personal**
Trigger: You fail a saving throw against acharm or fear effect
Effect: You reroll the saving throw. If you save, the enemy that caused the charm or fear effect takes radiant damage equal to your Charisma modifier.

Blessing of the Chalice — Knight of the Chalice Attack 20

Invoking the power of your order's oath, you infuse your blade with holy light to thwart your enemy.

Daily ✦ Divine, Radiant, Weapon
Standard Action — **Melee** weapon
Target: One creature
Attack: Charisma vs. AC
Hit: 4[W] + Charisma modifier radiant damage, and the target takes a -2 penalty to attack rolls (save ends). If the target is a devil, it also takes ongoing 10 radiant damage (save ends).
Miss: Half damage, and the target takes a -2 penalty to attack rolls until the end of your next turn.

MICHAEL PHILLIPPI

Questing Knight

"I measure my worth by that which I seek."

Prerequisite: Paladin

You have sworn a sacred vow to pursue a great quest that has challenged the devotion of divine champions for centuries.

As a questing knight, you must meet your god's demanding standards to prove yourself worthy of success. Depending on the nature of your deity, you might have to demonstrate outstanding courage, perseverance, humility, indomitability, wisdom, honor, fury, or piety. The object of the quest could be a lost relic, a hidden oracle, the words of a holy verse now forgotten, the destruction of an artifact inimical to your god, or the defeat of a legendary foe.

Because the trail leading to your ultimate goal sometimes grows cold, you need not abandon your current concerns entirely. Continue with your adventures, and strive to be the best you can be, but watch carefully for signs and portents that lead you onward in your quest.

Questing Knight Path Features

Resolute Action (11th level): When you spend an action point to take an extra action, you also make a saving throw with a +2 bonus.

Truth Sense (11th level): You gain a +2 bonus to Will against charm, fear, and illusion effects and a +2 bonus to Insight checks.

Knight's Resurgence (16th level): While you are bloodied, you can use your second wind as a free action on your turn.

For the DM: Devising a Quest

If a player chooses this path, you should provide a challenging quest that allows the other party members to contribute. A good structure is three clues scattered through adventures during the paragon tier.

For example, if the questing knight is seeking a lost crown, you might design a quest that ultimately leads to a crypt below a ruined castle. The first clue could be a signet ring belonging to a noble who served the ancient ruler, found among treasure in an otherwise unrelated adventure. The second clue might be a fresco in an abandoned shrine, depicting the noble wearing the ring and relating his story to a scribe. The third clue might be the scribe's long-lost book, which contains the name of the castle where the crown now lies.

Clues can serve as excellent hooks for intermediate adventures. For example, after finding the signet ring, some research might lead the questing knight to an old account of a traveler who visited the ancient noble's palace, which just happens to lie near the locale where you have set the party's next adventure.

EMRAH ELMASLI

Questing Knight Prayers

Strength of Ten — Questing Knight Attack 11

Your conviction lends you the force to repel nearby foes.

Encounter ✦ Divine, Force, Weapon
Standard Action — **Close** blast 3
Target: Each enemy in blast
Attack: Charisma vs. Fortitude
Hit: 2[W] + Charisma modifier force damage, and you push the target 3 squares. The target is also subject to your divine sanction until the start of your next turn.
Effect: After the attack, you shift to a square within the blast.

Quester's Discipline — Questing Knight Utility 12

Deceit, despair, and weakness find no purchase in your heart.

Daily ✦ Divine
No Action — **Personal**
Trigger: An attack that would blind, daze, dominate, stun, or weaken you hits you
Effect: The triggering attack's conditions are negated against you.

Virtuous Wrath — Questing Knight Attack 20

Your unflinching dedication is a dreadful bane to your enemies, who recoil from the strike.

Daily ✦ Divine, Fear, Reliable, Weapon
Standard Action — **Melee** weapon
Target: One creature
Attack: Charisma vs. Will
Hit: [4W] + Charisma modifier damage, and you push the target 5 squares. The target is weakened (save ends).

Scion of Sacrifice

"Your threats are meaningless to me. Nothing you say can save you from death at my hands."

Prerequisite: Paladin, *ardent vow* power

The core of your values and the code you follow are rooted in your willingness to give your life for a greater purpose. Your body and soul are strong, and you do not shrink from giving up some of that strength to help others. You strike out with divine fury that racks you with pain but imbues you with even greater strength. You measure your worth by the foes you defeat.

As a scion of sacrifice, you are zealous in the extreme, eager to meet the enemies of your faith regardless of the circumstances. When others pause and deliberate, you act—for better or for worse. However, you are not suicidal. If you encounter a foe clearly beyond your ability to defeat, you retreat to work toward the day when your power matches the enemy's. Or you might turn aside to aid companions who are in danger, or withdraw to carry the injured away from battle. But in most fights you are grim and fearless. Whether you fall in the effort to defeat a mighty foe or survive to face a new threat tomorrow lies in the hands of your god.

Scion of Sacrifice Path Features

Devastating Action (11th level): When you spend an action point to make an attack, the attack deals extra damage equal to your Charisma modifier. If you are bloodied, you also add your Wisdom modifier to the damage.

Unflinching Persistence (11th level): You gain an additional use of *ardent vow* each day.

Martyr's Strike (16th level): When an attack reduces you to 0 hit points or fewer, you can use an at-will attack power before falling unconscious.

Scion of Sacrifice Prayers

Scion's Sanction — Scion of Sacrifice Attack 11

You lash out against foes around you and dare them to strike back.

Encounter ✦ Divine, Weapon
Standard Action — **Close** burst 1
Effect: Before the attack, you can take damage equal to your level, which can't be reduced in any way. If you do so, the attack deals 2[W] extra damage.
Target: Each enemy in burst
Attack: Charisma vs. AC
Hit: 2[W] + Charisma modifier damage.
Effect: Each target is subject to your divine sanction until the start of your next turn.

Scion's Healing — Scion of Sacrifice Utility 12

You offer up part of your life force to restore your wounded ally.

Daily ✦ Divine, Healing
Minor Action — **Close** burst 10
Target: One ally in burst
Effect: You take damage equal to your level, which can't be reduced in any way. The target regains hit points equal to his or her healing surge value.

Punishing Flame — Scion of Sacrifice Attack 20

Divine flames flood over you, consuming nearby foes in a pyre of retribution.

Daily ✦ Divine, Fire, Implement
Standard Action — **Close** burst 3
Target: Each enemy in burst
Attack: Charisma vs. Reflex
Hit: 5d8 + Charisma modifier fire damage.
Miss: Half damage.
Effect: Until the end of the encounter, when any enemy within 5 squares of you deals damage (not ongoing damage) to any ally, that enemy takes fire damage equal to your Charisma modifier.

AMELIA STONER

Slayer of the Dead

"Stay in your graves, hungry dead! Or when I am done with you there will be nothing left to rebury."

Prerequisite: Paladin

The undead that crawl out of the earth and shamble from chill barrows are an unnatural blight upon the land. You have taken up the charge of destroying these horrors with the brilliant light of your faith. The undead are no longer the people they once were, and sending them back to their graves is the only way to respect those whose corpses walk again in undeath.

You were appointed to your holy task after undergoing sacred rituals and learning ancient prayers that invest you with the power to eradicate the walking dead. This paragon path is well suited to followers of Pelor, god of the sun and enemy of the creatures of darkness. Paladins of Ioun too are dedicated to foiling the plans of Vecna, who is the god of undeath as well as the keeper of foul secrets. However, many deities encourage their followers to dispatch the undead as violations of divine law, so slayer traditions are strong among the devotees of many gods.

Slayer of the Dead Path Features

Incandescent Action (11th level): When you spend an action point to make an attack, that attack deals extra radiant damage equal to 5 + your Wisdom modifier against the first target hit by it.

Scorn the Dead (11th level): You gain resist necrotic equal to 5 + your Strength modifier. The resistance increases to 10 + your Strength modifier at 21st level.

Slayer's Presence (16th level): When you bloody any undead creature or reduce it to 0 hit points, each enemy within 5 squares of you takes a -2 penalty to attack rolls until the end of your next turn. This is a fear effect.

Slayer of the Dead Prayers

Light of the Living — Slayer of the Dead Attack 11

Your strike flares with holy radiance, which sears nearby undead.

Encounter ✦ Divine, Radiant, Weapon
Standard Action **Melee** weapon
Target: One creature
Attack: Strength vs. AC
Hit: 3[W] + Strength modifier radiant damage. Each undead creature within 5 squares of you takes radiant damage equal to your Strength modifier and is subject to your divine sanction until the end of your next turn.

Life and Death Entwined — Slayer of the Dead Utility 12

The undead horror strikes at you, but your divine patron foils its loathsome touch and turns its aggression against it.

Daily ✦ Divine, Radiant
Immediate Interrupt **Personal**
Trigger: An undead enemy hits you
Target: The triggering enemy
Effect: You take no damage from the target's attack. Your next attack against the target deals extra radiant damage equal to one-half the damage you would have taken from the target's attack.

Bury the Dead — Slayer of the Dead Attack 20

The light of life gleams around you as you command the restless dead to return to their graves.

Daily ✦ Divine, Implement, Radiant
Standard Action **Close** burst 2
Target: Each creature in burst
Attack: Strength vs. Reflex
Hit: 4d8 + Strength modifier radiant damage. If the target is undead, it is also restrained (save ends).
Miss: Half damage.

MATIAS TAPIA

CHAPTER 5

Divine Options

ONE OF the most distinctive features of any DUNGEONS & DRAGONS campaign world is its pantheon, the collection of deities available for player characters, villains, and monsters to follow or oppose. Just as there are many deities in the D&D pantheon, so too are there many ways for characters to gain the gods' blessings, study their teachings, or demonstrate devotion to them. One dwarf paladin devoted to Pelor might select powers and feats that would be useful to any paladin, while another might choose radiant powers and feats related to them, reflecting Pelor's ascendancy as god of the sun. Both are capable characters, and each is a unique take on what a dwarf paladin of Pelor might look like.

With the options available to you in this chapter, you can customize your divine heroes to your own satisfaction. These options include the following material.

- **Divine Domains:** Deities often have several spheres of influence, represented by divine domains. You have access to feats, including divinity feats, associated with your deity's domains. This chapter presents over thirty divine domains and their related feats.
- **Your Deity and You:** How does your character's deity inform the way he or she thinks and acts? This section provides some roleplaying advice.
- **Divine Backgrounds:** This section provides several brief character backgrounds you can use or adapt to your own divine character.
- **New Feats:** Many new feats are presented here, providing you with new options for customizing your divine character. These include divinity feats related to evil deities, as well as feats specific to the avenger, cleric, invoker, and paladin classes.
- **Epic Destinies:** Ten epic destinies appear in this chapter, including the Chosen, the Saint, and Avatar, a destiny that involves you becoming an embodiment of your deity.
- **New Rituals:** The chapter concludes with several new rituals oriented toward divine characters.

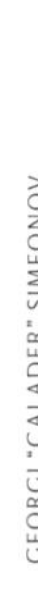

DIVINE DOMAINS

Each deity holds sway over certain aspects of existence. For example, Erathis is the god of cities and nations. She often represents law, order, authority, and invention. Aspects of existence such as these are summed up in domains, spheres of divine influence. Each deity is associated with two or three divine domains.

More than thirty divine domains are presented in this chapter, and the domains of the deities from the *Player's Handbook* and the *Dungeon Master's Guide* are noted. Erathis, for example, is associated with the civilization, creation, and justice domains.

Using Domains

Your divine character gains access to the domains of his or her deity, which means you gain access to those domains' feats. Each divine domain has a divinity feat and a domain feat associated with it. These feats follow the normal rules for feat selection.

If your character worships multiple deities with a common theme (such as the three gods of destiny, Avandra, Ioun, and the Raven Queen), you gain access to all their domains.

Divinity Feats

Characters who have the Channel Divinity class feature can gain additional Channel Divinity powers by taking divinity feats. As long as you have a particular divinity feat, you can use its power.

Domain Feats

Domain feats provide benefits when you use divine at-will attack powers associated with them. Each domain feat notes its associated powers.

If you have more than one domain feat associated with the same power, that power can benefit from only one domain feat at a time. You decide which domain feat applies each time you use the power. For example, if your cleric of Kord has the domain feats Power of Strength and Power of War and uses *priest's shield*, you choose which feat's benefit to apply.

CHANGING DOMAIN CHOICES

With your DM's permission, you can assign different domains to your character's deity. For example, in a campaign rife with giants, your dwarf paladin might choose to worship an aspect of Moradin that represents the ancient dwarven struggle for freedom from the giants. This version of Moradin has the freedom and war domains, instead of the creation and earth domains.

Deities and Domains

These tables show which domains are associated with each deity.

GOOD, LAWFUL GOOD, AND UNALIGNED

Deity	Domains
Avandra	Change, freedom, luck
Bahamut	Hope, justice, protection
Corellon	Arcana, skill, wilderness
Erathis	Civilization, creation, justice
Ioun	Fate, knowledge, skill
Kord	Storm, strength, war
Melora	Life, sea, wilderness
Moradin	Creation, earth, protection
Pelor	Hope, life, sun
The Raven Queen	Death, fate, winter
Sehanine	Love, moon, trickery

EVIL AND CHAOTIC EVIL

Deity	Domains
Asmodeus	Civilization, tyranny
Bane	Skill, war
Gruumsh	Destruction, strength
Lolth	Darkness, trickery
Tharizdun	Destruction, madness
Tiamat	Strife, vengeance
Torog	Earth, torment
Vecna	Knowledge, undeath
Zehir	Darkness, poison

Domain Descriptions

Each divine domain includes two feats associated with it: a domain feat and a divinity feat. The domain feats note which books their associated powers come from: the *Player's Handbook* (PH), *Player's Handbook 2* (PH2), or *Divine Power* (DP).

Arcana

The arcana domain rests securely within Corellon's sphere of influence. Other deities have interests in the arcane realm: Ioun wants to spread arcane knowledge as far as possible, Sehanine delights in arcane powers' potent illusions, and Vecna prefers that the secrets of arcana be granted only to a worthy few.

FOR THE DM: YOUR OWN PANTHEON

If you decide to assign divine domains to a pantheon you created, assign two or three appropriate domains to each deity. The domains' descriptions should help you choose which domains to assign to each deity. It's all right to assign the same domain to more than one deity. For instance, you might have a good deity of the war domain as well as an evil deity of that domain.

In contrast, Corellon glories in all aspects of arcane power and appreciates the use of it as the highest art. Any who create new arcane works or share lost secrets of the art can receive the Master of Magic's blessing, but those who have no dealings with the arcane may discover that Corellon has little interest in them.

As an unaligned deity, Corellon cares more for the elegance and potency of arcane magic than for the morality of its masters, but other gods might have different agendas. An evil deity of arcana might demand that it be used to exert dominance, while a good deity of arcana might command that it be used to seek truth.

Power of Arcana [Domain]

Prerequisite: Any divine class, must worship a deity of the arcana domain

Benefit: You gain a +2 feat bonus to Arcana checks.

When you use a power associated with this feat, that power is arcane as well as divine. After using the power, you gain a +1 bonus to attack rolls with arcane powers until the end of your next turn.

Powers: *divine bolts* (invoker *PH2*), *lance of faith* (cleric *PH*), *radiant vengeance* (avenger *PH2*), *virtuous strike* (paladin *DP*)

Arcana Ward [Divinity]

Prerequisite: Channel Divinity class feature, must worship a deity of the arcana domain

Benefit: You gain the Channel Divinity power *arcana ward*.

Channel Divinity: Arcana Ward — Feat Power

Your god's comprehension of arcane mysteries extends to shielding you from elemental forces.

Encounter ✦ Divine
Immediate Interrupt Personal
Trigger: You are hit by an attack that deals acid, cold, fire, lightning, or thunder damage to you
Effect: Until the end of your next turn, you gain resist 5 to a damage type of your choice: acid, cold, fire, lightning, or thunder.
Level 11: Resist 10.
Level 21: Resist 15.

Change

Avandra enjoys the winds of change and exhorts her faithful to follow where they blow. For Avandra, change represents ever-renewing opportunities. Each moment is a chance to alter the course, either personally or on a grander scale, and to take things in a better direction than in the past.

An unaligned deity might champion change in the form of evolution or the passage of time. Alternatively, a god might be seeking a particular change in the world or the cosmos. If that god is good or unaligned, the desired change—even if it is simply change for change's sake—falls short of tearing the structure apart, but an evil deity might elevate change precisely because of how it can destabilize people and societies.

Power of Change [Domain]

Prerequisite: Any divine class, must worship a deity of the change domain

Benefit: You gain a +2 feat bonus to Thievery checks.

When you use a power associated with this feat, you gain a +1 bonus to attack rolls with the next encounter or daily attack power you use before the end of your next turn.

Powers: *bolstering strike* (paladin *PH*), *divine bolts* (invoker *PH2*), *overwhelming strike* (avenger *PH2*), *recovery strike* (cleric *DP*)

Cycle of Change [Divinity]

Prerequisite: Channel Divinity class feature, must worship a deity of the change domain

Benefit: You gain the Channel Divinity power *cycle of change*.

Channel Divinity: Cycle of Change — Feat Power

With your god's help, you move the burden to where it can be borne with ease.

Encounter ✦ Divine
Minor Action Melee 1
Target: One ally
Effect: You transfer an effect that a save can end from the target to yourself or vice versa.

Civilization

Both Erathis and Asmodeus prize civilization as the most important force for greatness, but they seize upon the concept in different ways.

Erathis sees civilization as the means of bringing order and illumination to a dark and chaotic cosmos. For her, any culture of laws advances society better than the wild aspirations of individuals. Large and stable communities give people the chance to create the inventions that further propel the ascendancy of civilization as a whole.

Asmodeus understands civilization as a means of gaining power. Confused rabble roaming the wilderness make for easy conquests, but conquering them means bringing them under control. The laws, technologies, and structures of civil society provide the tools to pinion the weak beneath the boots of the mighty.

A good god of civilization might view it as the best way for people to help one another. The laws and shared responsibilities of societies give people the opportunities to show their better selves. In a world where cities are separated by vast areas of peril, expanding the reach of civilization can be a heroic task indeed.

Power of Civilization [Domain]

Prerequisite: Any divine class, must worship a deity of the civilization domain

Benefit: You gain a +2 feat bonus to Diplomacy checks.

When you use a power associated with this feat, you gain a +1 bonus to the damage roll for each enemy adjacent to you.

Powers: *leading strike* (avenger *DP*), *mantle of the infidel* (invoker *DP*), *priest's shield* (cleric *PH*), *valiant strike* (paladin *PH*)

Anthem of Civilization [Divinity]

Prerequisite: Channel Divinity class feature, must worship a deity of the civilization domain

Benefit: You gain the Channel Divinity power *anthem of civilization.*

Channel Divinity: Anthem of Civilization — Feat Power

You inspire your allies to work in concert to turn the tide of battle.

Encounter ✦ Divine

Minor Action — **Personal**

Effect: Until the end of your next turn, you or an ally of your choice within 3 squares of you gains an additional +2 bonus to attack rolls against any enemy he or she flanks.

Creation

Erathis and Moradin both claim the domain of creation, and their followers share an appreciation for works of craft. Yet each god places different emphasis on what they inspire their worshipers to create.

Erathis values creations that advance civilization. Faster ships to speed trade, great roads carved through mountains, new cities where no person had thought they might live—these bring Erathis joy. Even an invention as small as a new kind of hinge receives Erathis's sanction.

Moradin encourages others to bring works into being that will see generations of use. He was intimately involved in hammering the raw creation of the primordials into a durable and refined world that mortals could thrive in. Now that the work of original creation is done, his followers focus on the lasting works of hammer and forge, chisel and stone.

Other gods of creation likely make their own marks on the domain. A deity of creation and magic might focus on the invention of new spells or magic items. A god of creation and war might value inventions only for their destructive potential.

Power of Creation [Domain]

Prerequisite: Any divine class, must worship a deity of the creation domain

Benefit: You gain a +2 feat bonus to Religion checks.

When you use a power associated with this feat and hit one or more enemies with it, you or an ally of your choice within 5 squares of you gains a +1 power bonus to AC until the end of your next turn.

Powers: *bolstering strike* (paladin *PH*), *grasping shards* (invoker *PH2*), *radiant vengeance* (avenger *PH2*), *righteous brand* (cleric *PH*)

Creation Secret [Divinity]

Prerequisite: Channel Divinity class feature, must worship a deity of the creation domain

Benefit: You gain the Channel Divinity power *creation secret.*

Channel Divinity: Creation Secret — Feat Power

Your prayer has a chance of extending the magic contained within an item.

Encounter ✦ Divine

Free Action — **Personal**

Trigger: You use a magic item's daily power

Effect: Roll a d20. If you roll 10 or higher, the use of the daily power is not expended.

Darkness

Drow and darkness go together like spiders and webs, a fact often reinforced by priestesses of the dark elves' patron. Lolth commands her followers to use darkness as cover for their deceptions and attacks. No biting blade or cutting remark can be better delivered than from the shadows.

Zehir sees darkness in a broader scope. He delights in the darkness of ignorance and fear as well as the death of the light. Zehir's worshipers know they can stave off their patron's wrath by killing in darkness and by driving others to turn toward evil.

Darkness need not be the exclusive domain of evil gods. An unaligned or good deity of stealth could favor it, and so might a god of rest and rejuvenation.

Power of Darkness [Domain]

Prerequisite: Any divine class, must worship a deity of the darkness domain

Benefit: You gain a +2 feat bonus to Stealth checks.

When you use a power associated with this feat and hit an enemy with it, you gain concealment against the next attack made against you before the end of your next turn.

Powers: *ardent strike* (paladin *DP*), *overwhelming strike* (avenger *PH2*), *priest's shield* (cleric *PH*), *visions of blood* (invoker *DP*)

Darkness Consumes [Divinity]

Prerequisite: Channel Divinity class feature, must worship a deity of the darkness domain

Benefit: You gain the Channel Divinity power *darkness consumes.*

Channel Divinity: Darkness Consumes — Feat Power

You cause darkness to swirl around you and your allies for a moment.

Encounter ✦ Divine
Minor Action — **Close** burst 1
Target: You and each ally in burst
Effect: Each target gains concealment until the end of your next turn.

Death

The Raven Queen holds dominion over death. It represents her ultimate role in the cosmos, and she stands as its dispassionate symbol.

If they are true to her intent, the Raven Queen's followers advance death as the proper progression of the soul toward its ultimate destination. Death should be neither thrilling nor frightful. It comes as night to day and as naturally as winter bites at the heels of autumn. Those who break with that fate through undeath or other extraordinary means must be forcibly brought to their ends.

Other deities with death among their domains likely view it differently. An evil death god might be a tyrant who delights in the sorrow that death sows, whereas a good death god might be a compassionate guide to the next world, a stern judge of the dead, a guardian of the eternal gates, or a protector of tombs.

Power of Death [Domain]

Prerequisite: Any divine class, must worship a deity of the death domain

Benefit: You gain a +2 feat bonus to Religion checks.

When you use a power associated with this feat and hit a bloodied enemy with it, you gain a +2 bonus to the damage roll. The bonus increases to +3 at 11th level and +4 at 21st level.

Powers: *enfeebling strike* (paladin *PH*), *radiant vengeance* (avenger *PH2*), *righteous brand* (cleric *PH*), *visions of blood* (invoker *DP*)

Death Knell [Divinity]

Prerequisite: Channel Divinity class feature, must worship a deity of the death domain

Benefit: You gain the Channel Divinity power *death knell.*

Channel Divinity: Death Knell — Feat Power

Death comes to all, and your god counts on you to hasten the moment.

Encounter ✦ Divine
Minor Action — **Melee** touch
Target: One bloodied creature
Effect: If the target's current hit points equal 5 + one-half your level or fewer, it drops to 0 hit points. Otherwise, you can use one of your other Channel Divinity powers during this encounter.

Destruction

Gruumsh and Tharizdun share the destruction domain, but their outlooks have little in common.

Gruumsh exhorts followers to senseless carnage, burning, and the defilement of lands. His raging hordes scour the world, bringing cities down and dragging nations to their knees. Destruction is an end in itself, and the more violent the end, the better.

Tharizdun desires destruction on a grander scale. He is the god of cataclysms. No mere wildfire or volcanic eruption satiates his demands on his followers. The mad god seeks the world's end by whatever means possible. His crazed followers are often truly mad.

Other gods of destruction might be associated with natural disasters: storms, earthquakes, and the like. An unaligned god of destruction could be an uncaring agent of doom or a herald of the world's end, duty-bound to begin a cycle of cosmic rebirth by unleashing devastation upon the world. A good god of destruction might exist in a very dark world, where most of what exists is corrupt and must be wiped clean.

Power of Destruction [Domain]

Prerequisite: Any divine class, must worship a deity of the destruction domain

Benefit: You gain a +2 feat bonus to Intimidate checks.

When you use a power associated with this feat and hit an unbloodied enemy with it, you gain a +2 bonus to the damage roll. The bonus increases to +3 at 11th level and +4 at 21st level.

Powers: *ardent strike* (paladin *DP*), *bond of censure* (avenger *DP*), *grasping shards* (invoker *PH2*), *righteous brand* (cleric *PH*)

Path of Destruction [Divinity]

Prerequisite: Channel Divinity class feature, must worship a deity of the destruction domain

Benefit: You gain the Channel Divinity power *path of destruction.*

Channel Divinity: Path of Destruction — Feat Power

A snarled prayer is enough to invoke the power of the Breaker, the Mangler, the Destroyer—your god.

Encounter ✦ Divine
Free Action — **Personal**
Trigger: You roll damage for a melee attack
Effect: You reroll the damage and use either result.

Earth

Moradin and Torog oppose one another for many reasons, including their competing claims on the domain of earth. Moradin sees earth as the foundation of creation and a source of stability, wealth, and strength. He honors stone as the bones of the world and loves mountains as the domain's greatest symbols.

Torog has acquired power over earth during his imprisonment in the Underdark. First he drew the power of earth into the Underdark to provide islands of permanence in that ever-changing realm. Now he continues to scrape at the world above, clawing earth down into the unfinished creation of the Underdark where it can be used as a durable prison, a weapon of confinement.

Other earth gods are often some of the oldest deities and are frequently associated with the formation of the world. They are the carvers of mountains, the binders of stone, and the makers of law who fixed the work of the primordials in its place. An earth god might personify the earth itself as the soul of the world's physical shell. Many earth gods are associated with strength, stability, and time. Others have aspects of agriculture or mineral wealth. Evil earth gods are often jealous, destructive beings who demand placation and resent the exploration of the Underdark.

Power of Earth [Domain]

Prerequisite: Any divine class, must worship a deity of the earth domain

Benefit: You gain a +2 feat bonus to Athletics checks.

When you use a power associated with this feat and hit an enemy with it, that enemy is slowed until the start of your next turn.

Powers: *bolstering strike* (paladin *PH*), *overwhelming strike* (avenger *PH2*), *recovery strike* (cleric *DP*), *visions of blood* (invoker *DP*)

Earth Hold [Divinity]

Prerequisite: Channel Divinity class feature, must worship a deity of the earth domain

Benefit: You gain the Channel Divinity power *earth hold*.

Channel Divinity: Earth Hold — Feat Power

For a few moments, you give yourself up to your god's hold. Those around you sense the divine presence as fearsome gravity.

Encounter ✦ Divine

Minor Action — **Close** burst 2

Target: You and each enemy in burst

Effect: Until the end of your next turn, you are immobilized, and the other targets are slowed.

Fate

To many mortals, fate is inescapable. Their destinies are written before they're born, and throughout their lives, events conspire to lead them along their appointed path. A few mortals—particularly great heroes—sometimes overpower fate, but very few defy it indefinitely. Sooner or later all but the most extraordinary are caught up in fate's web.

The Raven Queen takes fate as her domain, acting as the guardian of destiny. In keeping with her cold nature, her vision of fate is grim, and she frequently resents great heroes for flouting their destinies. The irony of her situation is that she achieved mastery of fate by overcoming a mortal's destiny, so extraordinary heroes who survive long enough eventually find that fate begins to tip in their favor.

Ioun has fate as a domain for its aspect of prognostication. Ioun's followers seek to know and record the paths of events—in the past, the present, and the future. Her devotees hope to understand their own fates and to help those who do not comprehend their destinies to perceive what it is they are meant to do, for good or ill.

Power of Fate [Domain]

Prerequisite: Any divine class, must worship a deity of the fate domain

Benefit: You gain a +2 feat bonus to Insight checks.

When you use a power associated with this feat against a bloodied enemy, you gain a +1 bonus to the attack roll.

Powers: *astral seal* (cleric *DP*), *avenging light* (invoker *PH2*), *bond of retribution* (avenger *PH2*), *holy strike* (paladin *PH*)

Fate Rolls On [Divinity]

Prerequisite: Channel Divinity class feature, must worship a deity of the fate domain

Benefit: You gain the Channel Divinity power *fate rolls on*.

Channel Divinity: Fate Rolls On — Feat Power

In your god's presence, what was mere luck becomes destiny.

Encounter ✦ Divine

Immediate Reaction — **Ranged** 5

Trigger: A creature within 5 squares of you makes a saving throw

Target: The triggering creature

Effect: If the target failed the saving throw, it takes a -2 penalty to its next saving throw before the end of the encounter. If the target saved, it gains a +2 bonus to its next saving throw before the end of the encounter.

Freedom

Sehanine advocates that people follow their hearts without constraint, but Avandra stands as the symbol of true freedom. She commands the domain not to protect the selfish feelings of individuals but to defend the sovereign right of all people to take control of their destinies.

Avandra hopes that others use their freedom to do the right thing, and she stands against tyranny of any kind. Her followers keep alive flames of hope in oppressive societies, serving as the seeds of rebellion or peaceful reform.

It would be unusual for an evil deity to champion freedom, but the domain has dangerous aspects: anarchy, violence, and debauchery. An evil or unaligned god who promotes personal freedom above all other ideals could have the domain.

Power of Freedom [Domain]

Prerequisite: Any divine class, must worship a deity of the freedom domain

Benefit: You gain a +2 feat bonus to Acrobatics checks.

When you use a power associated with this feat and hit one or more enemies with it, you or an ally within 5 squares of you gains a +2 bonus to his or her next saving throw before the start of your next turn.

Powers: *holy strike* (paladin *PH*), *leading strike* (avenger *DP*), *righteous brand* (cleric *PH*), *vanguard's lightning* (invoker *PH2*)

Path of Freedom [Divinity]

Prerequisite: Channel Divinity class feature, must worship a deity of the freedom domain

Benefit: You gain the Channel Divinity power *path of freedom*.

Channel Divinity: Path of Freedom — Feat Power

Through your prayer, you remind your friends that they are always truly free.

Encounter ✦ Divine
Minor Action — **Close** burst 5
Target: Each ally in burst
Effect: Each target can choose to make an escape attempt against a grab as a free action or to make a saving throw against an immobilizing, restraining, or slowing effect that a save can end.

Hope

The hope domain doesn't exist for those who merely wish for something to come to pass; it stands for those who express an optimistic faith in the future. As such, Bahamut and Pelor share reign over the domain.

Pelor shines the light of hope into all hearts that accept his benevolent message. His followers express hope not just for a kinder future but for good harvests from their just labors. Pelor's hope is the faith that the sun will rise, that winter will end, and that compassion will flourish.

Bahamut claims hope among his domains in a different form. The Platinum Dragon's followers rely on the ideals of justice and honor as shields against the darkness that can claim souls. Their hope is that righteous action can prevent a drastic fall. Bahamut places faith not in the external world, but in the spirit of the individual.

Power of Hope [Domain]

Prerequisite: Any divine class, must worship a deity of the hope domain

Benefit: You gain a +2 feat bonus to Diplomacy checks.

When you use a power associated with this feat and hit one or more enemies with it, one ally within 5 squares of you gains a +1 power bonus to the next attack roll he or she makes before the start of your next turn.

Powers: *avenging light* (invoker *PH2*), *leading strike* (avenger *DP*), *righteous brand* (cleric *PH*), *valiant strike* (paladin *PH*)

Hope Remains [Divinity]

Prerequisite: Channel Divinity class feature, must worship a deity of the hope domain

Benefit: You gain the Channel Divinity power *hope remains*.

Channel Divinity: Hope Remains — Feat Power

Those who rise again fight with renewed vigor.

Encounter ✦ Divine
Free Action — **Close** burst 10
Trigger: You or an ally within 10 squares of you regains consciousness after being reduced to 0 hit points or fewer
Target: The triggering character in burst
Effect: The target gains a +2 power bonus to attack rolls, saving throws, and all defenses until the end of its next turn.

Justice

Justice lives differently in the mind of each person, and laws change with each ruler, but ideals of integrity and fairness exist in most societies—even among those who see such ideals as weaknesses. Two gods take up the banner of justice, placing it among their highest virtues.

Bahamut sees justice as the tool of good intentions. Laws and honor exist to protect those who cannot protect themselves and to prevent those who wield power from taking the path of evil.

Erathis views justice as the driving force behind civilization. Without law—without the shared understanding of what should and should not be—society dissolves into chaos.

Other gods of justice would place their own perspectives on the concept. A deity of justice and death might be concerned only with providing the proper rewards and punishments to souls. An evil deity of justice might be an unforgiving judge who cleaves to the letter of the law, relishing in the technicalities that entrap decent souls.

Power of Justice [Domain]

Prerequisite: Any divine class, must worship a deity of the justice domain

Benefit: You gain a +2 feat bonus to Insight checks.

When you use a power associated with this feat and hit an enemy with it, each bloodied ally within

10 squares of you gains a +1 power bonus to attack rolls until the start of your next turn.

Powers: *bond of censure* (avenger *DP*), *mantle of the infidel* (invoker *DP*), *righteous brand* (cleric *PH*), *virtuous strike* (paladin *DP*)

Immediate Justice [Divinity]

Prerequisite: Channel Divinity class feature, must worship a deity of the justice domain

Benefit: You gain the Channel Divinity power *immediate justice*.

Channel Divinity: Immediate Justice — Feat Power

You enforce balance with a flare of divine energy that lances your enemy.

Encounter ✦ Divine, Radiant
Immediate Reaction **Ranged** 10
Trigger: An enemy reduces your ally to 0 hit points or fewer or damages your unconscious ally
Target: The triggering enemy
Effect: The target takes radiant damage equal to 5 + one-half your level.

Knowledge

Ioun and Vecna take opposing perspectives on knowledge. Ioun believes that knowledge of any kind is for the benefit of all. Vecna encourages his followers to hide learning so that only their actions and his plans can profit by them. Ioun sees knowledge as a light that can illuminate the world. Vecna sees it as the secrets that can keep people bound in the darkness of ignorance.

Another god of knowledge might emphasize particular types of knowledge that god values. A deity of arcana and knowledge likely drives followers to discover the secrets of magic and the cosmos. A deity of knowledge and trickery emphasizes the power of using truth to make others believe lies.

If you serve a god of knowledge, you are naturally interested in discovering and preserving lore, especially the ancient or the esoteric. You might fill journals with descriptions of your travels and sketches of things you've seen.

Power of Knowledge [Domain]

Prerequisite: Any divine class, must worship a deity of the knowledge domain

Benefit: You gain a +2 feat bonus to History checks.

When you use a power associated with this feat and hit an enemy with it, you gain a +1 power bonus to all defenses until the start of your next turn.

Powers: *astral seal* (cleric *DP*), *grasping shards* (invoker *PH2*), *leading strike* (avenger *DP*), *virtuous strike* (paladin *DP*)

Sure Knowledge [Divinity]

Prerequisite: Channel Divinity class feature, must worship a deity of the knowledge domain

Benefit: You gain the Channel Divinity power *sure knowledge*.

Channel Divinity: Sure Knowledge — Feat Power

Some portion of your god's wisdom flows through you or your ally.

Encounter ✦ Divine
Free Action **Ranged** 5
Trigger: You or an ally within 5 squares of you makes a knowledge check and doesn't like the result
Target: The triggering character
Effect: The target makes the knowledge check again and uses the new result.

Life

All but a few deities have an interest in life as a domain, but only two place it among their primary concerns.

Melora stands as the world's advocate. If it originates in the world, and it breathes and draws sustenance, she champions its right to exist. Yet Melora does not value one of the world's living things over another. All have the right to play out the natural processes of struggle and survival. Melora does not control the world's primal spirits, but she recognizes their importance and has allied with the elder spirits many times. Primal peoples who would never consider worshiping another deity sometimes acknowledge Melora as a respected ally of the primal spirits.

Pelor brings focus to the cause of life in two different ways. He watches over the life of the fields and farms, and the harvests and herds. As his priests are wont to say, good food is sustenance for the soul. He cares also for the lives of good people and blesses those who show mercy and alleviate suffering.

Other deities of the life domain likely color their interpretation of the domain with their other concerns. There might even be a chaotic evil deity of destruction and the wilderness who promotes the life of ravenous beasts.

Power of Life [Domain]

Prerequisite: Any divine class, must worship a deity of the life domain

Benefit: You gain a +2 feat bonus to Heal checks.

When you use a power associated with this feat and hit one or more enemies with it, one ally within 10 squares of you gains 3 temporary hit points. The temporary hit points increase to 5 at 11th level and 8 at 21st level.

Powers: *avenging light* (invoker *PH2*), *bolstering strike* (paladin *PH*), *astral seal* (cleric *DP*), *radiant vengeance* (avenger *PH2*)

Pulse of Life [Divinity]

Prerequisite: Channel Divinity class feature, must worship a deity of the life domain

Benefit: You gain the Channel Divinity power *pulse of life*.

Channel Divinity: Pulse of Life — Feat Power

In the mortal world, death cannot be entirely denied. But it can be postponed.

Encounter ✦ Divine
Immediate Interrupt **Ranged** 10
Trigger: A creature within 10 squares of you makes a death saving throw
Target: The triggering creature
Effect: The target gains a +10 power bonus to the death saving throw.

Love

The domain of love includes friendship, romance, merriment, and desire. Sehanine accepts all of these as her province, but she places particular emphasis on the passions of new love and the changes it can create in the lives of people who thought their personal stories were set.

Most love deities are positive influences in the world, but some are known for being fickle. Other love deities might be cunning seducers or jealous beauties who delight in broken hearts.

If you serve a deity of love, you are probably a light-hearted and encouraging presence. Love has the power to melt the hardest of hearts, and you believe that your courage and compassion can change the world.

Power of Love [Domain]

Prerequisite: Any divine class, must worship a deity of the love domain

Benefit: You gain a +2 feat bonus to Diplomacy checks.

When you use a power associated with this feat and hit one or more enemies with it, you can choose to deal no damage and instead grant 5 temporary hit points to one or two allies within 5 squares of you. The temporary hit points increase to 10 at 11th level and 15 at 21st level.

Powers: *radiant vengeance* (avenger *PH2*), *recovery strike* (cleric *DP*), *sun strike* (invoker *PH2*), *virtuous strike* (paladin *DP*)

Loving Sacrifice [Divinity]

Prerequisite: Channel Divinity class feature, must worship a deity of the love domain

Benefit: You gain the Channel Divinity power *loving sacrifice*.

Channel Divinity: Loving Sacrifice — Feat Power

The loving tie between you and your friend allows you to take some of the pain he or she would have suffered alone.

Encounter ✦ Divine
Immediate Interrupt **Ranged** 5
Trigger: An ally within 5 squares of you takes damage
Target: The triggering ally
Effect: The damage against the target is reduced by 5, and you take 5 damage, which can't be reduced in any way.
Level 11: The damage is reduced by 10, and you take 10.
Level 21: The damage is reduced by 15, and you take 15.

Luck

Chance, coincidence, fortune, randomness—whatever you call it, luck is a powerful and unpredictable force. Avandra takes this powerful force in hand as a weapon against drab destiny and dark fatalism. For her followers, luck provides excitement and opportunity even in the face of terrible odds.

Another luck god might be a trickster figure, a troublemaker who injects an element of uncertainty into divine circles. Another might be a god of prosperity and good fortune, who rewards the virtuous and worthy. An evil deity of luck might take from it the aspect of misfortune and delight in accidents and disasters.

If you serve a god of luck, you believe in keeping your eyes open for the unexpected opportunity. After all, most people make their own luck by being prepared and decisive. If you're respectful, if you're ready, you'll see the moments when a divine hand arranges some small coincidence or decides some seemingly random outcome in your favor.

Power of Luck [Domain]

Prerequisite: Any divine class, must worship a deity of the luck domain

Benefit: You gain a +2 feat bonus to Acrobatics checks.

When you use a power associated with this feat, you can score a critical hit on a roll of 19–20.

Powers: *bond of censure* (avenger *DP*), *holy strike* (paladin *PH*), *lance of faith* (cleric *PH*), *vanguard's lightning* (invoker *PH2*)

Imminent Luck [Divinity]

Prerequisite: Channel Divinity class feature, must worship a deity of the luck domain

Benefit: You gain the Channel Divinity power *imminent luck*.

Channel Divinity: Imminent Luck — Feat Power

Your god gives you another chance at good fortune.

Encounter ✦ Divine
Free Action **Personal**
Trigger: You use a power that gives you a reroll, and the reroll is lower than the original roll
Effect: You don't expend the use of the power that gave you the reroll.

Madness

Those who know the name of Tharizdun attempt to avoid even thinking it, for fear of the thought's echoes in their minds. His worshipers are given to creeping suspicion, maniacal rage, or bizarre fixations. Lost in delusions and inner torment, they grovel before a divinity that exists to bring doom and the dissolution of all things.

A different god of madness might be one whose secrets are too much for the mortal mind to bear. Perhaps instead the deity claims madness as a domain because it comes from an insanity-inspiring place, such as the Far Realm, whose unnatural blessings overwhelm mortals wretched and foolish enough to seek them out. An unaligned deity of madness might take the form of a senile sage or a capering jester. There might even be a beneficent deity of madness and invention who offers inspiration through bouts of insanity.

Power of Madness [Domain]

Prerequisite: Any divine class, must worship a deity of the madness domain

Benefit: You gain a +2 feat bonus to Bluff checks.

When you use a power associated with this feat and hit an enemy with it, that enemy takes a -1 penalty to attack rolls until the end of your next turn.

Powers: *enfeebling strike* (paladin *PH*), *overwhelming strike* (avenger *PH2*), *righteous brand* (cleric *PH*), *visions of blood* (invoker *DP*)

Screaming Madness [Divinity]

Prerequisite: Channel Divinity class feature, must worship a deity of the madness domain

Benefit: You gain the Channel Divinity power *screaming madness.*

Channel Divinity: Screaming Madness — Feat Power

Ambushed by your dread god's madness, your enemy lurches into lunacy.

Encounter ✦ Divine

Minor Action — **Personal**

Effect: The next enemy you hit during this turn with a fear power hits itself with its melee basic attack the first time it makes an attack on its next turn. The enemy hits itself after its attack is resolved.

Moon

People place many different meanings on the moon. Some see it as a symbol of predictable cycles and time. Others take it as a sign of change, a symbol of magic, or an emblem of beauty and love. A deity of the moon might be seen as a hunter in the darkness, a patron of nightly revelry, or a god of ill fortune or savage madness.

Sehanine takes from the moon the aspect of shadows and masks. Its glow allows her followers to see dangers in the dark, and its darkness cloaks the dangers they present to others.

Sehanine's worshipers see her blessings in the moon's phases. The full moon shields the faithful from harm. A bladelike crescent bodes well for their attacks. And a dark moon presents opportunities to take what you will.

Power of the Moon [Domain]

Prerequisite: Any divine class, must worship a deity of the moon domain

Benefit: You gain a +1 feat bonus to Perception checks.

When you use a power associated with this feat and hit an enemy with it, that enemy takes a -2 penalty to the defense targeted by the power. The penalty lasts until the end of your next turn.

Powers: *bond of censure* (avenger *DP*), *enfeebling strike* (paladin *PH*), *hand of radiance* (invoker *DP*), *righteous brand* (cleric *PH*)

Moon Touched [Divinity]

Prerequisite: Channel Divinity class feature, must worship a deity of the moon domain

Benefit: You gain the Channel Divinity power *moon touched.*

Channel Divinity: Moon Touched — Feat Power

You glow with the healing light of the moon. The light waxes and wanes for a time.

Encounter ✦ Divine, Healing

Minor Action — **Close** burst 5

Target: You or one ally in burst; target must be bloodied

Effect: The target regains hit points equal to your Wisdom or Charisma modifier. At the start of each of your turns, roll a d8. If the roll is odd, the target gains temporary hit points equal to the roll, and if the target already has temporary hit points, the effect ends. If the roll is even, the target regains hit points equal to the roll, and the effect ends.

Level 11: Roll a d10 instead of a d8.

Level 21: Roll a d12 instead of a d8.

Poison

Zehir's words are venom, and his teachings poison minds wherever his priests' hisses can be heard. His followers value all kinds of poison: the toxins that debilitate or kill the body as well as the venomous ideas that ruin the mind and sap the spirit.

The followers of other gods might use poison, but for Zehir, poison itself is worthy of honor. His faithful pay homage to venomous creatures and often say prayers while applying poison to their objects or administering it for ingestion.

In your campaign, poison might not be the province of an evil god. Poison represents a hidden danger, so any deity accustomed to stealth and deception might take poison as a domain. But good and forthright gods likely avoid it.

Power of Poison [Domain]

Prerequisite: Any divine class, must worship a deity of the poison domain

Benefit: You gain a +2 feat bonus to Bluff checks.

When you use a power associated with this feat, you can choose to change its damage type to poison (the power gains the poison keyword and loses the keywords of its former damage types). If you do so, you gain a +2 bonus to the damage roll. The bonus increases to +3 at 11th level and +4 at 21st level.

Powers: *overwhelming strike* (avenger *PH2*), *enfeebling strike* (paladin *PH*), *grasping shards* (invoker *PH2*), *righteous brand* (cleric *PH*)

Original Poison [Divinity]

Prerequisite: Channel Divinity class feature, must worship a deity of the poison domain

Benefit: You gain the Channel Divinity power *original poison*.

Channel Divinity: Original Poison — Feat Power

Your prayer empowers your venomous attacks.

Encounter ✦ Divine
Minor Action — **Ranged** 5
Target: One creature
Effect: Until the end of your next turn, you gain a +2 power bonus to attack rolls against the target with poison powers.

Protection

Gods of protection wield their divine influence to minimize the effect of disasters, to guide those in peril to shelter, and to influence mortals away from overly destructive actions. Some protection gods inspire their followers to engage enemies through force of arms, while others work indirectly, shielding their chosen people with helpful weather, unexpected good fortune, or inspired champions.

Bahamut and Moradin share the domain of protection in a spirit of solidarity. Moradin emphasizes guardianship of home, family, and clan, while Bahamut takes a wider view of protecting society and good people wherever evil finds them. When danger comes, the followers of Moradin draw back to stand on solid ground, and Bahamut's faithful come forward to strike down threats.

Power of Protection [Domain]

Prerequisite: Any divine class, must worship a deity of the protection domain

Benefit: You gain a +2 feat bonus to Heal checks.

When you use a power associated with this feat and hit one or more enemies with it, one ally within 5 squares of you gains a +1 power bonus to all defenses until the start of your next turn.

Powers: *leading strike* (avenger *DP*), *priest's shield* (cleric *PH*), *valiant strike* (paladin *PH*), *vanguard's lightning* (invoker *PH2*)

Sure Protection [Divinity]

Prerequisite: Channel Divinity class feature, must worship a deity of the protection domain

Benefit: You gain the Channel Divinity power *sure protection*.

Channel Divinity: Sure Protection — Feat Power

You ensure that a moment of respite is not interrupted.

Encounter ✦ Divine
Free Action — **Close** burst 5
Trigger: You or an ally within 5 squares of you uses his or her second wind
Target: The triggering character
Effect: The target gains a +3 power bonus to all defenses until the start of his or her next turn.

Sea

The sea is a mighty force in the world. It offers the bounty of fish, the threat of storms, a means for commerce and exploration, and a wilderness in which ships and sailors sometimes vanish without a trace. A god of the sea can therefore be a protective figure who grants blessings to seafaring folk, a monstrous being who delights in drowning mortals, or a fickle divinity who helps or harms as the whim strikes. People see in Melora all three aspects.

Melora claims uncontested rule of the seas, and her whim is iron law. Yet she exercises little control over the vast waters of the world, preferring to allow events to unfold naturally. When she is roused to anger, her wrath comes in endless waves of destruction, and when brought to sympathy, she offers up astonishing treasures lost to the sea.

Power of the Sea [Domain]

Prerequisite: Any divine class, must worship a deity of the sea domain

Benefit: You gain a +2 feat bonus to Athletics checks.

When you use a power associated with this feat and hit one or more enemies with it, you can choose an effect: You make a saving throw against an effect that a save can end, or one enemy hit by the power takes a -2 penalty to the next saving throw it makes before the start of your next turn.

Powers: *bond of censure* (avenger *DP*), *divine bolts* (invoker *PH2*), *recovery strike* (cleric *DP*), *virtuous strike* (paladin *DP*)

Sea Surge [Divinity]

Prerequisite: Channel Divinity class feature, must worship a deity of the sea domain

Benefit: You gain the Channel Divinity power *sea surge.*

Channel Divinity: Sea Surge Feat Power

Your prayer calls forth a wave to carry you or your friend to safety.

Encounter ✦ Divine
Immediate Reaction **Close** burst 10
Trigger: You or an ally within 10 squares of you is pulled, pushed, or slid
Target: The triggering character in burst
Effect: You slide the target 2 squares.

Skill

A deity of the skill domain values excellence and precision in one's actions. The god's followers often seek mastery of some art or proficiency, spending much time in pursuit of perfection.

Bane demands martial skill from his followers, many of whom spend hours in drills and practice battles. If they are not hefting a weapon on a battlefield, his most faithful are studying theories of warfare or playing games of strategy to hone the military mind.

Corellon appreciates beauty and art, be it in song, story, sculpture, dress, or any form of decoration. Everyone seeking beauty in their actions prays to Corellon for the skill to bring their visions into existence.

As god of knowledge, Ioun offers the comprehension necessary to grow skilled and the deeper understanding that practice of a skill engenders. Sometimes dismissed by the ignorant as the patron of scholars, Ioun stands for truth and learning in all areas of thought and action.

Power of Skill [Domain]

Prerequisite: Any divine class, must worship a deity of the skill domain

Benefit: You gain a +1 feat bonus to trained skill checks.

You can use any power you have that is associated with this feat as a basic attack.

Powers: *divine bolts* (invoker *PH2*), *overwhelming strike* (avenger *PH2*), *righteous brand* (cleric *PH*), *valiant strike* (paladin *PH*)

Divine Excellence [Divinity]

Prerequisite: Channel Divinity class feature, must worship a deity of the skill domain

Benefit: You gain the Channel Divinity power *divine excellence.*

Channel Divinity: Divine Excellence Feat Power

Your prayer inspires excellence in yourself and your allies.

Encounter ✦ Divine
Free Action **Personal**
Trigger: You make a skill check
Effect: You gain a +2 power bonus to the skill check. Until the end of your next turn, you and each ally within 10 squares of you gain a +2 power bonus to checks using the same skill.

Storm

Slashing rain, roaring winds, brooding clouds, punishing hail—these are moods of Kord. People hear his laughter in thunder and fear the lightning of his fierce smile. Sailors seeking calm winds and farmers who hope for gentle rain beg Kord to vent his fury elsewhere. They engage in contests of strength and raise toasts in Kord's name to let him know they have neither forgotten his power nor taken his clemency for granted.

Like Kord, another god of storms is likely a deity of raging passions. A good god of storms might be thought of as scouring the world of evil, while a malignant deity of the domain would inflict storms simply out of cruelty.

Power of the Storm [Domain]

Prerequisite: Any divine class, must worship a deity of the storm domain

Benefit: You gain a +2 feat bonus to Intimidate checks.

When you use a power associated with this feat, you can choose to change its damage type to thunder (the power gains the thunder keyword and loses the keywords of its former damage types). If you do so, you gain a +2 bonus to the damage roll. The bonus increases to +3 at 11th level and +4 at 21st level.

Powers: *overwhelming strike* (avenger *PH2*), *righteous brand* (cleric *PH*), *valiant strike* (paladin *PH*), *vanguard's lightning* (invoker *PH2*)

Storm Sacrifice [Divinity]

Prerequisite: Channel Divinity class feature, must worship a deity of the storm domain

Benefit: You gain the Channel Divinity power *storm sacrifice.*

Channel Divinity: Storm Sacrifice Feat Power

If it is your god's will, the coming storm will strike as a blessing.

Encounter ✦ Divine
Minor Action **Ranged** 10
Target: One creature
Effect: You gain vulnerable 5 lightning and vulnerable 5 thunder. If the target has no lightning or thunder resistance, it gains vulnerable 5 lightning and vulnerable 5 thunder. If it has lightning or thunder resistance, it loses that resistance. These effects last until the end of your next turn.

Strength

Popular among barbaric peoples, the gods of strength are patrons to warriors and hunters. Violent and short-tempered, these deities act rather than reflect.

Blood-spattered Gruumsh glories in the slaughter of weaker foes, disdaining strategy and skill. He believes that the world belongs to those who can crush skulls in their fists or break bones with a bite. Strength is the license to do as you please, and it pleases Gruumsh when his followers use their might to destroy.

Kord acts as patron of strength to all who seek to avoid the wanton destruction urged by Gruumsh. Athletes, soldiers, laborers, and others who prize the power of the body pray to Kord, and so do those of weakness who are willing to act against the strong.

A strength god need not be so impulsive, and such a deity could be aligned with good. Perhaps your campaign has room for a god of strength and knowledge, patron of athletes and an asceticism seeking physical perfection. A strength god could instead be aligned with justice and promote the use of might for what is right.

Power of Strength [Domain]

Prerequisite: Any divine class, must worship a deity of the strength domain

Benefit: You gain a +2 feat bonus to Athletics checks.

When you use a power associated with this feat, you gain a +2 bonus to the damage roll. The bonus increases to +3 at 11th level and +4 at 21st level.

Powers: *avenging light* (invoker *PH2*), *holy strike* (paladin *PH*), *overwhelming strike* (avenger *PH2*), *priest's shield* (cleric *PH*)

Strength of the Gods [Divinity]

Prerequisite: Channel Divinity class feature, must worship a deity of the strength domain

Benefit: You gain the Channel Divinity power *strength of the gods.*

Channel Divinity: Strength of the Gods — Feat Power

From your god, to your ally, and into the enemy: a passage of strength and impact.

Encounter ✦ Divine
Minor Action **Close** burst 5
Target: One ally in burst
Effect: The target gains a power bonus equal to your Strength modifier to its next damage roll before the end of your next turn.

Strife

Tiamat rules the strife domain. It stands for her avarice and the greed she foments in her followers. Chaos too is her ally. When others cannot stand together, they are more easily torn apart.

The domain of strife exists for gods who act as thorns in the world's flesh, bloody troublemakers who don't want to get along with anyone else. Those people drawn to serve a strife god are attracted by the pure, driving ambition that the god represents—the desire to get ahead, regardless of the cost. Strife might be the single problematic domain of a god who is otherwise one of the world's defenders, representing the god's penchant for stirring up anger or a dangerous curiosity.

Power of Strife [Domain]

Prerequisite: Any divine class, must worship a deity of the strife domain

Benefit: You gain a +2 feat bonus to Bluff checks.

When you use a power associated with this feat, you gain a +1 bonus to the damage roll for each enemy within 3 squares of the target. The bonus increases to +2 at 11th level and +3 at 21st level.

Powers: *ardent strike* (paladin *DP*), *bond of retribution* (avenger *PH2*), *lance of faith* (cleric *PH*), *sun strike* (invoker *PH2*)

Sudden Strife [Divinity]

Prerequisite: Channel Divinity class feature, must worship a deity of the strife domain

Benefit: You gain the Channel Divinity power *sudden strife.*

Channel Divinity: Sudden Strife — Feat Power

You sow doubt in two enemies, causing them to question each other's loyalty. Their combat acumen suffers as a result.

Encounter ✦ Charm, Divine
Free Action **Ranged** 5
Target: Two enemies within 3 squares of each other
Effect: Until the end of your next turn, the targets take a -4 penalty to attack rolls while they are within 3 squares of each other.

Sun

The sun's influence and brilliance are obvious to all, acting as a daily reminder of Pelor's power and beneficence. The sun is the light of growth and renewal. It is warmth in winter and ensures good harvest come the fall. Pelor extends its light to all just as he hopes his followers extend their compassion to all. The sun also peels back the veil of night, and Pelor's followers see in that a metaphor for the light they must bring to shadowy deeds and dark hearts.

Sun gods frequently rule pantheons or stand as the first among equals. Although usually portrayed as benevolent or dispassionate deities, sun gods don't need to be good or unaligned. An evil sun god might be a bloodthirsty tyrant who threatens drought and fire unless slaked by sacrifices.

Power of the Sun [Domain]

Prerequisite: Any divine class, must worship a deity of the sun domain

Benefit: You gain a +2 feat bonus to Insight checks.

When you use a power associated with this feat and hit an enemy with it, that enemy gains vulnerable 3 radiant until the end of your next turn, after the power's effects are resolved. The vulnerability increases to 5 at 11th level and 8 at 21st level.

Powers: *lance of faith* (cleric *PH*), *radiant vengeance* (avenger *PH2*), *sun strike* (invoker *PH2*), *virtuous strike* (paladin *DP*)

Solar Enemy [Divinity]

Prerequisite: Channel Divinity class feature, must worship a deity of the sun domain

Benefit: You gain the Channel Divinity power *solar enemy*.

Channel Divinity: Solar Enemy — Feat Power

The divine sunlight playing across your enemies is a sign of the radiance to come.

Encounter ✦ Divine
Minor Action — **Close** burst 2
Target: Each enemy in burst
Effect: Each target gains vulnerable 5 radiant, or its vulnerability to radiant damage increases by 5.

Torment

Torog crawls through the gloom of the Underdark, his broken back hunched as his bleeding knees and elbows scrape their way through the earth. This tortured deity vents his imprisoned rage against existence as the god of torment. Patron of jailers, slavers, torturers, and sadists of all stripes, the King that Crawls takes pleasure in causing pain and in the agony inflicted by his devotees.

The torment domain typically belongs to evil deities, but your campaign might host a good or unaligned god subjected to torture. Mortals might ask such a divine martyr for the ability to endure the pains they face or to take on their troubles.

Power of Torment [Domain]

Prerequisite: Any divine class, must worship a deity of the torment domain

Benefit: You gain a +2 feat bonus to Intimidate checks.

When you use a power associated with this feat and hit an enemy with it, that enemy grants combat advantage to your next ally who attacks it before the start of your next turn.

Powers: *ardent strike* (paladin *DP*), *astral seal* (cleric *DP*), *overwhelming strike* (avenger *PH2*), *mantle of the infidel* (invoker *DP*)

Perfect Torment [Divinity]

Prerequisite: Channel Divinity class feature, must worship a deity of the torment domain

Benefit: You gain the Channel Divinity power *perfect torment*.

Channel Divinity: Perfect Torment — Feat Power

Your prayer prolongs your enemies' suffering.

Encounter ✦ Divine
Minor Action — **Close** burst 5
Target: Each enemy in burst
Effect: Each target takes a -2 penalty to saving throws until the end of your next turn.

Trickery

Cleverness, deceit, illusion, stealth—these are the tools of deities who hold sway over the domain of trickery. A god of trickery might be an irrepressible jokester whose misadventures serve to illuminate the follies and inanities of life; a shadowy patron to thieves and illusionists; or a cruel deceiver whose lies poison the world.

Sehanine and Lolth assert control over the domain of trickery, an uncomfortable allocation of power extant since before Lolth's rebellion. Though that conflict ended in an era long past, the followers of both deities open fresh wounds over it every year.

For Lolth, trickery presents the means of gaining and keeping power. Why fight foes when you can manipulate them?

Sehanine sees trickery in a more winsome light. Trickery can delight as well as devastate, and she encourages her followers to moderate one with the other as they pursue their destinies.

Power of Trickery [Domain]

Prerequisite: Any divine class, must worship a deity of the trickery domain

Benefit: You gain a +2 feat bonus to Thievery checks.

When you use a power associated with this feat and hit one or more enemies with it, you or an ally adjacent to that enemy can shift 1 square as a free action.

Powers: *avenging light* (invoker *PH2*), *overwhelming strike* (avenger *PH2*), *enfeebling strike* (paladin *PH*), *recovery strike* (cleric *DP*)

Trickster's Fortune [Divinity]

Prerequisite: Channel Divinity class feature, must worship a deity of the trickery domain

Benefit: You gain the Channel Divinity power *trickster's fortune*.

Channel Divinity: Trickster's Fortune — Feat Power

You slyly twist your foe's fate and try to turn its misfortune into your fortune.

Encounter ✦ Divine
Immediate Interrupt **Close** burst 5
Trigger: An enemy within 5 squares of you makes a saving throw
Target: The triggering enemy in burst
Effect: The target takes a -2 penalty to the saving throw. If the saving throw fails, you or an ally in the burst can make a saving throw.

Tyranny

Asmodeus seeks nothing less than complete dominion over all existence, and thus he jealously protects his control of the tyranny domain. Oppression, coercion, repression—these are the tools of the tyrant. Those who follow Asmodeus accept the domination of his agents or seek to gain power for themselves by crushing others in an iron grip.

Few adventurers devote themselves to the ruthless acquisition of power that the tyranny domain entails. However, tyranny might be the lesser of two evils in a setting that faces an even worse threat, such as demonic hordes or invasion from the Far Realm.

Power of Tyranny [Domain]

Prerequisite: Any divine class, must worship a deity of the tyranny domain

Benefit: You gain a +2 feat bonus to Intimidate checks.

When you use a power associated with this feat, the power's targets each take a -2 penalty to saving throws until the start of your next turn, whether or not you hit.

Powers: *astral seal* (cleric *DP*), *bond of censure* (avenger *DP*), *divine bolts* (invoker *PH2*), *enfeebling strike* (paladin *PH*)

Master of Tyranny [Divinity]

Prerequisite: Channel Divinity class feature, must worship a deity of the tyranny domain

Benefit: You gain the Channel Divinity power *master of tyranny.*

Channel Divinity: Master of Tyranny — Feat Power

Your enemies' weakness gives you strength.

Encounter ✦ Divine
Minor Action **Personal**
Effect: You gain a +2 bonus to attack rolls against bloodied creatures until the end of your next turn.

Undeath

Death is the natural end to mortal lives, but throughout the ages, some mortals have rebelled against this common fate. Undeath offers some mortals a way to cling to worldly existence long after they should have passed into the beyond. For most, undeath is a terrible curse that corrupts the soul.

Vecna clasps the secrets of the domain of undeath tightly to his bony breast. He envisions a world in which a chosen few rule over masses of undead, which are easily subjugated to his will. Although not all undead owe their allegiance to Vecna, the Maimed One keeps secret watch on the plans of unknown numbers of them, and many unwittingly do his will.

An evil god of undeath might usurp death as well, becoming a frightful master of all fates beyond life. More rarely, a good or unaligned god of undeath might be concerned with the preservation of ancestral spirits and the protection of burial places.

Power of Undeath [Domain]

Prerequisite: Any divine class, must worship a deity of the undeath domain

Benefit: You gain a +2 feat bonus to Religion checks.

When you use a power associated with this feat, the power's damage changes to necrotic (the power gains the necrotic keyword and loses the keywords of its former damage types). You also gain a +2 bonus to the damage roll. The bonus increases to +3 at 11th level and +4 at 21st level.

Powers: *bond of censure* (avenger *DP*), *enfeebling strike* (paladin *PH*), *grasping shards* (invoker *PH2*), *lance of faith* (cleric *PH*)

Undeath's Ally [Divinity]

Prerequisite: Channel Divinity class feature, must worship a deity of the undeath domain

Benefit: You gain the Channel Divinity power *undeath's ally.*

Channel Divinity: Undeath's Ally — Feat Power

At your touch, your friend's life begins to slip away, but he or she gains some of the resilience of undeath.

Encounter ✦ Divine
Minor Action **Melee** 1
Target: One ally
Effect: The target loses a healing surge but gains temporary hit points equal to his or her healing surge value + one-half your level.

Vengeance

Tiamat rises as the queen of vengeance. She exhorts her faithful to forgive nothing and avenge even the slightest wrong. Her worshipers believe that power can be respected only when it is exercised, and the way to gain power is by tearing down those who have what you desire.

A god of vengeance probably takes delight in revenge that far exceeds the original damage. Although an evil alignment is most likely, a god of vengeance might be an unaligned lord of strife. A good-aligned god of vengeance might be in a setting dominated by evil, where the forces of good seek redress for centuries of abuse.

Power of Vengeance [Domain]

Prerequisite: Any divine class, must worship a deity of the vengeance domain

Benefit: You gain a +2 feat bonus to Intimidate checks.

When you use a power associated with this feat and hit an enemy with it, that enemy takes 2 damage the first time it attacks you or an ally of yours before the start of your next turn. The damage increases to 3 at 11th level and 4 at 21st level.

Powers: *astral seal* (cleric *DP*), *avenging light* (invoker *PH2*), *holy strike* (paladin *PH*), *radiant vengeance* (avenger *PH2*)

Small Vengeance [Divinity]

Prerequisite: Channel Divinity class feature, must worship a deity of the vengeance domain

Benefit: You gain the Channel Divinity power *small vengeance.*

Channel Divinity: Small Vengeance Feat Power

You channel your god's essence and return pain to your foe.

Encounter ✦ Divine

Immediate Reaction **Close** burst 10

Trigger: You are bloodied by an enemy within 10 squares of you

Target: The triggering enemy in burst

Effect: The target takes 1d8 damage.

Level 11: 2d8 damage.

Level 21: 3d8 damage.

War

War is a powerful force in the world, the ultimate test of martial fitness. A war god can be an honorable champion who delights in demonstrations of courage, a cruel conqueror who revels in bloody triumph, or a harsh judge who measures mortals by how they meet their hour of doom.

Bane commands the domain of war for its aspects of conquest and strict military structures. Ordered battle plans and improvised strategies please Bane, as do masses of troops and tiny tactical units. Bane embraces every aspect of war and sees it as an end in its own right, an outlook shared by many of those devoted to him.

Kord sees war as the testing ground for strength. He values it as a storm of blood—a passion that rages in the heart of true warriors. Kord has little patience for strategizing and deception, and those who carry his standard into battle try simply to pit strength against strength, or they look to another power—such as Ioun, Bahamut, or even Bane—for the tactics they need to win.

If you are a devotee of a god of war, you regard battle as the principal test of your worth and devotion. And sometimes a fist in the face says more than a thousand honeyed words.

Power of War [Domain]

Prerequisite: Any divine class, must worship a deity of the war domain

Benefit: You gain a +2 feat bonus to History checks.

When you use a power associated with this feat against an unbloodied target, you gain a +1 bonus to the attack roll.

Powers: *bolstering strike* (paladin *PH*), *bond of retribution* (avenger *PH2*), *priest's shield* (cleric *PH*), *visions of blood* (invoker *DP*)

Path of War [Divinity]

Prerequisite: Channel Divinity class feature, must worship a deity of the war domain

Benefit: You gain the Channel Divinity power *path of war.*

Channel Divinity: Path of War Feat Power

You encourage your friends to throw themselves into glorious battle.

Encounter ✦ Divine

Minor Action **Close** burst 5

Target: Each ally in burst

Effect: Each target gains a +2 bonus to attack rolls and a -2 penalty to all defenses until the end of your next turn.

For the DM: Evil Feats

The *Player's Handbook* provides divinity feats only for good and unaligned deities. In contrast, this book provides divinity feats and domain feats usable with evil deities. Evil player characters don't mesh well with most D&D campaigns and the shared experience of the game table, so the evil-related feats, such as Perfect Torment, will prove most useful for DMs building evil NPCs. Evil-flavored domains, such as tyranny, are also useful for building complete pantheons.

In rare cases, a player character might try to walk the moral tightrope of worshiping an evil god while maintaining an unaligned alignment. This situation provides quite a few dramatic hooks, but such dramas usually end with only a few survivors. You should therefore think carefully before inviting such tensions into a campaign.

If you want to try running a campaign full of evil player characters, the new divinity feats and domain feats should prove invaluable. Quite a few of them capture the core evil experience—it's not necessarily hard to be evil, but it's hell being around other people who are evil.

Wilderness

During the world's creation, gods shaped the forests, the mountains, the plains, and the deserts. These vast landscapes form the foundation of life. The wilderness is the realm of primal spirits and fey powers, and Melora and Corellon divide their control of the wilderness domain on similar lines.

Melora concerns herself with the wilderness of the world, its cycles and the survival of its many beings: animals, plants, and spirits that are the source of primal power. Melora's view of nature is broad enough that she does not care if someone cares more for primal spirits than for her. Just as with her other domains, the sea and life, Melora has little impact on the wilderness so long as nothing dramatically affects its existence. Only when truly devastating threats loom will Melora marshal her resources to defend the world.

Corellon's interests are the wild places of the Feywild and the ancient forests that stand across the world. He most values locations of natural beauty, and his followers often protect them in his name, especially places of splendor in the Feywild.

An alternative wilderness deity might be an evil or unaligned power who emphasizes the harshness and cruelty of the wilds. A deity of trickery and the wilderness might act as patron to mercurial fey beings, offering other mortals infrequent protection from the pique of those mysterious beings.

Power of the Wilderness [Domain]

Prerequisite: Any divine class, must worship a deity of the wilderness domain

Benefit: You gain a +2 feat bonus to Nature checks.

When you use a power associated with this feat and hit an enemy with it, you and each ally adjacent to you ignore difficult terrain until the end of your next turn.

Powers: *overwhelming strike* (avenger *PH2*), *recovery strike* (cleric *DP*), *sun strike* (invoker *PH2*), *valiant strike* (paladin *PH*)

Grasp of the Wild [Divinity]

Prerequisite: Channel Divinity class feature, must worship a deity of the wilderness domain

Benefit: You gain the Channel Divinity power *grasp of the wild.*

Channel Divinity: Grasp of the Wild — Feat Power

You cause the environment to clutch at creatures in an area. Vines wrap around them, the earth softens under them, water churns about them–whatever is natural for the environs.

Encounter ✦ Divine
Minor Action — **Area** burst 1 within 10 squares
Effect: The area of the burst is difficult terrain until the end of your next turn.

Winter

The Raven Queen rules over winter as the uncaring marshal of its beginning and end. She pulls the white veil over the world with cold efficiency, and lets the world rise from the dead of winter only because the natural order demands it. The Raven Queen's servants see winter as a pure and fair means of culling the weak. It represents a time of hardship through which the world emerges stronger than before.

Mortals typically associate winter with darkness, hunger, and death, so many pray to a winter god out of fear, hoping to placate icy wrath. Those who adapt their lives to wintry environments might enjoy the protection of good god of winter. In lands where seasons change little, the winter god might be a god of the high mountains, where snow and ice never melt. An evil winter deity might dream about plunging the world into eternal ice but be held in check by a god of the sun and summer such as Pelor.

Power of Winter [Domain]

Prerequisite: Any divine class, must worship a deity of the winter domain

Benefit: You gain a +2 feat bonus to Endurance checks.

When you use a power associated with this feat, the power's damage changes to cold (the power gains the cold keyword and loses the keywords of its former damage types). You also gain a +2 bonus to the damage roll. The bonus increases to +3 at 11th level and +4 at 21st level.

Powers: *bond of censure* (avenger *DP*), *enfeebling strike* (paladin *PH*), *hand of radiance* (invoker *DP*), *lance of faith* (cleric *PH*)

Path of Winter [Divinity]

Prerequisite: Channel Divinity class feature, must worship a deity of the winter domain

Benefit: You gain the Channel Divinity power *path of winter.*

Channel Divinity: Path of Winter — Feat Power

At your prayer, you and your allies endure winter's chill.

Encounter ✦ Divine
Minor Action — **Close** burst 5
Target: You and each ally in burst
Effect: Each target gains resist 5 cold until the end of your next turn.
Level 11: Resist 10 cold.
Level 21: Resist 15 cold.

5

YOUR DEITY AND YOU

Each of the deities in the core pantheon has a unique outlook and a special mindset, just as do the devotees of those deities. This section provides advice on how to tailor the abilities and attitudes of your divine character so they are in concert with the god that he or she seeks to emulate.

In many of these passages, recommended trained skills are not all on the class list of every divine class. It's still possible for your character to become trained in such a skill, by taking either the Skill Training feat or a class-specific multiclass feat.

Avandra

You hope to become a quintessential adventurer, a walking symbol of the spirit of exploration as guided by Avandra's wishes. As you and your compatriots travel, you serve as a guide and a representative of the party. Though you give prayers and offerings to Avandra, you know it's more important to be assertive and take action. Nothing is more vile in your eyes than oppression and slavery, and you take up Avandra's mandate to right those great wrongs.

Choose powers—especially utilities—that grant movement or alter luck. Obtain training in skills that make travel easier in both civilization and wilderness, such as Diplomacy, Dungeoneering, Nature, and Streetwise.

Avenger: Less focused on a single goal than most other avengers, you travel across the world, finding your own targets. Those who enslave or confine others are your greatest foes. You might start your career fighting brigands who block a road and cap it fighting an archdevil who enslaves millions.

Cleric: Freedom is the core of your belief. While you might lead your allies, you are never domineering. Your devotion leads you to many lands, and the world is dotted with shrines you have built and consecrated, both humble and grand.

Invoker: You realize from the histories you've read that absolute freedom is far from ideal. It can cause pain as easily as joy, and it led to chaos in the times before deities ruled. Though Avandra encourages change, you believe she wants that change to be directed. Speaking with holy authority, you seek to bring change only for good and to drive the wicked to follow the will of the good deities.

Paladin: Those who expect a paladin to be a humorless, self-righteous soldier will be surprised by you. Though you are reliable and strong, you're hard to predict, and sometimes incautious. You never take prisoners, for it's better to be dead than bound.

Bahamut

Your philosophy exalts the good and righteous, the honorable and lawful, above all. Evil, no matter how powerful, must be opposed, and you will stand against any force of darkness. You make it your business to know the laws of any land you visit. The law can mask the workings of evil, and you cleave to the higher law—the divine law—set forth by Bahamut.

Pick powers that will best protect your allies, and possibly cold powers to mimic the frost of Bahamut's breath. Skills that overpower (such as Intimidate) and skills of understanding (such as Diplomacy and Insight) exemplify the strength and nobility of your deity.

Avenger: The retributive side of Bahamut intrigues you. You bring swift, bloody justice to those who transgress. With blade or bow in hand, you fight with the ferocity of a dragon.

Cleric: To protect the weak, you are willing to risk your life. Your divine power is a blessing, and you owe it to the world to safeguard those who have less power. You give aid to the person with the most need before you think of anyone else.

Invoker: You consider Bahamut to be a fragment of Io, the progenitor of dragons. As contradictory as it might seem, you pay tribute to Tiamat for the same reason. You use prayers to emulate Io's might, and the lawful code you follow is actually closer to Io's more brutish, prideful principles than to Bahamut's nobility and honor.

Paladin: None exemplify the way of the paladin as you do. You bring justice to your foes, but you do so with fairness and mercy. You allow no weakness in yourself, since you must stand as a paragon of law and honor.

Corellon

To serve Corellon is to serve enchantment—both the magic of beauty and the beauty of magic. You feel Corellon's favor when you find and foster magic and when you protect or create beauty. You take inspiration from exquisite things and seek ways to bring magic to others' lives.

As a worshiper of Corellon, you favor powers that emphasize the power of magic. Select showy powers, particularly those that deal radiant damage or force damage. Choose training in Arcana, Diplomacy, and Insight.

LEE MOYER (2)

Avenger: In an enchanted refuge you received your training and the investiture of your divine power. You didn't need the advice of others to tell you how to use Corellon's gifts. You heard your calling in songs and saw your path written across a starlit sky: Strike down those who destroy beauty, and tear through the web of Lolth's followers to stab at the heart of her plans. Death, too, can be a work of art.

Cleric: The splendor of the world and its peoples' creations inspires you, and you hope your deeds will inspire others to feel what you know in your soul. Corellon is a god of renewal, so you seek to restore and rebuild wherever destruction has wrought sorrow.

Invoker: You were granted a gift you're not sure you can ever repay. Thanks to Corellon, you can speak words of such grace that you command the attention of even the most hideous souls. With his magic behind your will, you feel compelled to share the joy your spirit feels. A magic so great should never be kept secret.

Paladin: Too often, ugly brutality ruins the gentle or glorious things in life. You chose the path of the paladin not for the song of the sword's arc, but for the sound of the next breath of a would-be victim bought by your weapon's strike against an attacker. Whether beauty takes the form of the most enchanting place in the world or the face of a kind soul, how could you not stand between it and destruction?

Erathis

The lights of civilization and invention are all that keep the world from descending into chaos and barbarism. You create new societies and protect those you find. To embody the virtues of progress, you study the histories of civilizations and learn some type of craft.

Choose powers that encourage teamwork by giving bonuses to allies, either directly or by imposing conditions on enemies. Take skills that encourage cooperation, such as Diplomacy, and ones you'll use in civilized areas, such as History and Streetwise.

Avenger: Rather than looking for new places to create civilization, you make existing cities run more smoothly. Frequently, this effort entails removing from power those who work against the goals of others (often criminal organizations).

LEE MOYER (3)

Cleric: You seek to forge alliances, broaden understanding, and ultimately bring disparate groups together to create new societies. Encourage the building of great temples in civilized lands, with shrines to many deities (to draw many people to the city).

Invoker: When the gods are strong, the world is ruled by law and great cities rise. You seek to pull the world from darkness and return it to glory under divine rule. Erathis's laws lay the groundwork that will bring law and prosperity to all.

Paladin: An aggressive, devout follower, you drive the progress of societies forward, delving into the wilds to reshape them into settlements that are both safe and civilized. You might even have an ambition to rule as a monarch one day.

Ioun

Serving Ioun means discovering and sharing secrets. Yet this quest ranges further than cobwebbed libraries and musty books. Your hunger for knowledge draws you to understand strategic thinking, foresight, and all forms of mental prowess.

As a worshiper of Ioun, you favor powers of prescience and those that deal psychic damage. Choose training in knowledge skills (particularly History), Insight, and Streetwise.

Avenger: Knowledge is a weapon, and you don't ever want to be caught unarmed. No secret is safe from you. Then again, neither are those who keep them. Vecna and his followers are a sickness that your blade can cut out of the world. You see your foes' future, and the prognosis for them isn't good.

Cleric: A secret dies with its keepers, but knowledge gains power when shared. Though you fight mortal foes, ignorance is your true enemy. You walk in a world unaware of its potential, so you strive to share your skills and learn the lessons others can teach you. You hope your example will lead others to take the right path.

Invoker: Ioun knows your mind, and your heart is turned toward her purposes. You know the peace of soul that comes from meditation and study. If others open their hearts to enlightenment, you're hopeful that they can share that peace. If not, you'll teach them the error of their ways.

Paladin: Knowledge shields people from many mistakes, but to take the proper path, one needs the wisdom to perceive it and the strength to stay the course. You know that many people will falter as they take the necessary steps, and it's your duty to make certain they don't fall.

Kord

As a follower of Kord, you serve as the fighting heart of your adventuring group—the character others can depend on to show great courage, to take risks, and to stand and fight against overwhelming odds. To show true devotion, you must act with bravery and skill, not simply pray at a shrine or carry a trinket of faith. You see no need to mince words, especially with those who are weak. Those who use subterfuge and honeyed words might show great skill, but such actions are fundamentally cowardly—not befitting a true adherent of Kord's teachings.

You prefer melee attacks and powers that deal lightning or thunder damage. Choose training in physical skills such as Athletics, Acrobatics, and Endurance.

Avenger: The teachings of Kord are always on your mind as you enter single combat. You focus on defeating one foe using only your personal might and skill, and you continually seek your next battle—your next victory.

Cleric: You shout out boisterous encouragement to your allies, providing emotional encouragement in addition to your magical boons. You lead by example, rushing headlong into battle and exhorting your allies to keep up with you.

Invoker: In ancient times, Kord's battles shook the world. You still feel the reverberations of those great fights and have an instinctual knowledge of the lord of battle's power. Though you might seem entirely different during travel or negotiation, in battle you enter a trance as you call on the strength of your god.

Paladin: You find it easy to follow Kord's teachings as a paladin, and your code of honor includes his commands. Although you seek battle and glory, you're never cruel, and you are quick to grant mercy to a foe that concedes defeat.

Melora

With a close connection to your animal instincts, you possess a mercurial temperament that alternates between the contradicting parts of nature. Sometimes you show grace and calm, but you also rage like a wild beast when in danger. Nature is your true home, and it's difficult for you to be confined in claustrophobic tombs or constructed tunnels.

Choose powers that bring out the savagery of yourself and your allies. Your skills should include those that help you persevere in the wild, such as Athletics, Endurance, Nature, and Perception.

Avenger: As an avenger worshiping Melora, you might be a member of an elite cabal of aberration hunters who have vast knowledge about the Far Realm and how to spot its influence. Until every aberrant spawn of that dread place is slain, you won't rest.

Cleric: You are the pack leader of your adventuring group, and you take on both the responsibility and power of an alpha animal. When fighting, you urge your allies to be merciless hunters.

Invoker: In the winding rivers, the lush jungles, and the rolling waves of the oceans, you see the care and skill the deities brought to creating the world. You revere and protect these natural wilds, considering them as important among the domains of the gods as any city or temple.

Paladin: Calling upon the strength of the oak and the power of the avalanche, you become a mighty protector of all living things. You remain vigilant, opposing anyone that attempts to destroy nature or slaughter beasts, beyond what is needed to survive.

Moradin

Your determination in the face of hardship is outweighed only by your loyalty to your friends. You apply your indomitable will toward crafting a better world. Order and goodwill clearly present the righteous path, and you try to exemplify these traits even in the worst moments.

As a worshiper of Moradin, you favor powers that aid allies and protect yourself. Choose training in Dungeoneering, Endurance, and History.

Avenger: Just as a smith beats weakness from metal or a sculptor chips away unwanted stone, you make the world a better place by carving out the bad parts. And as with any great work of craftsmanship, when you've finished making your mark on history, no one will mourn the missing pieces.

Cleric: Amid waves of chaos and destruction, you stand as solid as stone. Your solidarity provides an anchor for allies and presents an unfaltering wall to a tide of foes. You know that others look to you for guidance, and your steady hand gives them the confidence to take their own paths.

Invoker: Moradin fashioned your soul to further his will in the world, and you're determined to make great works with the materials your life provides. You're the keystone in these plans, while those around you need to be moved into place before their full roles can be realized.

Paladin: Anything worth making is worth protecting, especially friendship. Loyalty is your legacy, and you never break the oaths you forge. Come what may, your allies know they can depend on you.

Pelor

Pelor represents many things to many people, and so must you. You stand as the light to guide others out of darkness, and you offer redemption to those who seek it. Even so, you rise against darkness and see it put in

LEE MOYER (3)

its place. You serve Pelor best when you help others and protect them from evil.

As a worshiper of Pelor, pick powers that deal radiant damage or heal allies. Choose training in Diplomacy, Heal, and Nature.

Avenger: Pelor's priests often speak of showing compassion and kindness, but you know there is a difference between mercy and forgiveness. Those who truly see the light deserve its warmth. All others earn cold steel. When the path you walk seems dark, it is only because you stand in the shadows produced by Pelor's light.

Cleric: Your righteous stance is the light meant to lead others out of darkness. When your friends falter, you are beside them with the warm words and kind heart that illuminate the proper path.

Invoker: The warmth of summer ever fills your soul, and the world would be a better place if all could share the joy you feel. By sowing the seeds of empathy and goodwill, you're confident you'll reap a fine harvest. When you inevitably encounter resistance, you know Pelor's light shall reveal the errors of your enemies' ways. The sun causes crops to grow, but it can burn them too.

Paladin: Each sunrise brings a new day, and each day is a chance to start anew. Yet compassion for a foe is no excuse for allowing the innocent to come to harm. Your first duty is to protect those who choose the bright way. Only after innocence is shielded from evil does an evildoer deserve a second chance.

The Raven Queen

Death represents not an end but a transition. It holds no fear for you beyond the concern that it would cause you to miss opportunities to serve the Raven Queen. While you draw breath, you seek to help others with death, whether by comforting a mourner or helping someone find his or her way beyond.

As a worshiper of the Raven Queen, pick powers that deal necrotic damage or elicit fear. Choose training in Insight, Intimidate, and Religion.

Avenger: There is little passion in your killing, and no pity. Death is the threshold all must cross to meet their final destiny. Of course, some deserve to make that crossing sooner than others. That's where you come in.

Cleric: Fear and pride—these are the enemies of great deeds. You take advantage of these traits in your foes, and you quell them in your allies. You guide your companions on the path to greatness, but you know that their stories will eventually end.

Invoker: There is winter in your soul, as if ice flows through your veins. You see death in the faces of your closest friends, and even babes in their mothers' arms seem but guttering candles in a limitless darkness. You bear a power older than the Raven Queen, yet she granted it to you as her hand in the world. You are honored to take that mantle upon your shoulders, but sometimes it weighs heavily.

Paladin: You do not fear your own death, but your friends are another matter. You see in their deeds the hand of fate, and it is your duty to protect them until their deaths serve providence. You don't know how it all ends, but when your soul goes to meet the Raven Queen, you will not regret how you served her.

Sehanine

The moon's glow, the crisp leaves of autumn, the magician's trick, the kiss between lovers—all are signs of Sehanine's favor. You know this because you can feel her smile in your soul when you see them. You roam the world seeking your destiny, taking such omens as signals to guide your shadowy way.

As a worshiper of Sehanine, pick powers that allow you to avoid notice or escape trouble. Choose training in Bluff, Perception, and Stealth.

Avenger: Your soul has always lurked in the shadows. Even in the center of a crowded room, you felt as though you watched from hiding. Only the moon saw you for who you are. Only Sehanine answered the call you could not utter. Now beneath her bright smile you serve as her hidden blade, and when she clasps your soul in her hand, you strike.

Cleric: Life is a prank the gods play upon souls, but at least you're in on the joke. Fate, life, death—those ideas mean little when it comes down to it. The truth is that each moment is what you make it, and for you there's nothing better than spending those moments with friends. They don't always see what you find so funny, but with a little help from you, they can laugh at death too.

Invoker: Some would call you a trickster, others would call you a thief or a cheat, but they'd have to catch you first, and even then you'd figure out how to slip free. You know that the secret to life is living it well, and you use others as unwitting pawns in ways that amuse you. Sehanine approves, of course. If she didn't, you know she'd steal back the gifts she has given—because you'd do the same in her place.

Paladin: You can't say for certain where the boundary between right and wrong lies, but as you travel the road of life, you make sure to keep between those ditches. Yet there's one thing you and Sehanine can't leave behind, one thing that's worth going off your course for: love. Whether it's for the passion between two or the camaraderie of many, you'll stand your ground. Right and wrong don't mean a thing when you raise your shield—or draw your sword—for love.

LEE MOYER (3)

DIVINE BACKGROUNDS

The background section in Chapter 3 of *Player's Handbook 2* fleshes out the basics of character generation. It provides story hooks for a character's background and adds game benefits that reflect who you were before you became an adventurer.

Here are several backgrounds you can use or adapt to your divine character. After choosing your background elements, you can (with your DM's consent) select one of the following background benefits.

- Gain a +2 bonus to checks with a skill associated with your background.
- Add a skill associated with your background to your class's skills list before you choose your trained skills.
- Choose one language connected to your background. You can speak, read, and write that language fluently.
- If you are using a campaign setting that offers regional benefits (such as the FORGOTTEN REALMS® setting), gain a regional benefit.

CONVERT

You were a member of the clergy of a different deity, but something made you change your allegiance. What deity did you worship before? Was it an evil god or some false idol? Did some tragedy or miracle drive you to follow another god? Did you lose faith in your previous deity for some reason, or did you walk away from that life due to more worldly concerns? Did you meet someone who changed your mind? Do your old allies wish you well, or do they want you back?

Associated Skills: Insight, Religion

DISBELIEVER

In your early life, you never had much respect for gods, but something changed your mind. You still don't know if you can trust the gods you pray to, but you can't turn away from the powers they give. What happened in the past that made you wary of religion? What happened to provoke your return to worship? Are you a true believer now, or are you doing the god's work because of what you hope to gain?

Associated Skills: Bluff, Insight

DIVINELY INSPIRED

Following your divine path seems as natural to you as breathing air. You never heard the call to religion because it's always been in you. Even as a child, you heard voices others could not and saw signs no one else seemed to understand. Did you hide your connection to the divine, or did others know about it? Were you an outcast because of your odd behavior, or did the community look to you because of your gifts?

Associated Skills: Insight, Religion

FAMILY TRADITION

You come from a long family line with members devoted to religion. Does the tradition of worship in your family extend to everyone, or just certain members of the family? Are members of the family forced to adopt the tradition, or is the divine calling something happily shared by everyone? Has everyone worshiped the same deity? Are you breaking with tradition in some way?

Associated Skills: Diplomacy, History

FOLLOWED A CULT

You participated in a cult and worshiped a false god before you saw the true path. Did you follow a mortal demagogue, or was the cult dedicated to some magical creature or supernatural threat? Was the cult nefarious or simply misguided? How did you escape the cult and find your way? Does the cult still exist, or was it crushed or dispersed? Do you still secretly believe the cult's teachings, or do you hunger for revenge against those who lied to you?

Associated Skills: Stealth, Streetwise

FOUND RELIGION AMONG OTHERS

You gained your appreciation of your deity in a culture not your own, and you worship in a manner unfamiliar to your own people. Did you come to worship among another race or in some foreign culture? Was the place where you gained your appreciation for the faith in a distant land or on some other plane? What are the ways that you worship that others might find strange?

Associated Skills: Diplomacy, a skill another race gains a bonus to

HERETIC

You worship the same god or gods as others who share your choice, but you see those deities differently. You believe some legend in contradiction to common thought about your gods, or you practice rites in honor of your deity to which others object. What is it that you do or think that most people reject? Are you looking to make converts, or do you come from a heretical sect? Are you hunted by other faithful? Why did you take this difficult path when ordinary belief was open to you?

Associated Skills: History, Stealth

KYLE ANDERSON

Missionary Life

You or your parents struck out into the wilds to spread the word of your god. Did you travel all over, or stay in one place to preach to a particular group? Were you met with hospitality or hostility? How did you survive in your travels? Did you give up the work, or do you still seek converts? Do you count any converts in distant places as friends?

Associated Skills: Endurance, Nature

Out for Revenge

You follow your god not because you believe in what the god stands for, but because you and your deity have a common enemy. What individual, nation, or race do you desire vengeance against? What happened that made you so hell-bent on justice? How are other faithful likely to view your single-minded pursuit?

Associated Skills: Endurance, Intimidate

Penitent

You did something you're not proud of, a crime that still haunts your thoughts. What did you do? Were you a worshiper of your god when you committed the deed? Why is dedication to a deity the answer for you? Are those you wronged dead, or are they still looking for you? Did you really do something terrible, or do you just think you did?

Associated Skills: Stealth, Thievery

Touched by an Angel

You have encountered dangerous immortals for as long as you can remember, and a guardian angel taught you much of what you know about your god. What was the angel who watched over you like? Is the angel alive or dead? Why did the angel take an interest? What other immortals might interfere with your life?

Associated Skills: Arcana, Perception

Veteran of a Religious War

You fought hard for a divine cause but later turned away from that life. Why did you take up arms for your god? Is the war over, or are people still fighting it? Have you left that life behind, or do the feelings that brought you to battle for your religion still seethe within you?

Associated Skills: Athletics, Intimidate

Ward of the Temple

You grew up in a temple. You ran barefoot there and played games in the shadow of statues. Why were you left at the temple as an orphan or a ward? Are your parents still alive? Who took care of you, and is that person still alive? Where was the temple? Was more than one deity worshiped there? Did you have any rivals among the worshipers or the clergy?

Associated Skills: Heal, Religion

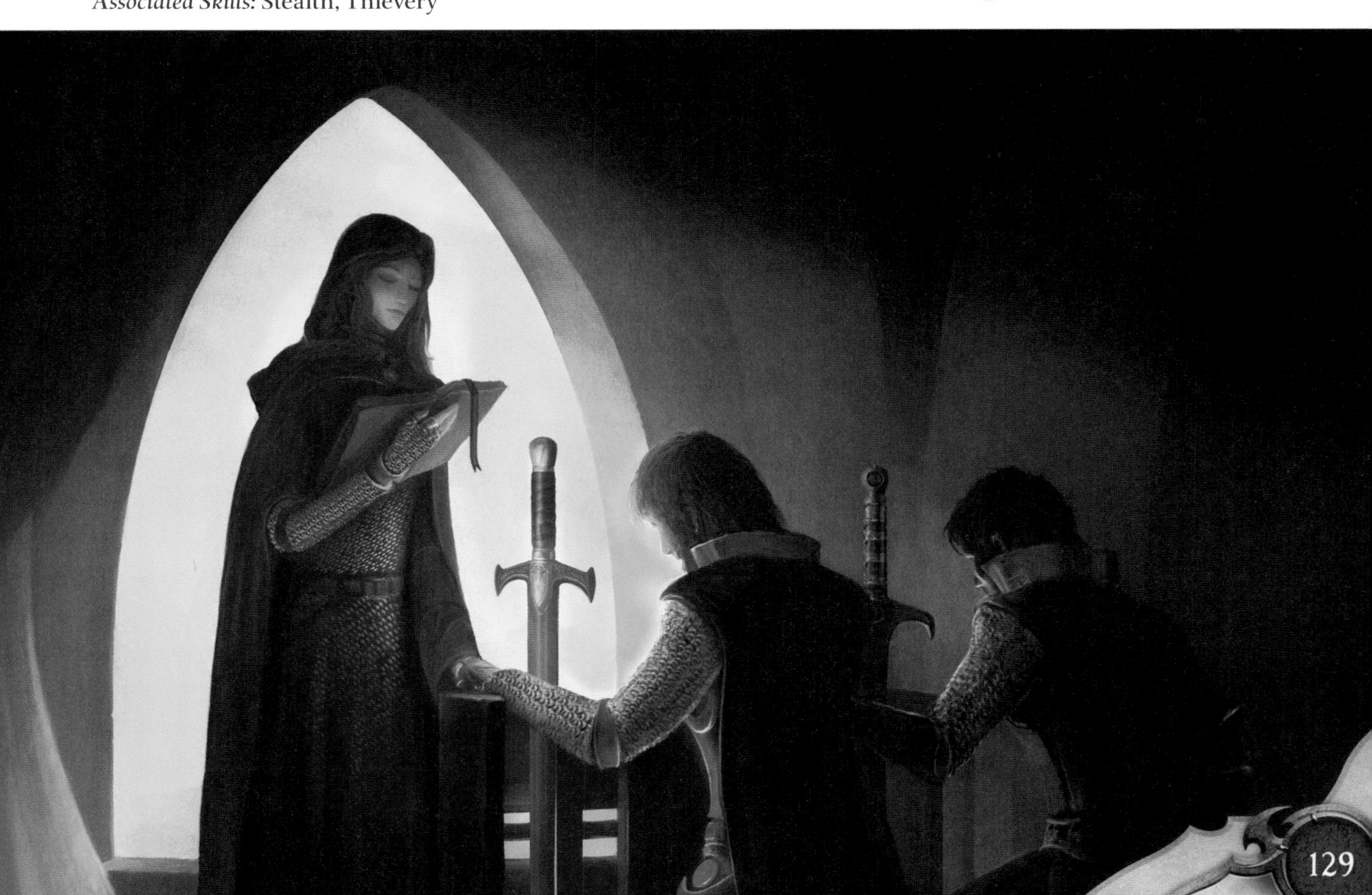

New Feats

Feats provide you with a powerful tool for describing your character's unique experiences, training, and natural knacks and talents. Two human clerics of Pelor might have similar ability scores and power selections, but if one chooses feats that reinforce healing powers and the other selects feats that give numerous options for Channel Divinity, they'll play differently at the table.

You must meet a feat's prerequisites, if any, to take the feat. If you ever lose a prerequisite for a feat, you can't use the feat until you meet the prerequisite again. A feat that has a class as a prerequisite is available only to members of that class, including characters who have joined the class through a class-specific multiclass feat.

Heroic Tier Feats

Feats in this section are available to characters of any level who meet the prerequisites.

Armor of Burning Wrath

Prerequisite: Invoker, Covenant of Wrath class feature

Benefit: Your *armor of wrath* power deals fire and radiant damage and gains the fire keyword. The target of your *armor of wrath* power takes a -1 penalty to saving throws until the end of your next turn.

Armor of Vengeance

Prerequisite: Avenger, Censure of Retribution class feature, *oath of enmity* power

Benefit: While you are adjacent to your *oath of enmity* target, you gain a +1 bonus to all defenses against all creatures other than that one.

Astral Enmity

Prerequisite: Deva, avenger, *oath of enmity* power

Benefit: If you use your *memory of a thousand lifetimes* racial power to increase an attack roll against your *oath of enmity* target, you deal extra damage equal to the bonus gained from the racial power.

Astral Preservation

Prerequisite: Deva, invoker, Covenant of Preservation class feature

Benefit: When you use your *preserver's rebuke* power, each ally within 2 squares of you gains a +1 bonus to all defenses against attacks made by bloodied creatures until the end of the encounter.

Avenging Allure

Prerequisite: Avenger, Censure of Unity class feature

Benefit: When you use your *bond of censure* power, add 2 to the number of squares you can pull the target.

Avenging Opportunist

Prerequisite: Human, avenger, *oath of enmity* power

Benefit: The first time in an encounter when you reduce your *oath of enmity* target to 0 hit points, you gain an extra move action that you must use before the end of your next turn.

Baleful Malediction

Prerequisite: Invoker, Covenant of Malediction class feature

Benefit: Whenever you use a divine encounter or daily attack power on your turn, each target hit by the power takes a -2 penalty to attack rolls against you until the start of your next turn.

Battle Healer

Prerequisite: Cleric, *healing word* power

Benefit: When you use your *healing word*, you regain hit points equal to your Strength modifier.

Blessed Scoundrel

Prerequisite: Halfling, any divine class

Benefit: When you use your *second chance* racial power and the enemy misses you with its attack, you can spend a healing surge.

Blessed Shifter

Prerequisite: Shifter, paladin

Benefit: When you use your *longtooth shifting* or *razorclaw shifting* racial power, you gain a bonus equal to your Wisdom modifier to melee damage rolls with divine powers until the end of your next turn.

Blessing of Avandra

Prerequisite: Halfling, cleric

Benefit: When you use your *second chance* racial power and the attack misses, one ally within 5 squares of you can spend a healing surge.

Blessing of Corellon

Prerequisite: Elf, cleric, *healing word* power

Benefit: When you use your *elven accuracy* racial power and the attack hits, one ally within 5 squares of you can spend a healing surge.

Breath of Life

Prerequisite: Dragonborn, cleric

Benefit: Your *dragon breath* racial power targets only enemies. Allies within the blast of your *dragon breath* gain temporary hit points equal to your Strength modifier.

Brilliant Darkfire

Prerequisite: Drow, any divine class

Benefit: When you hit a target with your *darkfire* racial power, the target gains vulnerability to radiant damage equal to your Charisma modifier until the end of your next turn.

Channel Might

Prerequisite: Paladin

Benefit: After you use a Channel Divinity power, you gain a +1 power bonus to your next melee attack roll made before the end of your next turn.

Clarity of Spirit

Prerequisite: Kalashtar, any divine class

Benefit: When you use your *bastion of mental clarity* racial power, you or one ally in the burst can spend a healing surge.

Closing Pledge

Prerequisite: Avenger, Censure of Pursuit class feature, *oath of enmity* power

Benefit: When you hit your *oath of enmity* target with a ranged attack, you can shift a number of squares equal to 1 + your Dexterity modifier as a free action, as long as you end that shift closer to the target.

Darkfire Vitality

Prerequisite: Drow, cleric

Benefit: When any ally hits an enemy that is under the effect of your *darkfire* racial power, that ally gains temporary hit points equal to your Charisma modifier.

Deadly Rebuke

Prerequisite: Invoker, Covenant of Preservation class feature

Benefit: When you use your *preserver's rebuke* power, add your Intelligence modifier to the damage roll of the attack that gains the bonus from the power.

Defensive Grace

Prerequisite: Cleric, *healer's mercy* power

Benefit: When you use your *healer's mercy*, you gain a power bonus equal to your Charisma modifier to all defenses until the end of your next turn.

Defensive Healing Word

Prerequisite: Cleric, *healing word* power

Benefit: When you use your *healing word*, the target also gains a power bonus to all defenses equal to your Charisma modifier against the next attack made against him or her.

Demonbane

Prerequisite: Any divine class

Benefit: When you use a divine power that normally targets undead, you can also target creatures of the elemental origin.

Demonbane Malediction

Prerequisite: Invoker, Covenant of Malediction class feature

Benefit: If you hit a creature of the elemental origin with your *maledictor's doom* power, that target also grants combat advantage to the next ally of yours who attacks it before the end of your next turn.

Devilbane

Prerequisite: Any divine class

Benefit: When you use a divine power that normally targets undead, you can also target creatures of the immortal origin.

Devoted Paladin

Prerequisite: Paladin, *lay on hands* power

Benefit: When you use your *lay on hands* on an ally, that ally regains additional hit points equal to your Charisma modifier.

When you select this feat, your number of healing surges increases by one.

Divine Approval

Prerequisite: Human, any divine class, Channel Divinity class feature

Benefit: When you use a Channel Divinity power, you can also make a saving throw as a free action.

Divine Assault

Prerequisite: Half-orc, paladin

Benefit: When you use your *furious assault* racial power, one ally within 5 squares of you gains a bonus equal to your Strength modifier to his or her melee damage rolls against the target until the start of your next turn.

Divine Distraction

Prerequisites: Avenger, Censure of Unity class feature, *oath of enmity* power

Benefit: When you are adjacent to your *oath of enmity* target, your allies gain a +1 bonus to damage rolls against that target.

The bonus increases to +2 at 11th level and +3 at 21st level.

HEROIC TIER FEATS

Any Divine Class	Other Prerequisites	Benefit
Blessed Scoundrel	Halfling	Spend healing surge with *second chance*
Brilliant Darkfire	Drow	Targets of *darkfire* gain vulnerable radiant
Clarity of Spirit	Kalashtar	You or ally spends healing surge when you use *bastion of mental clarity*
Demonbane	–	Powers that target undead also target elementals
Devilbane	–	Powers that target undead also target immortals
Divine Approval	Human, Channel Divinity	Channel Divinity grants you a saving throw
Elemental Blessing	Genasi	You or ally gains temporary hp when you use elemental manifestation
Fickle Servant	Changeling or doppelganger	+3 on Religion checks, and you can choose feats from any domain
Furious Devotion	Half-orc, Channel Divinity	+2 damage with divine powers after you use Channel Divinity
Healing Step	Eladrin	Grant temporary hp with *fey step*
Hidden Channeling	Gnome, Channel Divinity	Channel Divinity grants you concealment
Holy Savagery	Shifter, Channel Divinity	Channel Divinity grants you +1 to melee attacks when bloodied
Holy Speech	Fluent in Supernal	Extra success in skill challenges using Bluff, Diplomacy, or Intimidate
Infernal Blessing	Tiefling	Ally regains hp when you use *infernal wrath*
Kord's Resilience	Goliath	*Stone's endurance* extends to adjacent allies
Majestic Presence	Deva	Adjacent allies gain resist 3 necrotic and resist 3 radiant
Nimbus of Light	–	Allies gain +1 to attacks with radiant powers after you use a radiant power
Religious Dabbler	Half-elf	Use at-will power from another divine class as encounter power
Versatile Channeler	Channel Divinity	Gain another class's Channel Divinity power
Warforged Faith	Warforged	*Warforged resolve* also affects adjacent ally

Avenger Feat	Other Prerequisites	Benefit
Armor of Vengeance	Censure of Retribution, *oath of enmity*	+1 to defenses against creatures other than your *oath of enmity* target
Astral Enmity	Deva, *oath of enmity*	Bonus from *memory of a thousand lifetimes* also applies to damage rolls against your *oath of enmity* target
Avenging Allure	Censure of Unity	Pull target 2 extra squares when you use *bond of censure*
Avenging Opportunist	Human, *oath of enmity*	Gain extra move action when you reduce your *oath of enmity* target to 0 hit points
Closing Pledge	Censure of Pursuit, *oath of enmity*	Shift closer to your *oath of enmity* target after hitting it with ranged attack
Divine Distraction	Censure of Unity, *oath of enmity*	Allies gain bonus to damage your *oath of enmity* target when you are adjacent to target
Evade and Strike	Halfling, *oath of enmity*	If your *oath of enmity* target misses due to *second chance*, you gain +2 to damage against target
Fearsome Wrath	Half-orc, *oath of enmity*	Use *furious assault* to penalize attacks of your *oath of enmity* target
Fey Fate	Elf, *oath of enmity*	If you hit your *oath of enmity* target with *elven accuracy*, you gain +2 to damage against target
Feyborn Pursuer	Eladrin, *oath of enmity*	Teleport extra 5 squares with *fey step* if you end adjacent to your *oath of enmity* target
Oath Strike	*Oath of enmity*	Mark your *oath of enmity* target
Psychic Retaliation	Kalashtar, *oath of enmity*	Use *bastion of mental clarity* to change your *oath of enmity* target
Taunting Visage	Changeling or doppelganger, *oath of enmity*	Use *change shape* to gain combat advantage against your *oath of enmity* target
Unleash the Beast	Shifter, *oath of enmity*	Use racial power as immediate reaction when hit by your *oath of enmity* target
Vicious Darkfire	Drow, *oath of enmity*	Use *darkfire* against your *oath of enmity* target to give it vulnerability to all damage

Cleric Feat	Other Prerequisites	Benefit
Battle Healer	*Healing word*	Regain hit points when you use *healing word*
Blessing of Avandra	Halfling	If enemy misses due to *second chance*, ally can spend healing surge
Blessing of Corellon	Elf	If you hit with *elven accuracy*, an ally can spend healing surge
Breath of Life	Dragonborn	Your *dragon breath* gives temporary hp to allies
Darkfire Vitality	Drow	Allies gain temporary hp when they hit enemies under your *darkfire*
Defensive Grace	*Healer's mercy*	Bonus to defenses when you use *healer's mercy*
Defensive Healing Word	*Healing word*	Bonus to recipient's defenses when you use *healing word*
Dwarf Battle Priest	Dwarf, *healing word*	Gain temporary hp when you use *healing word*
Feyborn Fortune	Gnome, *divine fortune*	*Divine fortune* also affects one ally
Healer's Implement	–	Add holy symbol enhancement bonus to healing powers
Holy Resolve	Warforged	Bonus to healing you grant after using *warforged resolve*
Pacifist Healer	–	Your healing powers are better, but you're punished for damaging bloodied foes
Shared Perseverance	Human	When you grant a saving throw, your ally gains +1 to the roll

Invoker Feat	Other Prerequisites	Benefit
Armor of Burning Wrath	Covenant of Wrath	*Armor of wrath* gains fire keyword, and target takes -1 to saving throws
Astral Preservation	Deva, Covenant of Preservation	When you use *preserver's rebuke*, nearby allies gain +1 against attacks by bloodied creatures
Baleful Malediction	Covenant of Malediction	Enemies you hit with encounter or daily powers take -2 to attacks against you
Deadly Rebuke	Covenant of Preservation	Gain more damage with *preserver's rebuke*
Demonbane Malediction	Covenant of Malediction	Elementals you hit with *maledictor's doom* grant combat advantage to your ally
Elemental Rebuke	Genasi, Covenant of Preservation	Ally gains benefits when you use *preserver's rebuke*
Fey Preserver	Eladrin, Covenant of Preservation	Teleport ally 2 squares when you use *preserver's rebuke*
Infernal Malediction	Tiefling	Your attacks gain fear keyword when you use *infernal wrath*
Invoke Resilience	Human	Ally gains +1 to next saving throw when you use a divine power
Invoke Teamwork	Half-elf	Ally gains +1 to defenses when you use a divine power
Preserver's Call	Kalashtar, Covenant of Preservation	Pull allies 1 square closer when you use a daily divine power
Preserving Concealment	Gnome, Covenant of Preservation	Grant concealment to ally when you use *preserver's rebuke*
Wrath of Ages Past	Dwarf, Covenant of Wrath	Gain more damage when you use *armor of wrath* against enemies larger than you
Wrath of the Mountain King	Goliath, Covenant of Wrath	Knock target prone when you use *armor of wrath*

Paladin Feat	Other Prerequisites	Benefit
Blessed Shifter	Shifter	Gain more damage with melee attacks when you use shifting
Channel Might	–	You gain +1 to melee attacks after you use Channel Divinity
Devoted Paladin	*Lay on hands*	Gain 1 healing surge, add Charisma modifier to *lay on hands*
Divine Assault	Half-orc	Ally gains damage bonus against target of your *furious assault*
Divine Perseverance	Human	You gain +2 on your next attack after you succeed on a save
Draconic Challenge	Dragonborn	Your *dragon breath* places your divine sanction on enemies
Elemental Challenge	Genasi	Your *divine challenge* deals acid, cold, fire, lightning, or thunder damage
Group Defense	Half-elf	Allies gain +1 to defenses against creatures you mark
Mark of the Infernal	Tiefling	You can use divine sanction when your *infernal wrath* attack hits
Mighty Challenge	*Divine challenge*	*Divine challenge* deals extra radiant damage
Protector's Commitment	Cha 15	Gain +1 on attacks when you or target is adjacent to bloodied ally
Strength of Stone	Goliath	Ally gains resist all when you use *lay on hands* or *call of virtue*
Virtuous Recovery	–	Gain resist all when you spend healing surge
Warforged Example	Warforged	Allies can save against ongoing damage when you use *warforged resolve*

Divine Perseverance

Prerequisite: Human, paladin

Benefit: When you succeed on a saving throw, you gain a +2 bonus to your next attack roll made before the end of your next turn.

Draconic Challenge

Prerequisite: Dragonborn, paladin

Benefit: When you use your *dragon breath* racial power, you subject each enemy targeted by that power to your divine sanction. This divine sanction lasts until the start of your next turn.

Dwarf Battle Priest

Prerequisite: Dwarf, cleric, *healing word* power

Benefit: When you use your *healing word* on an ally, you gain temporary hit points equal to your Constitution modifier.

Elemental Blessing

Prerequisite: Genasi, any divine class

Benefit: When you use the racial power associated with your elemental manifestation, you or one ally within 5 squares of you gains temporary hit points equal to your Strength modifier.

Elemental Challenge

Prerequisite: Genasi, paladin

Benefit: When you deal damage to a creature by using your *divine challenge* power, you can change the damage type from radiant to acid, cold, fire, lightning, or thunder. Choose each time you deal damage with *divine challenge*.

Elemental Rebuke

Prerequisite: Genasi, invoker, Covenant of Preservation class feature

Benefit: When you use your *preserver's rebuke* power, you also grant a bonus to the ally attacked by the triggering enemy based on your current elemental manifestation.

Earthsoul: The ally gains a +1 power bonus to Fortitude and to saving throws until the start of your next turn.

Firesoul: The ally gains a +1 power bonus to Reflex and resist 5 fire until the start of your next turn.

Stormsoul: The ally gains a +1 power bonus to Fortitude and resist 5 lightning until the start of your next turn.

Watersoul: The ally gains a +5 power bonus to saving throws against ongoing damage until the start of your next turn.

Windsoul: The ally gains a +1 power bonus to speed and resist 5 cold until the start of your next turn.

Evade and Strike

Prerequisite: Halfling, avenger, *oath of enmity* power

Benefit: When your *oath of enmity* target misses on an attack you forced it to reroll by using your *second chance* racial power, you gain a +2 bonus to damage rolls against that target until the end of your next turn.

The bonus increases to +4 at 11th level and +6 at 21st level.

Fearsome Wrath

Prerequisite: Half-orc, avenger, *oath of enmity* power

Benefit: When you use your *furious assault* racial power against your *oath of enmity* target, the target takes a -1 penalty to attack rolls until the start of your next turn.

Fey Fate

Prerequisite: Elf, avenger, *oath of enmity* power

Benefit: When you use your *elven accuracy* racial power to reroll an attack roll made against your *oath of enmity* target and you hit, you gain a +2 bonus to damage rolls against that target until the end of your next turn.

The bonus increases to +4 at 11th level and +6 at 21st level.

Fey Preserver

Prerequisite: Eladrin, invoker, Covenant of Preservation class feature

Benefit: When you use your *preserver's rebuke* power, you can also teleport the ally who was hit by the triggering enemy 2 squares.

Feyborn Fortune

Prerequisite: Gnome, cleric, *divine fortune* power

Benefit: When you use your *divine fortune*, you also grant the +1 bonus to an ally within 5 squares of you.

Feyborn Pursuer

Prerequisite: Eladrin, avenger, *oath of enmity* power

Benefit: When you use your *fey step* racial power, you can teleport an extra 5 squares as long as you end adjacent to your *oath of enmity* target.

Fickle Servant

Prerequisite: Changeling or doppelganger, any divine class

Benefit: You can select domain feats for any domain, not just those for domains associated with your deity.

Also, you gain a +3 feat bonus to Religion checks.

Furious Devotion

Prerequisite: Half-orc, any divine class, Channel Divinity class feature

Benefit: When you use a Channel Divinity power, you gain a +2 bonus to damage rolls with divine attack powers until the end of your next turn.

Group Defense

Prerequisite: Half-elf, paladin

Benefit: Allies gain a +1 bonus to all defenses against creatures marked by you.

Healer's Implement

Prerequisite: Cleric

Benefit: When you grant healing with any of your cleric healing powers, add your holy symbol's enhancement bonus to the hit points the recipient regains.

Healing Step

Prerequisite: Eladrin, any divine class

Benefit: When you use your *fey step* racial power, one ally adjacent to either your original space or your destination space gains temporary hit points equal to your Intelligence modifier and can shift 1 square as a free action.

Hidden Channeling

Prerequisite: Gnome, any divine class, Channel Divinity class feature

Benefit: When you use a Channel Divinity power, you gain concealment until the end of your next turn.

Holy Resolve

Prerequisite: Warforged, cleric

Benefit: When you use your *warforged resolve* racial power, add your Strength modifier to the hit points regained by targets of your cleric healing powers until the end of your next turn.

Holy Savagery

Prerequisite: Shifter, any divine class, Channel Divinity class feature

Benefit: When you use a Channel Divinity power while you are bloodied, you gain a +1 bonus to melee attack rolls until the end of your next turn.

Holy Speech

Prerequisite: Any divine class, fluent in Supernal

Benefit: When you use Bluff, Diplomacy, or Intimidate in a skill challenge, you gain an extra success toward completing the skill challenge the first time you succeed on a skill check involving any one of those skills.

Infernal Blessing

Prerequisite: Tiefling, any divine class

Benefit: When you use your *infernal wrath* racial power, one ally adjacent to you regains hit points equal to your Charisma modifier and gains a +1 power bonus to his or her next attack roll against an enemy that hit you since your last turn.

Infernal Malediction

Prerequisite: Tiefling, invoker

Benefit: When you use your *infernal wrath* racial power, all attacks you make until the end of your next turn gain the fear keyword.

Invoke Resilience

Prerequisite: Human, invoker

Benefit: When you use a divine encounter or daily attack power on your turn, one ally within 10 squares of you gains a +1 power bonus to his or her next saving throw before the end of your next turn.

Invoke Teamwork

Prerequisite: Half-elf, invoker

Benefit: When you use a divine encounter or daily attack power on your turn, one ally within 10 squares of you gains a +1 power bonus to all defenses until the end of your next turn.

Kord's Resilience

Prerequisite: Goliath, any divine class

Benefit: While your *stone's endurance* racial power is active, allies adjacent to you have the same resistance that the power grants you.

Majestic Presence

Prerequisite: Deva, any divine class

Benefit: Allies adjacent to you gain resist 3 necrotic and resist 3 radiant. The resistance increases to 5 at 11th level and 10 at 21st level.

Mark of the Infernal

Prerequisite: Tiefling, paladin

Benefit: If an attack enhanced by your *infernal wrath* racial power hits, you also subject the target to your divine sanction. This divine sanction lasts until the start of your next turn.

Mighty Challenge

Prerequisite: Paladin, *divine challenge* power

Benefit: Whenever a target of your *divine challenge* takes damage from that power, it takes extra radiant damage equal to your Strength modifier.

Nimbus of Light

Prerequisite: Any divine class

Benefit: When you use a divine encounter or daily power that has the radiant keyword, you can create a zone of bright light in a close burst 1. The zone lasts until the end of your next turn. Allies within the zone gain a +1 power bonus to attack rolls with radiant powers.

Oath Strike

Prerequisite: Avenger, *oath of enmity* power

Benefit: When you use *oath of enmity*, you can mark the target until the end of your next turn.

Pacifist Healer

Prerequisite: Cleric

Benefit: When you use a divine power that allows a target to spend a healing surge, the target regains additional hit points equal to 1d6 + your Charisma modifier. The additional hit points increase to 2d6 + your Charisma modifier at 11th level, and to 3d6 + your Charisma modifier at 21st level.

Also, whenever you deal damage to a bloodied enemy, you are stunned until the end of your next turn.

Preserver's Call

Prerequisite: Kalashtar, invoker, Covenant of Preservation class feature

Benefit: When you use a divine daily attack power on your turn, you can pull each ally within 5 squares of you 1 square instead of using the normal benefit of your Covenant Manifestation.

Preserving Concealment

Prerequisite: Gnome, invoker, Covenant of Preservation class feature

Benefit: When you use your *preserver's rebuke* power, you can also grant concealment to the ally who was hit by the triggering enemy. The concealment lasts until the end of your next turn.

Protector's Commitment

Prerequisite: Cha 15, paladin

Benefit: When you or your target is adjacent to a bloodied ally, you gain a +1 bonus to attack rolls.

Psychic Retaliation

Prerequisite: Kalashtar, avenger, *oath of enmity* power

Benefit: When you use your *bastion of mental clarity* racial power, you can make the triggering enemy your new *oath of enmity* target as a free action.

Religious Dabbler

Prerequisite: Half-elf, any divine class

Benefit: Choose a 1st-level at-will attack power from a divine class other than your own. From now on, you can use either that power or the power you gained from your Dilettante racial trait as an encounter power (but you can't use both in the same encounter).

Shared Perseverance

Prerequisite: Human, cleric

Benefit: When you use a power that allows an ally to make a saving throw, the ally gains a +1 bonus to the saving throw.

Strength of Stone

Prerequisite: Goliath, paladin

Benefit: When you use your *lay on hands* or *call of virtue* power on an ally, the ally gains resistance to all damage equal to your Strength modifier until the end of your next turn.

Taunting Visage

Prerequisite: Changeling or doppelganger, avenger, *oath of enmity* power

Benefit: If you use your *change shape* racial power to assume the appearance of your *oath of enmity* target, you gain combat advantage against that creature until the end of your next turn.

Unleash the Beast

Prerequisite: Shifter, avenger, *oath of enmity* power

Benefit: If you are bloodied after your *oath of enmity* target hits you, you can use your *longtooth shifting* or *razorclaw shifting* racial power as an immediate reaction.

Versatile Channeler

Prerequisite: Any divine class, Channel Divinity class feature

Benefit: Choose a divine class other than your own and a Channel Divinity power available as a class feature for that class. Add that Channel Divinity power to your list of available Channel Divinity powers.

Vicious Darkfire

Prerequisite: Drow, avenger, *oath of enmity* power

Benefit: Whenever you hit your *oath of enmity* target with your *darkfire* racial power, it gains vulnerability to all damage equal to your Dexterity modifier until the start of your next turn.

WAYNE REYNOLDS

Virtuous Recovery

Prerequisite: Paladin

Benefit: Whenever you spend a healing surge, you gain resistance to all damage equal to your Wisdom modifier until the start of your next turn.

Warforged Example

Prerequisite: Warforged, paladin

Benefit: When you use your *warforged resolve* racial power, each ally within 5 squares of you can make a saving throw against one effect that deals ongoing damage and that a save can end.

Warforged Faith

Prerequisite: Warforged, any divine class

Benefit: When you use your *warforged resolve* racial power, one ally adjacent to you gains temporary hit points equal to your Constitution modifier and can make a saving throw against an effect that deals ongoing damage and that a save can end.

Wrath of Ages Past

Prerequisite: Dwarf, invoker, Covenant of Wrath class feature

Benefit: When you use your *armor of wrath* power against an enemy larger than you, add your Wisdom modifier to the damage dealt by the power.

Wrath of the Mountain King

Prerequisite: Goliath, invoker, Covenant of Wrath class feature

Benefit: When you use your *armor of wrath* power, you can choose to knock the target prone after pushing it.

Paragon Tier Feats

A character must be at least 11th level to select any of the feats in this section.

Armored by Faith

Prerequisite: 11th level, any divine class, Channel Divinity class feature

Benefit: When you use a Channel Divinity power, you gain temporary hit points equal to your Wisdom modifier.

Avenging Surge

Prerequisite: 11th level, avenger, Censure of Unity class feature, *oath of enmity* power

Benefit: When an ally hits your *oath of enmity* target, you gain temporary hit points equal to 3 + 3 per ally adjacent to that target.

Censure's Grip

Prerequisite: 11th level, avenger, Censure of Pursuit class feature, *oath of enmity* power

Benefit: When you have combat advantage against your *oath of enmity* target and hit it with an avenger power, your target cannot shift away from you until the end of your next turn.

Clinging Radiance

Prerequisite: 11th level, any divine class

Benefit: When you hit a target with a divine attack power that has the radiant keyword, the target loses any concealment or total concealment it has and cannot gain concealment or total concealment until the end of your next turn.

Contagious Challenge

Prerequisite: 11th level, paladin, *divine challenge* power

Benefit: When you hit an enemy marked by your *divine challenge*, you also subject one enemy adjacent to the target to your divine sanction. This divine sanction lasts until the start of your next turn.

Darkfoe

Prerequisite: 11th level, any divine class, Channel Divinity class feature

Benefit: When you use a Channel Divinity power, you and each ally within 10 squares of you gain resistance to necrotic damage equal to 5 + your Wisdom modifier until the start of your next turn.

Devout Guidance

Prerequisite: 11th level, avenger, *divine guidance* power

Benefit: When you use your *divine guidance*, the target gains a +3 power bonus to the second attack roll.

Divine Cleansing

Prerequisite: 11th level, cleric, *turn undead* power

Benefit: When you deal damage to at least one undead enemy with your *turn undead*, each ally in the power's burst can make a saving throw.

Eager for Blood

Prerequisite: 11th level, avenger

Benefit: During the first round of combat, your avenger weapon attacks deal 1[W] extra damage.

Extended Healing

Prerequisite: 11th level, cleric, *healing word* power

Benefit: The burst of your *healing word* increases by 5.

Focused Wrath

Prerequisite: 11th level, invoker, Covenant of Wrath class feature

Benefit: When you use your *armor of wrath* power and the triggering enemy is the only enemy in the burst, you deal 1d6 extra damage with that power.

At 21st level, this extra damage increases to 2d6.

Footsteps of Doom

Prerequisite: 11th level, invoker, Covenant of Malediction class feature

Benefit: Each target of your *maledictor's doom* power gains vulnerable 5 to all damage from fear attacks until the end of your next turn.

Forceful Covenant

Prerequisite: 11th level, invoker, Covenant of Malediction class feature

Benefit: Add 1 square to the distance that your Covenant Manifestation allows you to push a target.

What Is an Exarch?

An exarch is the champion or agent of a god, demon lord, or other being of great power. There is no one path leading to the title of exarch; an exarch might be someone who has adopted an appropriate epic destiny, a legendary monster, an archangel, or a damned or exalted soul of great power. Almost any epic character might become an exarch, regardless of his or her choice of destiny. However, characters who take the Chosen, the Demigod, or the Saint epic destiny are naturally suited to becoming exarchs.

The number of exarchs a deity employs, and their exact nature, varies wildly from deity to deity. Most deities have one or two exarchs in their service; some have no exarchs at all, and a few such as Pelor or Moradin have significantly more. For example, Moradin is the leader of the shining host known as the Morndinsamman, which includes the exarchs Berronar, Clangeddin, Dugmaren, Dumathoin, Gorm, Haela, Marthammor, Sharindlar, and Vergadain. At the other extreme, Avandra has taken no exarch into her service in ages. She chooses to interact directly with her followers, and she guides her mortal servants to battle against her enemies—not out of any sort of personal cowardice, but because she believes in allowing mortals to solve their own problems.

Choosing to become an exarch is a matter of mutual agreement between character and patron. Sometimes the prospective exarch approaches the deity and offers service, and other times the deity appears to a character with promise and offers patronage. A Chosen or a Saint is generally expected to serve as an exarch; characters of other destinies are generally free to seek or refuse patronage as they wish, although gods are not above manipulating promising Demigods into entering their service.

An exarch gains no special powers above and beyond any offered by his or her epic destiny or nature. However, an exarch has access to his or her patron and is expected to give and receive counsel when in the presence of that deity. In addition, most deities check up on their exarchs from time to time. An exarch off on some mission or adventure in the mortal world might be contacted through a dream or a vision, visited by a messenger angel or a physical manifestation, or sometimes summoned back to the deity's dominion. Some deities manage their exarchs' affairs closely, and others leave exarchs to act at their own discretion. An exarch doesn't have any innate ability to signal for his or her deity's attention, but in practice most deities provide their exarchs with rituals, magic items, or special powers to commune when necessary.

Greater Fortune

Prerequisite: 11th level, cleric, *divine fortune* power

Benefit: Your *divine fortune* changes from personal to close burst 1, and it affects you and all allies in the burst.

Honored Foe

Prerequisite: 11th level, paladin

Benefit: When a creature marked by you damages you, you gain temporary hit points equal to your Wisdom modifier.

PARAGON TIER FEATS

Any Divine Class	Other Prerequisites	Benefit
Armored by Faith	Channel Divinity	Gain temporary hit points with Channel Divinity
Clinging Radiance	–	No concealment with radiant prayer
Darkfoe	Channel Divinity	You and allies gain resist necrotic when you use Channel Divinity
Invigorating Critical	–	Ally regains hit points with critical hit on divine power
Pervasive Light	–	Enemies vulnerable to radiant take extra damage when you don't use a radiant power
Saving Grace	–	Give ally a saving throw with bonus instead of succeeding on your own saving throw

Avenger Feat	Other Prerequisites	Benefit
Avenging Surge	Censure of Unity, *oath of enmity*	Gain temporary hit points when ally hits your *oath of enmity* target
Censure's Grip	Censure of Pursuit, *oath of enmity*	If combat advantage and a hit, target cannot shift
Devout Guidance	*Divine guidance*	Target of *divine guidance* gains +3 to second attack roll
Eager for Blood	–	During first round of combat, weapon attacks deal extra damage
Pledge of Retribution	Censure of Retribution, *oath of enmity*	Gain +1 to next attack against *oath of enmity* target after you miss that target

Cleric Feat	Other Prerequisites	Benefit
Divine Cleansing	*Turn undead*	Each ally in burst can make saving throw
Extended Healing	*Healing word*	Add 5 to the burst of your *healing word*
Greater Fortune	*Divine fortune*	Change *divine fortune* from personal to close burst 1
Merciful Power	*Healer's mercy*	Each target of your healer's mercy can make saving throw
Radiant Vessel	–	Use radiant power to enhance your *healing word*
Swift Turning	*Turn undead*	Use *turn undead* as minor action instead of standard action

Invoker Feat	Other Prerequisites	Benefit
Focused Wrath	Covenant of Wrath	Gain extra damage if your *armor of wrath* affects only one target
Footsteps of Doom	Covenant of Malediction	Targets of your *maledictor's doom* gain vulnerable 5 to fear attacks
Forceful Covenant	Covenant of Malediction	Add 1 to push when you use your Covenant Manifestation
Invoker's Blaze	–	+2 damage with fire or radiant invoker powers (+4 when bloodied)
Invoker's Control	–	+2 to attacks against enemies that fail a saving throw against your divine powers
Warding Covenant	Covenant of Preservation	Ally you slide with Covenant Manifestation does not grant combat advantage

Paladin Feat	Other Prerequisites	Benefit
Contagious Challenge	*Divine challenge*	Place divine sanction on enemy adjacent to target you have challenged
Honored Foe	–	Gain temporary hit points when a marked foe damages you
Persistent Challenge	Cha 15, *divine challenge*	Maintain *divine challenge* even if you don't attack target
Resurgent Attack	Str 17	Gain +2 to attacks after you spend a healing surge
Touch of Salvation	Cha 15, *lay on hands* or *call of virtue*	Grant saving throw with bonus when you use *lay on hands* or *call of virtue*
Untiring Virtue	*Ardent vow, call of virtue,* or *lay on hands*	Gain additional use of *ardent vow, call of virtue,* or *lay on hands* when you reach a milestone

Invigorating Critical

Prerequisite: 11th level, any divine class

Benefit: The first time you score a critical hit with a divine attack power during an encounter, an ally adjacent to you or adjacent to the target regains hit points equal to 10 + your Wisdom modifier.

Invoker's Blaze

Prerequisite: 11th level, invoker

Benefit: You gain a +2 feat bonus to damage rolls with divine attack powers that have the fire keyword or the radiant keyword. While you are bloodied, this feat bonus increases to +4.

At 21st level, the feat bonus increases to +3 (or +6 while bloodied).

Invoker's Control

Prerequisite: 11th level, invoker

Benefit: When an enemy fails a saving throw against an effect caused by one of your divine attack powers, you gain a +2 power bonus to the next attack roll you make against that target before the end of your next turn.

Merciful Power

Prerequisite: 11th level, cleric, *healer's mercy* power

Benefit: Each target of your *healer's mercy* can make a saving throw.

Persistent Challenge

Prerequisite: 11th level, Cha 15, paladin, *divine challenge* power

Benefit: Once per encounter, if you fail to engage the target of your *divine challenge* on your turn, you can maintain that *divine challenge* as if you had engaged the target.

Pervasive Light

Prerequisite: 11th level, any divine class

Benefit: When you hit a target that has vulnerability to radiant damage with an attack that does not deal radiant damage, you deal extra damage equal to that vulnerability.

Pledge of Retribution

Prerequisite: 11th level, avenger, Censure of Retribution class feature, *oath of enmity* power

Benefit: If you miss your *oath of enmity* target with an attack, you gain a +1 bonus to the next attack roll you make against that target before the end of your next turn.

Radiant Vessel

Prerequisite: 11th level, cleric

Benefit: If you hit an enemy with a cleric attack power that has the radiant keyword, the next time you use *healing word* before the end of your next turn the target regains 2d6 additional hit points.

Resurgent Attack

Prerequisite: 11th level, Str 17, paladin

Benefit: When you spend a healing surge, you gain a +2 power bonus to the next attack roll you make before the end of your next turn.

Saving Grace

Prerequisite: 11th level, any divine class

Benefit: When you succeed on a saving throw, you can choose not to end the effect you saved against and instead allow an ally within 5 squares of you to make a saving throw with a bonus equal to your Wisdom modifier.

Swift Turning

Prerequisite: 11th level, cleric, *turn undead* power

Benefit: You can use your *turn undead* as a minor action instead of a standard action.

Touch of Salvation

Prerequisite: 11th level, Cha 15, paladin, *lay on hands* or *call of virtue* power

Benefit: When you use your *lay on hands* or *call of virtue* on an ally, that ally can make a saving throw with a bonus equal to your Charisma modifier.

Untiring Virtue

Prerequisite: 11th level, paladin; *ardent vow, call of virtue*, or *lay on hands* power

Benefit: Whenever you reach a milestone, you gain one additional use of your *ardent vow, call of virtue*, or *lay on hands* for today.

Warding Covenant

Prerequisite: 11th level, invoker, Covenant of Preservation class feature

Benefit: When you use your Covenant Manifestation to slide an ally, no enemy can gain combat advantage against that ally until the end of your next turn.

Epic Tier Feats

The following feats are available only to characters of 21st level or higher.

Beatific Healer

Prerequisite: 21st level, cleric, trained in Heal

Benefit: When you use a divine healing power, add your Charisma modifier to the hit points the recipient regains.

Crusading Wrath

Prerequisite: 21st level, Str 21, Wis 15, paladin, *divine strength* power

Benefit: When you use your *divine strength*, the next enemy you attack before the end of your next turn is subject to your divine sanction until the end of the encounter.

While the target is subject to your divine sanction, add your Wisdom modifier to the damage it takes from the divine sanction.

Devastating Invocation

Prerequisite: 21st level, invoker

Benefit: When you score a critical hit with an invoker power, each enemy within 5 squares of the target of the critical hit takes damage equal to 5 + your Wisdom modifier. The damage type is the same as that dealt by the critical hit.

Divine Health

Prerequisite: 21st level, any divine class

Benefit: You gain resistance to poison equal to one-half your level + your Wisdom modifier.

You can't become infected by any disease of level 30 or lower.

Divine Mastery

Prerequisite: 21st level, any divine class

Benefit: When you spend an action point to take an extra action, you also regain the use of a divine encounter power you have used during this encounter.

Enmity Shared

Prerequisite: 21st level, avenger, *oath of enmity* power

Benefit: When you use your *oath of enmity*, the target grants combat advantage until the end of your next turn.

Epic Turning

Prerequisite: 21st level, cleric, *turn undead* power

Benefit: When you use your *turn undead*, the size of the burst increases by 2, and each target is pushed even on a miss.

Fist of Heaven

Prerequisite: 21st level, avenger, *oath of enmity* power

Benefit: Your *oath of enmity* target takes a -2 penalty to saving throws.

Glorious Channeler

Prerequisite: 21st level, any divine class, Channel Divinity class feature

Benefit: Twice per encounter, you can use a Channel Divinity power, but not the same power twice.

Great Malediction

Prerequisite: 21st level, invoker, Covenant of Malediction class feature

Benefit: When you use a divine encounter or daily attack power on your turn, you can push each target hit by the power 1 square (instead of applying the normal effect of your Covenant Manifestation).

Guiding Rebuke

Prerequisite: 21st level, invoker, Covenant of Preservation class feature

Benefit: When you use your *preserver's rebuke* power, one ally within 10 squares of you gains a bonus equal to your Intelligence modifier on his or her next attack roll against the triggering enemy.

Heavenly Torrent

Prerequisite: 21st level, avenger, *oath of enmity* power

Benefit: The first time you score a critical hit on your *oath of enmity* target during an encounter, each ally can make a second attack roll and use either result on the next attack he or she makes against that target before the start of your next turn.

Icon of Hope

Prerequisite: 21st level, any divine class

Benefit: Bloodied allies within 10 squares of you gain a +1 bonus to saving throws.

Icon of Purity

Prerequisite: 21st level, any divine class

Benefit: You gain resistance to necrotic damage equal to one-half your level + your Wisdom modifier.

Indiscriminate Wrath

Prerequisite: 21st level, invoker, Covenant of Wrath class feature

Benefit: When you use your *armor of wrath* power, you can target each enemy in the burst, rather than only the triggering enemy.

Invoker's Aura

Prerequisite: 21st level, invoker

Benefit: Until the end of your next turn, after you use a Channel Divinity power, any enemy within 2 squares of you that hits you or any enemy that ends its turn within 2 squares of you takes radiant damage equal to 5 + your Wisdom modifier. No enemy can take this damage more than once per turn.

Paladin's Truth

Prerequisite: 21st level, paladin

Benefit: When you attack a creature marked by you, you ignore that creature's resistances and immunities.

EPIC TIER FEATS

Any Divine Class	Other Prerequisites	Benefit
Divine Health	–	You gain resistance to poison
Divine Mastery	–	Regain use of divine encounter power when you spend action point
Glorious Channeler	Channel Divinity	You can use Channel Divinity twice per encounter
Icon of Hope	–	Bloodied allies gain +1 bonus to saving throws
Icon of Purity	Trained in Religion	You gain resistance to necrotic damage
Punishing Radiance	–	Critical hit increases target's vulnerability to radiant damage

Avenger Feat	Other Prerequisites	Benefit
Enmity Shared	*Oath of enmity*	*Oath of enmity* target grants combat advantage when first chosen
Fist of Heaven	*Oath of enmity*	*Oath of enmity* target takes -2 penalty to saving throws
Heavenly Torrent	*Oath of enmity*	Grant allies rerolls on attacks against your *oath of enmity* target after you score critical ht on target
Righteous Focus	Censure of Unity, *oath of enmity*	Allies gain +1 to attacks against *oath of enmity* target while you are adjacent to target
Vengeance Recalled	*Oath of enmity*	On a miss, gain +5 damage against target

Cleric Feat	Other Prerequisites	Benefit
Beatific Healer	Trained in Heal	Add bonus to healing you grant with divine powers
Epic Turning	*Turn undead*	Increase burst by 2, and target pushed even on miss
Radiant Advantage	–	Enemies you deal radiant damage to grant combat advantage
Reactive Healing	*Healing word*	Use *healing word* as reaction to save dying ally
Shared Healing	–	You or willing ally can spend healing surge in place of the target
Supreme Healer	–	You heal two targets instead of one when you use *healing word*

Invoker Feat	Other Prerequisites	Benefit
Devastating Invocation	–	Deal extra damage to enemies near target when you score critical hit with invoker power
Great Malediction	Covenant of Malediction	Targets you hit with encounter or daily divine power are pushed 1
Guiding Rebuke	Covenant of Preservation	Ally gains attack bonus against target of your *preserver's rebuke*
Indiscriminate Wrath	Covenant of Wrath	Target all enemies in burst when you use *armor of wrath*
Invoker's Aura	–	Gain damaging aura after using Channel Divinity
Unbearable Malediction	Covenant of Malediction	Increase the distance you push target with *maledictor's doom*

Paladin Feat	Other Prerequisites	Benefit
Crusading Wrath	Str 21, Wis 15, *divine strength*	Place divine sanction on next foe you attack after using *divine strength*; add Wis mod to damage dealt by sanction
Paladin's Truth	–	Ignore resistance and immunity when you attack a foe you marked
Pious Champion	*Call of virtue* or *lay on hands*	Target two allies with *call of virtue* or *lay on hands*
Protecting Boon	Cha 21, Str 15, *divine mettle*	Target each ally in burst with *divine mettle*
Tireless Wrath	Str 21, Cha 15, *divine strength*	*Divine strength* lasts longer
Virtuous Company	Cha 21, Wis 15, *divine mettle*	Grant temporary hp to each ally who succeeds on a saving throw granted by *divine mettle*

Pious Champion

Prerequisite: 21st level, paladin, *call of virtue* or *lay on hands* power

Benefit: When you use your *call of virtue* or *lay on hands*, you can target one or two creatures. If you target two creatures with *lay on hands*, you spend one healing surge and each target regains hit points as normal for the power.

Protecting Boon

Prerequisite: 21st level, Cha 21, Str 15, paladin, *divine mettle* power

Benefit: When you use your *divine mettle*, you can target each ally in the burst.

Punishing Radiance

Prerequisite: 21st level, any divine class

Benefit: Whenever you score a critical hit with a divine attack power that has the radiant keyword, the target and each enemy within 5 squares of it gain vulnerable 10 radiant (or its existing vulnerability to radiant damage increases by 10) until the end of your next turn.

Radiant Advantage

Prerequisite: 21st level, cleric

Benefit: When you deal radiant damage to an enemy, you and your allies gain combat advantage against it until the end of your next turn.

Reactive Healing

Prerequisite: 21st level, cleric, *healing word* power

Benefit: You can use your *healing word* as an immediate reaction, triggered when an ally within 5 squares of you drops to 0 hit points or fewer. You must target the triggering ally with the *healing word*.

Righteous Focus

Prerequisite: 21st level, avenger, Censure of Unity class feature, *oath of enmity* power

Benefit: While you are adjacent to your *oath of enmity* target, your allies gain a +1 bonus to attack rolls against it.

Shared Healing

Prerequisite: 21st level, cleric

Benefit: When you use a power that allows an ally to spend a healing surge, you can instead have that ally regain hit points as if he or she had spent a healing surge, and you or another willing ally within 5 squares of you spends the healing surge instead.

Supreme Healer

Prerequisite: 21st level, cleric, *healing word* power

Benefit: When you use your *healing word*, you can heal two targets instead of one (either two allies or one ally and yourself).

Rites for the Deities

The people of the world and planes worship the deities in different ways. Some common practices are almost universal from culture to culture.

- When you are proven wrong, write down two copies of the truth you discover, keeping one and taking the other to a shrine to Ioun.
- After you take fruit, herbs, or wood from a forest, trace a star in the soil so Corellon's magic can replace what you've taken.
- Swear by Bahamut when you make an oath to bring someone to justice.
- When you agree to an alliance or a business arrangement, interlock your fingers like the teeth of two gears—forming the symbol of Erathis.
- Etch Avandra's symbol on a path to indicate a safe course or on a building to show it is a safe house.
- Shout at the heavens during a storm to prove your bravery to Kord.
- Wear golden jewelry during the day and silver at night, to please both Pelor and Sehanine.
- Inter a raven's feather with a corpse to keep undeath from claiming the body.

Tireless Wrath

Prerequisite: 21st level, Str 21, Cha 15, paladin, *divine strength* power

Benefit: When you use your *divine strength*, the effect applies to all attacks you make until the end of your next turn.

Unbearable Malediction

Prerequisite: 21st level, invoker, Covenant of Malediction class feature

Benefit: Whenever your *maledictor's doom* power allows you to push a target, you can add one-half your Intelligence modifier to the number of squares pushed.

Vengeance Recalled

Prerequisite: 21st level, avenger, *oath of enmity* power

Benefit: When you miss with an avenger power against your *oath of enmity* target, you gain a +5 bonus to damage rolls against that target until the end of your next turn.

Virtuous Company

Prerequisite: 21st level, Cha 21, Wis 15, paladin, *divine mettle* power

Benefit: When you use your *divine mettle*, you gain temporary hit points equal to your Charisma modifier for each ally who succeeds on a saving throw granted by this power.

Multiclass Feats

Some of these feats have paragon multiclassing in a particular class as a prerequisite. To qualify for such a feat, you must have chosen paragon multiclassing (*Player's Handbook*, page 209).

Channel of Faith [Multiclass Cleric]

Prerequisite: Any multiclass cleric feat, paragon multiclassing as a cleric

Benefit: You gain the cleric Channel Divinity powers *divine fortune* and *turn undead*. If you don't already have the Channel Divinity class feature, you can use a single Channel Divinity power once per encounter, and you're considered to have the class feature for the purpose of meeting prerequisites.

Channel of Invocation [Multiclass Invoker]

Prerequisite: Any multiclass invoker feat, paragon multiclassing as an invoker

Benefit: You gain the invoker Channel Divinity powers *armor of wrath* and *preserver's rebuke*. If you don't already have the Channel Divinity class feature, you can use a single Channel Divinity power once per encounter, and you're considered to have the class feature for the purpose of meeting prerequisites.

MULTICLASS FEATS

Name	Prerequisites	Benefit
Channel of Faith	Any multiclass cleric feat, paragon multiclassing as a cleric	Cleric: *divine fortune* or *turn undead* 1/encounter
Channel of Invocation	Any multiclass invoker feat, paragon multiclassing as an invoker	Invoker: *armor of wrath* or *preserver's rebuke* 1/encounter
Channel of Valor	Any multiclass paladin feat, paragon multiclassing as a paladin	Paladin: *divine mettle* or *divine strength* 1/encounter
Channel of Vengeance	Any multiclass avenger feat, paragon multiclassing as an avenger	Avenger: *abjure undead* or *divine guidance* 1/encounter
Divine Channeler	Wis 13, trained in Religion	Gain one Channel Divinity power from another class
Divine Healer	Wis 15	Cleric: training in Heal, Healer's Lore
Divine Secretkeeper	Wis 13, Int 13	Invoker: training in Arcana, History, or Religion, Ritual Casting
Hero of Faith	Wis 15	Avenger: training in one class skill, *oath of enmity* 1/encounter
Soldier of Virtue	Wis 15	Paladin: training in one class skill, *virtue's touch* 1/day

Channel of Valor [Multiclass Paladin]

Prerequisite: Any multiclass paladin feat, paragon multiclassing as a paladin

Benefit: You gain the paladin Channel Divinity powers *divine mettle* and *divine strength*. If you don't already have the Channel Divinity class feature, you can use a single Channel Divinity power once per encounter, and you're considered to have the class feature for the purpose of meeting prerequisites.

Channel of Vengeance [Multiclass Avenger]

Prerequisite: Any multiclass avenger feat, paragon multiclassing as an avenger

Benefit: You gain the avenger Channel Divinity powers *abjure undead* and *divine guidance*. If you don't already have the Channel Divinity class feature, you can use a single Channel Divinity power once per encounter, and you're considered to have the class feature for the purpose of meeting prerequisites.

Divine Channeler [Multiclass]

Prerequisite: Wis 13, trained in Religion

Benefit: Choose a divine class other than your own and a Channel Divinity power available as a class feature for that class.

If you don't already have the Channel Divinity class feature, you can use the selected Channel Divinity power once per day.

If you already have the Channel Divinity class feature, add the selected Channel Divinity power to your list of available Channel Divinity powers.

You are treated as having the Channel Divinity class feature for the purpose of meeting prerequisites. If you gain additional Channel Divinity powers by selecting divinity feats, you can use them in place of the power granted by this feat, but that doesn't change your normal limit on uses of Channel Divinity.

Special: This feat counts as a class-specific multiclass feat for the chosen class.

Divine Healer [Multiclass Cleric]

Prerequisite: Wis 15

Benefit: You gain training in the Heal skill.

You gain the cleric's Healer's Lore class feature.

In addition, you can wield cleric implements.

Divine Secretkeeper [Multiclass Invoker]

Prerequisite: Wis 13, Int 13

Benefit: You gain training in the Arcana skill, the History skill, or the Religion skill.

You gain the invoker's Ritual Casting class feature.

In addition, you can wield invoker implements.

Hero of Faith [Multiclass Avenger]

Prerequisite: Wis 15

Benefit: You gain training in one skill from the avenger's class skills list.

Once per encounter, you can use the *oath of enmity* power. You do not regain the use of the power if the target drops to 0 hit points.

In addition, you can wield avenger implements.

Soldier of Virtue [Multiclass Paladin]

Prerequisite: Wis 15

Benefit: You gain training in one skill from the paladin's class skills list.

Once per day, you can use the *virtue's touch* power.

In addition, you can wield paladin implements.

EPIC DESTINIES

Many epic-level divine characters can anticipate exaltation or damnation after death; as powerful stewards of divine causes in the mortal world, they are naturally among the favorites of the gods. The following epic destinies offer paths that transition the divine hero from the mortal world to the dominions beyond.

Avatar of Death

You know that life is fleeting, but death is forever. Your enemies would be well advised to remember that as they face you.

Prerequisite: 21st level, Death Knell feat

You are the mortal incarnation of a deity who holds sway over death. You are not simply Jozan the cleric; you are the Raven Queen, who for a time incarnates in the form of Jozan. Your body is a mere shell, a temporary vessel for the unthinkable might of a deity's soul. You were born to be the Raven Queen's mortal form, and as you grow in understanding and power, the light (or darkness) within you shines out for all to see. You might not have realized your true nature before, but now you know exactly what you are.

As an avatar of death, you incarnate the death aspect of your deity. Most likely this is the Raven Queen, but on rare occasions avatars of dead, dormant, or interloper gods arise—you might be an avatar of the dead god Nerull, or some other death deity contesting the Raven Queen's sway.

Good and evil are just words to you, for death makes all causes meaningless. You stare into the vacant sockets of long-dead kings, gaze across the soul-filled plains of the Shadowfell, and stand upon blood-soaked fields of battle. Through it all, you feel no sorrow, no remorse—only a grim sense of bemusement at mortal foolishness in the face of the inevitable. Adventuring is an amusing way to entertain yourself before life comes to an end.

Avatars Have Many Uses

Gods create avatars for many reasons. Some deities want to experience mortality and learn from mortal trials. Some use their avatars as agents and champions to battle their enemies in the world. Others send avatars as teachers and exemplars to their followers. Likewise, different gods might choose to incarnate their avatars in secret or to prophesy their arrival, to incarnate with full awareness of their true nature or to allow their mortal vessels to live well into life before becoming aware of themselves.

WILLIAM O'CONNOR

Immortality

You care little about the fate of your mortal shell, for you know that in time you will rejoin with your true self. After all, even gods must die in time. One or two previous incarnations have turned against the Raven Queen in ages past, using their powers to prolong their mortal existences. Whether you meet your fate with joy, resignation, or defiance is up to you.

Divine Reunion: When you complete your final quest, the purpose of your current incarnation is accomplished. The winds of oblivion sweep your body into nothingness, freeing your soul to return to its divine origin. You rejoin the deity whose incarnation you were, and you resume your existence in the eternal.

Avatar of Death Features

Foresight of Mortality (21st level): Your Intelligence score and your Wisdom score both increase by 2.

Death Comes to All (21st level): Your powers ignore necrotic resistance up to 20.

Deadly Revival (24th level): The first time each day you begin your turn dying or dead, you revive. You regain hit points equal to your bloodied value, and each enemy within 10 squares of you gains vulnerable 15 necrotic until the end of your next turn.

Harbinger of Demise (30th level): Enemies that end their turn adjacent to you and have 25 hit points or fewer die.

Avatar of Death Power

Inevitable Death — Avatar of Death Utility 26

Dark energy swirls about you and then explodes in a burst that encircles your enemies, causing their wounds to remain open.

Daily ✦ Divine
Minor Action — **Close** burst 5
Target: Each enemy in burst
Effect: The target gains vulnerable 10 to all damage and cannot regain hit points from healing powers or regeneration (save ends both).

Avatar of Freedom

Tyranny, slavery, oppression—these are your foes. You battle against those who think themselves above others.

Prerequisite: 21st level, Path of Freedom feat

You are the incarnation of a deity of freedom and liberation. Every word you speak, every action you take, is in exact accordance with your deity's will—because your choices are your deity's choices. In time you will abandon your mortal form and rejoin your eternal essence in the heavenly dominions, but until that time comes you are a champion, teacher, and example for all whom you and your deity hold dear.

As an avatar of freedom, you incarnate your deity's aspects of liberation. You might be Avandra or Melora in mortal form.

Regardless of your divine identity, you believe that the natural state of mortalkind is one free from oppression. You fight any force that seeks the enslavement of others and stand against deities bent on war and domination, such as Asmodeus and Bane. You believe that freedom of choice is the paramount freedom of all mortal creatures, and that destiny is not predetermined. You inspire the downtrodden with words of freedom, and you lead them in attempts to overthrow their vile masters.

MATIAS TAPIA

Immortality

As your life's tribulations come to a close and your Destiny Quest comes to an end, you are ready to free yourself of the shackles of mortality and physicality. Great struggles await you throughout the cosmos, and immortality represents an opportunity to continue your fight against the oppressive forces in the universe. As long as tyranny flourishes anywhere, freedom everywhere is threatened.

Divine Reunion: At the conclusion of your Destiny Quest, you abandon your current incarnation. Amid golden light and peals of thunder, your soul ascends to the heavenly dominions to rejoin your deity. You are once again Avandra, Melora, or a cosmic spirit of revolution—but you still recall your mortal persona. For ages to come the memories of your experiences and companions in your mortal existence influence your divine thoughts and actions.

Avatar of Freedom Features

Freedom of Mind and Body (21st level): Your Dexterity score and your Wisdom score both increase by 2.

Liberate the Mind (21st level): Allies adjacent to you gain a +2 bonus to saving throws against being dominated, immobilized, restrained, or slowed.

Liberating Revival (24th level): The first time each day you begin your turn dying or dead, you revive. You regain hit points equal to your bloodied value, and each ally within 10 squares of you ends any immobilizing, slowing, or restraining effect currently affecting him or her.

Agent of Freedom (30th level): You cannot be dominated, immobilized, slowed, restrained, or petrified. You ignore difficult terrain, and you can shift your speed as a move action.

Avatar of Freedom Power

Broken Chains — Avatar of Freedom Utility 26

Raising your weapon or implement high, you issue a proclamation that you shall not abide oppression. Your allies respond by shaking off their afflictions.

Daily ✦ Divine, Stance

Minor Action Personal

Effect: Until the stance ends, when an ally starts his or her turn within 5 squares of you, that ally can make a saving throw against each effect on him or her that a save can end.

Avatar of Hope

You steadfastly believe that hope lifts up everyone even in the darkest times. By word and deed, you spread hope wherever you go.

Prerequisite: 21st level, Hope Remains feat

As an avatar of hope, you are an aspect of a god of hope who has chosen to incarnate himself or herself in a mortal body for a time. You now know that you are both your deity and your own mortal shell at the same time. When you speak, when you act, your god speaks and acts through you. No matter what your name, you are a beacon of hope in a dark world.

Sorrow cannot abide your presence; you bring optimism and virtue to places of despair and sadness. You are an enemy of all the gods of evil, for they are destroyers of hope. You hold particular vehemence toward devils and demons—devils for their malicious practices, and demons for their recklessly destructive intentions. It's true that you've seen some terrible sights during your travels—murder, cruelty, slavery, war—but these horrors only fortify your determination. By your power, the points of light that lie within a sea of darkness burn a little brighter for a time.

Immortality

You have fought battles against despair all your life, bringing light to the darkest corners of the world. Your experience has taught you that people need only a little inspiration to find hope, so you have set yourself the task of providing an example, a legend, that will inspire people for ages to come.

Divine Reunion: When you complete your Destiny Quest, your soul bursts forth in a golden flame that consumes your mortal form, and you are reunited with your immortal self.

Avatar of Hope Features

Undaunted Will (21st level): Your Wisdom score and your Charisma score both increase by 2.

Indomitable Courage (21st level): You are immune to fear effects. In addition, you and any allies within 5 squares of you gain a +1 bonus to saving throws.

Hopeful Revival (24th level): The first time each day you begin your turn dying or dead, you revive. You regain hit points equal to your bloodied value, and each ally within 10 squares of you gains 20 temporary hit points.

Triumph of the Heart (30th level): Once per day, you can change the result of a single d20 roll made by an ally to 20. This requires no action on your part, but you must be conscious to do so.

Creating Avatars

Most deities have incarnated only a handful of avatars throughout the ages of the world, although some have never done so, and a few (for example, Moradin and Avandra) incarnate in every generation of mortalkind. Creating an avatar weakens a god for a time and can render it vulnerable to its enemies. Being in two places at once is difficult, even for a god. In the past, powerful devils or wicked mortals have managed to trap, coerce, or corrupt gods through their avatars. However, doing this is difficult in the extreme, since the deity can end its incarnation at any time and rejoin its true being.

Avatar of Hope Power

Elevate the Spirit — Avatar of Hope Utility 26

You conjure an angelic entity that infuses one of your allies' with hope and the mental fortitude to withstand attempts at control.

Daily ✦ Conjuration, Divine
Minor Action **Ranged** 10

Effect: You conjure an angelic figure in a square within range. The figure lasts until the end of your next turn. While the figure is in an ally's space, that ally gains a +4 power bonus to all defenses and can't be dominated. If an ally is affected by a dominating effect that a save can end while the figure is in his or her space, that effect immediately ends. As a move action, you can move the figure 5 squares.

Sustain Minor: The figure persists.

WAYNE REYNOLDS

Avatar of Justice

Your sole purpose is to balance the scales of justice, punishing the wicked and rewarding the good.

Prerequisite: 21st level, Immediate Justice feat

You are a god of justice incarnated in mortal form. All your life you have fought for justice, but now you know yourself for what you are. Your self-awareness merges with divine truth, and your consciousness becomes one with the concept of justice. In years to come, people will remember that you were your deity in the flesh, a shining champion who battled against wrong and a golden example of a righteous and courageous life well lived, but for now it is up to you to forge that legend.

In your true self you might be Bahamut, some other active deity, or even a dead deity such as Amoth—avatars of dormant deities, interloper gods, or cosmic principles sometimes appear in the world. Regardless of which deity you are the incarnation of, you grasp your destiny as a great lawgiver and a force for righteousness. As you take the guise of justice itself, divine knowledge guides you along the right course.

Immortality

Your path might involve the elimination of a major source of injustice, such as an evil deity. The evil gods and their worshipers scoff at justice, reveling in cruelty, theft, and murder. Destroying one of these deities brings the scales of justice closer to balance.

Divine Reunion: During your Destiny Quest, you begin to change. You no longer make decisions—you merely do the will of justice. When your final foe is vanquished, you abandon your mortal body, which falls to silvery dust and blows away in the wind. Your soul finds its way back to your eternal being and reunites, bringing with it all the joys, the sorrows, the wisdom, and the compassion you have learned in your mortal years. Your mortal existence might be done—but as a god of justice you well remember the lessons you learned during your time in the world, and temper your judgments with memories of your mortal experience.

Avatar of Justice Features

Justice's Mind (21st level): Your Intelligence score and your Wisdom score both increase by 2.

Just Consequence (21st level): When an enemy hits you or an ally adjacent to you, the next ally who attacks that enemy before the end of your next turn gains a +1 bonus to the attack roll.

Just Revival (24th level): The first time each day you begin your turn dying or dead, you revive. You regain hit points equal to your bloodied value. Each ally within 10 squares of you gains a +2 power bonus to attack rolls until the end of your next turn, and

each enemy within 10 squares of you takes a -2 penalty to attack rolls until the end of your next turn.

Instant Retribution (30th level): Each time an enemy within 5 squares of you scores a critical hit against you or one of your allies, the enemy takes damage equal to the damage it dealt with the hit.

Avatar of Justice Power

Word of Undoing — Avatar of Justice Utility 26

You deem an attack unjust, and reverse its effects.

Daily ✦ Divine, Healing
Immediate Reaction **Ranged** 10
Trigger: An ally within 10 squares of you is hit by an attack
Target: The triggering ally
Effect: The target takes no damage from the triggering attack and gains hit points equal to the damage he or she would have taken.

Trappings of Justice

You might choose to use symbols that represent justice as your insignia. Here are some of the most common symbols used by avatars of justice:

- Balance scales
- Flames (especially silver or white)
- Double-edged weapons (such as swords or battleaxes)
- Closed eyes or a blindfold

AMELIA STONER

Avatar of Life

Despite war, chaos, and hate, life endures, and you will ensure that it never falters.

Prerequisite: 21st level, Pulse of Life feat

You are the incarnation of a god, mortal and immortal beings united in the same flesh. You exist for the purpose of battling your true godly self's foes in the mortal world, of providing inspiration and hope to all who worship your divine being, and just possibly to learn a few things about what it means to walk in the world you helped to shape at the dawn of time. At the same time, you are also the mortal persona you have been throughout your current life, and you are destined to become part of the god you have served so well.

Avatars represent many different aspects of the gods, but you specifically embody the vital principle, the animating spirit of your deity. All life is sacred to you, and you are its divine protector. Your time as an adventurer has taught you how precarious life can be, whether it is the life of a butterfly struggling to escape its cocoon or a civilization living on the edge of lands inhabited by orcs and goblins. You hate taking life, but you recognize that it is the nature of the world that you must sometimes kill or be killed.

Immortality

As an avatar of life, you might be blessed with incredible longevity. Your calling could draw you to retire to a monastery or a temple to live in obscurity, protecting a small community from harm. You might be fated to heal some great sickness in the world, battling a magical plague or putting an end to some corruption or mockery of life that threatens the natural order. Or you might be compelled to venture across the planes, bringing an example of hope and healing wherever you go.

Divine Reunion: After you have completed your Destiny Quest and lived out the years appointed to you, you are called back to your true self. Lying down in a fair green meadow or forest clearing, you allow your body to crumble into dust, nourishing flowering vines and creepers. Your soul returns to your divine self, recalling the awesome power and understanding that comes with godhood. But some part of your mortal being still survives, since your memories, your cares, and your journeys are now your deity's too.

Avatar of Life Features

Life's Wisdom (21st level): Your Constitution score and your Wisdom score both increase by 2.

Unfettered Durability (21st level): When you roll a 20 on a saving throw, each ally within your line of sight can make a saving throw against one effect that a save can end.

RALPH BEISNER

Vital Revival (24th level): The first time each day you begin your turn dying or dead, you revive. You regain hit points equal to your bloodied value, and each ally within 10 squares of you can spend a healing surge.

Persistence of Life (30th level): You and any allies within 5 squares of you can use second wind as a minor action. If a character can already use second wind as a minor action, then the character can use it as a free action. When you or an ally within 5 squares of you uses second wind, twice the normal number of hit points are restored.

Avatar of Life Power

Font of Life — Avatar of Life Utility 26

Forming a circle with your fingers, you bring forth a sphere of divine energy that helps you and your allies continuously recover from wounds.

Daily ✦ Divine, Healing
Minor Action — **Close** burst 2
Target: You and each ally in burst
Effect: Each target gains regeneration equal to 5 + your Wisdom modifier until the end of the encounter.

Avatar of Storm

You ride the force of nature's fury, bringing wind and thunder and lightning with you. Where you go, the tempest goes.

Prerequisite: 21st level, Storm Sacrifice feat

You are two beings at the same time: a great mortal hero and the god of storms. You have always known you were different from the people around you, but now you understand what you are and why your heart sings when lightning flashes and thunder rolls in the distance. You are destined to walk the world in mortal form for a single brief lifetime, an inspiration to those who worship your true self and a terrible foe to those who oppose you. And after your incarnation ends and you reunite with your immortal being, people will look back on your deeds for centuries to come and see in them the hand of the divine.

As an avatar of storm, you are most likely an incarnation of Kord. However, minor storm deities or dormant powers sometimes incarnate as avatars, so you might be the mortal vessel of some other deity, or even a cosmic principle of storms and destruction.

Thunder and lightning are your weapons, and you wield them with all the fury and wrath of the most violent storm. Wherever you go, storms follow in your wake. You command them and use their power to bring your vengeance upon your enemies.

Immortality

Longevity is rarely important to an avatar of storm. You recognize that life and civilization are fleeting things in this world, and that enough wind and rain can wash away the existence of anything. You might wander into the wilderness to live in isolation or to revel in your communion with the primal forces of the universe. You might even challenge the Elemental Chaos, battling primordials for dominion over storms.

Divine Reunion: When you accomplish your final quest, your mortal existence comes to an end and you return to your divine form. Your body vanishes in a blinding thunderstroke, leaping upward into the dark storm clouds that gather overhead. Your ascension is marked by a thunderstorm of spectacular power. While your mortal life is at an end, your memories, your passions, and your struggles are all now part of your divine being.

Avatar of Storm Features

Strength of the Storm (21st level): Your Constitution score and your Strength score both increase by 2.

Stormhand (21st level): When you use a lightning or a thunder power, you can choose to turn its lightning damage or thunder damage into lightning and thunder damage (if you do so, the power gains the keyword of the second damage type if the power didn't already have it).

Thundering Revival (24th level): The first time each day you begin your turn dying or dead, you revive. You regain hit points equal to your bloodied value, and each enemy within 5 squares of you takes 2d10 + Constitution modifier thunder damage and is pushed 2 squares.

Windstrider (30th level): You gain a fly speed equal to your speed + 2, and you can hover.

Avatar of Storm Power

Gather the Storm — Avatar of Storm Utility 26

You stand at the heart of the storm, surrounded by rumbling thunder and crackling lightning that leaves nearby foes vulnerable.

Daily ✦ Divine

Minor Action — **Personal**

Effect: Until the end of the encounter, any enemy that ends its turn within 5 squares of you gains vulnerable 10 thunder and vulnerable 10 lightning until the end of your next turn.

KIERAN YANNER

Avatar of War

You know that peace cannot endure, and when it fails, you will be there to take over.

Prerequisite: 21st level, Path of War feat

Battle calls you, for you are the god of war. For a mortal lifetime you are incarnated in humanoid shape, sharing the existence and consciousness of a mortal hero. When you speak, you speak for your true divine self. When you act, you act as your godly essence directs. You exist to champion causes worth fighting for, to provide the people of the world with a shining example of valor and skill, and to teach people how to survive in a world filled with darkness and strife.

As an avatar of war, you are probably the incarnation of Bahamut, Kord, Bane, or possibly a dead war deity such as Tuern. However, war is a cosmic force that seems to have its own guiding consciousness, and you might in fact be the incarnation of the principle of war, or an eternal hero reborn to fight in every conflict spawned upon the mortal world.

Life as an adventurer has opened your eyes to the fact that strife and evil are ubiquitous. You have journeyed through many lands, both civilized and wild, and the only constant is the fragility of peace. Others work hard to stop war, but you believe it is the natural state of the world. You recognize that conflict is everywhere, and you embrace it. The machinations of usurpers, tyrants, and warlords will always drive civilization toward violence and destruction—but sometimes it is exactly this destructive force that gives rise to the most powerful and enduring of civilizations.

Immortality

The route to immortality is fraught with danger for an avatar of war. Due to a thirst for conflict, an avatar of war engages in many mortal contests. History tells the tale of several avatars of war cut down in epic battles—it could be that your fate is to forge a legend of a hero who only succeeded in dying well. The ultimate challenge lies in giving battle to the gods and primordials. Whether you hope to usurp power from Bane and conquer his home plane of Chernoggar or to rain destruction down upon surviving primordials, you carry in your ambition a war the likes of which hasn't been seen in a thousand years.

Divine Reunion: When your final quest is accomplished and your last foe lies vanquished at your feet, your mortal incarnation ends. Your body falls into gray dust and blows away to the sounds of ravens croaking and tattered banners flapping in the cold wind. Your soul ascends to the astral dominions to rejoin your divine being, bringing with it a lifetime of memories: battles won, battles lost, deeds of courage, acts of cowardice.

Avatar of War Features

Power in Conflict (21st level): Your Strength score and either your Intelligence score or your Charisma score increase by 2.

Master of the Battlefield (21st level): You never grant combat advantage.

Invoker of War (24th level): Your Channel Divinity power *path of war* grants a +4 bonus to damage rolls in addition to a +2 bonus to attack rolls.

Lord of War (30th level): Your first attack of each encounter that hits deals 25 extra damage.

Avatar of War Power

Rouse Conflict — Avatar of War Utility 26

You raise your weapon or implement and let out a rousing war-cry, invoking your powers of battle. Your shout and divine power stirs allies into action against nearby foes.

Daily ✦ Divine
Minor Action — **Close** burst 10
Target: Each ally in burst
Effect: The target can make an at-will attack as a free action. If the target has an unused divine encounter attack power, he or she can instead use that power as a free action.

WAYNE REYNOLDS

CHOSEN

Your deity makes you the living vessel of his or her power in the mortal world.

Prerequisite: 21st level, any divine class

Your deity selects you to serve as his or her agent in the mortal world. You watch over your deity's worshipers, protect sacred sites, and work to oppose your deity's foes. To prepare you for this task, your deity bestows upon you a spark of divine energy that grants you powers comparable to those of a demigod. As with the Demigod epic destiny detailed in the *Player's Handbook,* this divine spark increases your abilities and bestows great physical resilience. However, your epic destiny utility power is unique to the deity you serve.

Unlike a Demigod, you are sworn to the service of a particular deity. Some deities might leave you to pursue causes dear to them as you see fit, trusting in the good judgment you have demonstrated in your adventuring career. Other deities might task you with missions of importance to them, making sure that you keep their concerns foremost in your mind.

Not all deities have the power or the inclination to elevate a Chosen. Some deities can elevate several Chosen at once, but most have only a single Chosen at any given time. Deities most often bestow this honor on the most faithful of their worshipers, but a few gods take pleasure in selecting undeserving or fickle mortals for their earthly agents.

IMMORTALITY

Chosen often live for centuries. However, as you grow more powerful, the divine fire placed in your soul inevitably transfigures your mortal body. When no vestige of your mortal nature remains, it is time for you to join your deity in the astral dominions and champion his or her causes there. In your place, another deserving mortal can be raised up.

CHOSEN FEATURES

Chosen have the same features as the Demigod epic destiny.

Divine Spark (21st level): Two ability scores of your choice both increase by 2.

Divine Recovery (24th level): The first time you are reduced to 0 hit points or fewer each day, you regain hit points equal to half your maximum hit points.

Divine Miracle (30th level): When you have expended your last remaining encounter power, you regain the use of one encounter power of your choice. In this way, you never run out of encounter powers.

CHOSEN POWERS

Each Chosen has a specific level 26 utility power granted by his or her deity. The powers associated with gods who are either good, lawful good, or unaligned are described below.

Freedom Is Life — Chosen of Avandra Utility 26

Ribbons of glowing symbols flow out of you, linking you and your allies in a river of celestial light.

Daily ✦ Divine
Minor Action **Personal**
Effect: Until the end of your next turn, you and any allies within 20 squares of you gain a +10 bonus to saving throws.

Sheltering Wings — Chosen of Bahamut Utility 26

It is no shame to take refuge beneath the Platinum Dragon's wings.

Daily ✦ Divine, Healing
Minor Action **Melee** 1
Effect: You regain hit points equal to your bloodied value. One ally adjacent to you also regains hit points equal to your bloodied value.

High Arcana — Chosen of Corellon Utility 26

Corellon's mastery of the arcane allows you to choose between empowerment or defense for you and your allies.

Daily ✦ Divine
Minor Action **Close** burst 10
Target: You and each ally in burst
Effect: Until the end of the encounter, at the start of each target's turn, the target can choose to gain either a +2 power bonus to implement attack rolls or a +4 bonus to Fortitude, Reflex, and Will until the start of his or her next turn.

Anthem of Progress — Chosen of Erathis Utility 26

Erathis's grim efficiency inspires your comrades to their necessary work.

Daily ✦ Divine
Minor Action **Close** burst 10
Target: You and each ally in burst
Effect: Until the end of the encounter, each target can score a critical hit with any at-will attack on a roll of 16–20.

DIVINE ALLIES BRING DIVINE ENEMIES

As you might expect, your deity's enemies are yours as well. You, however, are a much more accessible target. Because very few beings can seriously entertain the idea of challenging Pelor, for instance, destroying the Chosen of Pelor is a more realistic and attainable goal. Most deities don't directly attack each other's Chosen, but they are certainly capable of instructing their own Chosen or lesser servants to do so in their stead.

Unerring Foreknowledge — Chosen of Ioun Utility 26

Hints of action and intention spread like gossamer trails that only you and your friends can perceive. Follow the trails and pierce the veils of time.

Daily ✦ Divine
Minor Action **Ranged** 10
Target: One ally
Effect: The target can take an extra standard action on his or her next turn.
Sustain Minor: Choose a different ally within range. That ally can take an extra standard action on his or her next turn. You cannot choose an ally as a target of this power more than once during an encounter.

Test of Strength — Chosen of Kord Utility 26

Strong? Worthy? Kord will judge.

Daily ✦ Divine
Minor Action **Melee** 1
Target: You and one enemy
Effect: The targets simultaneously hit each other with melee basic attacks as free actions. If your attack deals more damage than the enemy's, you can take a standard action as a free action. Any attack roll you make with this standard action has a +4 power bonus.

Wild Surge — Chosen of Melora Utility 26

Wild Melora blesses those who can kill for themselves.

Daily ✦ Divine
Minor Action **Personal**
Effect: Until the end of the encounter, you and any ally within 5 squares of you can score a critical hit with any daily attack power on a roll of 18–20.

Forge of Creation — Chosen of Moradin Utility 26

The fervor of Moradin's ancient workshops of creation inspires you and your allies as you hammer upon your foes.

Daily ✦ Divine
Minor Action **Personal**
Effect: Until the end of your next turn, you and any of your allies who hit with at least one attack regain their second wind if they have already used it during this encounter, regain one healing surge, and gain the use of another daily magic item power.

Celestial Balance — Chosen of Pelor Utility 26

Against the mightiest enemies, there is one hope: Pelor endures.

Daily ✦ Divine, Healing
Immediate Interrupt **Close** burst 10
Trigger: A creature within 10 squares of you spends an action point
Target: You or one ally in burst
Effect: The target can spend a healing surge and gains a +1 bonus to all defenses until the end of the encounter.

Death Is Nigh — Chosen of the Raven Queen Utility 26

The shadow of the queen's wing falls over your fight.

Daily ✦ Divine
Minor Action **Personal**
Requirement: You or one of your allies must have failed a death saving throw during this encounter.
Effect: Until the end of the encounter, you and your allies gain a +2 bonus to attack rolls.

Horns of the Moon — Chosen of Sehanine Utility 26

The goddess blesses and curses, sometimes in the same breath.

Daily ✦ Divine
Minor Action **Personal**
Effect: At the start of each of your turns until the end of the encounter, as a free action you choose one ally and one enemy within your line of sight. The ally you choose gains a +2 bonus to attack rolls until the start of your next turn. The enemy you choose takes a -2 penalty to all defenses until the start of your next turn.

WILLIAM O'CONNOR

Exalted Angel

Your wisdom, courage, and devotion have earned you an honor granted to only a handful of mortals across all the ages of the world—you are transformed into an angel.

Prerequisites: 21st level, any divine class

By the favor of the gods, you transcend mortality and join the angelic hosts. Your mortal flesh and blood are transformed into immortal substance; even though you still have your mortal appearance, your spirit shines inside your perfected body like a blazing fire in a crystal vessel. As an angel, you no longer age, and all the infirmities of mortality fall away. In time you learn to assume more and more of the appearance and powers of angels.

You are closely bound to the god who raised you up. You can continue to pursue the quests and goals of your mortal life, but from time to time your deity summons you to specific missions or dispatches you on important errands, and you are expected to answer any such call. Because you were once mortal, you can resume your mortal appearance whenever you wish, hiding your immortal nature. This attribute makes you a valuable servant, since you can go where other angels cannot; exalted angels often serve as spies or advise mortals on important matters without ever revealing their true nature.

Immortality

Even saints and other elevated souls know the bitterness of death, but you are spared that fate. From the moment of your ascension, you are immortal. For a time you walk the world, an agent of whatever cause your deity holds dear. But eventually you are called away to serve your patron in the astral dominions, leaving the affairs of your mortal life behind.

Exalted Angel Features

Angelic Nature (21st level): Your origin changes to immortal, and you cease to age. You gain the ability to speak Supernal, resist 15 fire, and resist 15 radiant. You are immune to fear attacks.

You gain a pair of angelic wings, which you can manifest or conceal as a minor action. While your wings are manifested, you can fly at a speed equal to your speed + 2, but you land at the end of your turn. If your turn ends while you are still flying, you swiftly descend and land without taking falling damage. While your wings are concealed, your angelic nature is hidden, and you resemble the mortal you once were.

If you already have wings from some other source (such as the favored soul paragon path; see page 23), these angelic wings take the place of the wings you previously gained.

Reborn in Light (24th level): Once per day, when you die, your body disappears in a flash of radiance. Each enemy within 10 squares of you takes 2d10 + Wisdom modifier radiant damage and is blinded (save ends). You reappear in a column of light at the end of the encounter at full hit points with all harmful effects ended.

Angelic Form (30th level): Attacks against you take a -2 penalty as long as you are not bloodied. Also, while your angelic wings are manifested, you can hover. (You no longer need to land at the end of your turn.)

Exalted Angel Power

Angelic Hosts — Exalted Angel Utility 26

You fly a short distance, while a host of minor angels appear to bear your comrades out of peril.

Encounter ✦ Divine
Move Action **Close** burst 10
Target: You and each ally in burst
Effect: Each target gains a +2 power bonus to all defenses until the end of your next turn. In addition, you fly your speed + 2 and land, and as a free action, targeted allies can fly 8 squares and land, without provoking opportunity attacks.

Saint

You are the perfected mortal servant of a god, a shining example of all your deity holds dear.

Prerequisite: 21st level, any divine class

In recognition of your faith, holiness, courage, and piety, you are elevated to sainthood. From the day you embark on this path, you can claim the title of Saint. Through dreams, omens, or angelic visitations, your deity makes your sainthood known to followers around the world. Those who share your faith hold you in the highest regard, while the enemies of your god naturally view you as the most terrible of foes. You might be a great crusader, a mighty prophet, or a revered sage. You set a sterling example of your deity's values and guidance.

Immortality

In the mortal world, you have only the years allotted by nature and fate. You could live to great old age, or you might die young as a hero or a martyr. When at last death draws near, you meet your end with joy—for now you go to the presence of the deity you have served so long and well. Your mortal body remains uncorrupted, and seems to be merely asleep; even the most gruesome wounds slowly vanish, leaving your body an imperishable symbol of divine grace.

Your immortality lies beyond this world, where you will stand among the highest of the elevated souls granted life after life in the divine dominions. In the dominion of your deity, you have a new, immortal body. You join his or her celestial court as a wise and valued counselor. Throughout the world you are regarded as an example of devotion and honor. When people face challenges and hardships similar to those you faced in your mortal life, they are heartened by your example.

Saint Features

Saintly Grace (21st level): You gain a +2 bonus to Fortitude, Reflex, and Will and resistance to necrotic damage equal to 15 + your Wisdom modifier. You cannot be dominated; any attack or effect that would dominate you dazes you instead.

Dark Saints

Although few saints serve evil gods, those that do are fearsome beings indeed. A dark saint gains resist radiant instead of resist necrotic at 21st level.

Sanctified Touch (24th level): When you enable a creature adjacent to you to spend a healing surge, the recipient can also make a saving throw. When you grant a saving throw to a creature adjacent to you, that creature can also spend a healing surge. When you use the Heal skill, any creature you grant a saving throw or stabilize with a successful Heal check can spend a healing surge.

Golden Halo (30th level): Holy light streams from your visage. Your halo gives off bright light within 5 squares, and you gain a +2 bonus to Diplomacy checks and Intimidate checks. You can suppress or resume your halo as a free action. In addition, when you use a divine healing power, the recipient regains 25 additional hit points.

Saint Power

Sanctified Revival — Saint Utility 26

A halo appears around your head, shining with bright golden light. A fallen ally is lifted up and healed by the heavenly light.

Daily ✦ Divine, Healing
Standard Action — **Close** burst 5
Target: One dead or dying ally in burst
Effect: The target is restored to maximum hit points, ends any one effect on him or her that a save can end, and stands up. Until the end of the encounter, the target gains a +2 power bonus to attack rolls and all defenses.

MAZIN KASSIS

NEW RITUALS

Countless minor rites exist in the various holy writings of the world's shrines and temples. Rituals, on the other hand, are powerful magical ceremonies that can summon and shape awesome, long-lasting magical effects. Although any character who has the Ritual Caster feat can master and perform the rituals appearing here, most are associated with the Religion skill, and therefore more easily accessible to divine characters than to others.

RITUALS BY LEVEL

Lvl	Ritual	Key Skill
1	Create Holy Water	Religion
3	Thief's Lament	Arcana or Religion
4	Iron Vigil	Religion
12	Hallowed Temple	Religion
12	Mark of Justice	Religion
16	Adjure	Religion
20	Succor	Religion
25	Ease Spirit	Heal

ADJURE

Filled with righteous authority, you order an immortal entity to serve you.

Level: 16
Category: Binding
Time: 1 hour
Duration: 8 hours or until discharged
Component Cost: 3,000 gp
Market Price: 7,500 gp
Key Skill: Religion

You command an immortal creature whose level does not exceed yours. The subject of this ritual must be able to see and hear you and must remain within 5 squares of you for the entire time necessary to perform the ritual. Because most creatures do not willingly submit to this ritual, you must usually make the creature helpless or restrain the creature by means of a Magic Circle ritual. Unless it is prevented from doing so, the creature can leave at any time. Finally, you must be able to communicate with the creature, or the ritual automatically fails.

To determine the extent of your authority over the subject, you engage in a special skill challenge during the time it takes to perform the ritual. The DCs for the checks in this challenge are equal to the subject's level + 10. Religion is the primary skill; each time you or an ally succeeds on a Religion check in the challenge, you or an ally can use Diplomacy, History, Arcana, or Intimidate for one subsequent check. Once you have amassed 3 failures or achieved 10 successes, the skill challenge ends. Consult the following table and apply the effect associated with the number of successes you achieved.

Number of Successes	Effect
0 or 1	The creature has authority over you and can issue one command that you must obey, a task that requires up to a day of effort.
2 or 3	You have immediate authority over the creature. You can command the creature to perform one task that takes no more than 5 minutes.
4 or 5	You have moderate authority over the creature. You can command the creature to perform a task that requires up to a day of effort.
6 or 7	You have significant authority over the creature. You can command the creature to perform a task that requires up to a week of effort.
8 or 9	You have great authority over the creature. You can command the creature to perform a task that requires up to a month of effort.
10	You have ultimate authority over the creature. You can command the creature to perform a task that requires up to a year and a day of effort.

When the specified task is completed, the ritual is discharged, and the creature (or you) is released from service. You can request any kind of service that does not compel the subject to obey multiple commands, force the subject to engage in combat, or ensure the subject's death. (The subject can engage in combat to achieve a task if it wishes, but combat cannot be required.) If the task is impossible, such as commanding a creature that cannot fly to soar into the sky, the creature can ignore the command.

CREATE HOLY WATER

The sparkling water you create seems proof against all impurities.

Level: 1
Category: Creation
Time: 1 hour
Duration: 24 hours
Component Cost: Special
Market Price: 50 gp
Key Skill: Religion (no check)

This ritual infuses astral radiance into a small quantity of ordinary water. The cost to do so depends on the level of the holy water you choose to create. You cannot create holy water of a level higher than your own. Aside from its effect on undead and demons, holy water acts as normal pure water in all ways. It can be distinguished from normal water with examination and a successful DC 15 Religion or Arcana check.

Holy Water			Level 1+
Undead and demons react poorly to the touch of this liquid.			
Lvl 1	20 gp	Lvl 16	1,800 gp
Lvl 6	75 gp	Lvl 21	9,000 gp
Lvl 11	350 gp	Lvl 26	45,000 gp

Alchemical Item

Power (Consumable ✦ Radiant): Minor Action. Make an attack: Ranged 3/6; +4 vs. Reflex; on a hit, the attack deals 1d10 radiant damage to an undead creature or a demon.
Level 6: +9 vs. Reflex; 1d10 radiant damage.
Level 11: +14 vs. Reflex; 2d10 radiant damage.
Level 16: +19 vs. Reflex; 2d10 radiant damage.
Level 21: +24 vs. Reflex; 3d10 radiant damage.
Level 26: +29 vs. Reflex; 3d10 radiant damage.

Ease Spirit

Death's memory fades as the spirit settles more firmly into the flesh.

Level: 25
Category: Restoration
Time: 2 hours
Duration: Instantaneous
Component Cost: 25,000 gp
Market Price: 70,000 gp
Key Skill: Heal (no check)

You designate one creature adjacent to you that is currently affected by a death penalty, such as that gained from the Raise Dead ritual. This ritual lessens the subject's death penalty by 1.

Hallowed Temple

A brilliant shrine appears in the area, welcoming those pure of heart and striking fear in those who know only corruption.

Level: 12
Category: Creation
Time: 1 hour
Duration: 8 hours
Component Cost: 520 gp
Market Price: 1,300 gp
Key Skill: Religion (no check)

The Hallowed Temple ritual creates a shimmering temple associated with your deity. The temple occupies a close burst 7 as it materializes around you. The structure incorporates as many appropriate artistic elements as you like: the exterior features iconography, stained-glass windows, and other decorative features, and the interior contains an altar, statues, or other appropriate items related to your faith.

The temple is comfortable, and creatures inside it feel close to your god. It is immune to damage. Access to the interior is through the temple's front (and only) door. The walls of the temple, including the door, are solid obstacles. The temple and all its contents (even items removed from the temple) vanish at the end of the ritual's duration.

Demons and undead cannot cross the temple's threshold. Any creatures within the burst (except for you) when the temple materializes are displaced to a space outside the temple as close to their former location as possible. If insufficient space exists either for the temple itself or for the displacement of creatures, the ritual cannot be performed.

Iron Vigil

Meditation and prayer are all the sustenance you need.

Level: 4
Category: Exploration
Time: 10 minutes
Duration: 8 hours
Component Cost: 35 gp
Market Price: 170 gp
Key Skill: Religion (no check)

You invoke your dedication to your god and let it wash your fatigue and needs from you. Iron Vigil fulfills your body's need for food and water when you perform it and allows you to remain aware and alert while taking an extended rest anytime during the ritual's duration.

REBECCA GUAY

Mark of Justice

Some lessons are best learned through suffering. Your magic ensures that the guilty creature continues its offenses only at great peril.

Level: 12
Category: Binding
Time: 10 minutes
Duration: Permanent
Component Cost: 1,000 gp
Market Price: 2,600 gp
Key Skill: Religion (no check)

You draw a mark on the subject of the ritual, who must be willing or helpless for the time it takes to perform the ritual. At the ritual's completion, designate an action or a kind of behavior that the mark forbids, and select one of the following penalties or another worked out by you and your DM. When the subject performs the forbidden action or displays the forbidden behavior, the subject is affected by the penalty for the next 24 hours. Example penalties include the following:

Ineptness: When the subject makes a successful d20 roll, it must roll again and use the second result.

Weakness of Flesh: The subject gains vulnerable 10 to all damage.

Curse of Solitude: The subject is blinded and deafened.

No matter the distance, you are aware when the subject triggers the penalty or when the penalty is lifted. The Remove Affliction ritual can end the effect of Mark of Justice, using twice your level as the penalty to the Heal check.

Succor

A site sacred to your deity is always open to those in need.

Level: 20
Category: Travel
Time: 8 hours
Duration: Permanent until discharged
Component Cost: 5,000 gp, plus 4 healing surges and a focus worth 5,000 gp
Market Price: 25,000 gp
Key Skill: Religion (no check)

You must perform this ritual inside a shrine, a temple, or some other site of religious significance to your deity. Succor attunes the ritual's focus to the site, linking the two until the ritual is discharged. After the time required to perform the ritual, the creature holding the focus can spend a standard action to activate the ritual's effect: At the end of the creature's next turn, the creature and up to eight willing creatures within its line of sight teleport to the holy site to which the focus was attuned, and the ritual is discharged. Succor crosses any distance and planar boundaries.

Any effect or condition that prevents teleportation also prevents this ritual from functioning (but does not discharge it).

Focus: Prayer beads, a holy book, or some other item of religious significance.

Thief's Lament

Those of criminal intent find their talents fail them when they enter the area protected by this magic.

Level: 6
Category: Warding
Time: 1 hour
Duration: 24 hours or more (see text)
Component Cost: 140 gp, plus 2 healing surges
Market Price: 360 gp
Key Skill: Arcana or Religion

Creatures in the warded area take a -5 penalty to Stealth checks and Thievery checks.

Your Arcana or Religion check determines the size of the warded area.

Skill Check Result	Warded Area
9 or lower	Burst 1
10–19	Burst 3
20-29	Burst 5
30-39	Burst 8
40 or higher	Burst 12

The warding effect lasts for 24 hours, but you (and not any assistants) can extend the duration by an additional 24 hours for each extra healing surge you expend just before the current duration expires. You need not be in the same area or even on the same plane to extend the duration. If you extend the ritual's duration for a year and a day without interruption, the effect becomes permanent.

GLOSSARY

This brief glossary contains game terms that appear in this book and are defined in a book other than a *Player's Handbook*.

attacking objects: With your DM's permission, you can use a power that normally attacks creatures to attack objects. See the *Dungeon Master's Guide,* page 65, for how to damage objects.

blindsight: A creature that has blindsight can clearly see creatures or objects within a specified range and within line of effect, even if they are invisible or obscured. The creature otherwise relies on its normal vision.

fly speed: If you have a fly speed, you can fly a number of squares up to that speed as a move action. To remain in the air, you must move at least 2 squares during your turn, or you crash at the end of your turn. While flying, you can't shift or make opportunity attacks, and you crash if you're knocked prone. See the *Dungeon Master's Guide,* page 47, for more about flying.

hover: If you have a fly speed and can hover, you can remain in the air without moving during your turn. You can also shift and make opportunity attacks while flying.

tremorsense: If you have tremorsense, you can clearly see creatures or objects within a specified range, even if they are invisible, obscured, or outside line of effect, but you and they must be in contact with the ground or the same substance, such as water or a web. You otherwise rely on your normal vision.

truesight: If you have truesight, you can see insivible creatures or objects within a specified range, as long as they are within your line of sight.

ABOUT THE DESIGNERS

ROB HEINSOO led the design of the 4th Edition D&D® Roleplaying Game. His 4th Edition design credits include the *Martial Power*™ supplement and the FORGOTTEN REALMS® *Player's Guide.* His other designs include *Three-Dragon Ante*™ and DUNGEONS & DRAGONS *Inn Fighting*™.

RICHARD BAKER is an award-winning game designer who has written scores of D&D adventures and supplements, including *Manual of the Planes*™, *Divine Power*™, and *Draconomicon*™ 2. Rich is also a best-selling author of FORGOTTEN REALMS novels, including *Swordmage* and *Corsair* in the Blades of the Moonsea series.

ROBERT J. SCHWALB works as a freelance designer for Wizards of the Coast; his recent credits include *Martial Power*™, *Draconomicon*™, and *Player's Handbook*® 2. Robert lives in Tennessee with his incredibly patient wife, Stacee, and his pride of fiendish werecats, but is happiest when chained to his desk, toiling for his dark masters in Seattle.

LOGAN BONNER traded the Great Plains of Kansas for Seattle when he landed a job at Wizards of the Coast. His design credits include the FORGOTTEN REALMS® *Player's Guide* and *Adventurer's Vault*™, as well as various *D&D*™ *Dungeon Tiles* and *D&D*® *Miniatures* products.

SHARE YOUR ADVENTURES.
SHAPE YOUR WORLD.
Explore Faerûn with a band of adventurers gathered from around the globe and make a *real* impact on the world of Toril.
The RPGA's Living Forgotten Realms® campaign offers dozens of official D&D® adventures every year—adventures that will help guide how the Realms will continue to evolve.
And best of all, you can do it wherever you play D&D®—at home, your favorite game store, anywhere—even a convention.
DUNGEONS & DRAGONS®
LIVING FORGOTTEN REALMS
RPGA NETWORK
All trademarks are property of Wizards of the Coast LLC
©2009 Wizards.